DALTON KANE
AND THE
GREENS

DALTON KANE
AND THE
GREENS

J. S. BAILEY

A DALTON KANE NOVEL

PROLOGUE

usic thudded through the tiny spaceport terminal as Dev Chakrabarti held a champagne glass aloft before his drunken friends and colleagues, many of whom swayed in time with the beat. Confetti littered the floor and the padded chairs where passengers would wait for a lift offworld, and it was a godawful mess that Dev would have to clean up later, but right now he was too inebriated to care.

"Thanks again for coming, everyone!" he slurred. "This has been a—*hic*—hell of a party!"

"Anything for you, Dev!" cried someone from the back of the room.

Dev poured back the remainder of his champagne in one gulp. "I couldn't have asked for a better fortieth birthday. *Hic.* Who made the cake?"

"I did!" Nydia Stone, who worked with him in the space traffic control room, beamed. "I remembered vanilla's your favorite."

"You all surprised me good." Dev plonked himself into one of the chairs. "I never would have guessed you'd throw me a party at work."

"There isn't enough room for one at home," commented his wife, Leesa, who'd been standing off to one side chatting with some of Dev's aunties who'd tired of dancing with the younger people. "And Nydia assured us there were no incoming flights this evening."

"It's Molorthia Six," said Dev. "When do we ever have incoming flights?"

This was met with a roar of laughter, and Dev's own sudden mirth made his stomach lurch. "I need to step out a moment," he said, setting his glass on the floor and trying not to heave. He rose, one hand on his stomach, and hurried out of the terminal into the short corridor leading to the breakroom and the space traffic control room. He had nausea pills in his messenger bag along with an assortment of other remedies he liked to have on hand in case of emergencies. Now where had he put it?

He poked his head into the breakroom.

No messenger bag.

Please don't let me puke, he thought as he raced into the space traffic control room and spotted his bag sitting on the chair he occupied during the occasional instances when ships entered and departed the Molorthia System. He unzipped the bag with a zeal borne of necessity and downed two nausea pills before all of the cake and champagne did him in, and he sighed in relief as his queasiness subsided in an instant.

Modern day medicine. Gotta love it.

Dev rubbed the back of his hand across his mouth and straightened, ready for Round Two. He left the space traffic control room and rejoined his party, feeling like a new man.

He never saw the five large blips that had appeared in the three-dimensional holographic rendering of the Molorthia System floating in the center of the room, and on several of the flat screens on the walls surrounding it. The blips had already crossed the orbit of Molorthia Seven—a rocky, inhospitable world swathed in chlorine gas—and were closing in rapidly on Molorthia Six, where the humans lived.

More champagne was poured as the blips entered Molorthia Six's atmosphere and settled down north of the planet's equator, far from the spaceport and out of sight of any witnesses.

If Dev had noticed them, things might have turned out quite differently—but then there wouldn't have been a story.

PART 1

CHAPTER 1

Dalton Kane hated meetings.

He suspected that whoever invented them had done it to see if anyone would notice a punchline. But, as sheriff, he was required to participate in said meetings as requested, and he wasn't in a position to argue about it no matter how much they made him want to stab his eyes out with a paperclip.

Luckily for him, today's meeting was with Carolyn Kaur, Richport's mayor, and she promised it would be brief.

So.

He looked at his reflection in the small hand mirror he kept in his desk drawer, decided he looked as much of a bastard as ever, and dragged a greasy comb through his sunbleached hair to make it look like he'd at least tried. Then he stood, squared his shoulders, and strode out of his office with a swagger of forced masculinity to greet his superior.

He didn't spot Carolyn at first. His gaze roved briefly over the desks and filing cabinets that sat in neat rows in the main part of the police station. Cadu Mão de Ferro, the emergency operator, sat at his desk swirling a pen around on a piece of paper waiting for calls to come in, and Debbie Harper . . .

Dalton's eyes went wide.

Debbie Harper had brought a salad.

Again.

He ground to a halt as the reason for Carolyn's visit fled his mind. Time itself slowed to a near-standstill, and his vision darkened around the edges until Debbie and her lunch were all he could see.

The mousy-haired office assistant sat hunched over her desk, forking a glob of dressing-soaked plant matter into her mouth. Dalton could hear the languid crunch as she bit into it, watched as she stabbed into her bowl and brought another forkful of the substance toward her mouth.

His heart fluttered in his chest like a moth caught in a window screen, not that they had any moths here on Molorthia Six.

Spots danced mockingly through the air before him as his consciousness started to go.

Debbie took another bite.

A faint ringing began to sound in Dalton's ears, and he thought, *Sonofa*bitch.

Dalton came to feeling something cold and damp pressing against the side of his head.

His eyes snapped open. Everything towered over him as if he'd shrunk, and it took him a few seconds to realize this was because he lay sprawled across the wooden plank floor like a drunk in the gutter. The battered gray filing cabinet to his left had toppled over, belching papers across the planks, and Dalton's head and shoulder smarted in time with his heartbeat.

Ah, he thought.

"Dalton, are you okay?" Carolyn Kaur asked in a low tone. The brown-skinned woman held a self-activating icepack in one hand, and a first-aid kit lay open on the floor next to her. Her dusty, black business suit had a smudge of fresh blood on one sleeve.

He squinted past her and saw Debbie standing by her desk with her arms crossed in defiance while Cadu Mão de Ferro gave her a scolding.

The salad was nowhere in sight.

"But I *have* to start eating better!" Debbie whined to Cadu. "My doctor said!"

"You know you can't bring that kind of stuff in here," Cadu said, perhaps too gently. "Not after what happened to the sheriff's family."

"I taste blood," Dalton said, looking back to Carolyn, who'd pressed the icepack against his head again.

"You bit your lip when you fell. I saw the whole thing happen. Your legs turned into jelly, and bam."

Dalton narrowed his eyes again. The door to the lobby had been propped open, and an industrial-sized fan parked a meter or so away from the doorway riffled papers on the scattered desks.

Vaguely, he remembered that Carolyn had come here to talk to him about something. But then there had been the salad.

He pulled himself to his feet, his face setting itself into a scowl so deep, it might become permanent. He stormed from the office area and out through the lobby without even going back for his Stetson.

Outside in the dusty street where the only colors were

brown, tan, gray, and a little bit of red on some shop signs, Dalton began to feel more like himself again, whatever that meant. The gleaming sun beat down upon him so heavily that he could already feel his ears thinking about blistering. His brown leather trench coat would keep the sun off most of the rest of him, at least.

He couldn't bring himself to go get his hat. Not after what everyone had seen him do.

"Dalton, wait."

He turned his head enough to see Carolyn hurrying out the entrance to the police station in her high heels.

His expression felt like stone. "What do you want, Carolyn?"

She frowned at him, her eyes dark wells of concern. "A few people have come to me worried about the smoke on the horizon. I thought you should send someone to check it out."

She hadn't been kidding when she'd said the meeting would be brief. "Smoke?" Dalton craned his neck, unable to see anything but buildings and sand. "In which direction?"

"To the north." She paused. "And the northeast. Mostly the north, though. I figured you'd noticed it already."

He gave her a dull glare. He may have spotted some smoke that morning on his way in, but hadn't thought much of it—sometimes things just burned. "Maybe the folks up in Paris are celebrating Bonfire Night already."

Carolyn opened her mouth as if to say more but then shook her head. "Clearly, this isn't the right time to be talking to you. Is this about that damned salad?"

A tendril of dread scuttled down Dalton's spine the

moment she spoke *that* word. Instead of answering, he set his jaw and turned on his heel, then stomped away from her.

Maybe she'd understand a little better if she'd been there. They *all* might understand a little better. But only Dalton had been there, and Summer Kane, too, but he sure as hell wasn't going to go talking to Summer about it. He'd rather lay down naked in a bed of fire ants in the noonday Molorthian sun. Not that they had any fire ants.

As Dalton's boots sent up puffs of dust with every angry footfall, he patted the loaded water pistol in its holster on his hip and felt one microscopic shred of relief.

Whenever Dalton found himself in a temper, he preferred to take long and moody walks around his domain, scowling at anything that looked happier than he did. This had, over time, bestowed him with the reputation of World's Most Formidable Sheriff, which would not last long if word got out that he'd fainted over salads again.

He turned down Holy Street, where a Sikh gurdwara sat next door to the province's busiest mosque, which sat next to a pint-sized Roman Catholic cathedral and across the street from the First Baptist Church of Richport, the Free Will Baptist Church of Richport, The First Synagogue of Richport, Heavenly Fire Church, The Church of Jesus Christ of Latter-day Saints, St. Nicholas Greek Orthodox Church, The Church of Chris (a sandstorm had blown the T off the sign), and Hindu Temple of Richport.

The village atheists met once per week at Slim's Café to discuss whatever their book club was reading.

"Hey, Sheriff!"

Dalton drew up short. Spinning to the left, he spotted citizens Gurmeet Singh and Lennox McTavish perched together in the shade on the front stoop of Desert Sands Gurdwara which, like most of the other dwellings in town, had been built of sand-colored adobe designed to deflect the scalding heat.

Gurmeet gripped a stringed instrument that somewhat loosely resembled a short, squat guitar, while Lennox shyly hugged a set of bagpipes.

"Good day, Sheriff!" Gurmeet said brightly, undeterred by Dalton's glare. "Nice to see you out here today." The man's white turban reminded Dalton of the fact that the top of his own Stetson-less head was currently undergoing a slow roast.

Dalton grunted and casually joined them in the shade. "Same, I suppose."

"Your lip is bleeding, sir."

"Bit it. What's that?" He nodded at the instrument.

Gurmeet practically beamed at him—he'd always been too cheerful for his own good. "It's my grandfather's sarangi! I've been practicing. Lennox thinks we ought to start our own band once I get good enough."

Lennox, a raven-haired Scotsman who'd arrived on Molorthia Six as part of a fresh batch of settlers five years earlier, flushed with a faint embarrassment. "Aye, we've been practicing together all morning." His accent still held traces of his native Scottish brogue, which he tended to dial down in public since there were no other Scotspeople around to understand him properly.

Dalton suspected that, given the influx of settlers from so many different backgrounds, Richport itself would be developing its own unique standard accent within two or three more generations that nobody else on Molorthia Six would understand, like a modern-day Bronx with fewer bodegas.

"Do you want to hear how we sound so far?" Gurmeet asked, his eyes glimmering hopefully as his fingers moved toward the strings.

Dalton held up a hand. "Not today, Mr. Singh. I'll . . . wait until you've gotten better at it."

Disappointment shone in Gurmeet's eyes, but only for a moment. "Ah, that's too bad. Oh! A ship arrived last night," he said. "From Pelstring Four, people are saying."

Dalton furrowed his brow. "Pelstring Four? Who is it, more settlers?"

"I don't know. But Mrs. Abernathy next door says she thinks one of them is a salesman."

"A salesman." Dalton repeated the word with a measure of distaste. The last time a salesman had arrived in town from offworld, Dalton himself had had to rescue him from the roof of the town hall, where he'd taken refuge after an angry mob had gone after him. And he'd been selling *air conditioners*.

"That's what she says," Gurmeet went on.

Dalton looked up at the sky and shook his head. "God help him."

Dalton did not encounter any salesmen during the rest of his walk, though he did spot gray-haired citizen Gwendolyn Goldfarb standing outside the supermarket shouting "Fire in the sky! Fire in the sky!" at anyone who would listen.

When Dalton returned to the police station, Debbie Harper wouldn't make eye contact with him.

"You're fired," he said as he passed her desk. "Cadu, make sure we get a job posting up in the next paper."

Cadu rolled his eyes and jotted a note down on one of his papers. "Got it."

Nothing else happened for the rest of the day. Slow days meant peace and harmony; two things Dalton craved like his fellow citizens craved ice water and cloud cover.

Slow days meant he wouldn't have to use his water pistol.

As dusk began to fall, Dalton trudged off to the farthest eastern reaches of town, where his small, adobe house sat behind a picket fence that used to be white but had since faded into a sort of peely, sandy gray. Inside, he shrugged off his trench coat and hung it and his Stetson on hooks just inside the door. He left his holster on, not wanting it out of sight, and went into the bathroom to attend to his scorched ears.

In the mirror, his skin looked like it belonged on a lobster. Dalton plucked up a jar of expired sunburn cream and, wincing, rubbed it on his ears, his nose, and his cheek-bones. His hair, naturally a light brown, was sunbleached all the way to blond at the tips. Cadu Mão de Ferro, a vintage television and film buff, informed Dalton that he looked like a desert-baked John Constantine from some old show put out by DC Comics several hundred years ago.

Dalton failed to see the resemblance.

His temple still throbbing from where he'd bashed it on the filing cabinet, he ate a small dinner of steak and potatoes, worked on a crossword puzzle for a good half-hour, then retired to his room, where he stripped down to his briefs.

After making sure his blinds were pulled, he lay on his side in bed and gazed at the family photograph sitting on his bedside table. In it, he, his wife, and his girls had struck goofy poses in front of one of the Weird Sisters, a collection of vaguely-humanoid rock formations in Crater Valley west of Paris.

Then he closed his eyes and folded his hands together, grateful no one could see him.

"Please," he whispered. "Just bring them back to me. You've done it before to other people—I've read about it in your book. So, please . . . bring back my family. I don't think I can survive another day without them."

CHAPTER 2

Daylight roused Dalton from a dream where treelike beings chased him through the darkness, his right shoulder aching like it usually did in the mornings. He rolled over and gazed hopefully at the space beside him on the bed, but it remained unoccupied, just as it had been for five years now.

Like he'd really expected to see Darneisha lying there beside him. He wouldn't be hearing any excited squeals from the other bedroom down the hallway, either, because Kendra and Imani were just as dead as their mother.

He thought about picking up his comm and calling Summer to talk through some of his feelings, but he refused to subject himself to such torture. His brother's wife had been a nagging thorn in his flesh for too many years. The fact she was the only other survivor was a cosmic joke that had not been lost on Dalton.

Dalton fried himself two sausage patties for breakfast, got dressed, and set out for work.

The front door of the police station was already unlocked when Dalton arrived, and Cadu sat at his desk holding his comm unit and looking quite grave.

"You'll have to speak more clearly," Cadu said over the wail coming through the comm. "I can't help you if I don't know what's going on."

"Cut myself!"

"You'll need to stem the bleeding while you wait for the medics to get there. Where is your cut?"

"Hand—was peeling an avocado, and the knife slipped. Oh, God! What if I *die*?"

Cadu's black hair stood up in a tuft where he'd already run a hand through it, and his dark brown skin glistened with sweat as he very calmly walked the man through what he needed to do.

Dalton did not envy Cadu his job.

He let himself into his already-stifling office, where he picked up his Mega Tough crossword puzzle book and continued where he'd left off the day before.

At half past ten, there came a knock on his door. "What is it?" he called, and a chagrined-looking Cadu poked his head around the corner.

"Another call just came through on the emergency line," Cadu said. "They said there's a salesman handing out pamphlets in the town square."

Gurmeet had been right about one of the new arrivals. "What's he selling?" Dalton asked, thinking of air conditioners. He mopped a trickle of sweat off his forehead with the sleeve of his trench coat.

"I don't know, but he has quite a few people upset. You'd better check it out before he ends up on the roof like the other guy."

Dalton rose and jammed his Stetson over his sunburned ears. "Consider it done."

The town square lay six blocks from the police station. On his way there, Dalton rehearsed what he planned on saying to the newcomer: *Richport has a No Solicitation ordinance, established to protect all salespeople and citizens alike, so please stop selling whatever it is you're selling.*

Shouts up ahead alerted Dalton to the salesman's precise location. He shoved his way through the gathered throng and spotted a gangly South Asian man wearing khaki slacks and a pale pink dress shirt, amiably conversing with Alma Vaidya, one of the book club atheists who met at Slim's Café every Thursday evening at eight.

Alma, a stocky woman in her fifties, leveled a glare at the man that would have made warriors tremble in their boots. "I have no need for anything you're trying to sell."

The salesman appeared in no way deterred. "Our tanning beds come with the best new features," he went on in a smooth English accent as an apple core sailed through the air and hit him in the shoulder. "They have an internal cooling system to keep you comfortable while you tan, and they even have built-in satellite radio."

"Why in the bloody hell would anyone in Richport need a tanning bed?" cried Henry Halpern, Dalton's barber, lurking close by. "Richport *is* a tanning bed!"

"Our tanning beds allow one to tan comfortably from the comfort of one's own home," the salesman said calmly.

Dalton stifled a snort. "Excuse me," he said, shoving past a few more people who stood blocking his way.

He reached the salesman and cleared his throat. "You. Newcomer."

The salesman turned and brightened, no doubt believing Dalton had some interest in his wares. "Why, hello there! I'm Chumley Fanshaw, from Sunspotz Tanning Beds. So great of you to come out here today!"

Chumley thrust a business card into Dalton's hand. He glanced down at it and read to himself: *Chumley Fanshaw, purveyor of fine tanning beds from Sunspotz. Look great, feel greater!*

An electronic address had been printed across the bottom. Dalton slid the card into his pocket in case he'd have to use it as evidence in a trial for Chumley's future murderer.

"You've gathered quite the crowd here," Dalton commented.

"Oh, I know." Chumley's cheeks flushed as if he were impressed by his own feat. "I didn't expect such a response."

"You realize most of them probably want to kill you."

"Kill *me*?" Chumley brought a hand to his chest. "Why would they do that?"

"You've never been in Richport before, have you?"

"This is my first time on Molorthia Six. It's kind of an odd planet, isn't it?"

Dalton kept his tone guarded as he said, "What makes you say that?"

Chumley scratched the back of his neck, which was probably already starting to blister since he didn't have a hat. "It's just that most colony planets settle the temperate zones, but all the settlements on Molorthia Six are in the equatorial desert. It certainly would have made my job easier, having cities farther south or north."

Dalton clapped him on the shoulder. "I think you should research your markets a little better before spending a fortune on spacefare. Now I'm afraid you'll have to stop what you're doing, because solicitation happens to be against the law here in Richport."

"Oh." Chumley's lips formed a disheartened frown. "Is that right?"

"I'm the sheriff. It's right."

"What should I do, then? Set up a pop-up shop and sell tanning beds from there?"

"I think," Dalton said, "you'd better pack your bags and head somewhere else. Molorthia Eight is covered in ice."

"Isn't Molorthia Eight uninhabited?"

"It won't be if you go there."

Before Chumley could muster a reply, the comm unit clipped to Dalton's belt let out a squawk. "Dalton?"

He fumbled with it a moment and held it to his ear. "Cadu? What is it?"

"It's the Greens, sir," Cadu said, as evenly as if he were imparting the weather. "They've just invaded Falcon Ranch."

The comm nearly slipped through Dalton's sweaty fingers. "Invaded?" His voice came out in a croak.

"Can you make it out there, or do you need me to send someone else?"

Dalton patted for the water pistol hanging from his hip, and swallowed. "I'll go," he heard himself say. To Chumley, he said, "Book the next shuttle out of here. I don't want to scrape what's left of you off the hardpan."

Chumley's mouth gaped open in an O. Dalton turned on his heel and dashed back toward the police station through the surprised throng as fast as if a Green were chasing him.

Two rust-colored quads with deep-tread tires had been parked behind the station. One had a dead battery, and the other just barely growled to life when Dalton thrust a key into its ignition. It gave a lurch before gliding smoothly forward, and he slapped the siren button so all the nincompoops still clogging the town square would get out of his way before they turned into life-sized bowling pins.

He breezed past an alarmed Chumley Fanshaw, who *still* hadn't taken Dalton's advice and left.

The edges of Richport soon gave way to rocky, reddish-tan sand that swirled up from the desert floor in plumes to mark Dalton's passage. None of the roads on Molorthia Six were paved, and since Falcon Ranch lay somewhat off the beaten path, Dalton opted to eschew the road altogether and shot off in a northwesterly direction approximating the shortest distance between the ranch and the town.

He sped past the Lady Liberty rock formation, which looked a bit like a statue holding a torch if you imagined hard enough. At its base lay a few scattered bronze boom-stones the wind had uncovered—he'd have to get a team out here to collect the explosive minerals before someone blew themselves up being stupid.

Off to the north, plumes of smoke rose into the air from below the horizon, just like Carolyn had said.

More smoke lay dead ahead, coming from Falcon Ranch.

He gritted his teeth. It was times like this when he wished their police force was bigger than just him, Cadu, and a handful of unqualified volunteers who came and went with the wind. How could he, one miserable man, fight back against the Greens and win, especially when he'd fainted the day before just from seeing Debbie's lunch?

Her lunch had taken him by surprise, though. This time, he came prepared.

The main ranch house came into view past a low

ridge—an adobe structure of ample size that made Dalton's own house look like a pillbox. A pasture full of lavender-colored grass, watered via an underground aquifer, was populated with several dozen field beasts swishing their tails in agitation.

Smoke rose from several singed clumps of desert scrub smoldering near the barn, one of those rare Molorthian structures built of imported wood that would have cost the builder a fortune. Doris Kelso, the stocky owner of Falcon Ranch, stood with her back pressed against the barn's outer wall, gripping a smoking flamethrower in one trembling hand.

The quad threw up a spray of pebbles and dirt as Dalton ground it to a standstill, and he vaulted from it with his water pistol clenched tightly in his fist.

"Oh, Sheriff, thank God you're here," Doris said, looking strangely unrelieved in spite of his timely arrival. "I called as soon as I saw them coming, and then—"

"Where are they now?" Dalton saw nothing leafy and emerald-colored in their vicinity, but that didn't mean the Greens weren't being furtive.

Doris pointed toward the southwest. "They were heading that way, across open ground toward the Rosa."

"How many?"

"Four; two tall and two shorter. They . . ." She swallowed. "They vaulted the pasture fence and drank from the beasts' trough, then gathered up fistfuls of grass and shoved it into some sacks. They even scooped extra water into what looked like canteens, if you can believe it."

Dalton's insides felt colder than the ice fields of Molorthia Eight. "You're sure there were only four."

"I'm positive. But Sheriff, what does it mean? Is my ranch going to be some sort of . . . of *rest stop* for those things?"

Instead of answering, he regarded once more her flamethrower, and then the smoldering patches of desert scrub. "You fired at them," he said. "Did they seem . . . frightened?"

"Only a little. They seemed more concerned about replenishing their supplies."

Dalton was about to say more when a faint swishing sound reached his ears.

His heart nearly stopped mid-beat.

"Sheriff?" Doris asked, eyes widening in alarm.

"Get inside," he hissed. "Now!"

Doris didn't need to be told twice. She launched herself from the barn's shadow, seized Dalton's free hand, and nearly tore his arm out of its socket hauling him toward her back door, which she threw open and then slammed shut and bolted once they were both safely inside.

Dalton got down on his hands and knees and peered slowly above the nearest windowsill, still gripping his water pistol. The window gave him the perfect view of the pasture, which would have looked idyllic on any other occasion.

"Doris?" he whispered. "Where are the other people who work here?"

"I gave them the day off," she said in a low voice. "They're at the water park in Pleasant Springs. They won't be back until nightfall."

"Good," he said, and continued to watch and wait. Doris

poked her head up beside his. It was sort of nice having the company. He'd never wanted to die alone.

Soon, a four-meter-tall being shuffled into view from the right, and Dalton nearly let out a shriek. He'd never even *seen* one that big before. Its forest-colored legs were as thick and sturdy-looking as the trunks of Earth trees, and its two sets of arms ended in hands sprouting rows of emerald, twig-like fingers that looked flimsy but had the strength to peel the roof off a car. Leaves sprouted from the whole length of its body much in the way that scales grew from a minnow.

The creature's four eyestalks protruded from the top of its leafy head, surveying its surroundings as it drew to a stop next to the pasture fence. Some sort of primitive canvas sack had been slung over one of its shoulders, and the creature pulled it open and withdrew an earthy-brown canteen like the ones Doris had mentioned before.

"Should we kill it?" Doris hissed.

"Wait," Dalton said, hardly daring to blink.

The creature stepped over the pasture fence as if it were a man stepping over a paving stone. It knelt down and stuck its face into the trough to drink, and once it had its fill, it dunked its canteen into the water and screwed the cap back on.

Then it rose, turned, and faced the herd of mooing field beasts, which might have been called cows had they lived on Earth, except for the fact they'd been genetically-modified to survive the harsh desert climate and now grew to half the size of normal cows and ate only the lavender grass.

Dalton slid Doris's window open about three centimeters, then shoved the barrel of his water pistol through the gap.

"Water won't hurt them, Sheriff," she said to him.

He grunted. "It's not water."

"Then what—"

The creature lunged at the nearest field beast with lightning-quickness and seized it in its four arms. The field beast let out a bone-chilling squeal as the creature sank its two rows of razor-sharp fangs into its neck.

The poor thing started to struggle but immediately went limp.

Dalton aimed his water pistol at the creature and squeezed the trigger.

The pressurized jet of liquid shot outward in a fifteen-meter line, which splattered against the creature's back.

It let out a roar, dropped the dead field beast, and whirled to face the house, its eyestalks glowering with murder as it spotted Dalton and Doris peeking above the windowsill.

It charged, blood dripping from its mandibles.

Dalton sprayed the rest of his ammo into the creature's face, if you could call it a face. The creature roared again as it went down, its leafy flesh already dissolving into a chartreuse sludge.

Within sixty seconds, it stopped moving.

"It's weed killer," Dalton said.

He shoved the empty water pistol back into its holster and spoke into his comm unit. "Cadu? This is Dalton, calling in from Falcon Ranch."

His voice sounded calm. Too calm, which meant he was probably going into shock, or something just as horrible.

"Yes?" came Cadu's voice.

"Send out as many people as you can with reinforced fencing. They're using Falcon Ranch as a rest stop." He scrunched his eyes shut, hating the truth of the matter. "The Greens are on the move."

Chumley Fanshaw settled back on the divan in his room at Hotel Richport, the town's poshest place of lodging, sipping on a glass of champagne he'd had room service bring up to him with his dinner. After he'd showered the desert grit out of his hair and off his skin, he'd slipped into his favorite silk dressing gown, which felt so much nicer than having a layer of sand plastered to his body.

He really ought to have picked a different name to use here, since he was hiding. Call himself Bill, or Curtis, or Sanjay, or something. He still had time to come up with an alias, probably, but would he even remember to respond to it?

He set down his glass and refocused his attention on the guidebook he'd purchased at the town's small spaceport upon his arrival. For a guidebook about the whole planet, it didn't say much. The number of human residents living on Molorthia Six numbered close to a hundred thousand, which amounted to the population of a small city on Pelstring Four, but it made sense, given that Molorthia Six had been colonized for only a century.

The guidebook displayed a map of the planet's nine cities—Richport, Paris, Pleasant Springs, Acropolis, Mount Olympus, Washington, New New Delhi, Cloud City, and Fred—and listed a few other notable sites, such as caverns, hot springs, and unique rock formations shaped like various aspects of the human anatomy. There was no unified government among the cities, which sprawled out across a thousand miles of equatorial desert; but there did seem to be two unofficial "provinces" imaginatively-named "East Desert" and "West Desert."

Richport, Paris, and Pleasant Springs were located in East Desert Province. Perhaps the other two towns would be more accepting of tanning beds, and if not, he could book a transport that would take him across the rocky sands to the other province.

A person had to make a living somehow, especially when one was on the run and in need of funds.

When Chumley grew bored of the guidebook, he lay it down on the table and moved toward the window, champagne glass in hand.

Chumley peered down at the quiet, unpaved street, adjusting his dressing gown to make sure he remained decent. A few solar-powered outdoor lights had flickered on in the past hour, and in their soft glow, he could see townsfolk making their way toward the pub where he'd first begun passing out business cards and brochures.

He still couldn't understand why they'd taken so unkindly to him, but he supposed it came with the territory. These people would be close-knit, and he was a stranger to them, which meant he'd just have to get to know them better and instill in them a sense of trust before he tried Round Two.

While he continued to watch the ground, a tall, furtive shape down below him drifted from one shadow into another, and when Chumley tried to get a better look at it, it had gone.

It had seemed too tall for a typical man, and moved in a manner most alien.

He stared down at the remaining champagne in his glass, frowned, and swallowed the rest of it, then went to the room's sideboard and poured himself another.

Lying on the divan once more, Chumley's tired brain continued to stew in an alcohol-induced haze. Molorthia Six . . . he'd learned about it in school like all the other kids as part of the required unit about colony worlds. The colony on Jeptune Three, for example, was scattered across a chain of fertile islands since that planet boasted no larger land masses. Killian Six's colony had to build reinforced homes due to frequent, violent earthquakes.

There had been something unique about Molorthia Six, too, but he couldn't put a finger on it. Was it a vicious monsoon season? No, that was Orbus Prime. So maybe it was—

A short-lived scream carried up from the ground floor, derailing his train of thought.

Chumley sat up, blinking.

Pounding footsteps followed another scream.

He frowned. His flight from Pelstring Four to here had also contained one elderly Earth couple and a younger family with four small children, all of whom had checked into Hotel Richport as well. Were the children roughhousing down there?

Now someone was yelling.

Chumley wavered to his feet and walked in a sort of meandering arc to the door of his suite, then poked his head out into the hallway.

The staircase lay several meters to his right. The man he recognized as the hotel manager stood at the top of the stairs holding an honest-to-god flamethrower like a tough guy in an old action movie.

While Chumley watched, a ten-foot-tall walking plant strode up the staircase. The hotel manager let loose with a gush of flame that took the plant right in the chest.

The chest?

More walking plants appeared in its place, their long, jointed limbs reaching out toward the manager, who tried in vain to fire the flamethrower again, but it seemed to have jammed or run out of fuel, for it made a feeble clicking sound.

The plants stepped over their burning comrade, and the one in front plucked the manager right off his feet and bit into his neck with vampiric ferocity. Blood spurted across the floor, the walls, the ceiling, the potted ferns standing sentry on either side of the hallway, and even across Chumley's own face.

The champagne glass slid from Chumley's hand and rolled across the carpet, and it took him too long to realize that the screaming he heard now came from his own mouth.

Dalton had retired early after drinking himself into a stupor following the morning's jaunt to Falcon Ranch. He'd kept Doris company until two dozen villagers arrived with all the extra-tall fencing the hardware store had on hand. They'd spoken for a while, but he was so shaken by what he'd seen that he had no recollection now of the things he and Doris had said to each other.

He hoped it hadn't been something embarrassing. He had an image to keep.

Dalton had just started to drift off into sleep when a faint whine from somewhere outside made his eyes snap open. Frowning, he rose and slid open his bedroom window to confirm what he already knew.

The town's sandstorm sirens were wailing like hell's banshees. (Did hell have banshees? He felt too drunk to remember.) Scowling, he slid the window closed and latched it. Sandstorm season wasn't due for another month, and though there was the occasional outlier, he had the hunch that the only reason they could possibly be going off now was if someone had set them off manually.

The moment Dalton lay back down on his bed, his comm unit crackled to life. "Hey, Dalton? Are you awake?"

It was Cadu. Dalton snatched the comm off his bedside table. "I'm awake," he growled, anger masking his profound concern. "What the feck is going on out there?"

"It's the Greens again," Cadu said. "I heard screaming outside, and once I knew what was going on, I rushed to the station and switched on the alarm. Carolyn is going door to door warning people to stay inside."

A wave of dizziness nearly sent Dalton sprawling as he hopped up and jammed his feet into his boots. Realizing it would be best to put on trousers before leaving the house, he kicked his boots back off, plucked that day's outfit out of the laundry hamper, and dressed as quickly as inebriation would allow.

Cadu was still saying something to him, but Dalton could hardly follow his words.

"I'm coming," he said, his voice slurring. "Hang tight."

He'd already reloaded his water pistol upon arriving home that afternoon. Giving it a superstitious pat, he clambered into his trench coat and fled the house on foot, wishing he'd brought the police quad home with him, although then he would have had to pull himself over for Driving While Intoxicated.

The sky flickered off to the west, right over the downtown district, and the acrid smell of smoke wafted through the night air. Dalton realized he'd left his comm in his bedroom. Too late to go back and get it now.

As he passed the post office, Dalton was nearly flattened by a small armada of land rovers packed full of fleeing people who evidently had not listened to Carolyn. Swearing, he got his bearings and rounded a corner onto Main Street, where the mighty Hotel Richport, which had stood strong for fifty years, was more ablaze than Methuselah's birthday cake.

Hotel Richport had not been constructed of adobe. Its painted, wooden walls had gone up like kindling. He could feel the heat from it even a block away.

Screams filled the air in a bone-chilling chorus. Citizens dashed every which way, some of them with scorched clothing. Marsha Soderberg, Richport's only firefighter, had hooked an extra-long garden hose to a tap in one of the buildings across the street from the burning hotel, and the weak spray of water hissed uselessly in the flames, like someone trying to tame an erupting volcano with a plant mister.

Dalton didn't see Greens anywhere. He saw only masses of distraught people, which made his scowl deepen.

The sandstorm sirens continued their earsplitting wail. Cadu sidled up beside Dalton in the street, his face long.

"What's going on here?" Dalton demanded. "Where are the Greens?"

"I don't know." Cadu swallowed and glanced up at the three-story hotel. "I only just got here from the station. Should I have turned the alarm off?"

"Doesn't matter. How did this fire start?"

"I think someone inside the hotel must have tried to stop the Greens with a flamethrower, and it got out of hand."

Dalton continued to regard the burning building as the roof caved in. A few volunteers were dousing the neighboring adobe buildings with buckets of water to help prevent marauding flames from spreading next door.

Since no Greens appeared to have survived the blaze, Dalton felt himself relax.

But only a little.

"Oh, it was simply *awful*."

Dalton's ears perked at the sound of the salesman's voice, and he turned to see Chumley Fanshaw speaking to a group of haggard onlookers, wearing a singed pink dressing gown and matching slippers. Droplets of blood had dried on his face, though it did not appear to be his own.

"Excuse me," Dalton said to Cadu, and strode toward the salesman.

Chumley, detecting his approach, turned to regard him. "Sheriff!" he exclaimed. "Thank God you're here!"

Dalton didn't smile—like there was anything he could do now that the hotel was turning into a pile of ash. "You were staying at this hotel?"

"Yes."

"What happened?"

Given the blood on Chumley's face, Dalton suspected he knew the answer.

"Plants," Chumley croaked, red-eyed. "They came up the stairs like *people.* And they killed the manager *right in front of me.*"

"How did you get away?"

"I ran track in school." Chumley appeared sheepish. "I'm such a coward. There could be people trapped in there, and I left them all to die." He ran his hands over his face and kept them there. "Oh, God. I've never watched anybody die like that before."

Dalton felt a shred of pity for the man. There had been a time in his own life when he'd never seen anyone die before, and he missed that like amputees missed their limbs.

"Is there anyone you can call?" Dalton asked. "Friends, family?"

Chumley shook his head. "I don't have anyone." Then his eyes widened. "Oh, no."

"What?"

"My things! I've got to get back up there!"

He started toward the hotel as the second floor caved into the first floor. Dalton grabbed him by the arm before he could get any farther, and Chumley let out a surprised, strangled cry.

"You're not getting your things," Dalton said.

Chumley seemed not to comprehend him. "I mean, *all* my things were in there! All my cash—everything I owned!"

"Are you insured?"

Chumley gave him a look that said, *are you kidding me?*

"Surely you have a bank account," Dalton said.

"Not one I'd prefer to access at the moment. I keep all my cash with me. It doesn't leave a paper trail."

Dalton arched an eyebrow. "In that case, I'd call your employer and see if they'll pay you early. Unless you're strictly on commissions."

Chumley let out a giggle tinged with hysteria. "There is no employer."

"Then where do the tanning beds come from?"

The *are you kidding me* look returned to Chumley's bloody face. "Did you see me lugging around a trailer full of tanning beds? I bet you didn't, because *there are no tanning beds.*"

Jigsaw pieces were beginning to assemble themselves inside Dalton's weary head. "You're a conman," he said. It was more of an observation than an accusation. Dalton felt much too tired to arrest him.

"Yes!" Chumley exclaimed so loudly that several people still gawping at the fire turned their heads. "So you'd better throw me in jail, because now I can't even pay for a room!" He stuck his face in his hands.

Maybe it was still the alcohol coursing through his system, maybe it was his deepening fatigue after a long, turbulent day, but Dalton didn't have the energy to deal with the man anymore. He groped one hand into the inner pocket of his trench coat, withdrew his wallet, and sifted through it until he found a one-hundred-pound note, which he thrust into Chumley's soot-stained hand.

"Now I don't know if this is just another con, or if you really did lose everything in that blaze," Dalton said, "but either way, you can use this to book a room at Sands Inn over on Mission Street. It's not as swanky as the Hotel Richport, but at least it still exists."

Chumley's eyes widened. "How do I get there?"

Dalton pointed at the next intersection to the west. "Turn left onto Mission Street. Sands Inn is on the left. You can't miss it."

"Oh, thank you, thank you!" A wave of tears cascaded down the man's cheeks, and he hurried off, dressing gown fluttering behind him.

Dalton refocused his attention on the glowing remains of Hotel Richport, his stomach tightening.

The Greens had invaded Doris Kelso's ranch.

The Greens had invaded the hotel.

Why had they begun to move? Would none of his people be safe again?

One thing he knew with a sickening certainty.

This was far from over.

CHAPTER 3

Dalton's body felt as though it had been cast from lead when he peeled himself off the top of his bed in the morning. What a dream he'd had! Greens attacking Doris's animals, and even more of them slaughtering the good people of Hotel Richport? Must have been an aftereffect of seeing Debbie's lunch.

He glanced at the photo of Darneisha and the girls, showered, pulled on his clothing, and fried up some eggs for his morning meal, wolfing them down on the go since he'd overslept by half an hour.

To his surprise, Cadu, Carolyn, and Carolyn's personal aide, a small-framed androgyne named Errin Inglewood, were gathered in the police station meeting room when Dalton arrived.

Coffee brewed in a pot in the corner. The smell of it made Dalton's mouth water.

"Morning." Dalton plopped into a lopsided swivel chair and plunked his booted feet onto the edge of the table. "Are we talking about that smoke again?"

Carolyn leveled an unimpressed gaze at him. "You're the one who asked me and Errin to be here."

Dalton reached into one of his trench coat pockets and pulled out a wooden toothpick, which he stuck between his teeth. "*I* scheduled a meeting?"

"You did."

"And?"

"And," Carolyn went on, her stare unwavering, "I don't think it's proper for you to be so damned lackadaisical when six people are dead."

Dalton bit down on the toothpick so hard, it splintered between his incisors. Very calmly, he removed the pieces and stuffed them back into his coat pocket. "These six people . . ."

"Were killed when the Greens attacked Hotel Richport last night. You saw the aftermath; you called me from the station after it happened. Don't you remember?"

Dalton's eyes closed. He supposed that bad dreams had been too much to wish for.

After a silent count of ten, he said, "What do we know about the . . . situation?"

Errin cleared their throat. Today, the thirtyish, sandy-haired aide had dressed in a pale blue shirt and black slacks so free from dirt and grit that it had to be an optical illusion. "Of the six deceased," they said, pale face drawn with lines of exhaustion, "three were from Earth, and three lived here in town."

"Who?" Dalton croaked, sitting up a little straighter and removing his feet from the table.

Errin glanced down at the datapad in front of them. "Horace Kilburn, the hotel manager; Corvus Hightower, a front desk clerk; and Maria Beauregard, who stopped by the hotel to pick up a friend who'd been staying there. The offworlders were Larue Chancy, Krishanna Lopez, and Grainey Kirk, all visiting from Australia." They cleared their throat and looked up at Dalton, as if silently entreating him to do something. "Seven more people from the hotel are being treated for burns and lacerations including my sister Jeanette, who works in the laundry room." Their fair skin paled even further.

"Is she going to be okay?" Dalton kept his tone neutral.

"Most likely." Errin's expression didn't change—ever the professional.

Dalton forced himself to breathe deeply for a few seconds even though tension was squeezing his lungs flat. "Do we know why the Greens attacked the hotel?"

"Eyewitnesses said the Greens went for the fountain in the lobby before they did anything else," Errin said, eyes downcast. "They must have smelled the water from outside and stopped in for a sip before they went on a rampage. If the Rosa had been full, we might never have known they were coming this way."

"But what brought them into town in the first place?" Cadu asked, breaking his own contemplative silence. "What could we possibly have here that they don't?"

"Could be they're at war with each other and the losers turned tail and ran," Dalton mused, hoping it wasn't true. "It's not like we know anything about their society, or if they even have one."

"They seem to function on basic animal instinct," Errin said. "They may have tools like sacks and canteens, but their primary focus seems to be on survival. And they eat meat."

Carolyn scooted her chair forward an inch or two. "I think this is connected to the smoke up north."

"Forest fire?" Cadu asked.

"It's possible. We'll have to put a message out to any

incoming shuttle pilots and ask if they see anything on their way down."

Errin tapped at their datapad and said, "We don't have any shuttles due today."

Dalton banged a fist on the table. "We need to work faster than that! If we don't—"

There came a loud rapping on the frame of the open doorway leading out to the main part of the police station. Dalton swiveled his chair to see who'd had the gall to interrupt so important a discussion and nearly did a double-take when he saw it was Chumley, still in his scorched dressing gown and slippers, his gleaming black hair in disarray.

"Erm, excuse me," Chumley said, glancing from Dalton to Carolyn and then back again. "I wondered if I could speak to the sheriff."

Bags hung under Chumley's eyes. At least he'd wiped the blood off his face.

Dalton gave him a cool look. "About what?"

"I don't have anywhere to go!" Chumley wrang his hands together in front of him. "The front desk lady at the inn kicked me out this morning when I went down for breakfast and she recognized me from the town square."

Dalton shook his head. "You need charity, go beg it from one of the churches."

"But last night you gave me—"

Dalton slammed his fist on the table again, unable to hide his wince at the pain lancing through his joints. "Forget about last night! Now get out of here so we can figure out how to stop the Greens from killing anyone else."

Chumley's deep brown eyes welled with tears, and his

mouth quivered as if he were a toddler who'd been forcibly removed from his favorite teddy bear. Without another word, he turned on his heel and padded out of the meeting room. Dalton could hear the door to the lobby click shut a moment later.

Good riddance.

Cadu, Carolyn, and Errin regarded him with arched eyebrows. Dalton removed one of the toothpick shards from his pocket and gnashed it hard. "Now, where was I?"

"Dalton," Errin said with evident hesitation, "there are eight thousand terrified citizens out there wondering when the next attack is going to happen. How are we going to protect them?"

"We'll establish a watch," Dalton said.

"Consisting of who?" Carolyn asked.

"Whoever has the biggest flamethrowers. We can use boomstones, too—I saw some out near Lady Liberty that need to be picked up."

"Are these people going to be paid?"

"That's not for me to decide."

Carolyn sighed and gazed down at the tabletop in front of her with a sort of weary resignation. "I suppose we can organize shifts to patrol the outskirts of the city."

"I'll start making calls as soon as we get back to the office," Errin said as they stood. "Dalton, is there anything else you'll need us to do?"

"You might want to put in an order of extra flamethrowers and fuel." Dalton patted his holster. "And weed killer."

"Oh, *why* did I come to this stupid little planet?" Chumley sobbed as he rounded a corner onto yet another unfamiliar street. He was hopelessly lost in the grid of adobe dwellings, most of which resembled sand-colored boxes of varying heights; and every time he considered stopping and asking for directions, whichever townspeople he'd been about to approach wrinkled their noses and glared as if daring him to give it a try to see what happened.

His stomach rumbled, and his mouth felt so parched, he could hardly swallow. If only he could get some water, he might be able to brainstorm his way out of this mess.

But he was in a desert. Water wouldn't likely be free, anywhere, and right now free was all he could afford.

A wave of lightheadedness made Chumley stop in his tracks and put his hands on his knees to steady himself. He felt like a tiny plant trying to grow through a crack in the pavement on a summer day—withered and useless.

If he still had his Cube, everything would be fine. But the Cube had been lost in the fire along with everything inside it, including his wardrobe, his childhood mementos, his minibar, and his refrigerator full of bottled Crystalline Ice, which would feel downright refreshing right now.

The buildings on this street rose three or four floors, the upper levels of which boasted balconies festooned with laundry drying in the bright Molorthian sun. A woman pinning bras to a clothesline on one of the balconies scowled down at him and spat. It evaporated before it hit him.

"Could . . . could I have a glass of water, please?" Chumley croaked, his voice a ghost of its usual self.

A door above him slammed. He blinked, and the woman was gone.

He forced himself onward, keeping an eye out for a church. Would churches around here offer free water? He hoped so, or there wouldn't be a Chumley Fanshaw dying of thirst for much longer.

The townspeople would probably love that. He'd been naïve to think the sheriff would help him again after last night. The man probably gave him the money to get him out of his hair.

"Hey, mister."

Chumley turned. A boy of perhaps twelve stood in the street behind him, wearing a wide-brimmed hat that kept the sun out of his eyes.

"Hello," Chumley said, faintly, as the ground swayed.

"You're the salesman," the boy said. His callused, weather-worn hands hung at his sides.

"I'm Chumley Fanshaw."

"You sell things. We saw you in the town square."

"Levi, who're you talkin' to?" a man asked before Chumley could form a reply. Footsteps behind him made Chumley turn, putting his back to the boy. A man roughly Chumley's age had planted his hands on his hips and was looking Chumley up and down, sneering at his ruined dressing gown.

"I'm lost," Chumley whispered. "Can you tell me how to get to a church?"

The man cracked a malicious grin showing several missing teeth. "You were the one disturbing the peace."

"I was just trying to do my job." Not that it was a real job, but this man didn't need to know that.

"You have anything to do with the Green attacks?"

"What? No!" Chumley pulled his dressing gown tighter around himself, wishing it could protect him.

"Awful funny, they attacked right after you showed up." The man stepped closer to Chumley. "It's like even the savages sniffed you out."

Chumley sensed his situation was about to deteriorate even further when another man and a woman appeared on the front step of the nearest dwelling, looking gleeful much in the way piranhas do when someone has thrown them a juicy steak.

He recognized them as a couple to whom he'd given his fraudulent tanning bed information.

"We heard you survived the Green attack," the woman said, folding her arms.

"I run fast," Chumley said.

"Let's see just how fast," her partner said, and suddenly two men and little Levi were charging at him all at once, fists raised.

Stars danced in Chumley's eyes, and the next thing he knew, all he could taste was sand and blood.

Dalton had been working on his crossword puzzles again when Cadu stepped into his office, looking chagrined.

Dalton slapped the book shut, his heart stuttering in a sudden panic. "Green attack?"

"Um . . . no," Cadu said. "There's been a disturbance over on Wax Street. It's your salesman friend again. He's made some people unhappy."

"You've got to be kidding me." Dalton rose and jammed on his Stetson. The last thing he needed was a mob to defuse.

He marched past Cadu and hopped on one of the quads parked out back, then nearly hit Gwendolyn Goldfarb when she stepped out into the street in front of him just as he was gunning it up to full speed.

Gwendolyn wore a fluorescent pink wide-brimmed hat that kept most of her wrinkled, nut-brown face in shade, and a matching kaftan that fluttered in the light wind. "Two broken halves make a whole," she crooned as she hobbled toward the nail salon on the other side of the road.

Dalton scowled and stomped his foot into the accelerator. The woman was going to get herself killed if she didn't snap out of her daydreams and start paying attention to the world around her.

It took him five minutes to reach Wax Street, which had accumulated a small crowd in the center of it like ants swarming a discarded bit of candy. Dalton disembarked from the quad and strutted toward the gathering, flashing his tarnished badge even though everyone in the city knew him.

"Out of the way, out of the way," he snapped. "Now what do we have here?"

He noted that many of the twenty-odd people clustered in the center of the street looked a bit ruffled, as if they'd been engaged in some overexuberant physical activity shortly before his arrival. A few, like Bennett Smith and his son, Levi, looked a shade guilty.

Dalton didn't see Chumley. He must have been trying to keep a low profile to avoid imminent arrest.

When no one was forthcoming in moving, Dalton

shoved his way past the Smiths, the Wus, the Nguyens, and the Kaouds, who parted like a reluctant Red Sea. He was fully prepared to give an intense verbal berating to one Mr. Chumley Fanshaw, but he found his mouth hanging open in silent yet abject horror.

Chumley lay crumpled and unmoving in the center of the dusty thoroughfare. His dressing gown was gone—mercifully he'd been wearing a pair of designer briefs underneath it, which were now ripped in several places. He appeared reasonably well-toned, yet his strength had not been able to save him. Both of his eyes were swollen shut, his nose appeared a bit more crooked than it had earlier, and blood had run from his nose, over his lips, and onto the dirt.

Shit, shit, SHIT.

Shaking, Dalton crouched down and put two fingers against the man's neck, grateful when he felt a pulse.

"Who did this?" he asked softly, without rising.

At first, no one spoke. Levi Smith shuffled his feet, and Ramsey Wu became very interested in the time on his wristwatch.

"I assume this man just beat himself all up," Dalton said.

The silence continued.

Dalton drew himself to his full height and growled, "I can arrest the whole lot of you if nobody speaks up!"

"We . . . we found him lying there," said Bennett Smith. "He, uh, didn't look too good."

Bennett had fresh blood on his knuckles. So did Benjy Kaoud and Ramsey Wu.

Dalton strode right up to Bennett and seized him by the collar. "Did you, now."

Bennett let out a squeak that might have been words, or just a noise.

"It's a rough part of town," Ramsey said, stepping in and turning his hat over in his hands. "He had it coming."

But Dalton knew who had it coming, and it wasn't the poor bastard lying in the street. In one swift movement, Dalton brought a fist back and slammed it into Bennett's insolent little face, sending the man crashing backward into the others.

"You can't do that!" Ramsey cried, rushing in to help his accomplice to his feet.

"Can't I?" Dalton held up a quivering finger and shook it. "If I find out you've done this to anyone else, ever again, I'm deporting you back to Earth without trial on the next shuttle. Is that clear?"

A few heads nodded. Bennett, Ramsey, and Benjy shot him looks of pure loathing before drifting away, no doubt to plot further mayhem.

Dalton gritted his teeth and crouched down beside Chumley once more. He had to get him out of here before the crowd decided they didn't like sheriffs, either.

When Dalton realized that some of the crowd remained like vultures waiting for a piece of the kill, he shouted, "Go home, or I'll arrest every last one of you!"

The stragglers glared at him and dispersed. Dalton refocused his attention on Chumley, whose chest rose and fell with shallow breaths.

"Hey," Dalton said in a low voice.

Chumley groaned, but his eyes didn't open.

"Mr. Fanshaw—Chumley—I need you to wake up."

"Mmmwake," Chumley said. He remained still.

"You'll need to come with me."

Silence.

"Mr. Fanshaw?"

Belatedly, Dalton recalled Chumley mentioning that he'd been driven from the inn when he went down to get his breakfast. Perhaps he hadn't had the chance to eat any before his eviction.

Perhaps he'd had nothing to drink, either.

Dalton patted his trench coat pockets and found his emergency flask. It had been a few days since he'd put anything fresh in it, but the stale liquid would have to do.

He shook the flask, then said, "Mr. Fanshaw, I have some water here. You'll need to sit up to drink it."

Chumley's swollen eyes fluttered open, unfocused. Dalton held out a hand and helped him into sitting position, then handed him the flask. "Drink all of it," he said. "When we get to my place, you can have more."

The words slipped from his mouth before he could think. Chumley admitted to being a conman. He would probably rob Dalton blind while he slept and be offworld before he knew what had hit him.

As if Dalton had anything worth stealing.

Chumley accepted the flask with trembling hands and spilled half the water down his front. "Th—thank you," he spluttered. "They . . . they . . ."

"Don't wear yourself out. Where's your dressing gown?"

Chumley made a weak gesture with one arm. Dalton followed the angle of it and spotted the dressing gown slung over an electric line in front of one of the flat complexes, high out of reach.

"Right, forget about that," Dalton said. "We're going to get on my quad, and I'm going to take you to my house where those fecking punks can't get their hands on you."

Chumley's head bobbed up and down in acknowledgment. Dalton helped him to his feet and then guided him over to the quad. It took a few tries for Chumley to swing his right leg over the seat, and then Dalton clumsily clambered on behind him, his face burning less from the midday heat and more from the embarrassment that he had a gangly, mostly-naked man parked in front of him while half the street watched from their windows.

Dalton craned his neck to see over Chumley's shoulder, set his jaw in determination, and stepped on the accelerator, wondering what exactly he'd done to make the universe hate him so.

He avoided the busiest parts of town and kept his gaze fixed straight ahead anytime he detected onlookers. Chumley started to lose consciousness a few times and slumped uncomfortably against Dalton's front, and it was with immense relief that they arrived in front of Dalton's house ten minutes later.

As Dalton guided him toward the door, he glanced toward the north and saw yet a new plume of smoke unfurling into the air from below the horizon.

He frowned, unlocked the door, and began attending to his guest.

CHAPTER 4

Chumley had been on more than his fair share of benders at university and even in the years since then, but nothing compared to how he felt when he cracked his sore eyes open. It was like knives had been inserted beneath his skin in various places. His head, for example. And most of his face.

It felt like someone had tied him to the back of a lorry and dragged him through a few thousand miles of boulders.

Something cool pressed against his forehead. He lifted a hand and patted his fingers against what felt like an icepack. Craning his neck even further, he noted that he wore a clean pair of pajama shorts.

He appeared to be in an unfamiliar living room. The off-white curtains had been drawn, but he could still make out the outlines of shelves and another sofa.

He remembered feeling deliriously thirsty, but his mouth felt fine now, as if he'd been recently hydrated.

Footsteps made Chumley shift his attention to the left. A man stood in the open doorway between this room and the next.

"Hello?" Chumley rasped.

"You're awake. Good."

It was the sheriff. Chumley hadn't recognized him without the long coat and cowboy hat. His pulse spiked, and he scrambled into sitting position, looking for his shoes, then remembering they'd been lost in the fire.

And God only knew what had happened to his slippers.

"It's all right," the sheriff said, striding into the room and seating himself in a chair on the other side of the coffee table. The man's light brown hair had faded into the color of straw at the ends, and his gray shirt and dark slacks looked equally faded from use.

The shorts were probably his.

"Am I in trouble, Sheriff?" Chumley asked.

His host smirked. "Loads of it. How are you feeling?"

Chumley touched a hand to his chilled forehead. The icepack had fallen into his lap when he sat up, and he set it aside. "Sore," he said.

"You caused quite the scene over on Wax Street."

"I did?" Chumley strained to remember. He thought there might have been a kid, and some men. "I was looking for the churches. For water."

"Let me know if you need more. I can tell you're from a temperate climate."

Chumley nodded. "I was born north of London. I've been on Pelstring Four for a while, though. They have nice summers."

Dalton stared at him. Chumley averted his gaze, uncomfortable.

"I want the truth from you," Dalton said at length.

"The truth?"

"Who are you, and what are you doing on my planet?"

"I already told you."

Dalton folded his arms. "You're Chumley Fanshaw, and

you pretend to sell tanning beds to con people out of their money. You say you only carry cash, which was burned up along with everything else you owned." He paused. "I don't buy it."

"What do you mean?"

"You're wearing designer briefs, so I have a hard time believing you're in as much trouble as you say you are."

Chumley felt his cheeks turn scarlet. "I paid for them with cash at a charity shop. They still had the original tags."

"Do you have cash stashed anywhere else? On Pelstring Four, perhaps?"

"I swear I don't. I . . . sort of fell on hard times." Harder, now, it seemed. Every time Chumley hit rock bottom, yet another rock bottom had lain below it like levels in a rock bottom skyrise. "I had cash with me when I came here. I assume it all burned."

"Hmph." Hidden gears turned behind Dalton's gray eyes. "You seem to be in a dilemma."

Chumley swallowed, and the smirk returned to the sheriff's face. "The only way you can get off this rock is if you earn your keep long enough to save money for a shuttle ticket. However, the good people of this city will skin you alive the moment you step out my door, and few of them are about to go hiring you. You are, as they say, up a creek."

Chumley picked up the icepack and jammed it into his suddenly-throbbing temple. "Then what am I going to do?"

Dalton's smirk turned wicked. "I've been thinking."

"And?"

"I'm going to put you to work."

"Doing *what*?"

"We're understaffed at the police station. Greens keep invading us so the mayor is instituting a city watch, but it won't be enough. If you work for me, you'll be as protected as you're going to get. People respect lawmen here."

It took Chumley's frazzled brain a few tries to comprehend what Dalton was saying. "I can't be a police officer!" he exclaimed, rising on unsteady legs. "I don't have that kind of training!"

"Neither did I in the beginning. You'll learn the ropes like I did. Consider it a penance for breaking the law."

"This is cruelty!"

"Cruelty would be me leaving you to the folks outside. Now I think you're probably a pathetic person, and I think it'll give me a migraine having you stay here, but I'm an officer of the law, and I can't abide with murder."

"Are there a lot of murders here?"

"Not too many. You want to know why we have a No Solicitation ordinance?"

Chumley was sure he didn't, but he said, "Why?"

Dalton looked thoughtful for a moment. "These people, these Molorthians, are a different sort of folk. I say that because I came here too, a long time ago. Molorthia Six isn't like other places. You won't see rich folk or poor folk, because here we're just folk. Someone opens a business, it's because it's needed. Half the goods are probably bought with bartered items anyway. But if a salesman comes along?" Dalton's smile reminded Chumley of a shark's.

"I think I understand now." Chumley swallowed. "The ordinance is for my own protection."

"That's right."

"Isn't there an ordinance against homicide?"

"Of course. But when has that ever stopped a murderer?"

Chumley blinked at him, wondering if Dalton had noticed his own contradiction. "I knew I should have gone to Killian Six instead."

"No point in lamenting that."

"I just can't work for the police. It's—it's *wrong!*"

Dalton shrugged. "I can't keep an eye on you twenty-eight hours a day unless you're on my payroll."

Chumley's shoulders drooped. "I don't have a way around this, do I?"

"Not unless you can conjure up a shuttle ticket—and I'm not buying you one; I gave you enough money already. Now what do you want for dinner?"

Dalton fried up four beef patties slathered in Worcestershire sauce and chopped onions, pondering the various sorts of trainings he'd have to put his guest through. He'd lent Chumley an old shirt in addition to the shorts, and the conman sat at Dalton's table with his head in his hands, devoid of all hope.

"So, when do I start my training?" Chumley asked as Dalton set a plate in front of him five minutes later.

"First thing in the morning. You'll come with me to the station and I'll get you a badge so people know not to mess with you. Need ketchup?"

Chumley eyed his beef patties, sitting on buns Dalton had bought fresh from the bakery earlier in the week, and said, "Yes, please."

Dalton grabbed the ketchup from the fridge and plunked it on the table, then bit into his own patty sandwich. After swallowing, he said, "I'll take you out to the firing range before lunch tomorrow and see how well you can aim a water pistol. It's my favorite way of dealing with *them*."

Chumley's brows knit together. "You squirt water at them?"

"Weed killer. It's less risky than flamethrowers or boom-stones. You saw what flamethrowers did to the hotel."

"What you're saying is, these plants have caused trouble before."

"Not often, but often enough. Until this week, it'd been a year or so since I had to deal with one. It got tangled in some fencing outside a homestead about five kilometers south of here. They called me in to put it out of its misery."

"I'm in hell." Chumley shoved his plate away from him and ran his hands through his hair.

"You've got the climate about right. Being on the force around here isn't that bad, though. We can go weeks at a time without any major incidents."

Dalton's comm, which had been laying on the countertop next to the range, squawked to life as if on cue. "Dalton? You there?"

It was Cadu, of course. Dalton snatched up the device. "What is it now?"

"Gwendolyn Goldfarb is causing some problems over on the corner of Broadway and Cactus. Just come over and give her a good talking to. She might actually listen to you."

We'll see about that, Dalton thought. "All right," he said. "We'll be there soon."

"We?" Cadu asked, but Dalton had already pocketed the comm.

"Well, Deputy, it seems we have a job to do." Dalton bared his teeth in a grin and shoved his plate into the refrigerator. "Think you can handle it?"

Chumley groaned.

Shadows began to grow long, and the temperature had started its much-needed evening plummet by the time Dalton ushered a whining Chumley out the door.

"They're going to kill me as soon as they see me!" he said as Dalton led him around to the parked quad.

"Not if you stay with me."

"I don't have a badge yet!"

"If anybody kills you, I'll see to it myself that they're force-fed to the Greens. Now get on."

Chumley made an unmanly noise and mounted the quad. This time Dalton got on in front of him and said, "You might want to hang on."

Dalton gunned the quad out of his yard. He felt Chumley's hands instinctively latch onto the back of his trench coat. A few onlookers gawked as Dalton navigated the grid of streets, and they came at last upon a scene most surreal.

Dalton dismounted on Cactus Street, frowning.

Behind him, Chumley said, "What the hell?"

Gwendolyn Goldfarb, whom Dalton had nearly flattened in the street that very morning, stood in the center of the thoroughfare with her arms spread wide and her head thrown back, as if awaiting a flying saucer to come along and beam her up. Her hat was gone, but now she wore a neon orange shawl over her kaftan that made Dalton's eyes hurt.

"Stay close," Dalton muttered to Chumley, then approached the old woman with caution.

Her lips were moving. Faint words spilled from them.

"Worlds of hurt," she breathed. "So much pain, and for what? They teem, they thrive, but for how long? Save us!" Her voice rose in pitch until she nearly screamed the final word. "Save us all! They're coming!"

Her words chilled Dalton's veins into ice. "Who's coming, Gwendolyn?"

She didn't even acknowledge his presence. Her eyes appeared to have rolled back into her head, showing only the whites. "It will be death to us all."

"What does she mean?" Chumley worried, lingering near Dalton's side. "What's wrong with her?"

"She got lost in the desert a few years back and lost her mind. She's always going on like this."

"Should we get her to a doctor?"

"I don't know yet."

Dalton stepped forward and put a hand on Gwendolyn's arm. She flinched and peered at him with dark eyes. "Sheriff Kane!" she exclaimed. "Fancy seeing you here! What am I doing in the center of the street?"

"You said something is coming."

"I did?" She blinked at him like someone stepping into the sunlight after a long day indoors.

"What's coming?" Chumley asked. "Is it more of the . . . the Greens?"

Gwendolyn drew back a step. "How should I know what the Greens are doing?" She brushed a smudge of sand off the front of her shawl, turned tail, and sauntered off past several bewildered onlookers as if nothing unusual had just happened.

Dalton strode over to Helmut Jones, a teller at his bank, who stared after Gwendolyn in astonishment. "What was she saying before we got here?" Dalton demanded.

Helmut scratched at his beard. "I couldn't hear much, but I think she said something about lights."

"Lights?"

"She's crazy, Sheriff. You know that."

Dalton frowned after Gwendolyn's dwindling figure. She'd said something before that niggled at the back of his mind. He rewound his thoughts past rescuing Chumley from Wax Street, past the hotel fire and the attack at Falcon Ranch, and let out a small gasp.

"Fire in the sky!" Gwendolyn had cried outside the supermarket during Dalton's walk to clear his head after the salad incident. It seemed she had shouted it almost continuously from the moment he'd caught sight of her until he'd rounded the corner onto another street.

The very next evening, Hotel Richport had gone up in flames.

Surely it was a coincidence.

But what if it wasn't?

They're coming, Gwendolyn had said just now. *It will be death to us all.*

Dalton let out a curse.

"What is it?" Chumley asked.

Some of the people near them had spotted Chumley, who sported two black eyes from the assault over on Wax Street. Dalton made a point of looking menacing so they would stay away from his reluctant deputy. "We need to alert the new city watch," Dalton said, pulling out his comm. "Right now."

The sun had dipped below the horizon by the time Errin Inglewood and an assortment of armed citizens met up with Dalton and Chumley just to the north of town.

Dalton had retrieved two pairs of night vision goggles from the police station and passed one to Errin.

Errin slipped the goggles into place over their eyes, the straps making their sand-colored hair stick up in tufts. "I'm not sure I understand the point of this. We already have three volunteers patrolling the perimeter."

"Call it a very good hunch," Dalton grunted. "The town was attacked just after nightfall last night. I won't let it happen again. Strength in numbers, you know."

"Shouldn't we have extra people posted on all sides of town, then? Not just the north?"

"North is where most of that smoke is." He snapped his own goggles on and withdrew his loaded water pistol. "If more Greens are coming, that's the direction they'll be coming from." His heart stuttered, and he turned so Errin couldn't see the fear on his face.

Dalton felt a tap on his shoulder. "Erm, Sheriff?"

"What?"

"I can't see anything." Chumley coughed lightly. "How am I supposed to kill a Green when I can't even see?"

"I was getting to that. Errin?" Dalton nodded toward Carolyn's aide, who picked up a giant bulb mounted on a tripod to show to Chumley, who of course couldn't see it.

"The moment Dalton or I see movement out here, we flick on the floodlight and take the Greens by surprise," Errin said. "Then we fire."

"Won't the floodlight overload those goggles? And won't it blind the rest of us, since our eyes aren't adjusted to light?"

Chumley's worried expression appeared a sallow green through the goggles. He held his own water pistol at his side, barrel pointed toward the ground. Weed killer trickled from it in a slow drip.

"Errin, could I talk to you alone for a minute?" Dalton asked.

They nodded. "Certainly, Sheriff."

The two of them stepped away from Chumley and the four other volunteers they'd rounded up.

"The salesman is right," Errin said in a low tone, looking up at him. "If we use the floodlight, we might incapacitate ourselves. I say you and I keep these on—" they tapped at their goggles— "and tell everyone exactly where to fire the moment we see a Green."

"Too much could go wrong that way."

"It's not perfect, but it's the best we can do on such short notice."

Visions of bloodthirsty leaves and branches flashed through Dalton's head, and he counted to ten while drawing slow breaths so he wouldn't have a panicked meltdown in front of everyone. "Right," he said at length. "No floodlight, then. You hear that, everyone?" he called back at the others. "We're not using the floodlight. If Errin or I say fire, start firing."

Luckily, all of them were armed with water pistols, so accidentally shooting a comrade would not result in immediate combustion.

He and Errin rejoined the others. His heart thudded harder as he imagined the leafy hordes charging toward them under cover of darkness, and his mind's eye replayed the beasts clambering over picnic tables and around playground equipment while screams rent the air.

Dolls and action figures had lain abandoned on the ground. Sand castles had been flattened among puddles of blood.

He forced his eyes back open, not realizing he'd closed them.

He was a different man now.

He could do this.

But can you? a little voice asked inside of him. *Because that salad . . .*

"Errin, keep your eyes peeled," Dalton barked. "Chumley, you come and stand beside me. Joe and Edith, you take up positions on the other side of Errin. Abdul, you stand on the other side of Chumley, and Helen, you stand between me and Errin."

Someone let out a sob, and Dalton was startled to realize it wasn't Chumley, but Joe, who ran a repair shop over on Sunrise Street.

"Are you going to be all right?" Dalton asked him in a low voice.

"I don't know." Joe's voice quavered. The man kept his gaze fixed straight ahead toward the open desert. "I thought I could do this, but . . . but then I remembered Piney Gulch. Your cousin Darius was a good friend of mine."

Dalton nodded in understanding. "You can go home, if you want. I won't make anyone do anything they're not comfortable with."

"Except for me," Chumley snapped, his tone bitter.

"I'll stay," Joe said. "I want to help. My neighbor's in intensive care after the hotel attack. It's the least I can do."

"Okay, then." Dalton squared his shoulders. "If Errin or I say to fire, you know what to do."

The seven of them fell silent and waited.

Dalton kept his eyes wide, scanning the horizon from left to right and back again. Nothing moved out there except the low-growing desert scrub, which was not nearly lush enough to ever be confused for the enemy.

An hour passed. Dalton heard Chumley's stomach growl. He remembered they hadn't finished their dinners.

Errin withdrew their comm from their pocket and spoke into it in low tones. "Marshall, are you picking up anything yet?"

"Negative," came the voice of one of the mobile patrols scouting around the edge of the city. "It's deader out here than Crypt Valley. You?"

"Same," Errin said. "Where are you?"

"Southwest side, close to the Rosa. I haven't seen a thing."

"Just keep your eyes open," Errin said, throwing Dalton a glance.

"I'm getting tired, and I have to be up for work in five hours."

"Just keep looking, Marshall. If you don't see anything else in the next hour, you can go home."

Dalton could hear Marshall's grumble loud and clear on the night air. Errin tapped at the buttons on the comm and said, "Ash? Do you see anything yet?"

"Nope," the comm replied. "You?"

"Not a thing. What's your current position?"

"I'm just now passing the ballfields. There's a stray cat slinking around out here, but nothing bigger than that."

"Excellent. Keep us posted if you see anything else."

"Will do."

Errin then proceeded to call yet another one of the citizens patrolling the perimeter. "Maxine? How are things over your way?"

The comm emitted only silence.

"Maxine, do you copy?"

Dalton's chest tightened. Maxine had been toting a flamethrower nearly as long as she was tall the last he'd seen her. If she'd met some sort of foul play . . .

"Maxine, *do you copy*?" Errin repeated, their tone growing more anxious. Then they swore. "Her comm must be out of order."

"What if it isn't?" Joe asked. "What if *they've* got her?"

Errin tapped more buttons on the comm. "Marshall, it's me again. Have you heard from Maxine?"

"Can't say I have," Marshall replied. "Is something wrong?"

"She isn't answering her comm."

"I'll try her and see if it works for me." Marshall fell silent, and thirty agonizing seconds later, his voice came on again. "I've got nothing, but I'll be on the lookout for her."

Sweat ran down Dalton's scalp even though the temperature outside had grown quite pleasant.

Save us all! They're coming! Gwendolyn had wailed.

The woman knew something, no doubt about that. But how did she know? What was her source of information? Did she even know she knew?

He was peripherally aware of Errin contacting Ash, who also had not seen Maxine during the past couple of hours.

Out on the horizon, something that wasn't desert scrub moved.

Dots sparkled on the edges of his vision.

Don't faint, he ordered himself.

"Errin, look," he whispered, and nodded straight ahead of him.

Errin put away their comm and drew in a short breath. "What is it?"

"I'm not sure."

Whatever it was appeared low to the ground, perhaps half a kilometer in front of them. It held still, then made a quick if lopsided lurch toward the right.

"Is it a juvenile Green?" Errin asked. "It's not tall enough to be an adult."

"I don't know." Dalton fiddled with a button on the side of his goggles and zoomed in as far as it would go. Under night vision, the thing looked chartreuse and somewhat plastic bag-shaped.

An underdeveloped juvenile, perhaps—or even a baby?

He had to find out.

"Stay," Dalton ordered his comrades in a low tone, then crept forward with his water pistol at the ready.

His heart climbed higher into his throat with each step. He reminded himself he was doing this for the eight thousand souls in the sleeping city behind him.

Up ahead, the object had grown stationary and only fluttered at sporadic moments, coinciding with the soft gusts of wind susurrating over the rocky ground.

Dalton narrowed his eyes and held his water pistol in a two-handed grip in front of him as he continued his cautious approach.

Twenty steps later, he saw why the object looked like a plastic bag.

It was a plastic bag.

Which had snagged on a wiry desert bush.

PAM'S PLEASURE PALACE, read the block letters printed on the side, and below that in smaller print read, *Where everyone goes home a winner.*

Bloodcurdling screams cut through the air behind him, and the view through the goggles went blank.

Blinding light lanced his corneas when Dalton tore the goggles from his face. He tried in vain to blink the tortuous afterimage from his vision and sprinted blindly toward his companions, using the sounds of their dying agony to guide him.

Through the afterimage, he watched a tongue of flame lick horizontally through the night.

Flame?

When Dalton was fifteen meters from Chumley, Errin, and the others, the screams morphed into cries of outrage.

"What do you think you're *doing*?" a woman shrieked.

"I ... oh, gosh, *sorry!*" Someone made a spluttering, retching sound. "I didn't think ..."

Though the floodlight still dazzled Dalton's eyes, he could see enough now to tell that Errin stood with their hands on their knees, and Maxine, the missing city watch volunteer, stood close by brandishing a smoking flamethrower. The ground smoldered a meter away from them.

"What happened back here?" Dalton demanded. "Who turned on that light?"

"I did," Joe said weakly. "I heard a noise, and ... and ..."

"And they all sprayed weed killer at me," Maxine said.

"I didn't," said Chumley. "I sprayed weed killer at Joe."

"It went in my *mouth*," Joe whined. Then, "I've been poisoned!"

Dalton ground his teeth together. "Someone kill that damned light so I can think straight."

The floodlight winked out. Dalton patted his coat pockets and found a penlight inside one of them, then clicked it on and aimed at it the nearest person, who turned out to be Abdul.

"Are you all right?" Dalton asked him.

Abdul nodded and nervously rubbed at his beard. "I seem to be."

"Good. Take Joe to the hospital so they can wash his mouth out with soap." He turned to Maxine. "Why didn't you answer your comm?"

The fiftyish woman frowned. Splotches of herbicide

covered the front of her leather jacket, but it didn't look like any had gotten on her face. "I didn't know anyone was trying to call me. The battery must be dead."

"Next time we head out on our watch," Dalton said, "we're all going to make sure we have a full charge in all of our equipment first. If we'd brought flamethrowers too, you'd be dead."

Maxine bowed her head. "It won't happen again, sir."

Dalton stared back out toward the northern horizon, where the bag remained stuck to the bush. "Go home, all of you. My hunch was wrong. There will be no attack tonight."

"Even me?" Maxine asked.

"Even you."

"But you saw something out there," said Edith, who had folded her arms. "If it wasn't a baby Green, what was it?"

"Plastic bag. Simple mistake."

"Dalton," Errin said gently, "you and Carolyn wanted—"

"I don't care what we wanted. We shouldn't have come out here." Dalton ground his teeth together, wishing he had more toothpicks. "Chumley, let's go home."

He'd taken three long strides when something off to his left caught his eye. He halted, frowning, and squinted, automatically raising his water pistol in defense.

"What is it?" Chumley asked, hovering half a meter behind him.

"Someone's standing over there." Dalton struggled to get a good look, but his vision still dazzled with afterimages. He might as well have been blind.

Errin stepped in closer, the top of their head just above and to the right of Dalton's shoulder. "I don't see anyone."

Dalton pointed at a human-shaped pale blur. "Right there. Looks like they're in light-colored clothes. You!" he called. "Are you part of the watch?"

There came no reply. Dalton fumbled for the penlight and aimed it at the person, who whirled away from him and faded into the shadows.

"Well, they weren't a Green, at least," he said, and turned back to Chumley, Errin, and the others, all of whom appeared equally baffled. "What?"

"Who wasn't a Green?" Errin asked. "There wasn't anyone there."

CHAPTER 5

Just before fourteen o'clock midnight, Dalton and Chumley trudged through the door and reheated their unfinished patty sandwiches, which they consumed in a contemplative silence in Dalton's kitchen.

Dalton already dreaded going into work in the morning. News traveled fast in Richport. He was probably already a laughingstock because of the bag.

But didn't he have a right to be jumpy?

Some of the vitality had returned to Chumley's bruised face once he'd finished his meal, but Dalton had the sense that something was still bothering the man.

"Are you all right?" Dalton asked.

Chumley's unfocused gaze turned into a glare. "Did you really just ask me that?"

"Sorry. You looked troubled."

"Maybe I just lost all my belongings in a fire, watched a man get murdered by plants, and got the stuffing beaten out of me."

Well . . . maybe it had been a silly question, after all.

"I'm sorry," Dalton said. "I imagine things must be very hard for you right now." Darneisha would have been proud of him for that one. She'd always told him he should do more to make people comfortable.

Chumley blinked at him. "Why did anyone even settle

this planet in the first place, with those things running around out there?"

Dalton leaned back in his chair and folded his arms. "You really didn't read up on Molorthia Six before you came here, did you?"

"Do I look like a scholar? The spacefare was on sale. I thought, frontier planet with hardly any population? Those people could be easy marks! So off I went, and here I am." Chumley's cheeks flushed beneath the bruising. "So, tell me about Molorthia Six. What do I need to know?"

Dalton closed his eyes and breathed in deeply as he dredged up memories of school lessons. "The planet was first discovered two hundred years ago. Survey ships arrived fifty years later. 'Fertile land!' they proclaimed. 'Perfect climate for humans!' They were here a week, marked it safe for human habitation, then moved on to the next planet on their list."

"And they didn't . . . notice anything unusual?"

"According to their reports, their entire visit passed without incident."

"Good lord," Chumley breathed, and ran his hands through his disheveled black hair.

"The first settlers arrived a hundred years ago," Dalton continued. "They landed about four hundred kilometers southeast of here, in one of the most fertile regions of the planet. They started chopping down trees and whatnot to make room for their settlement, and that's when the Greens attacked." Though Dalton had not yet been born, it still made his skin clammy just thinking about it. "They slaughtered half the colonists in one night. The survivors fled into the desert, hoping the Greens wouldn't follow."

"Did they?"

Dalton shook his head. "The Greens chased the humans from their land, and the settlers built their city in the desert instead."

Chumley's brow furrowed in contemplation. At length, he said, "Why didn't the survey crew see any Greens?"

"We think the Greens in their vicinity got scared and were holding still to avoid notice."

"But why did they attack the settlers?"

"The settlers thought they were trees. They tried to chop them down."

"Good lord," Chumley said again. "They must think we're monsters."

"*They're* the monsters," Dalton spat. "You saw what they can do."

A tremendous shiver racked Chumley's body. "I might be inclined to agree with you."

He yawned, and Dalton had the sense it was time to draw this conversation to a close. "It's late," Dalton said, rising. "You and I both need some shuteye. I'll show you where you can sleep."

Dalton headed out of the kitchen toward the hallway, Chumley following at a distance. Dalton closed his eyes and drew in a breath when he arrived in front of the door to Kendra and Imani's old bedroom, then gently pushed it open.

"Sorry it's not in order right now," he said, stepping aside so Chumley could enter. "I can clean it later."

Then he ducked past Chumley before he could see inside the room himself, and shut himself inside his own bedroom to pass yet another lonely night with only the picture of him, Darneisha, and the girls to keep him company.

Chumley frowned after Dalton, who'd zipped out of the way as if he were fleeing a Green, then shook his head and stepped into the bedroom.

The walls were painted a sort of fuchsia pink, and a set of bunkbeds with white frames had been pushed against the right-hand wall. A matching white dresser sat near it, and after Chumley had closed the bedroom door behind him, he slid the top drawer open and frowned when he regarded a child's stick-people drawing of a family standing in front of a house with a stereotypically-peaked roof. The other drawers were empty, but several boxes had been stacked in the closet, marked with cryptic words like "Imani" and "Kendra."

Ah, Chumley thought. *Of course.*

He kicked off the shoes Dalton had lent to him and flopped onto the bottom bunk, fully-dressed.

What a *day*. What a life, really. He did not miss creditors banging down his door on Pelstring Four, demanding that he pay up or face the consequences. Yet how could he pay, when he'd spent every last dime and then some on Gran's care and the funeral?

Shut your mind off, he ordered himself. *Just shut it off and get some sleep. Pretend the killer plants were just a dream. You've had nightmares before. That's practically what your whole life has been, anyway. One solid string of nightmares.*

Chumley rolled toward the wall, then realized he'd left

the light on. Wearily, he trudged across the room, slapped the switch, staggered back to the bed, and winced as he felt the twinges of yet more bruises he'd sustained that morning, which felt so long ago now.

And maybe it had been long ago. The days on Molorthia Six contained more hours than the ones on Pelstring Four and Earth. He was too tired to remember just how many. Felt like about a thousand.

He stared at the underside of the upper bunk which, in this darkness, was indistinguishable from the shadows.

What if the creditors or the Feds found him here?

No, they wouldn't do that. He paid for passage in cash and used a fake passport.

But what if they found him anyway and dragged him kicking and screaming back to Pelstring Four? He couldn't go to jail. Terrible things happened in jails—he'd heard the stories, same as anyone.

Yet terrible things happened on Molorthia Six, too. Although, if asked to choose between imprisonment and staving off carnivorous vegetation, well . . .

Which potential nightmare *was* worse, anyway?

Of course, if he *were* imprisoned, he could always . . . no, that would be a terrible idea. Prisons monitored their prisoners. If he tried that trick, everyone would see, and know.

It felt too uncomfortable lying on his back, so Chumley shifted to his right side. The pillow beneath him smelled of dust, and he sneezed, then winced again, because it used more bruised muscles.

"Gran," he whispered into the darkness, "if you can hear

me, please send me some help. I . . . I don't think I can . . . "
Warm tears sprang into his eyes, and he wiped them away
with the back of his hand. "I don't think I can survive
anywhere, anymore. Not without money, that is."

As much as he craved it, sleep seemed to be the last
thing his body wanted. Maybe he was too tired to sleep. Had
happened before, oddly enough, and he'd only ever found
one thing capable of curing it.

Somewhat blindly, Chumley rose, feeling his way across
the room to the light switch. He blinked against the abrupt
glare and slipped on his borrowed shoes, then made his way
out to the hallway.

He paused by the front door, his chest tightening as he
remembered this was not the tranquil world of Pelstring
Four, with its gentle breezes smelling of honey and flowers.

Going for a nighttime walk on Molorthia Six might be
suicide.

Better take a water pistol with him, just in case.

Hoping he wasn't being an utter fool, Chumley pocketed the glorified squirt gun he'd left on the coffee table and
stepped out into the darkness, then breathed in lungsful of
crisp desert air that eased some of the tension in his chest.
Downward-facing streetlights placed at sporadic intervals
along the road lent faint illumination to his surroundings, as
did the two pale moons hovering off toward the east, so he
needed no extra light to see by.

He set off in a westward direction, keeping an eye out
for anything large and leafy. An imported palm tree growing
near an intersection a few blocks from the sheriff's house
made his heart spring into his throat, but then he allowed

himself a nervous giggle when he realized it was as likely to eat him as was a bowl of spinach.

Maybe, like lightning, the Greens would attack here only once.

Well, twice. They'd attacked a ranch, too, though he'd heard only an animal had died.

It didn't take him long to come across the wreckage of the burned hotel, which resembled the ashy remains of a large campfire.

Could his Cube have survived the heat? It was encased in metal, after all, but fires had been known to melt steel girders when they got hot enough.

His room had been on the western side of the dwelling. Chumley stepped over charred boards that had once been the hotel's front wall, crunched through several feet of charcoal, spotted something shiny in the glare of the nearest street lamp, and sighed when he saw it was only a twisted spoon.

He clambered over several more burnt boards jutting up into the air like a row of jagged teeth. Rubble shifted beneath his feet, and he winced at the unexpected heat rising up from beneath it all. This rubbish was still smoldering!

Swearing lightly under his breath, he retraced his steps and made it back out to the unburned street.

He would have to search for his Cube once the fire went out completely. Maybe he could check again tomorrow, if he got the chance.

Chumley's internal compass brought him in a loop back out to the edge of town, where the sheriff's house sat alone. He knew that sleep would remain elusive, so instead of returning indoors, he crept behind the house and sat on a patio table that would provide a view of the low-lying mountains off to the east during the day.

Even though he'd kicked the habit a few years earlier due to health concerns and his own lack of funds, he itched for a cigarette. That would get him to sleep all right. Perhaps he could negotiate for a pack of cigarettes to come with his weekly pay . . . ?

Something out in the desert moved.

Chumley sat up straighter, eyes as wide as they could go, praying the movement he'd seen had been his imagination.

Then he heard the swishing, as if something with many thin, loose sections were dragging itself over the ground.

A scream froze in Chumley's throat as his vision focused on the source of the swishing.

Striding across the sand, from north to south, was a long line of Greens, perhaps only a hundred yards away from the sheriff's back porch. They traveled single-file and gave Chumley no notice, but he withdrew the water pistol from his pocket anyway and held it in front of him with one trembling hand. He tried to count them, but there were too many. It looked like an entire forest had gotten tired of being rooted to the ground and formed a caravan so it could go out and see the world.

He wasn't sure how long he stood out there, watching them. A tiny part of him wondered if he should go inside and wake the sheriff so he could sound the alarm, but he found himself unable to tear his gaze from the silent, mobile ranks.

His night-adjusted eyes allowed him to focus on individual Greens and make out details about them. Many carried large packs on their backs, and some held smaller specimens in their arms that might have been their children. Some of the Greens sprouted more leaves than the others, some less; some had four arms and some had six, and a couple even warbled faint notes like dirges.

One even pulled a wagon bearing a mound of lumpy, leaf-wrapped bundles. Its wheels made a faint *creak-creak-creak* as it crossed the sand.

"The plants go marching one by one, hurrah, hurrah," Chumley murmured, and tried not to let a crazed giggle escape into the night air.

Why weren't this bunch attacking the city? More than a hundred must have passed him by already, and they would need food and water like the others. He'd seen with his own eyes how violent they could be—he would never forget the hotel manager's death right in front of him for as long as he lived.

When the ranks finally dwindled into nothing and the last Greens receded into the distance, Chumley slunk back into the house, wide-eyed, and bolted the door.

He took the water pistol to bed with him.

CHAPTER 6

"Sleep all right?" Dalton asked as he flipped pancakes at his stove the next morning.

"Like a baby," Chumley said. Dalton had heard him taking a lengthy shower early on, which might prove to be a problem if that became a typical habit. Nothing worse than an empty cistern on Molorthia Six.

Well, almost nothing worse.

Dalton grabbed a stick of butter out of the refrigerator. "Heh. In my experience, that means you were up every hour wailing for milk."

Chumley raised an eyebrow. "In your experience?"

Dalton turned so his back faced his guest. "Well. People talk."

Amazingly, he himself had slept like a cadaver all the way through the night. He hadn't done that since—well, since Darneisha and the girls were still around.

"But you've got kids, though, right? I mean, the bunkbeds."

Dalton swiveled back to him. Chumley was tracing the grain of the wood on the table with one forefinger.

"They're not here," Dalton said. "If that's what you're worried about."

"Custody battle, I assume."

"Something like that."

Chumley gave an understanding nod. "That's too bad.

Knew a bloke back on Pelstring Four who fought his ex for *six whole years* just to have the right to see his boys every other weekend. Nasty bit of business. He won, though, in the end. So there's hope for you, maybe."

"Maybe." Dalton clenched his jaw, swallowed, and switched off the burner. "All right, Deputy. Eat your breakfast, and we'll head over to the station."

Carolyn was already waiting for him inside the station, sitting at the meeting room table with a box of donuts and a drink carrier full of paper coffee cups from Slim's Café. She wore a gray skirt and blazer, and her tightened expression made it look as though she'd recently eaten something sour.

Errin sat on the opposite side of the table, giving Dalton a grimace that Carolyn didn't see.

"Good morning, Dalton," Carolyn said coolly, then nodded at Chumley when he followed him into the meeting room.

Dalton plunked himself into a swivel chair and folded his arms. Chumley gave him a nervous glance and took the seat beside him, probably worried that Carolyn might recognize him and throw him to the dogs. "What do you want?" Dalton asked, ignoring any niceties. "I've got a new deputy to train today."

"So I've heard." Carolyn nodded at Chumley for a second time. "Welcome to the force. May you use your brain better than our sheriff uses his."

"Thanks," Chumley mumbled, keeping his gaze fixed on

the table. His black eyes didn't look any better than they had the previous evening. Probably hurt like hell, too.

Carolyn cleared her throat and continued. "Dalton, I've received no less than three complaints about your conduct last night. I've been told that you anticipated a Green attack because, and I do quote, *Gwendolyn Goldfarb* was raving gibberish in the middle of the street? And then you sent most of the watch home, which defeats the entire purpose of having a city watch to begin with!"

The room grew hotter by a few degrees. "It seemed logical at the time."

"You do realize Gwendolyn is insane."

"I . . . might acknowledge that fact."

Carolyn's dark eyes seemed to crackle as she glared at him. "How could any reasonable human being hear a madwoman shouting nonsense and think, 'Ooh, maybe she's *predicting the future!*'"

Dalton dug in his pocket and located one final, tiny shard of toothpick.

It wasn't big enough to chew on.

He put it back into his pocket and silently counted to ten.

"Gwendolyn predicted the hotel fire," he said, calmly.

Carolyn blinked. "Did I really just hear you say that?"

"She kept spouting something about a fire in the sky. Then the hotel burned."

"Funny, then, that our hotel was on the ground, not in the sky. Now do I have to place you on administrative leave while you go sort yourself out, or are you going to wake up and do your job right?"

Across from her, Errin mouthed, "I'm sorry she's like this today," but Dalton knew Carolyn was right. He'd been a fool, plain and simple. Logical people didn't think Gwendolyn Goldfarb could predict the future, because there was no such thing as predicting the future.

Dalton made another silent count to ten. "It won't happen again, Carolyn."

"Good. If you hadn't gotten that particular bee in your bonnet, then Maxine wouldn't have nearly killed your little band of volunteers with her flamethrower. Errin told me everything."

Errin's pale cheeks flushed, and they made a point of appearing highly interested in a hangnail on their left thumb.

"Is there anything else you'd like to yell at me about this morning?" Dalton asked. "I've got things to do."

One side of Carolyn's mouth quirked into a smile. "No, but I did bring coffee—the real stuff, not that swill you and Cadu brew here. And have a donut!"

"Your boss didn't seem very happy with you," Chumley commented as he and Dalton clambered off the quad just outside the firing range gates which, along with the chain-link fence, stood three meters tall. A drab, canvas canopy shaded the entire area, making it perhaps a degree cooler than if they were standing in the sun.

At first, Dalton couldn't think of what he meant, but then he laughed. "Carolyn? She's the mayor. Has to keep me in line, because who else will? You've still got your water pistol, right?"

Chumley stuck a hand in his pocket and withdrew the plastic yellow weapon, which they'd filled with water at the station to conserve their weed killer supply. "I've been wondering about the Greens. After what you said about them last night."

"What about them?" Dalton strode toward the gate, undid the padlock, and let himself inside. Black and white targets with bullseyes had been set up at varying distances inside the fenced-in area, and it was Dalton's hope that Chumley would be able to hit every target by the end of the day.

"I mean, what if they aren't all bad?"

"Of course they're all bad. That's why we live in the desert. We're like walking filet mignons to them."

Chumley frowned, and Dalton wondered what sort of bee had gotten into *his* bonnet.

"Sorry," Chumley said. "Maybe I think too much."

"Right. Now I want you to stand here—" Dalton gestured at an X painted on the concrete floor— "and try to hit that target there." He pointed at the closest target, only four meters away.

Chumley moved into position, lifted the water pistol, aimed, and fired.

The stream of liquid sailed past the target, half a meter off the mark.

Chumley's shoulders slumped.

"Again," Dalton ordered him. He sat down on a wooden bench near the gate and folded his arms while he watched, remembering how Warren Prentiss, the last deputy he'd trained, had been just as terrible on his first day.

Warren, bless him, had lasted a year before tiring of the oven-like climate and catching a shuttle back to northern Alaska where, apparently, the sun didn't come up at all for two whole months during the winter.

Chumley let out curses when his second and third attempts at hitting the target failed just as miserably as the first. "Sheriff, I'm out of ammo."

"Good thing there's a hand pump down the street."

"You mean I have to go fill it up myself?"

Dalton smiled. Chumley glowered at him. "Which way is it?"

Dalton pointed, and Chumley muttered something profane as he marched off toward the pump, which sat outside Heavenly Fire Church, a hundred meters away.

While he waited for the man to return, Dalton leaned back and closed his eyes, then flailed to attention when his sister-in-law's voice crackled through the comm unit in his pocket.

"Dalton? Are you there?"

He didn't say anything. Maybe if he stayed quiet, she would go away.

"I know you're listening," she said, and sniffled. "You never want to talk. Can't figure out what I ever did to make you ignore me so much. Did Rob say things about me when I wasn't there? Because he was a good husband, and I can't imagine what he would have told you."

Dalton stared at the target straight ahead of him and imagined the bullseye turning into Summer's face.

"I just want to talk, Dalton," Summer continued. "You know I've got no one else. I can't stand it anymore. Dr.

Kiyosaki says I should go back to Earth, but it's not home, not like it was to you and Rob. Do you ever think about going back there? Dalton?"

He sighed and pushed a button on the comm. "I'm busy, Summer."

"You *are* there!" Her relieved laugh made Dalton uncomfortable. "Maybe you could come by tonight? I can make dinner."

"I'll be busy tonight, too. Nice day, Summer."

He switched the comm off, praying that nobody important would need to get hold of him within the next couple hours.

"Who were you talking to?" Chumley asked when he returned to the firing range with his refilled pistol.

"Nobody important," Dalton grunted. "Now let's see if you can do better this time around."

"I don't think I'm going to get better at this." Chumley pulled off another shot and watched as the spray of water dampened the concrete a meter short of the target. "I couldn't even hit the pub dartboard back home." He squeezed the trigger again and swore. "It's already half empty. Couldn't we have brought a tank to fill, or something?"

"Wouldn't fit on the quad." Dalton was still imagining Summer's face decorating the center of the nearest target. "Hold on a minute." He thought, and thought again, and smiled. "Is there anyone you can't stand?"

Chumley regarded him with a frown. "I'm sure I can think of someone."

"Pretend they're the target. See if you can't hit that."

"You're kidding me."

"Just try it. See what happens."

Chumley bared his teeth and turned back to the target with the pistol raised.

He aimed.

Pulled the trigger.

The stream of water thudded against the plastic front of the target, not on the bullseye, but close enough to make Dalton grin.

He applauded, and Chumley faced him, his expression unreadable. Chumley lifted the pistol again and shook it. "It's empty."

"You know what to do."

"But it's so *far* . . ."

Dalton was about to tell him to suck it up, then decided he could at least reward the man for dampening the target for the first time. "Here," he said. "Use mine until it's empty. Ought to save you a trip." He slid his own water pistol out of its holster and passed it to Chumley, who'd pursed his lips at him.

"Thanks," Chumley muttered, and shot at the target again. He missed the first shot but hit closer to home with the second and third. When he held up Dalton's empty pistol, he said, "Now this one's empty, too."

"Now you can go fill them both."

As his new deputy stomped off toward the hand pump once again, Dalton slid his latest crossword puzzle book and a pen out of his trench coat pocket, then got to work.

Approaching footsteps made him lift his head. At first he thought Chumley was returning with the refilled water pistols, but no, two people strode in from the open desert in the opposite direction.

Dalton rose to get a better look.

The duo was both clad in flowing, white robes and had veils draped over their faces, though he could tell by their statures that one was likely male, the other female.

Nobody in all of Richport dressed like these two, and they reminded him of the figure he'd spotted out in the darkness after the plastic bag incident. Were they newcomers like Chumley?

He strode out of the fenced-in area to greet the faceless couple as they passed the range. "Good morning," he said, not too cheerfully. "Is there anything I can help you with?"

The couple halted in their tracks, unmoving. They might as well have been statues hidden under sheets. Their white-gloved hands hung loosely at their sides—Dalton counted five fingers on each one. Definitely human, then, or close to it. But why did they conceal themselves? Ordinary citizens had nothing to hide.

"I don't recognize you," Dalton said. "I assume you're new to town."

The pair said nothing.

"Hablo ... un poquito de español," Dalton continued, not entirely sure if what he'd said was grammatically correct. "¿Me entienden?"

The only sign that the strangers were alive and not androids was the soft fluttering of their veils as they breathed in and out.

He switched to Hindi, another language he'd struggled through in school before deciding it would be best for everyone if he just stuck with English. "Kya aap hindee bolate hain?"

He might as well have been speaking Greek to them. Unless they spoke Greek, which he couldn't know, since he neither spoke it nor knew what it sounded like.

Dalton resisted the mad urge to tear the veils from their faces so he could see if they were someone he knew playing a prank on him. He didn't want to be placed on administrative leave for harassment.

More footsteps crunched behind him as Chumley returned with refilled water pistols.

"Sheriff?" Chumley came up to his side. "What's going on?"

"Damned if I know. They don't understand me."

"Who doesn't understand you?"

"Who do you think?" Dalton made a gesture at the couple, only to discover they were no longer there.

His skin crawled as he made a 360-degree turn, searching for glimpses of white and seeing none. Where on Molorthia Six had they gone?

"Maybe you ought to sit down," Chumley said, his expression uncertain. "It's awfully hot out here. Do you need me to get you something to drink?"

Dalton hardly listened to him. "They must have dematerialized. But where did they *come* from?" He hadn't even heard of technology like that, and it spooked him to think of how out of touch he must be, living on a backwater world like this one.

To Dalton's surprise, Chumley grabbed his arm and dragged him back through the gate, then pointed at the bench Dalton had so recently vacated. "You're acting delirious. You should sit."

Dalton did not sit. "How am I acting delirious? That couple was walking by, all in white, and I stopped them because I didn't know who they were. You have to do that sort of thing when you're sheriff."

Chumley's face became grim. "You were talking to thin air. At first I thought you were on your comm, but you weren't holding it." He bit his lip. "This is like last night, when you saw someone none of us could. Have you been under any extra stress lately?"

"I'm not 'seeing things,' if that's what you're implying."

Chumley gave Dalton a look of pity. "Look, you need fluids, and rest, or something. I can work on target practice on my own."

"Don't tell me how I should be treating myself."

"You were talking to people who weren't there! And what about yesterday, when you thought the old lady was predicting the future? Is that normal, too?"

Dalton wished he had a fresh toothpick to gnash between his incisors. "Someone else must have seen them. They could be a threat." He turned toward the nearest dwelling; a bungalow with heavy drapes drawn tight behind its square, recessed windows. The closest churches on Holy Street lay a fair distance away from them, but maybe someone there had excellent vision.

Dalton set off toward Holy Street at a jog, remembering halfway there that he could have just hopped on the quad to speed things up.

Gurmeet Singh and Lennox McTavish were heading away from him toward the center of town, carrying oddly-shaped cases likely containing their musical instruments.

"Wait!" he called at their backs.

The pair stopped; turned.

"Sheriff!" Gurmeet said brightly. He wore a flowing white shirt over white slacks, but Dalton knew he hadn't been one of the vanishing intruders. "What can we do for you today?"

Dalton drew to a stop, panting. It was never a good idea to run in this kind of heat. "Have either of you seen anyone in a white robe and veil wandering around here this morning?"

Gurmeet and Lennox exchanged glances. "Like a dressing gown?" Lennox asked.

"Not quite like that." He strained to think of a better way to put it, but the sweltering air was getting to him, and he'd left his Stetson down at the firing range. "They wore flowing robes. Gloves, too. I couldn't see their skin."

"Robes, plural?" Lennox frowned. "How many people are you looking for?"

"Two. Possibly one man and one woman."

"What did they do?" Gurmeet asked, lowering his instrument case to the ground.

Chumley caught up to them then, hardly looking winded after his sprint. "Sheriff, what are you telling them?"

Dalton scowled at his trainee deputy. "I'm telling them what I saw."

"But—"

He silenced him with a shake of his head. "If you two see *anyone* fitting that description, you alert the station at once. Understand?"

The musicians nodded, uneasy.

"Good. You may go about your business."

Lennox leaned in and whispered something in Gurmeet's ear. They both frowned, and Gurmeet said, "Of course, Sheriff."

The pair walked away from them, speaking in low tones and throwing the occasional glance back over their shoulders.

"I need to report this to Carolyn," Dalton said, more to himself than to Chumley. "See if she can't get the city watch on the lookout for those people."

He made an about-face to head back to where he'd parked the quad, but Chumley remained rooted to the spot, arms folded.

"What?" Dalton asked, his tone sour. "This is a matter of security."

Chumley's expression had become drawn. "At my last eye exam," he said, "the doctor told me I have 20/10 vision. Granted that was five years ago, but he said I'm one of the lucky few to have vision that crisp without enhancements."

"What does that have to do with anything?"

"I saw you talking to thin air. Open a book across the room from me, and I can tell you every word on the page. There weren't any people in white. There weren't any *people*."

It was difficult not to feel unnerved, when Dalton felt equally certain that the robed figures had indeed existed. "Footprints!" he exclaimed, snapping his fingers. "They'll have left footprints."

He sprinted back the way he'd come and began to examine the dusty ground outside the firing range fence. There were indeed footprints—many, many of them—and he immediately matched one set to his own boots, and another to Chumley's, which were also Dalton's boots that he'd lent to him.

The other sets—two, to be precise—led out into the desert, just the way he'd seen the couple arrive.

"Look," he said, pointing at the dirt. "Explain that."

Chumley bent down, looking as though he were only doing it to humor him. "So, someone came this way earlier. It doesn't mean it was your ghosts."

"Is that what you're calling them?"

Chumley shrugged. "Seems fitting."

"Here's the thing," Dalton said. "You feel that?"

"Feel what?"

"It's called *wind*. Footprints don't stay intact too long out here unless we've had a freak rainstorm that turns them into concrete. Wind wipes them away like they were never there. Watch."

An aptly-timed gust sifted sand particles into the depression left by one of the intruders' feet.

"I'm going to follow these as far as I can before they're gone," Dalton said, setting off into the open desert, feeling like a detective in one of those silly old Earth shows Cadu loved so much. Give him a magnifying glass, and he could start calling himself Sherlock Kane.

The two sets of prints continued for nearly sixty meters until they stopped with an unnatural abruptness.

"There's nothing out here, though," Chumley said, scanning the horizon, where more smoke plumed into the sky. "Where would they have come from?"

"I'm telling you, they must have dematerialized when you were coming back with the pistols. Which means that in order to get here, they materialized first, maybe even right here." Dalton gestured at the ground. "That's why the prints just stop."

"Or, the wind wiped the older prints away already."

"I don't think so." Dalton ran a hand over his hatless head, having the sudden, surreal sensation he was living inside a dream.

He followed the prints back to the firing range and retrieved his Stetson from the bench inside the fence.

"Get on," Dalton said, motioning for Chumley to join him on the quad. "We can call it a day."

Chumley, his mouth drawn in a thin line, mounted the quad behind him. "Erm, Sheriff? If there really were people materializing out in the desert, why couldn't I see them?"

Dalton stomped on the accelerator. "No idea, but I'm going to find out."

CHAPTER 7

Dalton had never imagined that Carolyn's face could grow so cold.

She stood behind her desk in her air-conditioned office down the street from the police station, hands firmly gripping the back of the chair in front of her. It felt so heavenly between those walls, Dalton didn't think he could ever bring himself to leave in spite of the deep trouble he seemed to be getting into with his superior.

"Human intruders," she repeated.

"They might not have been *human* humans," Dalton said, clutching his Stetson in front of him because he didn't know what else to do with his hands. "But they were humanoid. Two arms, two legs, ten fingers."

"And you didn't see them at all." Carolyn looked past Dalton to Chumley, who'd unfastened the top two buttons of his shirt and was basking in the stream of air issuing from a nearby vent.

"I saw tracks," Chumley said. "Whatever that means."

Carolyn appeared to mull her words over carefully before speaking them. "Dalton, I'm concerned you might be experiencing a psychotic break."

"*What?*" The hat slid out of Dalton's hands and plopped to the floor. He didn't pick it up.

"You witnessed two Green attacks one right after the

other. I know what that means to you, and I'm deeply sorry, but you just haven't been thinking rationally. Enlisting a salesman to be a deputy, for one, and you know the rest."

"If I hadn't enlisted him, they'd have killed him," Dalton said, sourly.

"You could have paid for his passage back to wherever he came from, instead. Surely that would have been easier on you both."

Dalton glanced back at Chumley, whose face had turned into a mask of inexplicable fear.

"I don't have the extra money for spacefare right now," Dalton said, which wasn't entirely true.

Some of the lines of anxiety vanished from Chumley's face.

"And that's fine," Carolyn went on. "But the fact is, I just found out Naomi Schwartzman is on her way here, which means we need to make the absolute best impression possible."

Dalton's insides went clammy. "She's coming . . . here? To Richport?"

"Yes." Carolyn allowed herself a smile. "If she's feeling extra generous, she might gift us with free air conditioning units and solar panels to power them."

"Who's Naomi?" Chumley asked, sitting up straighter.

"She's in charge of Frontier Care United," Dalton said. "They go out to all the poorer colony worlds and make donations if they think the residents need them."

"The last I heard," Carolyn said as her eyes glimmered, "FCU helped build ten thousand earthquake-proof homes on Killian Six this past year. Imagine how many air conditioners they might donate to us if they think we deserve it."

She let her words hang in the air like juicy morsels. Dalton personally tried not to allow himself the luxury of sitting in air conditioning too often so he wouldn't grow spoiled and never step outside again, but he had to admit that Carolyn's office held an almost intoxicating coolness. He'd need a blanket if he stayed in here much longer.

"What do we have to do?" Chumley asked, his tone soft but hopeful.

"We have to appear like a functioning society, for one," Carolyn said. "We can chalk the hotel fire up to an unfortunate accident—it was wood, after all. But I don't want to hear a peep from anyone about any Green attacks. I'm going to make a public announcement about it tonight, telling everyone to keep their lips sealed if they know what's good for them. Naomi's shuttle arrives tomorrow."

"Won't they give us more stuff if it looks like we're in trouble?"

"That's not quite how they work. They consider it a waste of money if whatever they donate gets destroyed."

"We can ask them about the fires though, right?" Chumley asked. "They might see something important on the way down."

Carolyn had started shaking her head before he'd finished speaking. "I don't want them to think there's any trouble here. As soon as they approve us, *then* we can continue our investigation into the fires. It's for the best."

Well . . . the fires didn't seem to be affecting Richport directly, in any case. They were only sending bloodthirsty Greens fleeing in their direction.

"Is FCU visiting any other cities?" Dalton asked.

"I've heard they're making stops in Paris and Cloud City. The better the impression we make here, the better life could be for everyone on the planet—I heard a rumor that the colony on Marris was denied any assistance because the governor frowned too much. You do understand how important this is, right?"

It was difficult not to.

"Suppose trouble just happens while she's here," Dalton said.

A manic gleam appeared in Carolyn's brown eyes. "I won't let that happen. I want you to take the rest of the day off, Dalton. You and Chumley both. You're going to get some sleep, and tomorrow when Naomi and her people arrive, you're going to be all smiles and manners, none of that brooding cop bullshit." Carolyn looked to Chumley. "And you go out and buy some clothes that fit. I can see your ankles from here." Carolyn dug in her blazer pocket and pulled out a crinkly hundred-pound note, which Chumley goggled at as if it were gold.

He took it and pocketed it, uttering a soft, "Thank you."

"It's barely even noon, and you want me at home?" Dalton asked, struggling to maintain an even tone.

"If any trouble arises between now and tomorrow morning, Errin will be there to help. They volunteered on the force ten years ago, and they know how to deal with interpersonal disputes. Perk of working with me." She flashed bright, white teeth at him.

"Errin is an aide," Dalton said.

"And Chumley is a salesman. You tell me who's more qualified to keep the peace. Chumley, there's a charity shop over on Boulder Avenue where you can buy used clothing. If either of you need anything, call me."

"See any more people in white?" Chumley asked when he and Dalton stepped out into the noonday sunshine, sarcasm tinging his voice.

Dalton swept his gaze from left to right. A rickety, solar-powered bus painted with a Desert Van Lines logo lurched its way down the street, and Sumeet Johnson, a postal worker, lumbered down the sidewalk gripping a bulging sack of mail.

"Hey, Sheriff!" Sumeet called. "See any spooky grocery bags yet today?"

Dalton turned away from the postal worker, his face burning with humiliation.

Chumley smirked at him. "How do I find Boulder Avenue?"

"Head north from here for two blocks, and it's a block and a half ahead on the right. Do you really want to risk shopping by yourself?"

Chumley absently adjusted the seven-pointed deputy's badge Dalton had given him earlier that morning. Slightly tarnished, it was pinned to his shirt right over his heart. "I'll have to try. If anyone wants to hurt me, I have a few moves I can use."

"Moves." Dalton imagined Chumley ineffectually aiming a water pistol at a disgruntled sales clerk.

"You don't really know me, Sheriff. The only reason I

couldn't defend myself yesterday was because I was dying of dehydration. Thanks for rescuing me, by the way."

"You're welcome." Dalton paused. "You're really sure . . . ?"

"I'll manage."

It seemed there would be no arguing with him. "Well, then. Happy shopping."

He turned away from Chumley, mounted the quad he'd left outside Carolyn's door, and headed toward home, keeping a lookout for more of the people in white. The city looked as normal as it always did, with its adobe structures and dusty citizens going about their business.

On a day like this, one could almost believe that nothing bad could ever happen in Richport. If Naomi Schwartzman arrived this very moment, she'd be pleased at the rugged determination of the colonists who'd eked out an existence in such a hostile climate, tapping into the underground water supply when the Rosa River ran dry and building homes with walls thick enough to keep out the majority of the heat.

But not all of the heat, Dalton thought. The air conditioning in Carolyn's office called to him even now, beckoning for him to turn the quad around and spend the rest of the day soaking up the chill like a human sponge.

Ahead of him, a figure in a neon kaftan stepped out into the street.

He braked.

It was Gwendolyn Goldfarb.

God help him.

"Ghosts," she murmured, turning her head toward him. Today she wore an immense pair of sunglasses that concealed half her face. "They watch us with secret eyes, plotting, destroying."

Her words conjured the image of the robed pair he may or may not have encountered outside the firing range.

"There's no such thing as ghosts, Gwendolyn," Dalton said, hearing a slight tremor in his own voice. He wished he could see her eyes behind the sunglasses; whether she appeared coherent or not.

"But they believe in you, Sheriff."

She continued her way across the street, the epitome of calm.

Dalton wished he could say the same for himself.

CHAPTER 8

Dalton still thought about the white-clad intruders as he came through his front door and regarded his vacant living room; the empty sofas yearning for someone to come along and warm them. Richport had always been an ordinary place with some obvious exceptions, and the presence of the intruders made him wonder what else might be going on unseen right under his nose.

He didn't have too many memories of Earth. The ones he did have largely featured him and his older brother, Rob, clambering over rocks along the northern Cornish coast, finding shells wedged among them and taking them home to add to their collections. He remembered cloudy weather and rain, and storytelling around the fireplace in the evenings.

His father, an Arizona native who'd met Dalton's mother while on extended holiday, pined for a drier climate and suggested they transplant the entire family to the budding settlement on Molorthia Six. With such a vast universe to see, why should they stay in Cornwall?

The family had uprooted themselves with both trepidation and excitement. They'd settled in the Molorthian city of Paris, where they lived for the next five years while other branches of the Kane clan departed Earth and joined them; and then they'd moved down to Richport when Dalton's father accepted a new job managing the city's largest bank.

Life for the Kane family became ordinary to the point of boredom, but they got along well enough, and they were all comfortable in spite of the scorching heat.

Now, though . . .

Dalton shivered as he thought again of the white-clad specters. Gwendolyn had clearly seen them, too, and he didn't like the idea of having something in common with her.

He hung his trench coat and Stetson on the hooks near the door, undid his bootlaces, and sank, bewildered, onto the sofa along the farther wall.

Idleness like this made him antsy, and sitting around for the rest of the day was bound to turn him into a jittering, nervous wreck. He had to *do* something, dammit, and something useful, before his mind cracked worse than Gwendolyn's.

Then he thought, *Aha.*

He retrieved his comm unit from the pocket of his coat, switched it back on, and keyed in a number he hadn't used in a while.

"Annaliese?" he said in a brusque tone. "You there?"

After a pause, a deep feminine voice came through, slightly husky from a few decades of smoking. "Dalton Kane? Is that you?"

Dalton allowed himself a grin. "I think so. How are things up your way?"

"Hold on a minute, hon." There came a scraping sound, a series of footsteps, and the soft thud of a closing door. "All right, I'm back. You hear Naomi Schwartzman is on her way?"

"I did," Dalton said. "You folks wouldn't have anything to hide from her, would you?"

"Um," Annaliese said.

The speed of Dalton's pulse ticked up a notch or two. "Um, what?"

"What do you mean?"

"You said 'um.' That means something."

"Nothing important." Annaliese cleared her throat. "How are things in Richport? We heard about the hotel burning down. Damn shame. I stayed there a couple times. They had a nice buffet."

"You didn't happen to hear *why* it burned down, did you?"

"Wood does that, last I heard."

"Wood especially does that when someone's fending off a bunch of Greens with flamethrowers indoors."

A peculiar thud crackled from the comm, as if Annaliese had just dropped hers on the floor.

"Sorry," Annaliese said. "What did you say?"

"Greens attacked the hotel. People died. We can't let Naomi Schwartzman know anything is wrong here."

"Holy sands, Dalton. How many?"

"Greens?"

"Fatalities."

Dalton swallowed. "Six, I think they said."

"No es bueno."

"No kidding. So, what about you? Wondered what you lot thought of all that smoke up in your direction."

"You can see the *smoke*?" Annaliese blurted.

"It's a bit obvious."

Annaliese let out a huff. "It's coming from the forests. I sent out two teams to go investigate earlier this week, and none of them have reported back. I don't know if that means . . . well, there's no need to speculate so soon. Just wish we had a copter so we could get a good look at things from up in the air." Desperation crept further into her tone with every word she spoke. "Dalton, I don't know what's happening, and I don't know how we can hide it from the FCU people when they get here."

"Maybe we shouldn't."

"Are you *crazy*?"

Dalton shrugged, though Annaliese couldn't see him. "Has anything else happened up your way I should know about?"

"Only what I've said. Well, that and the fact a few of the outlying ranches saw some Greens scampering the hell south like the devil was after them. Wonder if they're the ones who got your hotel."

Dalton frowned. "Let me know if you have any more trouble, you hear?"

"Loud and clear," Annaliese said. "And the same goes for you."

They exchanged farewells. Dalton severed the connection between them, then wiped the sweat from his forehead with the back of one hand. His nose itched again, but he wouldn't apply more sunburn cream until he'd finished his off-the-clock correspondence.

He keyed in another number and said, "Janelle, do you copy?"

Nobody responded. Dalton drummed his fingers on his knee while he counted off sixty seconds, then tried again.

Still no answer.

Frowning, Dalton rose and went to the north-facing

window in his living room. He slid aside the drapes and regarded the sandy plain and the few low mountains, counting four separate plumes of smoke clouding the horizon in various directions.

The closest forests lay a hundred and twenty kilometers to the north. Paris, the city where Annaliese led the police force, sat a scant fifty kilometers from the forests—too close for Dalton's liking, which was why he visited Paris only when he absolutely had to.

He shuddered to think of what might have happened to the teams Annaliese sent to investigate the fires. Paris wasn't as large as Richport, so he could only guess at how ill-prepared the teams might have been before they went in. Had they forged suits of armor by which they could protect themselves from the Greens? Did they drive into the forests with armored vehicles? Where on Molorthia Six could anyone even *get* an armored vehicle?

If they were lucky, maybe FCU would donate one or two of them. Which of course would mean they'd have to know about the recent Green attacks, which Carolyn would never allow.

His hands balled into fists, and he went back to his comm unit to call Janelle again.

"Dalton?" the woman panted when she finally picked up. "Is everything okay?"

Her tone sent a chill directly into Dalton's heart. "Why do you ask?" He tried to sound casual, as if the threads of his sanity weren't on the verge of unraveling.

"The last time you called, someone's entire herd of field beasts had escaped their enclosure and went stampeding through town. You wanted advice on how you all could round them up."

Dalton grimaced. "I'd forgotten about that."

"It was only eight weeks ago."

"Things happen. Do you have a minute?"

"Sure. What can I do for you?"

"You've heard that FCU is landing here tomorrow."

"I did! I was just talking with the mayor about it. He gave us a rundown of how we should . . . manage things once they show up here in Cloud City."

"What sort of things?" Dalton kept his tone neutral.

"We've had a problem with looters the past couple weeks. Someone cleaned out the general store in the middle of the night about ten days ago, and we have no suspects. Then the same thing happened at the hardware store and the Hindu temple."

"Hate crimes?"

"Oh, I doubt it. The people who run the general store are druids, and an ex-priest runs the hardware store."

"Could cameras have caught anything?"

A soft snort issued from the comm. "Remind me again, Dalton, which planet are we on? Hey, maybe FCU will donate security cameras so we don't have to deal with this rubbish anymore!"

"What did they take from the Hindu temple?"

"About half a dozen gold-plated statues. Ganesh, and a few other gods I can't remember. It's all in the police report, if you want me to mail it to you."

Dalton raised his eyebrows. "How big were these statues?"

"The biggest ones were close to two meters tall. We

don't know how they got them out of there without anyone noticing."

"What did they take from the stores?"

"Oh, just what you'd expect. Funny thing is, there were no signs of forced entry. It's like the thieves are ghosts."

"*What?*"

"My people are working on it, Dalton. No need to worry."

"You haven't seen any strangers in white wandering around, have you?"

There came a pregnant pause. "Not that I'm aware of. Why?"

"There ... may have been a report of strangers here in town. Nothing important. Forget I asked."

"What aren't you telling me?"

He coughed a few times and opted to change the subject. "You haven't had any Greens running amuck, have you?"

"In Cloud City? No way. We'd have sent an alert out immediately if we had. That's not something to just sweep under the rug, is it?"

"Not at all," Dalton said. Paused. "We've had two Green attacks already. People died. Carolyn doesn't want FCU to know."

"That's terrible! How many—hold on a minute, someone's knocking on my door." He heard a clunk, and indistinct murmurs. Then, "Dalton, I've got to go—someone's just looted the elementary school and taken all the desks. Good luck with the FCU people, okay?"

"You too," Dalton said, ending the call and wondering just what was happening to his planet.

Finding the charity shop proved easier than Chumley had expected, though he felt like a sardine swimming through a current of sharks as he traversed the grid of streets to get there. He made sure his new deputy badge stood out prominently on the front of him, praying it would ward off attacks like a blessed crucifix against vampires.

He received plenty of dirty looks, but nobody hurt him.

The charity shop sat on the ground floor of an adobe structure that rose several stories into the sky; the uppermost of which were probably flats full of more glaring people. When he stepped through the door into the somewhat less-stifling interior, he caught a whiff of that charity-shop smell that seemed intrinsic of every charity shop in which he'd ever set foot, regardless of region or planet. It was the smell of a thousand fragments of disparate lives, thrown together in a depressing clutter of had-beens.

Some days he felt like the human equivalent of that.

"Can I help you, sir?" asked the twentysomething sales clerk, glaring at him from behind the counter. Their dark hair stood up in spikes dyed pink at the tips, and they wore a black t-shirt with white letters that read, "This is my happy face."

Chumley recognized them as one of the people he'd handed a tanning bed brochure to on the day of his arrival. "Just browsing," he said, darting past the gender-neutral aisle toward the men's section. "I'll let you know if I need anything."

Honestly, these people's attitudes were simply abominable. He hadn't even had the chance to properly con them before they'd unleashed their fury.

He located a rack of button-down shirts that predated some of the dinosaurs and riffled through them one after the other, finding a mauve one that still bore its original store tags. This he removed from the rack and draped over one arm before proceeding through the rest of the shirts, finding a handful more suitable enough for his tastes.

Halfway through his perusal of the trouser section, movement in the corner of his eye caught his attention, and he did a double-take.

Standing in one corner of the charity shop were two white-robed people wearing white veils and white gloves that completely obscured any identifying features.

He nearly dropped the bundle of clothes draped over his arm.

"Oi!" he shouted. "Who are you?"

The figures froze in place.

"Who are you shouting at?" the clerk asked, rising from the stool behind the counter and craning their neck to see better. "You're the only one in here, besides me."

Chumley rubbed his eyes with one hand; blinked.

The people in white were still there.

"Oh, erm, you're—you're right," he stammered. "Can't imagine what I was thinking."

The two figures glided toward the exit without a sound. Chumley made quick inventory of the items in his arms—four shirts and two pairs of trousers—and darted after them, tossing the hundred-pound note toward the counter as he passed it. The money fluttered to the floor like a lonely piece of confetti.

"Keep the change!" he cried to the bewildered clerk, who might feel more warmly toward him now that he'd paid nearly triple for his clothes.

The shrouded couple pushed their way outside. Chumley swept up his pair of new trousers that had begun to drag the floor, did an awkward little dance as he avoided a hanging display of belts he hadn't seen until the last second, and plunged into the sunshine and sweltering heat, wincing at the retina-searing glare.

He glanced to the left. To the right. Straight ahead.

The shrouded couple were gone.

"Oh, *biscuits*," he said. His gran would have been proud of that. She'd never liked it when he swore.

Spotting a glimpse of white in the distance, Chumley sprinted toward the left, which was east, but immediately lost sight of the mysterious pair. Who could they *be*? Invisibility technology had been banned for centuries due to safety concerns. Could someone have invented their own faulty invisibility shields that enabled some to see them and others not to? What would anyone hope to accomplish by creating such a device?

Chumley peered down alleyways and side streets, nearly got flattened by a passing lorry when he forgot to look both ways before crossing an intersection, and decided that he'd either gone the wrong way, or the couple had vamoosed, or turned invisible again, or something.

There wasn't anything he could do but find the sheriff and tell him what he'd seen.

He wondered if Dalton would believe him.

Dalton had begun pacing back and forth across his living room after he'd concluded his calls with his fellow keepers of the peace, having more questions now than answers. Buildings being looted without forced entry? Sounded like an insurance scam to him, but who knew?

Footsteps outside made him turn to the door. He schooled his expression into a mask of disapproval just in time for Chumley to barge in and drop an armful of charity shop clothing onto the floor. Dalton could smell it from where he stood and was about to point Chumley in the direction of the washing machine when he noticed the look on his deputy's face.

"I saw them," Chumley said, breathlessly. "The people you saw earlier."

Dalton folded his arms. "You're sure."

"They were inside the charity shop. The clerk didn't see them, but I followed them outside, and they'd disappeared. I ran all the way back here to tell you."

God in heaven. "Spies," Dalton muttered. "They have to be spies. Nobody with good intentions is going to go snooping around my city invisible."

"They're not very good at being invisible, though, are they?" Chumley mused. "And what would spies want here in Richport?" His cheeks flushed, then paled. "What if it's the people from FUC?"

"That's FCU," Dalton snapped. "Why would they send invisible spies to peek in on us?"

"They could be like secret shoppers; get a feel for the place without anyone expecting them."

"And you think what, they'll report to Naomi Schwartzman when she and her crew get here?"

Chumley shrugged. "It's possible, isn't it? Who else would be keeping an eye on us?"

Dalton frowned. He could think of no one, honestly, and he felt himself relax. "You know," he said, "I think you're probably right."

Chumley's eyes widened. "Really?"

"Don't see why not. You're right, there's nothing here in Richport anyone else would want, except maybe a good curry." Idly, Dalton thought of the mysterious looting over in Cloud City. But that was Cloud City, not Richport.

And Janelle had mentioned nothing about the people in white.

CHAPTER 9

The next morning, Dalton and Chumley convened in Carolyn's office along with Errin Inglewood and Cadu Mão de Ferro. Paper cups of coffee steamed from their places in a cardboard drink carrier, and a fresh box of donuts sat beside them.

Dalton and Chumley had agreed to say nothing more to Carolyn about the people in white, considering the plausible possibility they had some connection to FCU, and Dalton didn't think it would be the best of ideas to worry the mayor unnecessarily. Let her keep thinking Dalton had been seeing things. It would be better for everyone in the long run.

Carolyn, her black hair wavy and gleaming, stood ramrod straight behind her desk again. Dalton didn't think he'd ever seen her actually sitting at it. "This is a momentous day," she said, her eyes twinkling with zeal. "You know I only ever want what's best for this city. We may not be as dazzling as Mumbai or London on Earth, or as affluent as Kingston or Nuevo Pradesh City on Pelstring Four, but we've got guts, grit, and determination, and I say we deserve FCU assistance just as much as anyone on any colony world."

Errin gave a polite clap. Dalton wondered how many times Carolyn rehearsed her speech before everyone arrived.

"What will you need us to do?" Dalton asked.

"I've already ordered the sanitation workers to sweep the

streets of any garbage. You, Cadu, and Chumley should just stand around looking tough but pretty. You're all handsome people; you should look good for any publicity photos they'll want to take."

Dalton, Cadu, and Chumley turned toward each other and looked each other up and down wearing matching frowns. Chumley had chosen to wear a mauve button-up shirt and slick, gray trousers that looked brand-new in spite of being secondhand. He'd put mousse in his black hair that morning before heading out, making him look more like a bruised fashion model than an officer of the law.

Cadu looked rumpled, as usual, as if he'd come straight here after rolling out of bed. He absently tucked his sand-colored shirt into his trousers and straightened his shoulders. "All right, Dalton. How do I look?"

Dalton squinted at the emergency operator. "You look like Mogotsi Molosiwa in *Rise of the Killer Meerkats*."

Creases formed in Cadu's brow. "You mean the part where he's running from the swarm and rolls down the hill into the bubbling mud pit?"

"That's the one."

"I didn't realize you were paying attention."

"I remember every awful fecking movie you've made me sit through."

Chumley gave a light cough and looked to Carolyn. "Is there anything else we should be doing aside from . . . what you said?"

"I'd rather not have my police force actually have to *do* something while FCU is here," Carolyn said, "since that means there would have to be a problem for all of you to take care of. We do not need any problems. And for God's sake, don't forget to smile."

Dalton tried to force his expression into something that wasn't a glower, but his facial muscles didn't seem to want to budge.

"Don't worry," Errin said gently. "If you all want to help, you can join me in the town square in—" they checked their plain, black wristwatch— "half an hour to help set up the stage and podium. Ms. Schwartzman will want to make a speech, of course."

Speeches were, perhaps, even worse than meetings. "Suppose I can help with that," Dalton said.

"Shouldn't I stay inside the station in case any emergencies get called in?" Cadu asked.

Carolyn bit her lower lip with great thought. "That's a good point. Stay on call, though, in case we end up needing you for anything."

Cadu dipped his head in acknowledgment.

"FCU will be staying at the Oasis Bed and Breakfast for the days they're here in Richport," Carolyn continued. "When they've concluded their visit here, I would like for you, Dalton, to escort them to Paris, so you might protect them from anything untoward they might encounter on the way there."

Dalton raised his eyebrows. "Just me?"

"You, and whoever you think is most qualified to help. I want to make sure they stay safe. If anyone asks why you're going with them, you can make up some bullshit answer that sounds good."

"Ms. Kaur?"

Carolyn blinked, then glanced down at the shiny, silver comm unit lying atop her desk. She plucked it up between thumb and forefinger and said, "Yes? Who is this?"

"This is Dev Chakrabarti. Um . . . FCU just landed here, at the spaceport. They said they made good time. Um . . . what should we do?"

"Treat them like royalty, of course!" Carolyn snapped, the color deepening in her cheeks. "I'll head out to greet them right now. You lot, get to work on that stage."

Errin plucked up a cup of coffee and a donut, then made a gesturing motion with their head indicating that Dalton should follow. Dalton opted to skip the coffee for the time being; it would only make him jittery and need to use the toilet too many times while he was busy ass-kissing the FCU people.

Chumley took a coffee for himself and started chugging it almost immediately as the three of them shuffled out of the office.

"Wow," he said. "That actually isn't as bad as I expected for a colony world."

"Better watch what you say," Dalton said. "Carolyn's cousin Slim runs the coffee shop."

Errin led them down a corridor into a wide storage room filled with long sheets of composite flooring of a pale brown color meant to imitate wood. "We can carry these sections out the back here and around the side of the building," they said, having already consumed their entire donut. "They sit on top of these big blocks, and here's the steps."

Dalton regarded the concrete blocks, each of which

looked about as heavy as one of the Egyptian pyramids. He attempted budging one. It didn't move.

"Teamwork," Errin said, wheeling over a hand truck. "I'll hold this in place while you and Chumley maneuver one onto here. I'd help lift if I had any muscles." They flexed a skinny bicep in demonstration.

Dalton looked over at Chumley, still chugging coffee, and sighed.

He could already tell this would be a fabulous morning.

Dalton longed for Carolyn's office air conditioning by the time he and Chumley had arranged the massive blocks in the appropriate places in the town square. Errin helped heave the lighter composite boards over top of them and fastened them into place with pins.

"There," Errin said, taking a few steps backward and admiring their handiwork. "What do you think?"

Dalton put his hand on his chin. His healing sunburn was itching his nose again, and he resisted the urge to dig at it. "Podium's off-center," he said.

"Seriously?" Chumley said.

"Carolyn will notice."

Chumley rolled his eyes, ascended the portable set of steps, and dragged the podium roughly two centimeters to the right. "Better?"

Dalton gave a curt nod. He attempted another experimental grin. It was like trying to make one of the faces on

Mount Rushmore smile, not that he'd ever seen Mount Rushmore.

"What was that face for?" Errin asked. "The podium looks fine to me."

"What Carolyn said. About smiling." Dalton couldn't help it, he had to scratch his sunburned nose, and flakes of dead, white skin came away when he did and fluttered to the ground.

"You're having trouble with it?"

"It's not a thing I'm used to." He lowered his voice so Chumley wouldn't hear him. "You understand, right?"

Errin dipped their head in a show of empathy. "I lost people that day, too, you know. It's not an easy thing to forget."

Dalton had nearly forgotten—Errin's cousin Paulson had been married to Dalton's cousin Marrietta. The couple had had two children. All gone, now, just like everyone else.

"I've seen you smile," Chumley said, joining them at ground level.

Dalton threw him a look of irritation. "When?"

"You probably weren't thinking about it," Errin said. "Can you think of something happy? It could be anything—eating a piece of chocolate cake; winning a million pounds."

Dalton closed his eyes and imagined walking into his house to see Darneisha sitting on the sofa reading bedtime stories to Kendra and Imani, wearing her favorite ochre dress and a blossom tucked behind her ear. The thought lit up his entire being for the briefest of instants before he crashed back down into the unrelenting gloom of the present.

Instead, he thought of driving up to the forests, glugging

a tanker of fuel over every speck of organic matter, lighting a match, and watching the bastards burn.

"You're smiling!" Chumley exclaimed.

Yes, Dalton thought. Yes, he was. And as long as he thought about what he'd love to do to the Greens himself, he didn't think he'd be able to stop.

Several hundred curious citizens already lined the sidewalks when the caravan from the spaceport lurched into town carrying Naomi Schwartzman and her cronies. Dalton, lurking near the stage with his hands clasped behind his back and his healing sunburn itching him worse than ever, kept an eye on the throng to make sure nobody got out of hand. Chumley stood at the opposite corner of the stage, squinting at the crowd in mild trepidation, but everyone seemed too excited about the approaching caravan to give Chumley any extra notice.

Dalton had missed Carolyn's broadcast to the town. He wondered what she'd said to encourage them to behave.

Errin had dragged a few of the nicer-looking chairs out of Carolyn's office and lined them up along the back of the stage. They'd slathered their fair skin with sunblock, donned a wide-brimmed-hat, and were fanning themself with a black folder Dalton remembered seeing on Carolyn's desk.

Good idea, Dalton thought. It might pay to have everyone look sweltering and miserable in front of the FCU people. He could practically feel his new air conditioning unit now.

The soft rumble of the caravan's engine echoed off the

adobe buildings as it approached. Dalton straightened his shoulders and imagined himself feeding Greens into a woodchipper.

Errin hurriedly set the folder down on the podium and stood beside it, short but proud in their pale blue shirt and spotless slacks. Dalton wondered if Errin knew that a glob of sunblock had plastered a curl of their sandy hair to their forehead, and if Carolyn would say anything about it later.

The caravan pulled up in front of the stage. Dalton wondered what Naomi Schwartzman would think about the dents and dings in the caravan's body, and the peeling paint that had once been a gleaming white. He felt sure someone could have scrounged up a nicer-looking transport for the visitors, but he supposed this had been another strategic Carolyn thing intended to conjure extra sympathy.

Brakes hissed as the caravan parked. Dalton could see a flurry of motion through the row of squarish windows, and then the door slid open to reveal Carolyn chatting with a tall, imposing woman who could only be Naomi Schwartzman.

Ms. Schwartzman's skin was a rich, olive tone, and her jet-black hair had been piled atop her head and sprayed so heavily, it was probably solid. She wore a black pantsuit and blazer—she'd be roasting out here in no time—and a gaze that held more clinical interest than charity.

Four additional suited persons emerged from the caravan after Naomi. Dalton didn't recognize any of them. More FCU people, then.

He pictured himself dropping a nuke on the Greens from orbit.

"Ms. Schwartzman, I'd like to introduce you to Mr.

Dalton Kane, our sheriff," Carolyn said, leading the woman in his direction. "Sheriff, this is Naomi Schwartzman of Frontier Care United."

"It's a pleasure meeting you." Dalton gently shook the woman's hand. It felt like ice. His nose and ears itched. He imagined a Molorthia Six with no vegetation at all, just a vast desert, safe and sound.

"Likewise, Mr. Kane," Naomi said in an unfamiliar accent. Her gaze slid past him like water running off an oil slick. Dalton was not disappointed.

"And this is Mr. Chumley Fanshaw, our new deputy," Carolyn said, bringing Naomi over to Chumley, who'd put on one of Dalton's old trench coats over his mauve shirt, which he'd left rakishly unbuttoned at the top. He'd opted to go hatless, presumably to show off his moussed hair.

"Nice meeting you, ma'am," Chumley said, giving her hand a shake.

Naomi studied his face. "What happened to you?"

"Accident. It, erm, comes with the job." Chumley coughed, and Naomi immediately lost interest in him as well.

Carolyn then led Naomi up onto the stage. "And this is Mx. Errin Inglewood, my personal aide, who has saved my sanity on more occasions than I can count."

"It's truly an honor to meet you," Errin said to the woman.

Naomi then leaned down and murmured something to Carolyn, who nodded and stepped back, motioning for Errin to join her in front of the row of chairs, though neither of them sat. Naomi's cronies ascended the portable steps and lined up beside them, looking impassive.

Naomi herself stepped up to the podium and tapped at

the microphone to test its functionality. Dalton flinched at the amplified sound as it issued through the large speaker directly behind him.

"Greetings, good citizens of Richport," she said. "As you may know, I am Naomi Schwartzman of Frontier Care United. For the past forty-six years, our organization has dedicated itself to the betterment of every worthy human colony world. Our funding is made possible through generous donors who wish to see humankind succeed no matter where they may live in the universe. This week, we are here on Molorthia Six to assess your colony's most vital needs. We will be spending time here in Richport as well as some of your other settlements to observe your ways of life and conduct interviews with citizens as part of that assessment.

"With me this week are my colleagues Myron Estevez, Anastasia Sheen-Smith, Gopal Shah, and Olivia Newkirk. They will be helping me collect data about your colony."

The four FCU cronies dipped their heads as their names were called. Already bored by the formalities, Dalton refocused his attention on the crowd, where parents held their children aloft to get a better look and couples whispered excitedly among themselves, no doubt dreaming of whatever luxuries FCU might bestow upon them.

Naomi continued to ramble for some time, citing their successes on other colony worlds where they'd installed solar panels, wind turbines, new plumbing, and the like. Dalton's sunburn itched worse than ever, which was when he realized he'd forgotten to apply fresh ointment that morning before leaving the house.

"Does anyone have any questions?" Naomi asked, at last.

Dalton snapped back to attention as a hand near the middle of the crowd shot into the air.

Naomi gave a thin smile. "Yes?"

"Are you going to give us any swimming pools?" asked a young voice. Dalton couldn't see who it was, but it sounded like one of Imani's old friends from school, which made his chest tighten.

He quickly thought of collecting seashells with his brother Rob back in Cornwall, then banished the images when he realized they were too painful.

This smiling thing was going to become a problem.

Naomi appeared slightly taken aback by the question. "What this colony receives will be based on our careful assessment of colony needs. We cannot guarantee any particular donation before the assessment has taken place."

"What about air conditioners?" a man called without raising his hand.

"What about them?" Naomi asked, her eyes narrowing further.

"We need to keep cool!" someone else shouted from the crowd. "Adobe only does so much to keep the heat out."

"If you'd wanted to keep cool that badly, you wouldn't have terrorized that air conditioner salesman to death!" another person butted in. "I was all ready to pay him, and everything!"

"If you'd hated the heat that badly, you shouldn't have moved to this planet in the first place!"

Chumley threw Dalton a worried glance from his position at the other corner of the stage. Dalton shook his head to indicate *not now*. His waning faux-smile left his face entirely as he took two intimidating steps closer to the crowd and glared his best glare.

Nobody paid any attention to him.

"Does anybody *else* have any questions?" Naomi asked, her tone as frigid as the day was hot.

"What about a new movie theater?" another citizen called out from somewhere off to Dalton's left. "The one we've got here is falling apart. The projector broke last week during the middle of *James Bond 200*!"

Dalton peered back at the stage in time to see Carolyn stride forward and take the microphone from Naomi. "Our good friends at FCU have had such a long journey; I'm sure they're looking forward to a bit of rest," Carolyn said, using her best PR tone.

A flurry of motion made Dalton turn his head. Gwendolyn Goldfarb broke free of the throng, kaftan fluttering as she ran, hatless, down the street, shouting, "Grapefruit! Grapefruit! Where in the bloody hell did they find grapefruit?"

Dalton let her go. If she wanted to act crazy, at least she was doing it away from everyone else.

A few other citizens asked questions of a somewhat more serious nature, and Dalton started to relax, chaos averted.

Two minutes later, Cadu Mão de Ferro's voice crackled out of the comm unit in Dalton's pocket, much too loudly for his taste. "Um, Dalton? Bit of a problem . . ."

Dalton gnashed his teeth together and moved away from the stage. "What?" he hissed into the comm.

"Well, um, Maxine of the city watch just called in a report."

"She's on patrol right now?"

"Carolyn thought it would be a good idea. Cover all our bases, that kind of thing."

"What's the report?"

"Well … she's out on the eastern edge of town, right behind your place."

Dalton could feel his knuckles going white as he gripped the comm. "So what?"

"She says she's found evidence that Greens have passed through recently."

He shuddered at the sound of *that* word. "What sort of evidence?"

"Maybe you should just come down here."

"I'll be there in a minute."

Dalton pocketed his comm, lifted his head, and froze.

Nearly everyone in a two-block radius was staring at him.

He tried to think of something happy but drew only a blank.

"Greens are attacking again?" someone asked, tremulous.

"Did someone say *Greens are attacking*?"

"Oh my God, they're gonna kill us!"

Dalton watched, mortified, as the crowd surged in a sudden terror. People collided with each other as they chose different directions to escape in, and panicked cries filled the air in a dissonant chorus.

It was the closest thing to a mob Dalton had ever seen.

"There's no attack!" Dalton shouted. "Calm down, all of you!"

But Maxine had seen something. What if there had been a minor attack he'd missed, being here in the middle of town?

What if someone else was dead? And near his house!

His own panic rising, Dalton rushed to Chumley's side. His deputy's eyes had gone round, and he'd drawn his loaded water pistol even though there wasn't anything to shoot at.

"What in the world is going on here?" Naomi exclaimed behind them as more people scattered. Children were crying, adults were shouting, and Dalton just *knew* Carolyn was going to kill him and love every moment of it.

"What do we do?" Chumley whispered.

"Remain calm!" Dalton bellowed to the crowd. "I order you all to remain calm!"

He might as well have been telling a sandstorm to hold still for him.

"Dalton?" Cadu said from the comm. "A stampede just rushed past the station, and Gwendolyn Goldfarb walked in, singing something about grapefruit."

Dalton felt torn. He needed to get to the station to learn what Maxine had found, but he also needed to get this crowd under control before anyone got trampled.

But that's what he had a deputy for, right?

"Chumley, you stay here to maintain order," he said. "I'm going to the station."

"Me?" Chumley looked vaguely seasick.

"Yes, you! Now get on with it!"

Dalton set off toward the police station without looking back. He could hear Chumley feebly raise his voice to address the crowd as Dalton twisted and sidestepped and elbowed and ducked his way through it.

He burst through the police station door ten minutes later, his shoulder and his side throbbing from the crowd's frantic jostling. Gwendolyn sat hunched in a chair, eyes round and glazed.

"Exodus," she murmured, peering up at Dalton.

Dalton scowled at her, then at Cadu, who stood near his own desk with his comm in hand. Cadu held the device out for him to take. Dalton snatched it up and said, "Maxine, what the hell is happening out there?"

Carolyn burst through the police station door half a second before Maxine could answer, her hairdo crooked and murder glinting in her eyes.

"I'm doing my rounds like I was supposed to, Sheriff," Maxine said, voice shaking. "And I found leaves."

Dalton's mouth opened and closed a few times before actual sound came out of it. "Leaves?"

"They're a little shriveled and buried in the sand, but I can tell what they are. They grow on the Greens."

"Why would they pull off their own leaves?" Dalton asked, feeling too stunned to use his critical thinking skills properly.

"I doubt they did, Sheriff. I did a botany course my senior year of university. They shed their leaves like we shed our hair. And ... well, there's so many out here, half-buried, it looks like some large number of them passed through here. Maybe one, two days ago? I can bring them in as evidence."

Carolyn tore the comm out of Dalton's grip. "Maxine, this is Carolyn," she said. "What is your precise location?"

"I'm on the eastern side of town, a little way out into the desert. I can see the sheriff's back porch from here, ma'am."

"Stay precisely where you are," Carolyn ordered. "We're coming out to take a look at this."

"We?" Dalton had officially run out of things to smile about. "You're not on the force."

"I have an image to keep in front of our visitors, and I'll do whatever I damn well please to maintain it."

To Dalton's ultimate chagrin, Naomi Schwartzman herself pushed her way inside the station, followed by her colleagues, a highly-flustered Errin Inglewood, and one tear-streaked Chumley Fanshaw, who had a fresh bruise forming on his left cheek.

"They wouldn't listen to me," Chumley moaned. "And now someone's gotten out a flamethrower!"

Dalton felt utterly helpless as everyone in the room stared at him, their expressions demanding answers he didn't have.

"Dalton, Chumley, you two will come with me to meet Maxine," Carolyn said, her tone grave. "Ms. Schwartzman, words cannot describe how deeply sorry I am this has happened in front of all of you. This is not the way things usually are in our city, I can promise you that."

"I see," Naomi said. Her expression remained neutral. Dalton imagined her jotting down mental notes to store away for later, none of them good.

"Cadu, see if you can't keep the peace out there while we investigate whatever is going on on the east side," Carolyn went on. "Errin, you go with him and see what you can do. As for her . . ." She trailed off, looking at Gwendolyn. "Hell if I know."

Gwendolyn blinked up at Carolyn. "Grapefruit is full of vitamin C," she whisper-sang. "Good for you, and good for me."

Dalton wished that a bolt of lightning would shoot down

from the heavens and incinerate him on the spot to spare him this humiliation.

"I'm on it, ma'am," Cadu said, giving Carolyn a little salute and darting out of the police station, Errin on his heels. Dalton heard him let out a shrill whistle to capture people's attention, but he doubted anyone would listen. When an entire city's survival instinct kicked in and sent them scattering, there was little anyone could do but watch.

"See?" Maxine said, scraping aside sand with one booted foot. "Leaves."

Dalton bent down somewhat dizzily to examine what she'd unearthed. Several bright green, waxy leaves did indeed lay half-buried in the loose soil, and he banished wild visions of each one growing into a full-bodied Green before their very eyes, vengeful and hungry and full of teeth.

Naomi Schwartzman and her people observed him from a distance tapping notes into datapads, because of course they'd all had to come with them as part of their "assessment."

"How could you have failed to notice an army of the damned things marching past your house?" Carolyn said, her hands planted on her hips. "It's your *job* to notice this kind of thing."

Dalton glared at her as he straightened. "Clearly, they either came through in the middle of the night, or when I wasn't home. And how do we know it was a lot of them? Maybe two or three got into a scuffle and pulled out all of each other's hair. Er, leaves."

"It was a lot," Chumley murmured.

Dalton rounded on him, and Chumley flinched backward. "What did you say?"

"I saw them, night before last. I couldn't sleep and came outside, and . . . they weren't hurting anybody. Honest." Sweat started to distort Chumley's carefully-coiffed hair.

"And what, pray tell, were they doing?" Carolyn asked. Dalton felt grateful not to be on the receiving end of that glare, which had grown icy enough to freeze the entire desert into a skating rink.

"Walking," Chumley said. "Single-file. I was afraid at first, but they didn't notice me."

"Tell us more about these creatures," Naomi said, stepping forward with her datapad, which she'd withdrawn from somewhere inside her blazer. "I understand they're called Greens?"

"They're the native wildlife," Carolyn said. "They stick to the forests and mind their own business if people don't come near them."

Naomi glanced down at the shriveled leaves in the sand. "I see."

"They've been known to attack and kill, at times," Carolyn went on. "We've been on full alert the past few days after being subject to two random attacks. Our security efforts have been ramped up since then, hence Maxine here being out on patrol."

Maxine, whose short, brown hair stood up in random, dusty spikes, dipped her head in acknowledgment. "It's an honor to serve," she said, throwing Dalton a glance from the corner of her eye. She wore army fatigues and still toted her flamethrower, looking every bit the soldier.

Naomi typed something into her datapad.

"Mr. Fanshaw, *why* didn't you report the Greens to anyone the moment you saw them?" Carolyn asked.

Chumley fidgeted like an antsy child confined to a classroom desk, put on the spot by the teacher. "Because they weren't attacking anyone."

"You had no way of knowing they wouldn't."

"I know, but . . . they were carrying things. Sacks, canteens. One even had a wagon full of stuff." He gave Carolyn a sheepish grin that she did not return in kind.

"How many?" Carolyn asked.

Chumley's smile faltered. "Pardon?"

"How many Greens did you see pass by here?"

Chumley swallowed and tugged absently at his shirt collar. "Not sure."

"Why don't you take a guess?"

"Erm. Let me think."

Dear God, don't let him say anything stupid, Dalton thought. He could already sense the last fraying remnants of his own reputation teetering at the edge of an abyss, and all it would take was one final, soft push to send it plummeting over the edge.

Naomi waited with her finger poised over her datapad. Maxine absently traced a line in the sand with the toe of her left boot, and Carolyn's complexion was rapidly changing from its normal brown into something more like a pickled beet.

"There might have been a hundred," Chumley said at last. "Possibly two. Or three."

Carolyn blinked. "You're telling me that you, the new deputy, saw up to three hundred Greens traipsing past you, and you did *nothing*?"

"I kept an eye on them. They weren't like the Greens I saw at the hotel. These just seemed . . . well, peaceful."

Dalton put a hand to his forehead and closed his eyes. His pulse beat out a steady tattoo in his eardrums. Odd, how calm he felt, like a prisoner quietly accepting his fate as he stepped up to the gallows.

"Mr. Fanshaw," Carolyn said, "I am placing you on administrative leave so you can receive proper training."

"But nothing happened!" Chumley looked to Dalton, pleadingly. "Back me up, here!"

Dalton opened his mouth to speak, but no sound came out. None of this could be happening. He was still asleep, in bed, and FCU hadn't even landed yet.

"And Dalton, I'm placing you on administrative leave as well," Carolyn said. "Indefinitely."

"*What?*"

"You heard me." There was no humor in her tone, no kindness, no compassion.

"How was I supposed to know he was sitting out here watching the damned things?"

"And therein lies the problem," Carolyn said. "Maxine, grab as many of those leaves as you can, and meet us all back at my office with them when you've finished."

"Yes, ma'am," Maxine said, bending down to begin her task.

"As for you, boys . . ." Carolyn looked from Dalton to Chumley. "I don't want to see either of you again for the rest of the day. If you need me, call Errin. They're more forgiving than I am." She made a gesture and turned toward town, and Naomi and her lot followed her like a troop of corporate soldiers.

Dalton felt his shoulders droop as he watched them all go.

"Sheriff?" Chumley asked, stepping up beside him.

"Seems kind of silly calling me that now, doesn't it?" Dalton held out a callused hand, and Chumley eyed it warily before giving it a tentative shake. "Nice to meet you, Chumley. You can call me Dalton."

CHAPTER 10

Dalton didn't often spend time in his cellar, but right now it was the closest thing he'd ever get to proper air conditioning. The air down there hovered at a respectable 26 degrees Celsius, a whole six degrees cooler than his living room upstairs.

"So, what are we going to do now?" Chumley asked from the aubergine loveseat shoved against the far cellar wall.

"Hell if I know." Dalton took a swig of his whiskey and stared up at the rafters. "Carolyn'll feel sorry for me in a few days; she always does."

"You don't seem very angry about it." Chumley had declined Dalton's whiskey and instead sipped on an old bottle of champagne Dalton found in the back of the refrigerator.

Dalton shrugged. He'd drank so much already his fingers and toes were tingling. "Never wanted to be sheriff in the first place."

"Then why did you take the job?"

"Old Man Sondhi was retiring, and I needed something to do. He said it was easy; you just tell people what to do and call it a day."

"Don't you have to be elected sheriff?"

"Not on Molorthia Six."

Chumley tilted his head to one side, or maybe the whole room was tilting. "What did you do before you were sheriff? You never said."

"Had a shop. Couldn't bring myself to run it anymore. Sold it."

Chumley was starting to slouch over. He picked up the champagne bottle again and glugged some more of it, spilling a few dribbles on his shirt. "Wish I could nip out for a rolly," he muttered, plunking the bottle back onto the wooden crate sitting beside the loveseat.

Dalton straightened. "Pardon?"

"Cigarette," Chumley said. "I wish I had a cigarette."

"Oh, right. Give you lung cancer."

"Give me something to do, more like." Chumley paused. "Aren't you from England, too?"

Dalton's lips twisted into a frown. "How do you know?"

"I can hear a bit of it in your voice. Your accent ... it's like someone painted over it with American and a few other things."

"That's Molorthia Six for you," Dalton said. "It's a melting pot, and England was a long time ago. You should have heard me when we had neighbors from Kentucky. Everything was y'all, y'all, y'all."

Chumley offered him an intoxicated grin. "Oh, that's like when I was living with Gran, and our neighbors were from Yorkshire." His smile faltered, and he partook of more champagne. "Gran's parents came from Chandigarh, but my granddad was an Englishman through and through. I was named after him."

Dalton's molasses-slow thoughts had finally succeeded in

the tiniest of revelations, and he said, "Hold on a sec. I'll be right back."

He swayed as he climbed the stairs, gripping the banister for good measure. He rummaged through a few kitchen drawers until he found what he was looking for, then returned to the cellar, tossing a half-crushed pack of cigarettes and a lighter to Chumley.

"They're a bit stale, but you can have them," Dalton said, flopping back onto the creaky old armchair. Sudden vertigo made him scrunch his eyes shut.

"Thanks." Chumley fumbled out one cigarette and lit it. "Ugh, these are *bad*."

They sat in silence, each consumed with his own thoughts. Once Chumley's cigarette had burned down to a nub, he sat forward and said, "We should save our reputations."

Dalton snorted, feeling fractionally more coherent. "Are you going to buy Carolyn a bouquet of flowers and tell her how sorry we are?"

"It's my fault we're both in trouble." Chumley bowed his head. "I want to make things right."

"It's *our* fault." Dalton paused, thoughtful. "What do you have in mind?"

Creases formed in Chumley's forehead. "I keep thinking about the Greens."

Dalton tensed. "What about them?"

"I saw the ones that attacked the hotel. They were awful, murdering those people. But the ones outside the other night were different. They had kids with them. Plant kids, I mean, not people kids. And some of them were singing."

Dalton could feel his eyebrows shoot up toward his hairline. "You're out of your fecking mind."

"But they were! And it sounded so sad. They all seemed sad. I mean, I'm no expert on plant psychology, but I've seen documentaries about refugees, and that's exactly what they looked like."

"They're running from the fires. Wild animals even do that."

"Wild animals don't pack up their belongings and bring them with them."

"You said they had a wagon?"

Chumley nodded. "Full of things, yes. It had wheels and everything."

"Don't make them sound so human."

Chumley's shoulders bobbed in an inebriated shrug. "Just telling you what I saw." He frowned, tilted his head again, and said, "Fecking?"

"Hmm?"

"You said 'fecking' a minute ago. Is that Irish?"

Dalton slouched sideways in his armchair to get more comfortable. "Did I? Yeah, it's Irish. We had neighbors from Kill . . . Kill . . . Kilkenny, too." His vision blurred. "How do you want to save our reputations? 'Cause I got nothin'."

"We can put out the fires so the Greens stop evacuating their land."

Dalton found himself sitting bolt upright and feeling almost sober. "What?"

Chumley's eyes glistened with a sudden intensity. "You want to protect the town, right?"

"And what, you and I are going to just walk up to a

raging wildfire and dump a few buckets of water on it, call it a day?"

Chumley bit his lower lip. "Well, not us, specifically. But we can go there and see what's going on, then come up with a plan based on whatever we see. Does anyone on this planet have a copter?"

"Nobody in this town does."

"We can at least see how big the fires are and hire a fleet of copters to dump water on them."

Dalton thought about it. "Carolyn was just asking me the other day if I'd send someone up that way and have a look at things. But how are we going to find a fleet of copters capable of hauling water on Molorthia Six? Hell, where are we going to get *water*? The Rosa's been dry for months."

"There must be a lake somewhere. Or an ocean?"

"Not close enough to here for it to make sense."

"Frontier Care United, then," Chumley said, with conviction. "It's the biggest need here right now, more important than air conditioners."

The man was absolutely right. "We need to tell Carolyn what we're doing." Dalton rose, and his body remembered that he'd drank a significant portion of alcohol over the past hour. He gripped the arm of the chair and felt the cellar floor rocking beneath him. "Maybe in a while, though. Carolyn sees me like this, she'll kill me all over again."

"This is a terrible idea."

"But you said!"

"I was *drunk!*" Dalton stood in his living room facing Chumley, who'd changed into a fresh outfit that still smelled like the charity shop from which it had been purchased. "Driving up to the forests is suicide!"

"But we have to find out what's really going on up there." Chumley's expression remained resolute. "I saw how violent the Greens can be. I also saw how peaceful they can be."

Dalton kept shaking his head. "So you saw a group of pacifists. Fact is, you have no way of knowing what you'll run into up in the forests. You haven't heard anyone mention anything about Piney Gulch since you've been here, have you?"

"I've been a little busy getting the stuffing beaten out of me. Why?"

Dalton cleared his throat a few times. "Piney Gulch is a small oasis at the bottom of a ravine about twenty kilometers from the southern edge of the forests. It was one of the only places with vegetation that the Greens wouldn't touch. A hot spring bubbled up in the middle of it, and people built cabins and a playground and a picnic shelter there to attract visitors. Folks who ran it made a killing in rental income."

"Right." Chumley's brow furrowed.

"Five years back, people rented out the entire oasis for a big family reunion. They had games, campfires, barbecues, you name it. Everyone was having a grand old time until the Greens showed up." Dalton closed his eyes and silently counted to ten. "There were forty-eight people at Piney Gulch that day. Two survived."

Chumley's eyes widened. "What happened to the survivors?"

Dalton coughed, lightly. "The man who survived lost his

arm when a Green tore it from its socket and ate it in front of him. He crawled into a tunnel on the playground that the Greens were too big to fit inside, praying for a quick death."

"And the other survivor?" Chumley asked faintly.

"She was using the toilet when the attack started. She heard the screams and stayed inside while she called for help. Her husband and kids were killed while she hid in a stall with her comm unit." Dalton coughed again. "A rescue team arrived in time to save the man from bleeding to death. The Greens had fled already. He spent three weeks in intensive care, having a new arm grown from his own stem cells." His shoulder prickled at the memory. "That's what will happen to you if you go barging like a fool into their forests."

A sickly pallor had washed over Chumley's face.

"Stay here, in Richport," Dalton said. "I'll call around to the other cities; see if there isn't a copter someone can send out that way."

"Maybe that is a good idea," Chumley said, at length.

"I'll go ahead and start making calls."

Chumley sighed morosely as he ran a soggy rag over the gray, laminate countertop in Dalton's kitchen. He'd offered to help clean while Dalton spoke with his colleagues, but he would have much rather been out looking for the remains of his Cube.

Was he wrong to think the Greens he'd seen marching single-file through the night were of friendlier stock than the ones that invaded the hotel?

He paused in his work to light up another stale cigarette. He puffed on it thoughtfully and strained to hear fragments of Dalton's conversation issuing from the gap beneath the closed bedroom door. "... are you sure that ... but this is urgent! ... you're kidding me ..."

There came a click as Dalton turned his doorknob. Chumley made a point of scrubbing very hard at a stain.

"I've got bad news," Dalton said, stepping into the kitchen. An ashen pallor had settled over his face.

"No copters?"

"Oh, I wouldn't say 'none.' Folks over in Mount Olympus have one they use for aerial tours, but it's broken down and they're waiting for the replacement parts to come in from Earth. Only other place that's got one is Fred, and they use theirs to fly emergency victims to the hospital."

"What about airships?"

Dalton shook his head.

"Hot air balloons?"

Dalton scowled at him.

"What are we going to do, then? Just wait for the next attack?"

"We'll talk to Carolyn," Dalton said. "See if she has any better ideas."

"And if she doesn't?"

"Then you and I get to drive north after all and see what's going on for ourselves."

Carolyn appeared most displeased when Dalton and Chumley stepped into her office later that afternoon.

She'd appeared even more displeased when Dalton laid out their plan.

"I'm not sure you two understand what 'placed on indefinite leave' and 'talk to Errin, not me' means," she said, standing behind her desk once more. One of Naomi Schwartzman's FCU cronies sat in the corner taking notes, to Dalton's mild annoyance.

"We won't be doing it in any official capacity. Since we don't have the means to fly, we wondered if we could acquire a city vehicle. Unless you have a better idea." Dalton flashed his teeth at her. She didn't smile back.

"Lending you a city vehicle is out of the question," Carolyn said. "Not while you're on leave. Right now, you're just another civilian."

"Then how are we going to take a look at what's going on up there?" Chumley asked. "You want to find out, don't you?"

Carolyn's mouth twitched. "I'd already asked Dalton to do something about it, but that was before the Green attacks. There has to be a better option than this."

"We can't fly, that's for sure," Dalton said.

Carolyn remained silent for at least an entire minute, during which Dalton and Chumley glanced at each other with equal parts hope and dread.

"You're absolutely right," she said softly. "I'm just as curious as you are about what's causing those fires, and it's important we get to the bottom of this before anyone else gets hurt. Since you can't fly and you can't use a city vehicle, you'll have to find a vehicle of your own to take."

Dalton dipped his head. "I understand."

"Dalton, are you *sure* you'll be able to handle something like this? Because I know your history, and I don't want this to have a bad effect on you."

"This will be surveillance only. We drive in, take a look around, and report back our findings. Should be easy enough if the Greens haven't learned how to outrun a bus."

"Where are you getting a bus from?"

"Well, not a bus, exactly." Dalton grimaced.

"Okay." Carolyn frowned, briefly. "If you can find your own transport, I'll lend you a few power packs so you can keep your comms fully charged and remain in full contact with us the entire time. You might be an insufferable bastard, but I really don't want to lose you out there."

That might have been the kindest thing she'd ever said to him. "We'll find transport," he said. "Don't you worry."

"Where are we getting a vehicle from?" Chumley asked when they emerged from Carolyn's office. The gleaming sun hung closer to the western end of the sky, and the temperature had dropped about half a degree.

"My sister-in-law has a motorhome she doesn't use but won't sell. Figure she won't mind if we take it out for a spin."

He climbed onto the quad, Chumley getting on behind him.

"When you say sister-in-law . . ."

"She was my brother's wife."

"So, she's your ex-sister-in-law."

"Yeah." Dalton put the quad into gear. "You could call her that."

Summer Kane lived on the edge of a gully about two kilometers southwest of town, in an adobe house flanked by a grove of artificial palm trees that the late Robert Kane had paid a fortune to have imported from Pelstring Four. They looked real, though, and the sight of them made Dalton's nerves twitch when he coasted up to the house.

Chumley stood and stretched. "Nice place she's got."

"She writes articles for some holistic magazine," Dalton said. "Don't be surprised if she gives you a bottle of essential oils to test out for her."

They approached the dwelling via the curving cobblestone path. Various succulents from Earth grew in pots and in window boxes, reminding Dalton all too much of his former profession.

The front door flew open before Dalton had the chance to knock. A fortyish woman with curly strawberry-blonde hair stood before him in an ankle-length turquoise skirt patterned with swirls and a white tank top that displayed her amply-toned arms.

"Dalton!" she exclaimed. "To what do I owe the pleasure?"

Pleasure, Dalton thought. *Ha.* The first time Rob had brought Summer over for dinner, she'd informed everyone that if they didn't switch over to a strictly organic diet immediately, they would all die of cancer.

She had been wrong.

"We need to borrow your motorhome," Dalton said, skipping over the small talk he dreaded.

Summer squinted at him, then looked past him at

Chumley. Her expression brightened once more—she must not have been in town recently enough to know about Chumley's antics. "And who's this?"

"Chumley Fanshaw," Chumley said, dipping his head. "And you are . . . ?"

Summer scowled at Dalton. "Really, you didn't even tell him my name? I'm Summer Kane, Dalton's only living—"

"Can we borrow the motorhome?" Dalton cut in. "It's for police business. We need to see what's going on up in the forests, and Carolyn won't lend me transportation."

Summer blinked a few times. She wore some sort of bluish crystal pendant around her neck, no doubt to ward off bad vibrations.

"You do still have the motorhome, don't you?" Dalton asked.

"Of course I still have it!" She let out a little sniff, no longer cheerful. "Not like I'd get rid of it when it was Rob's pride and joy. I haven't changed a thing about it, either, so it still has scribbles on the walls inside from Ricky and Chandra. I just can't *believe* you'd only come out here to borrow something, and not to see me, your only living—"

"Is it still in the garage?" Dalton asked.

Dalton swore he saw tears well up in Summer's green eyes, but only for a moment. "Yes," she said in a softer tone, then brightened a third time, her rollercoaster of emotions making Dalton a trifle dizzy. "Come this way."

Chumley lifted one eyebrow at Dalton, who set his face into its general glower as Summer headed around the side of the house with the two of them in tow.

"Do you remember the time we all drove out to see the

Weird Sisters?" Summer asked as they passed some of the ultra-realistic fake palm trees. "Poor little Chandra had the stomach virus and threw up in front of a whole crowd of tourists."

"I remember."

"And Imani tried to climb some of the rocks all on her own, and she fell and cracked her wrist! Darneisha always called that The Vacation from Hell. If only we'd known."

They reached the free-standing adobe garage, and Summer grabbed the handle at the bottom of the metal bay door and yanked it upward with a metallic screech to reveal a shiny silver pill-shaped vehicle sitting on six wide tires with deep treads. "Here you go, motorhome, just like you want. Solar panel on top is still intact, last I checked. It's got bedding and dishes and everything you'll need." Summer gave Dalton a sidelong look. "You want to use *this* to drive into the forests?"

"It's not my first choice, but we don't have any other options."

"Not even a copter," Chumley said, shaking his head. "I would have preferred a copter."

"Who are you again, exactly?" Summer asked him.

"I'm the new deputy. Sort of." Chumley shifted his feet, uncomfortable. Dalton was glad he wasn't the only one. "Erm, does it have air conditioning?"

"Of course! But you can't run it nonstop, or the solar panel won't be able to keep up and you'll lose power until it gets enough new juice. It should only take you a couple hours to drive up to the forests, though, so you should probably be fine. I'd give it fifteen minutes of AC at a time with fifteen-minute breaks in between; that always worked for us. Any other questions?" Summer put her hands on her hips and looked back and forth between them.

"I don't think so," Dalton said, then added, "Where are the keys?"

"Already in it. Best way for me to keep track of them, not that I need them anymore, do I?"

"You could still travel if you wanted to," Dalton said, not rising to the bait. He had no desire to Discuss the Past, and Chumley didn't need to be privy to every last aching detail of his life.

Summer pursed her lips. "With who?"

"Whoever you want." Dalton stepped forward and opened the driver side door of the motorhome, spotting the keys lying on the upholstered seat.

He turned back to her. She'd folded her arms, and her green eyes glimmered like bits of jade.

"Chumley?" he said. "You can drive the quad back into town while I finish things up here. Meet me at Carolyn's office."

Chumley's eyes had narrowed. "Sure thing, Sheriff—erm, Dalton."

The deputy turned on his heel and crunched back over the rocky hardpan toward the quad. Once Dalton heard its soft motor sputter into life, he looked Summer in the eye and said, "So, you doing all right?"

Her expression grew a tad colder. "Does it look like it?"

"You know I don't like talking about any of this," he said.

"You never liked talking to me about anything to begin with."

"I don't like talking to most people."

"Well, *I* for one am supposed to talk about my feelings," she said. "My therapist says so. But nobody wants to hear them. It's like I was only supposed to be sad for a little while, and now that it's been five years, I'm supposed to be all back to normal, like nothing ever happened." Her eyes reddened. "They're the first thing I think about every morning, and the last thing I think about every night as I fall asleep. Sometimes I just wish I could . . ." She swallowed. "Forget it all. But that would be unkind to them. Don't you think?"

Dalton felt a tremble enter his bones. Being around Summer made everything too real again. "I think," he said, "that Rob and all the others are beyond caring what anyone thinks."

"Surely you don't believe that."

He shrugged, heaved himself up into the driver's seat, and slid the key into the ignition, but before he started it, Summer said, "Do you still think about Darneisha and the girls?"

"Every waking moment." His jaw clenched, and Summer stepped aside when he twisted the key and the solar-powered engine spluttered into life. It wouldn't hold a charge long here in the shade, so he eased the vehicle forward until it was completely out of the garage and let it idle a few moments in the evening sunlight.

"Thank you for lending us the motorhome," he said, glancing down at her to see a tear running down her face. "I'll try to get it back to you all in one piece."

What an odd family, Chumley thought as he parked the quad behind Dalton's house and began his walk toward Carolyn's office. He couldn't be one to judge, though, as his cousin Bhavisha would spend every family gathering discussing scientific evidence that the creation of agriculture had been the beginning of the downfall of humanity, and his Aunt Priyanka touted an equally-fervent belief that most, if not all authority figures were in fact members of an as-yet-unidentified species of shapeshifting lizard.

Chumley straightened his shoulders, tapped at his chest to reassure himself that his deputy star was still pinned there despite the fact he'd been placed on administrative leave, and held his head high anytime he passed someone on the sidewalk.

It was only when he saw the ruins of Hotel Richport that he realized he'd taken the wrong street. Four people were loading charred boards onto a flatbed lorry, and a folding table had been erected next to it, covered in misshapen objects Chumley couldn't identify from that distance.

One member of FCU stood nearby, wearing shades and taking notes.

With some trepidation, Chumley approached the workers, who paused to regard him.

"Excuse me," Chumley said. "I was wondering if—"

"You're that salesman," spat one man wearing a hardhat, safety goggles, and heavy work gloves covered in black grime.

"Deputy, now." He pointed lamely at his star, then flicked his gaze to the FCU representative, who might have been the one named Olivia Newkirk. Surely these dolts wouldn't try to hurt him in front of a visitor. "Erm, have any of you found anything unusual in the wreckage?"

The worker jerked his head in the direction of the table. "We put the salvageable stuff over there. It's not a lot. Fire ate through this place like it was made of paper."

"Oh. Thank you." His heart heavy, Chumley went to the table to regard its blackened contents. Lying atop it were a comm unit, a hoop earring, three matching candlesticks he remembered seeing on a sideboard in the hotel lobby the day he'd checked in, a set of military dog tags, a wine glass with a hairline crack running down one side, and two datapads.

He slunk back over to the workers, who were lifting a chunk of burnt drywall onto the bed of the lorry. "Excuse me again," he said. "Did any of you happen to see a small, metal cube, about this big?" He held up his hands to demonstrate the size.

Two of the workers glared at him.

"I was staying here when the fire started," he added quickly. "The Cube is . . . a paperweight. It means a lot to me, and I was hoping . . ."

"It's that way." The first worker he'd spoken to jerked his head toward the rubble behind him. "Saw it glinting in the sun, but we still have to move a load of rubble before we get to it."

Chumley's heart skipped several beats. "You . . . seriously?"

But the workers had continued with what they were doing and chose to ignore him as if he'd never been there.

Before Chumley could advise himself to be careful, he'd vaulted over a fallen crossbeam, crunched through what had probably been the ground floor's ceiling, clambered over a mound of ash, and saw, impossibly, his Cube, partly covered by yet another fallen board, but wholly recognizable as his most prized possession.

He took a step closer to the Cube, tripped over more rubble, landed on his stomach, reached out one hand, and closed his fingers around the thing he thought he'd lost forever.

His hands shaking as he sat up, he tapped the Cube three times on one side, watched the hidden button emerge from the otherwise smooth surface, and pressed it. The holographic archway he'd yearned for for days appeared before him, and he rose, unable to contain his joy, and stepped through it.

CHAPTER 11

It took Dalton at least twenty minutes to get the hang of maneuvering the bulky motorhome over the uneven ground, and the shadows grew even longer by the time Dalton made it back into town. In front of Carolyn's office, Errin Inglewood was setting unmarked wooden crates on the ground next to Chumley, who even at first glance seemed a different man from the one who'd left Summer's house on the quad such a short time before.

Dalton parked the motorhome along the curb and got out.

"What's all this?" Dalton asked Errin, who brushed sweaty bangs out of their eyes when they straightened.

"Supplies," they said. "A little gift from me and Carolyn. Well, mostly me—she's lending you the power packs, of course. But I thought you could use provisions and a first-aid kit. You never know what might happen out there."

Dalton peered into one of the open-topped crates and saw boxes of freeze-dried fruit and beef jerky tucked down into it. "Thank you," he said. Then, turning to Chumley, who wore yet another fresh outfit, he said, "What do you look so happy about?"

"Nothing! I mean, we're taking action. It could help a lot of people." Chumley's cheeks flushed. A squarish bulge in the left pocket of his trousers made Dalton arch his eyebrows, but he decided it wasn't his place to pry.

Carolyn stepped outside to join them, her heels clacking on the sidewalk. "Here, take these," she said, passing a metal case into Dalton's hands. "I'm lending you two extra comm units and two extra chargers so you'll have no excuse for breaking communications with me. I want you to keep checking in once you've made it to the forests, you hear?"

Dalton dipped his head. "We'll keep you up to date on everything we see."

"Good. Bon voyage, boys."

Dalton looked over to Chumley, who'd suddenly turned apprehensive.

This was it, then.

"You ready?" Dalton asked him.

"Sure," said Chumley. "I invade the lairs of man-eating trees all the time."

"Help me put all of this stuff in the motorhome. Then I'm stopping at home to get a couple changes of clothes, and we can be off."

Chumley complied by hefting a crate into his arms and carrying it into the motorhome. Dalton looked from Errin to Carolyn, hesitated a moment as he wondered if he'd survive to see either of them again, and proceeded to load the motorhome with the rest of the crates. Once he and Chumley had finished, Dalton gave Carolyn and Errin a solemn salute and hoped they didn't notice his hands shaking.

"Wish us luck," he said, then gestured for Chumley to join him inside.

"Isn't it a bit late to head out?" Chumley asked, strapping himself into the plush passenger seat to Dalton's right.

"We can get a head start this way, and we won't have to

worry about running the AC so much since it won't be as hot."

Chumley mulled this over and nodded. "Don't forget to pick up the weed killer at your house."

"I wouldn't dream of it."

Dusk had fallen. Dalton angled the fully-stocked motorhome so the high beams pointed toward the north. His fingers tightened around the steering wheel as the vehicle idled in place.

"Do you need me to step on the accelerator for you?" Chumley asked.

Dalton shivered. "I'm ready." He could do this, dammit. He was the bloody sheriff.

He pressed the accelerator with his right foot. The motorhome eased forward at three kilometers per hour. The dashboard panel indicated that the system held a 75% charge, which would drain significantly overnight but climb right back up again once the sun rose.

He didn't anticipate there being any problems. The motorhome was only ten years old; it had a good, long life left in it.

"The thing about the forests," Dalton said, "is that they're so much cooler than the desert. Once we reach vegetation, we won't even need the AC as much."

"Uh-huh," said Chumley. Dalton could still see the strange bulge in his pocket, even in his peripheral vision.

"It's just a shame the Greens have to live here at all," Dalton went on. "This colony could be booming by now if we could live in an area that doesn't roast people alive. We could have real cities, long walks in the shade . . ."

"If you hate Molorthia Six that badly, you could leave," Chumley said. "There are dozens of planets nicer than this one, no offense."

"Ah, but this one is home."

Ahead of them, a stray cat slunk from right to left. Dalton watched it stop a moment to sniff at something on the ground before vanishing in the night.

"Dalton, if you need me to drive, I can."

Dalton twitched, then realized the motorhome was idling in place again.

He didn't remember braking.

"I'll manage," he grunted, feeling a flash of irritation as he pressed on the accelerator. Dalton brought them up to roughly fifty kilometers per hour—a sensible speed far less likely to cause them to bust an axle on uneven ground.

He kept an eye on the dashboard compass so he could maintain a northerly direction. Chumley lapsed into silence beside him. Dalton glanced over and saw that the man's eyes were shut.

He smiled as he remembered a time when little Imani had dozed off in the passenger seat on one of their longer family trips, then silently cursed himself for allowing himself the emotion.

Dalton slowed the motorhome to forty kilometers per hour when the ground sloped uphill a short distance. Once it leveled out again, he glanced at the power indicator and felt his heart stutter to see it had dropped down to 52% in less than fifteen minutes.

Something emerald flashed in the vehicle's high beams.

Dalton slammed on the brakes.

Chumley flailed beside him and gripped the arms of the passenger seat, fully alert. "What's happening?"

Dalton pointed toward the windshield with one quaking finger.

Chumley leaned forward, squinting, and gasped.

Perhaps thirty meters ahead of them lay a Green. Unlike the others Dalton had the misfortune of meeting, this one lay on the ground, partly curled in on itself. The high beams revealed that at least two of its limbs had been blackened like charcoal.

"It's hurt, isn't it?" Chumley said in a whisper.

"Looks like it."

Chumley opened and closed his mouth a few times before saying, "Should we see if we can help it, somehow?"

Dalton snorted. "What are you going to do, slap a sticking plaster on it and tell it to take it easy for a few days? It's a fecking *plant*."

"It's a 'fecking' plant that walks and makes tools. I want to talk to it."

"You can't be that stupid."

Chumley folded his arms. "It's clearly injured, and might even be dead, for all we know. It might be wise to learn more about these things if I'm going to be traipsing right into their land."

"What are you going to learn from a dead Green?"

"I don't know. That's what I'm going to find out." Chumley withdrew his water pistol from its holster and stepped out into the night.

Dalton swore and followed suit.

The vehicle's high beams did a sufficient job of illuminating the general vicinity, which consisted mostly of sand, rocks, and more desert scrub. Dalton kept his eyes and ears open for signs of an impending Green ambush as he stepped closer to the prone bit of vegetation.

Chumley drew up short four meters from the Green. "It's not dead."

It took every ounce of Dalton's will to step up beside him.

Two of the thing's limbs were indeed blackened nubs, and most of the leaves on the left side of its body had been burned away. One of its four eyestalks was severed at the base, but whether that injury was old or a recent one, Dalton didn't know.

Two of the remaining eyes flicked open to regard the two men. They weren't white with a colored iris, like human eyes. These looked like yellow-green marbles bearing thin slits in the centers, like a snake's.

Chumley took one tentative step forward, then another. Dalton did likewise but made sure to glance behind him in case more Greens were coming.

"Hello there," Chumley said in a soothing tone. "I see you've had some trouble."

The Green blinked at him but didn't try to get up.

Chumley stepped forward another meter and stopped just short of the beast, then crouched down on the ground beside it.

The Green shook, its remaining leaves rattling like brittle twigs.

"Do you mind if we take a look?" Chumley asked.

At that moment, Dalton noticed the canteen lying half-buried in the sand beside it. Gingerly, he took the canteen and shook it—empty. Despite not being man-made, its purpose was all too obvious, which chilled him deeply for a reason he couldn't fully explain.

"Nasty bit of a burn you've got," Chumley said, leaning closer and shining a penlight on the Green to get a better look. Where had Chumley even gotten a penlight? Not that it mattered.

Chumley reached out one shaking hand and laid his fingers on one of the less-damaged leaves, then jerked his arm back with a gasp.

Dalton flinched. "What happened? Did it burn you?"

"No . . . it's weird. Something with my head."

"You mean your hand."

"No." Frowning, Chumley touched the Green again, and in the glare of the high beams, Dalton watched his face grow pale.

Chumley pulled his hand back again and then rubbed both of them together.

"Mind sharing?" Dalton turned toward the darkness again. They were still alone, though he couldn't shake the feeling of being observed from a distance.

"It's hard to explain," Chumley said. "You should touch it, too."

"I am not touching that thing."

"It doesn't hurt."

"I've touched a Green before. Well, one touched me."

"And when was that?"

"When it ripped my arm off and ate it."

Chumley stared at him.

"Maybe you should just try describing what you felt just now."

"Ah. Erm." Chumley blinked. "It was like, my head opened up, like a barrier slid aside for a moment. Maybe it's how they communicate with each other! Psychic vibes, or something."

"Psychic vibes."

"Maybe that's not the best way to describe it. If you'd just poke it with one little finger . . ."

"Absolutely not." Although Dalton couldn't deny he was intrigued by the matter. "If you think this thing is psychic, maybe figure out if it can tell you what's been happening up in its homeland and save us the trip."

To Dalton's horror, Chumley said, "Good idea!"

Before Dalton could mention he'd only been kidding, Chumley had laid his entire hand against the Green's side.

In the old movies Cadu Mão de Ferro forced him to watch, this would have been the moment where the inert monster rose up in all its glory and swallowed the dimwit whole.

Beads of sweat broke out on Chumley's forehead. "Hello there again. I'm a friend, I think. I just want to know what happened to you and your people. Do you call yourselves people? I heard your lot making music, and I think only people do that."

Dalton wanted to roll his eyes but found himself transfixed by the fact that Chumley was not yet dead.

"Oh my God," Chumley whispered. "I think I'm getting something."

"You're kidding."

"No, no . . . I'm getting little glimpses of it. Great, silvery things falling from the sky. No, that's not quite right . . . the things, they hover in the sky and rain down bad rain on everything."

Dalton felt his eyebrows rise. "Rain down bad rain?"

"I'm communicating psychically with an alien plant, Dalton. There's going to be a language barrier. Hold on . . . everything the bad rain touches goes up in flames. The monsters watch and laugh."

A faint chill wafted through Dalton's veins. "What sort of monsters?"

"It's hard to tell. Our friend here is sending me mostly impressions of what it experienced. It thinks the monsters are demons."

"Plants believe in demons."

"This one does, at least. Wait a minute—oh no." Chumley pulled his hand back from the creature, which had ceased trembling, and said, "It's gone."

Dalton stared at the inert plant. "That fast?"

"We're lucky we got to it when we did. I'm sorry, friend." Chumley addressed that last bit to the Green. "What should we do with its body?"

"We're going to leave it right where it is." Dalton pulled out his comm unit and keyed in Carolyn's number. "Carolyn, there's a dead Green just north of town. It's half-burned; it's a miracle it made it down this far before keeling over."

"Are there others?" Carolyn asked.

"Not that we've seen. We're leaving the body where it is; you can send someone up here in the morning to collect it. I'm sending you the coordinates now." Every comm unit came equipped with its own positioning system, and all it took was the press of a button to relay that data to the recipient.

"Coordinates received," Carolyn said a moment later. "I'm pulling them up on my datapad now . . . good Lord, you two didn't get very far yet, did you? Let me know if you run into more of them."

"We will."

Once Dalton had pocketed the comm unit, Chumley said, "Why didn't you mention the psychic connection?"

Dalton turned and began the short walk back to the motorhome. "Because it's Carolyn. With her, some things are best left unsaid."

CHAPTER 12

When Dalton got behind the wheel of the motorhome once more, he noted with dismay that the system's power had plummeted to 38%.

They were barely twelve kilometers out of Richport.

"Problem?" Chumley asked, buckling himself in.

"Hoped we'd get farther than this tonight." Dalton brought the vehicle up to thirty kilometers per hour, hoping the slower speed would keep the power from draining so quickly.

When the power level dipped below 35% a few minutes later, Chumley cleared his throat and said, "So, your arm."

"I don't want to talk about it."

"You brought it up."

"I was making a point."

"Did a Green really eat your arm?"

"I *said*—"

"Right, right. I shouldn't have asked." Chumley turned his head toward the passenger window. "You said there were only two survivors."

"You strike me as someone who's not nearly as stupid as you act."

"I suppose that's a compliment."

"If you say so."

"Fine. I just thought since we're working together, that maybe, well, we should be open with each other about things."

"What for?"

"To create rapport, or something."

"I'm not creating rapport with you. Now shut up before I drive this thing off a cliff."

Chumley fell silent.

The power level fell to 34%.

They were now fifteen kilometers north of Richport.

They had a long way to go.

Dalton's soft snoring would not allow Chumley to drift off to sleep, so he grudgingly stepped out of the parked motorhome and lit up one of the few remaining stale cigarettes Dalton had given him.

Stars blanketed the ink-black heavens like jewels—he could see the pale, yellow dot that was Sol, Earth's sun, twinkling amid a distorted Sagittarius, and it made him feel a little sad to think of how far he'd come since the beginning.

Random rock formations stretched upward from the ground like ruddy obelisks. To the south, a faint glow on the horizon indicated the location of Richport, and to the north, another glow spoke of fire and destruction.

Just how large did a fire have to be to be visible from that far away? It had been hard to discern specific details from the dying Green's thoughts, but Chumley guessed it would have to be a cataclysmically raging inferno far larger than anything he could imagine.

Had someone taken pity on Molorthia Six and opted to rid the planet of the Greens once and for all? It seemed a bit extreme, but mad rulers of old had burned whole cities just to rid them of antiquated infrastructure, and plenty of tyrants had turned to genocide and called it societal advancement.

But who were the tyrants here? Humans? Other Greens? Someone else they didn't know about? There had been some article Chumley read perhaps only a year or two earlier, something that had pertained somehow to this situation, but as much as he strained to remember what he'd read, the more the facts of it remained elusive. He'd probably been drunk when he read it.

Don't forget you have your Cube now, a tiny voice reminded him. *Why keep wondering when you have that?*

Good point.

Chumley finished his cigarette, flicked the butt out onto the sand, and tiptoed back into the motorhome so he wouldn't wake its cranky driver.

He'd tucked the Cube beneath his pillow for safekeeping. He removed it now, glanced to Dalton to make sure he was still asleep, then activated the holographic archway leading into his portable universe before setting the Cube back onto the thin, cot-like mattress.

Chumley had not been lying when he'd told Dalton he'd lost everything in the hotel fire. Well, he *had*, unintentionally, since all his belongings were here now save for the few that had been left out in his hotel room, but he hadn't known that at the time. Losing his Cube was as good as losing all his belongings, because that's where he stored them.

The holographic archway flickered as Chumley stepped through it into a room that did not exist anywhere in the known universe.

It wasn't an overly large room; only about twenty feet per side. He'd done his best to decorate it like the room he'd had as a child before everything had gone to shit, so the full-sized bed was shoved into the corner beneath two dozen glow-in-the-dark stars dangling from the ceiling on near-invisible strings. The room also contained a minibar, a wardrobe, a computer workstation where he printed out his fake brochures and business cards, a shelf full of knickknacks, a small exercise machine that kept him trim enough to outrun the police if needed, and one hamster cage, currently unoccupied.

One doorway led to an attached bath, and another provided access to the veranda, which (since the portable universe was much, *much* smaller than the real deal) looked out onto a holographic garden populated with rosebushes and privet hedges. Chumley poked his head through this latter doorway to see a holographic night sky spread out above it, resplendent with the constellations as seen from Pelstring Four.

It looked the same as when he'd checked earlier. Good to see that the fire hadn't even disrupted the portable universe's current settings. The one time he'd accidentally dropped the Cube into the toilet at Major Tom's Bar and Grill near the spaceport on Axaloon, the veranda had looked out onto a holographic seascape filled with narwhals for a week.

Chumley closed the door and threw open the drapes on the two windows that gave view of the veranda. Then he withdrew a glass, a corkscrew, and a bottle of chardonnay from behind the minibar and took them over to his worksta-tion, where he uncorked the bottle and filled the glass while he waited for his computer to wake up. He swirled the wine in the glass and took a sip, then leaned forward and switched on the security screen beside the main computer screen.

It showed Dalton, unmoving, on his bunk.

Good.

He cracked his knuckles and typed "burning planets" into the database search box, then leaned back in the swivel chair while he watched the screen populate with results:

1. Wildfires in the Streetha Plains of Vu-Ong Twelve enter third week; thousands evacuated as drought continues.

2. Fourteen-year-old charged with arson in Omicron Delta's Prime City after being found responsible for the apartment fire that spread through four city blocks, killing three people.

3. Controlled burn in Glades National Forest ensures new growth for coming year.

Chumley rubbed his chin. Controlled burn? Was that what he'd been thinking of? He still wasn't sure. He'd heard somewhere as a kid that certain types of plants could only reproduce if they caught fire first, and some parks here and there amongst the settled planets set areas on fire to clear out old growth and invasive species.

It seemed so unlikely on Molorthia Six. Not enough people lived here to care about how well the forests were doing, especially when the forests tried to eat them.

Speaking of which . . .

He turned to the other screen. Dalton had rolled over and jammed a pillow over his head, but he still appeared to be asleep. Chumley couldn't help but notice the man's arms, which were bare since Dalton had gone to bed shirtless.

Had Dalton been pulling his leg about the arm thing just

to give him a hard time? Why would anyone even do that? But if Dalton had been telling the truth, that meant . . . but that was too unbearable to think about. Only two survivors?

Chumley cleared the search terms from the main screen and typed "Piney Gulch Molorthia Six" in their place.

1.   Piney Gulch, a scenic gorge in the northeastern desert region of Molorthia Six, is a popular vacation spot for desert-dwellers who yearn for peaceful, Earth-like forests.

That was all. Maybe if Chumley was close enough to civilization for the database to gather updates from the local net he'd learn more, but he didn't really think so. These desert types didn't have the media lurking around like piranhas, waiting to dig their teeth into the next juicy story they could sensationalize beyond any semblance of reason.

Only two survivors.

Chumley thought of the woman who'd lent them the motorhome and shivered.

He thought of the empty bunkbeds in Dalton's house and shivered some more.

On the security screen, Dalton was rolling over again.

Chumley drained the rest of the wine from his glass. He'd better get back out there before the sheriff woke and wondered where he'd scampered off to.

He shut down his computer and stepped back through the holographic archway into the real universe.

"See, I told you the power would climb back up in no time," Dalton said as they cruised over a patch of bumpy ground the next morning. Multiple plumes of smoke blackened the sky in the distance, and Dalton had angled toward the largest one.

"I didn't doubt you." Chumley sat in the passenger seat with his arms folded across his chest. They hadn't turned the air conditioner on yet, and the temperature inside was climbing just as rapidly as the system's power.

They'd reached rockier terrain within ten minutes of setting out after a quick breakfast. A three-pronged rock formation jutted from the ground off to their left—Dalton recognized it as Chicken Foot, which lay thirty kilometers north of Richport. It felt both good and terrifying to be so much closer to the forests.

When it got too hot for comfort, Dalton switched on the air conditioner—ironic, how desert-dwellers kept them in their motorhomes but not in their houses—and then wondered how the FCU people were getting on back in Richport. Were they really connected to the people in white? They'd given off completely different vibes from the invisible intruders, so Dalton was no longer certain.

"Is it getting darker?"

"What?"

Chumley leaned closer to the windshield. "I'd swear it's getting darker."

"I'm wearing shades, and the sunlight's still trying to sear off my eyes."

"Take them off."

Dalton was about to object when something ticked softly against the driver's side window, and the entire vehicle gave an unexpected lurch.

He yanked off the shades just in time for a shadow to pass over them.

"Dalton? Are you there?"

It was Errin Inglewood's voice, barely masking worry. Dalton dug one-handed for his comm unit, which Chumley plucked off the floor and handed to him. "I'm here," Dalton said. "What is it?"

"Our sandstorm sirens just started going off."

"But it's too early for—"

"Wildfires can disrupt normal atmospheric conditions. What's your current location?"

Dalton braked and put the motorhome in park as the left-hand side of the vehicle ticked more frequently. He relayed the location back to Errin using the comm's positioning system, then said, "Do we know how big this storm is?"

"Just by looking, we think it's . . . ometers wide." Errin's voice dissolved in a burst of static. "No other reports . . . other towns . . . moving toward . . . theast?"

The sky continued to dim. The motorhome rocked in place. Chumley's knuckles turned pale from gripping the armrests so tightly.

Dalton glanced out the window toward the southwest, regarding the kilometers-high wall of airborne sand barreling toward them.

He'd been too preoccupied with looking at the smoke ahead of them to even notice it coming.

It slammed into them within seconds, turning the sky and everything else around them such a dark shade of brown it was nearly black. The wind shrieked like ten thousand ghouls, and fine particles of sand found their way through the tiniest gaps and sifted into the vehicle.

"Errin?" Dalton shouted into the comm unit. "Errin, do you copy?"

The comm unit only hissed.

"How long do these things last?" Chumley asked, making an admirable effort to appear calm.

"Up to five days."

"We can't be stuck in here that long!"

Dalton rose and went into the kitchenette, pulling two dishcloths out of a drawer and dampening them with water from the sink. "Put this over your face and breathe through it," he said, tossing one of the cloths to Chumley. "It filters out the particles you'd be breathing otherwise. It can cause lung problems."

Chumley's eyes went round as he put the cloth over his mouth and nose. Dalton did the same with his own cloth, then shut off the engine.

They wouldn't be going anywhere for a while.

Not like he'd been in a huge rush to get to Green territory, anyway. Maybe getting stuck in the sandstorm here was saving his life.

The storm raged onward.

"What's the shortest one of these things can last?" Chumley asked when the outside world grew to the color of pitch. Dalton couldn't see his own hand in front of his face and sneezed in spite of the cloth protecting him.

"About two hours." Dalton sneezed again. "I wouldn't count on it, though."

"What are we supposed to do if we're stuck in here for five days?"

"Sing songs, talk about our feelings."

More static burst from the comm unit, making Dalton jump. He patted around for it, and once he'd located it, held it up to his protected face and said, "Is anyone there?"

Words in a language unknown to Dalton spilled into the room: "*Pip-pip! Ammru gugaa'a shora . . .*"

Dalton tapped the comm. "Who's there?"

"*. . . jejeshu ku'a himms . . .*"

"I take it you don't understand that," Chumley said.

"Do you?"

"Aside from the obvious one, I speak a little Gujarati and Punjabi because of my family, but that's not either of those."

"It's not Hindi or Spanish, either. Who is this?" Dalton demanded of the speaker as they continued to carry on. "Why are you contacting me?"

"I think it's picking up a stray signal," Chumley said. "I used to have a radio that randomly spouted jargon I couldn't make sense of. I thought it was haunted until my gran told me it was picking up signals from the lorry drivers on the motorway."

"But we're in the middle of nowhere," Dalton said. "There shouldn't be anybody out here to give off a signal for us to pick up."

"So, someone else is stuck in the storm, too."

"Then why can't we understand them?"

"You said this planet is a melting pot. Do you have a way to home in on the signal, see if someone out here needs help?"

"Suppose I can try." Dalton felt his way into the kitchenette and blindly pulled open drawers, feeling for anything shaped like a flashlight. He struck gold in the third drawer down and clicked it on.

Now that he could see, he examined his comm unit and tried to remember if this one featured a trace function. The voice continued to speak in garbled bursts as Dalton located the menu on the tiny comm screen and scrolled through it, finding options like "Group Call" and "Sleep Mode."

When he selected the option for "Trace Caller," nothing happened.

"Of course," he muttered.

"Hmm?"

"If it's a stray signal coming through, it won't be able to latch on to where the signal is coming from. The trace can only work if someone intended to call us."

Chumley twisted around in his seat to look at him. "They'd have to be close, though, right?"

"You'd think."

"Well . . . we could get moving again; turn the headlights on and see if we can see anyone through all of this."

The comm unit fell silent. The voice hadn't really sounded urgent. In fact, there hadn't been much emotional inflection at all, which seemed kind of odd for someone trapped in a sandstorm.

"I can try to move this thing," Dalton said, "just to see if we can find our way out the other side of it." He hated the thought of having to do it. He didn't think there had been anything treacherous in front of him before the sand blotted out all visibility, but what if he was wrong and drove over an exposed boomstone, or hit a rock formation? Surely it would be safer to stay put and ride out the storm.

But we could be stuck here for days, otherwise.

Grudgingly, Dalton got back into the driver's seat and started the engine. The interior and exterior lights came on, illuminating copious quantities of sand still seeping in through cracks that Dalton couldn't see.

The headlights shot through the sand as far as they would go, which was about three meters.

"Here we go," Dalton said, and set the vehicle into motion.

Very, very slow motion.

He kept the towel over his face with one hand while he steered with the other. The vehicle rocked and lurched so violently that Dalton almost couldn't keep it straight, yet they were still making progress, small as it may have been.

Chumley glared at the filthy maelstrom. "It doesn't look any lighter yet." He lowered the cloth from his face, immediately sneezed, and hastily replaced it. "If anyone had told me two weeks ago that I'd soon be witnessing plants murdering a man, spotting ghosts that no one else can see, and getting myself stuck in a sandstorm, I'd have said they'd had one too many Soul Rippers during Happy Hour at Major Tom's Bar and Grill."

"Soul Rippers?"

"They're made from Kaktian Rum. One shot can drop a man twice my weight if he hasn't eaten anything first."

"Mm." Dalton kept his eyes wide, seeking out any obstacles that might hinder their trip. This part of the desert was supposed to be mostly flat, "supposed" being the operative word.

"I can buy you one sometime," Chumley went on.

"Why would you want to buy me a drink?"

"You seem like you could use one."

Dalton had no response for that. He was too busy trying not to drive them off any cliffs he might have forgotten about.

They continued in that creeping, lurching fashion for a time that felt like hours. The gloom neither lightened nor darkened, and the ceaseless wind howled like a thousand angry banshees.

Since the sun could not penetrate the storm and give them any extra juice, the power Dalton had been pleased to regain ticked lower, and lower, and lower.

"I'm turning the interior lights off," Dalton said, flipping a switch that plunged them into gloom relieved only by the illumination of the high beams.

The foreign voice burst from his comm unit again. "*Pip-pip! Annjui mish himms.*"

"I wish it would stop doing that," Dalton said. "The way I see it, if you're going to land on Molorthia Six, you should at least know Hindi, Spanish, or English so someone can understand if you're sending out a distress call or not."

"Or Gujarati or Punjabi," Chumley pointed out.

"Those too."

"Maybe they're not human."

Dalton shivered. "I met some Heemins once."

"Here?"

"It was on a spaceport layover when my family was coming here. I thought they were human until I saw their eyes. That can scare a kid, you know."

"You must not have gotten out much."

"Aliens don't really visit Cornwall."

Chumley moved in the darkness beside him, and a sudden burst of ancient electropop music from the dashboard speakers nearly ruptured Dalton's eardrums.

"I didn't mean to push anything!" Chumley shouted.

Dalton flicked the lights back on. Chumley had dropped his face cloth and was scrambling at the dash.

Dalton recognized the cacophony as "Just Dance" by Lady Gaga, an old Earth-based singer whom Summer had been obsessed with some years before.

"It's the dial right in front of you! Turn it to your left, and it'll—"

Dalton never got to finish his sentence. The motorhome shuddered, and the ear-blistering music was not loud enough to mask a great shrieking like metal peeling back from itself.

Gravity changed directions. Dalton, who had not buckled himself into the driver's seat, found himself lying on top of Chumley, who was squashed against the passenger side door.

Lady Gaga told them it would be okay as Dalton killed the blaring sound system with the slap of a hand. He clambered over the side of the passenger seat and stood against the main side door, which was now his floor.

"Dalton?" Chumley coughed. "I think you should look at this."

Dalton turned. An error message flashed above the power indicator: *Warning: solar panel disconnected. Please reconnect solar panel before complete system failure.*

Dalton said a word that his daughter Imani had said before Darneisha grounded her for a week.

He scrambled for his comm unit, keyed in Carolyn's number. "Carolyn? Carolyn, come in, please!"

The device emitted only static.

He keyed in Errin Inglewood's number. "Errin? Are you there? We have an emergency!"

More static.

"Storm's disrupting the signal." Dalton fought to keep his rising panic at bay. "I'll try calling Paris."

He tried the numbers of a few of his contacts in that neighboring city closer to the forests. Either the signal couldn't get through at all, or every human on Molorthia Six had inexplicably begun to hiss.

"Maybe we should try reconnecting the solar panel," Chumley suggested.

"You might not have noticed," Dalton said, "but this vehicle is lying on its side. Even if we can reconnect it, we won't be able to get it on its wheels again."

"But we'd have power."

Dalton grunted. "Fine. We'll see if we can't repair it. But we'll need goggles." He walked over to the cabinets, which were basically now the floor. Dealing with the drawers below the cabinets proved sort of an issue, however, since sliding open full drawers against the pull of gravity tended to result in a struggle and then a mess. Among the mess, Dalton located three pairs of swim goggles and tossed one to Chumley, who promptly slid them over his eyes.

"Try to keep the cloth over your face," Dalton said, slipping on his own pair of goggles and tucking one corner of the cloth beneath it so he could use his hands. The only logical door through which they could exit was the driver's side door, which now comprised part of the ceiling.

He went to the door, which lay just a bit out of reach from where he stood. "You'll have to give me a boost," he said. Chumley clambered his way and laced his hands together as a sort of step, and Dalton stuck one booted foot onto them and heaved himself upward.

He pulled on the door handle above him, bracing himself for the storm, and shoved the door open.

The howling wind practically yanked the door out of his hand. The hinges groaned as the wind bent them to an angle they weren't supposed to attain. Dalton hooked his fingers around the doorframe and pulled himself up and out of the motorhome, onto its side, feeling sand particles stinging his few bits of exposed skin.

He lay on his stomach and reached a hand down for Chumley to take. Chumley, slightly taller than he was, stood on the side of the passenger seat to give himself a boost, and Dalton got hold of his hand and helped pull him from the vehicle.

"Why do I feel like we're going to regret this?" Chumley asked, hopping down from the side of the motorhome onto the ground, which bore scant illumination from the high beams. The cloth on his face fluttered beneath the hand pinning it there.

Dalton didn't answer. He patted his coat pocket for the flashlight he hoped he remembered to stash there, then pulled it out and clicked it on. He motioned for Chumley to follow him around to the other side of the vehicle, then drew up short when he saw the motorhome's roof.

"Ah," Chumley said, joining him.

The solar panel wasn't just disconnected.

It was missing.

Dalton aimed his ineffective flashlight beam toward the east; the direction in which all this was blowing. Sand stung his ears, his cheekbones, and his hands. He could barely see two meters in front of him. The solar panel was probably kilometers away by now, forever out of reach.

He would not risk walking blindly out into the desert to find it.

Chumley huddled close to the side of the motorhome, which was technically the roof. Dalton could see where the wind had yanked the solar panel from its fittings, and spotted a few disconnected wires flapping in the gale.

"What are we going to do?" Chumley asked.

"We're going back inside to ride this thing out."

"But it could be days!"

"Good thing we brought provisions."

It was an extra effort climbing back on top of the prone motorhome without blowing away, and even more of an effort to yank the door closed. Dalton strained every muscle in his body to get the door to latch into place, but the wind had warped the hinges so badly that all he could do was leave it open and hope the sand didn't smother them.

"Get into the very back," Dalton said, stepping across the cabinets into the sleeping area. He walked along the wall between the upper and lower bunk, stepped up to the bathroom door, and yanked it open. "In here."

Chumley didn't protest. Still keeping the cloth pressed

over his face, he followed Dalton into the cramped room and closed the door above them.

The motorhome's bathroom contained a sink, a narrow shower, and a chemical toilet, none of which were currently in the proper position to function as intended.

"Never thought I'd have to take a shit sideways," Chumley giggled as he pulled off his goggles and rubbed his eyes. He sat cross-legged on the tile shower wall and put his head in his hands. Dalton sat beside him with his knees drawn to his chest.

The wind continued to howl.

"You'd think," Chumley said at one point while they waited, "that your people would have a better warning system about this sort of thing."

Dalton shrugged. "We have sirens. When high winds hit the sensors twenty kilometers outside of town, it triggers the sirens to go off. You and I are just too far away to hear them."

"Maybe Frontier Care United ought to give you something a bit higher-tech."

"Like a fancy colony ship that can haul everyone off this rock to somewhere nicer."

He felt Chumley shift beside him. "I thought you said Molorthia Six was home."

"That gives me the right to complain about it."

Hours passed. Dalton made a few more attempts to contact Carolyn, Errin, and the folks over in Paris, without success.

He ventured into the kitchen at one point to unearth some of the food and water they'd brought with them, trying not to worry too much about the fact that nearly the whole front end of the motorhome had filled with sand. His flash-light revealed that the wind had torn the driver side door clean from its hinges. It and the solar panel were probably off having a party somewhere.

"How is it out there?" Chumley asked when Dalton handed him a packet of mixed nuts and dried fruit.

"Not good." Dalton sipped at a bottle of water.

"Should I be worried?"

"Nah. We have enough provisions to last us until the storm's over, and once the skies have cleared, I can get through to Carolyn and have her send out a rescue crew."

"And we still won't have seen what's causing the fires."

"Maybe it's better this way."

Chumley glumly tore open his bag and popped a handful of snack mix into his mouth. Dalton could hear crunching as Chumley chewed.

He bit off a chunk of the jerky strip he brought for himself, but Dalton's appetite had blown away with the door and the solar panel.

A raspy cough made Dalton jerk awake. He rubbed his eyes and frowned at the door above his head, and then remembered what had happened.

He sat up. Faint light spilled around the edges of the closed door. Chumley stirred beside him on the tile wall of the motorhome's cramped shower, muttering something about biscuits.

Dalton paused; listened.

He allowed himself the ghost of a smile.

"Rise and shine," he said, shoving open the bathroom door and clambering out into the morning light. It had been a full twenty-eight hours since the storm hit, and they'd survived.

He looked at the condition of the motorhome and said a bad word.

"What is it?" Chumley mumbled, poking his head up through the doorway. "Oh."

Sand had drifted as high as a meter at the front of the motorhome and petered out into a fine layer of silt at the back. The passenger seat was completely buried.

Dalton pulled out his comm unit. "Carolyn? Do you copy?"

"Loud and clear, Dalton. How are you doing?"

His eyes stung with tears of relief at hearing another human voice. "We . . . had an accident. Can you send someone up here to get us?"

"I can try, but . . ." Carolyn coughed. "Richport's a mess right now, as I'm sure you can imagine. That's the worst storm we've had in two years. Errin's out on a plow helping clear the streets, and I've got about a dozen people lined up outside my office asking for favors—not to mention Naomi and her lot are still hovering around here like flies. I can't guarantee I'll be able to send anyone for hours."

"Well, don't make it take too long," Dalton spat. "The wind ripped the solar panel off the top of the motorhome and turned us on our side. We're completely stranded."

"I'm sorry, Dalton, but we have to follow up with three missing persons reports and reconnect the power for half the town. We'll get to you as soon as we can."

"Carolyn!"

The comm fell silent, and Dalton stared at it, dumb-founded. "I don't bloody believe it."

He dug another box of provisions out of the accumulated sand and opened a fresh packet of jerky.

Chumley twisted his slender hands together. "Why won't she help us?"

"She knows I can handle myself just fine." Dalton ate his jerky, angrily.

"We can't stay out here all day! I mean, there's always . . . oh, never mind."

"There's always what?" Dalton asked.

Chumley just shook his head.

Fifteen minutes ticked by. The air grew hotter, like an oven. Sweat ran down Dalton's scalp. He thought, and thought some more, and decided it was too much effort.

"*Pip-pip! Mehelu answaa him pahare.*"

The voice spoke from Dalton's trouser pocket, where he'd tucked the comm unit after Carolyn had cut him off. He pulled it out, stared at it a moment, and pushed the button. "Hello?"

"*Pip-pip! Kalaa oom himms.*"

His pulse spiked as he looked to Chumley, whose dark eyes had gone round. "Hello? Can you hear me?"

"*Pip-pip! Melaa'a konash.*"

Dalton's heart continued to thud. That had sounded like a response!

"What language are you speaking?" Dalton asked. Then, in what was most likely butchered Spanish, said, "*¿Cuál es su lengua?*"

More unfamiliar words spilled forth from the comm unit.

"I don't think that's a stray signal this time," Chumley said in a grave tone. "If someone's talking to you directly, they could be anywhere on the planet, right?"

Dalton rubbed his nose. Only a few sunburned flakes peeled off this time. "It's got a range of up to 1,500 kilometers, I think."

"So there might not be anyone close by to rescue us."

"Wouldn't say that. Although," Dalton added, "if it is the folks whose stray signal we were picking up before, then they might be close after all."

"It did seem to be the same language."

"Too hard for me to tell."

"All that *pip-pipping* was sort of a giveaway. I'm going outside to see if I can see anyone."

"Have at it," Dalton said, making himself comfortable sitting on the closed bathroom door. "I'll stay here and not die of sunstroke."

Chumley may have been on Molorthia Six for several days now, but the heat still smacked him like a thousand-degree croquet mallet every time he stepped into the sunlight.

As he strode down a newly-sculpted dune, he patted his pocket for his Cube and withdrew it. Casting one glance behind him to make sure Dalton hadn't changed his mind and was following him, Chumley activated the Cube's holographic archway and then hurried into his portable universe. He didn't take the time to bask in the cooler air; he began yanking open drawers until he found the pair of binoculars he'd been looking for.

Chumley stepped back out into the desert, picked up the Cube, deactivated the archway, and pocketed the whole device before Dalton peeked outside and discovered Chumley's little secret.

He held the binoculars to his eyes and made a 360-degree sweep of the desert. Tall shapes in the distance made his heart leap for a moment until he realized they were cacti, not approaching Greens.

He didn't see any signs of people.

Chumley focused the lenses on the smoke pluming on the northern horizon. It was still farther than anyone could go on foot. Not that he'd want to get there on foot, given the resident plant life. But if he could get somewhat closer …

He tucked the binoculars inside his shirt, then climbed back up onto the motorhome and hopped down through the opening above the sideways driver's seat.

"Back already?" Dalton asked. He still sat on the closed bathroom door, looking moody.

"I'm just getting a few things. I'll walk as far as I can and then come back to report my findings."

"I already know what you'll find. Sand. Maybe a rock or two. Watch out for the boomstones, though; if you step on them, they explode."

"Seriously?"

"It's something to do with the mineral content. We clean up all the ones we can find near town."

"Well, that's brilliant."

"They're the lumpy bronze ones. Just watch where you step."

"Is there anything else I should worry about out there?"

"You might run into a few sand serpents. They're mostly friendly unless you get near their burrows."

Chumley grabbed a hat and put it on before he could develop second thoughts about this whole endeavor, then slipped on his borrowed trench coat and loaded its pockets up with bottled water and food. He exited the vehicle again and set off in a northerly direction, keeping an eye out for anything that wasn't desert.

Sweat oozed from every pore of Chumley's skin—he'd have to take a shower in his portable universe by the end of the day. Should he tell Dalton about the portable universe? Dalton didn't seem the sort who'd want to steal it, but you could never be too sure about people. Portable universes weren't exactly a mainstream commodity, and it was only by pure chance that Chumley had come about getting one in the first place.

He passed a few bronzish rocks and sidestepped them, not knowing if Dalton had been kidding. He didn't see any snakes.

As Chumley contemplated turning around and going back, a faint, whirring sound somewhere behind him made his skin prickle. He scanned the horizon in all directions, saw nothing out of the ordinary, and decided it must have been in his head.

Saguaro cacti loomed ahead on his left. *Imports*, Chumley thought. That's what humans did, wasn't it? They found a new place to live, and rather than accepting it as it was, they had to turn it into someplace it wasn't. The ancestors of these wild cacti had probably arrived with early waves of settlers who'd wanted to emulate the deserts of the American southwest.

Something glinted ahead of him in the sunlight.

Chumley halted in his tracks and looked through his binoculars again.

The glinting thing appeared to be a metal structure, much larger than the ruined motorhome. Two figures moved about it, but he couldn't make out many details at that distance, which was probably at least three kilometers.

Chumley grinned, turned tail, and sprinted back toward the motorhome, taking care not to step on any exploding rocks.

It took him half an hour to get there, panting.

"Dalton!" he cried, vaulting himself up onto the "roof" of the useless vehicle. "Dalton, I've found people!"

He heard no response as he made his awkward way through the opening into the sand-filled cockpit. "Are you still in here?"

The sheriff no longer sat on the bathroom door. Chumley negotiated his way through the mess and rapped on it. "Dalton?"

Frowning at the continuing silence, Chumley pulled the door open.

The sideways bathroom was empty.

Chumley checked inside the closet across the corridor from the bathroom, which now lay above him like a ceiling, just to see if Dalton had gotten bored and tried to defy gravity. Several boxes and a citronella candle fell on his head for his efforts.

He got more bottled water and went back outside.

There were footprints in the sand beside the motorhome. Chumley recognized some of them as his own, and another set that could only be Dalton's. He followed the second set for several meters until it met up with two other sets that made Chumley's blood turn to ice, for those other sets had appeared out of nowhere.

They disappeared, too.

Like ghosts.

Chumley whisked his comm unit out of his pocket and keyed in Dalton's number. "What's happened?" Chumley asked. "Where have you gone?"

"*Pip-pip! Imruu himms a' kolaa,*" said the comm unit. "*What?*"

He thought he heard a muffled groan somewhere in the background.

Chumley's heart raced. Dalton had been rescued, dammit, and hadn't even attempted to let him know about it! Whoever else was out there with them must have spotted the motorhome and spirited Dalton away from it.

Having no other course of action to take, Chumley headed back toward the metal building he'd spotted earlier. Maybe they'd sent someone out on a hovercraft, hence the disappearing footprints. It would explain the whirring sound, too. If Dalton was inside the metal building, then all would be well.

Chumley didn't run this time. His reserves of energy were waning.

When it felt as though he'd been walking for two hours, he checked the horizon with the binoculars and couldn't see the dwelling anywhere.

His forehead creased. He'd always been fairly decent with directions, and he'd passed the same clump of saguaros not too many minutes earlier. So where had the building gone? Was it not a building at all, but a vehicle that had looked like a building? It wasn't fair they'd left him behind out here to die, just when he was starting to feel useful again.

He heard a sudden sound and whirled.

A figure dressed entirely in white stood there, holding some pistol-like weapon in a gloved hand.

"What are you—" Chumley started to say as he instinctively raised his hands, but the weapon fired, and the next thing Chumley knew, he was sitting in a beach chair wearing only what nature had given him while several handsome people waited on him hand and foot, and since he knew his luck would never allow that to happen in the real world, he knew he had to be dreaming, which also meant he was probably not dead, so at least he had that going for him.

CHAPTER 13

Just when he was really starting to enjoy it, Chumley's dream changed, and he was kneeling beside the dying Green out in the desert, placing a hand against one of its blackened stumps of a limb.

A thousand images and sensations whirled through his head, some pleasant, and some far from it. Verdant fields stretching from one horizon to the next, swooping birds unlike any he'd ever seen, ranks upon ranks of Greens stretching their limbs to the sky as their song filled the air . . .

He felt a hand on his and glanced to his right as the dream made another abrupt shift like someone changing the channels.

Dalton, sunburned and hatless, huddled against a gunmetal-gray wall, gripping Chumley's right hand in his left one. The man's eyes were over-dilated and out of focus, and tears trickled down his weather-beaten cheeks.

Chumley tried to pull his hand away from him, but Dalton wouldn't let go.

"Oh, Darneisha," Dalton moaned. "I wish you were here."

"Darneisha was your wife?" Chumley asked. He flicked his gaze to his left, spotting a sealed metal doorway, and then to the right, where two dozen school desks were inexplicably stacked against the wall next to a golden statue of Ganesh and a crate overflowing with boxes of drywall screws. Just what was his subconscious mind trying to represent here?

Dalton nodded. "Greens ate her, you know. They ate all of them." He slid his hand out of Chumley's and rubbed his eyes. "You know Alpha Centauri?"

Chumley could only frown—this dream was taking a particularly strange turn. "What about it?"

"Darneisha loved astronomy. She said . . . well, you know the Alpha Centauri System is the closest one to Earth. People knew about Alpha Centauri from the time they crawled out of the mud, but didn't know it was binary until the 1600s. Darneisha told me."

"That's nice." Chumley pinched his arm, wishing to wake up so he could figure out why the person in white had shot him.

"Darneisha always said, she said that was the two of us," Dalton went on. "Alpha Centauri is two stars orbiting each other so close, you can't even tell without a telescope. She said she and I were those two stars. And now she's *gone*, and what does that make me?"

The sheriff fell silent. Chumley wondered why this dream wouldn't just hurry up and change back to the beach one.

Time passed. Chumley gradually became aware that the place they were in was vibrating, ever so faintly. He also noticed a porthole through which he could see a bit of sky. His frown deepening, he crossed the metallic space toward the round window and held his face to it.

They were up in the air. The land was transitioning from sand to rockier terrain covered in low-growing plants that didn't appear to be mobile. After perhaps ten minutes, the airship banked, causing the room to tilt, and Chumley gasped.

For as far as he could see, the ground was blackened with broken trunks jutting up feebly from the uneven ground, and heavy machinery trundled along shoving it into piles.

He could smell the char even from up in the air.

Chumley pinched his arm again.

Nothing happened.

Then the metal door behind him slid open.

Swallowing, Chumley turned.

Dalton, still in a daze from whatever they'd doped him up with, lifted his head when the room's single door opened.

A figure dressed entirely in white stepped inside, and the door whooshed shut behind them. They looked exactly like the invisible intruders he and Chumley had both spotted in Richport, and Dalton knew deep down that they had nothing to do with FCU, since FCU was not known for luring people out of their vehicles and tranquilizing them for no apparent reason.

When Dalton had heard people outside the stranded motorhome, he thought someone had shown up to rescue him, which just went to show what one got for hoping.

The figure lifted the veil from their face, revealing icy violet eyes and pale cheeks that managed to look just as frigid.

They weren't human.

"Greetings," they said in a masculine voice with an unidentifiable accent.

Dalton scowled up at his alien captor. His vision doubled for a moment before resolving back to normal. "You speak English."

"Yes. We intercepted some of your transmissions before we took you. We assume you do not speak Haa'anu."

Chumley, who'd been standing near a porthole with a hand on his chin, looked as though he'd seen a whole platoon of ghosts. "Haa'anu?"

The man—Dalton assumed it was a man—grinned, displaying two rows of thin, razor-sharp teeth. "You have heard of us, then."

"You're planet-killers."

"I'm a businessman, hardly a planet-killer. My name is Kedd."

Dalton tried to stand up, but he must have gotten a much higher dose than Chumley, because his legs wouldn't cooperate. "Care to enlighten me?"

A subtle sort of rage trickled into Chumley's expression. "Haa'anu is a language of the Haa'la people of Leeprau. Loads of them make their money by scalping planets into dust. One of the news outlets on Pelstring Four broadcast a nasty piece about them."

Dalton tried to process this—he'd heard of the Haa'la but knew little about them. "When you say 'scalping' ..."

"They sent a fleet of miners to the Gem of Antaka last year, dug out everything that made it beautiful, and turned it to ash. The Feds arrested the ones who didn't get away. Not that it made a difference at that point."

Kedd managed to look offended. "That was one of our competitors."

"But now you're doing it to Molorthia Six," Chumley went on. "Why?"

Kedd shrugged. "We have powerful scanning equipment. Your planet is rich with raw materials, but unfortunately the resident life forms get a bit feisty if you try to get near them, so we started burning their forests to the ground for our own safety. We've already cleared two million square kushkims of land and installed our drills. We plan to burn the rest of this zone over the next one hundred forty-four days."

Dalton didn't know how big a kushkim was, but two million sounded like an awful lot. "You're burning all the vegetation," he said.

"We believe it's safer that way." Kedd sounded grave, and his lips drooped into a frown. "We lost sixty workers during our first week here. We'd heard the rumors about the locals, of course, but thought they might have been exaggerated."

Conversely, Dalton found himself grinning. "You're doing this planet an immense favor."

Chumley whirled upon him, mouth falling open. "You can't be serious."

"I am. Kedd, we ought to give you an award."

Chumley folded his arms. "It's because of the fires this lot started that the Greens fled through your town and murdered your people."

That gave Dalton pause. He closed his eyes and snuggled up closer to the wall.

"Oh, for goodness sake," Chumley said. "So, you're burning the planet down to drill for minerals. Why did you capture us?"

Kedd shrugged. "You were getting too close to one of our listening posts."

"What's a listening post?"

"It's where we go to monitor human communication channels. Bureen and I heard your transmissions, came across your derelict transport, and tranquilized your friend, and you know the rest of the story. Where were you headed?"

Dalton opened his mouth to tell the man they'd intended to find out what was causing the fires, but Chumley spoke first. "We were on our way to Paris but got turned around in the sandstorm. Nasty bugger. Never seen one like it before."

You don't say, Dalton thought.

Kedd nodded. "And what were you to be doing in Paris?"

"Well . . ." Inexplicably, Chumley blushed. "It was supposed to be a romantic getaway, just the two of us. There's a little place up there that . . . well, it doesn't matter now, does it? You've captured us. Well done."

Dalton glared at Chumley, vowing to kill him at the first available chance.

"We apologize for the inconvenience," said Kedd. "But you must understand why it was necessary."

"What will you be doing to us now?" Dalton asked.

"Killing us, I suppose," Chumley said, eyes downcast.

Kedd made a scoffing sound. "If we wanted to kill you, we would have done that out in the desert and burned your bodies. We'll be putting the two of you to work once we reach Nydo Base headquarters."

"Doing what?" Dalton asked.

Kedd's grin spread wide. It said, *Don't you want to know?*

The small airship began its descent from the sky about twenty minutes later and landed beside a hangar in a charred valley that had most likely been full of old-growth forest a few months earlier. An impressive block of office buildings sat in a row beside a stream full of sludgy, gray water, and when Kedd and his associate, a stony-faced Haa'la woman named Bureen, shuffled Dalton and Chumley out of the airship, Dalton could hear the low hum of mining equipment in the distance.

The air stank like a campfire, though nothing nearby was aflame.

Off to their left lay a long, one-story building that might have been flats for the workers. More white-clad figures milled about near the entrance, some of them in hard hats.

"How many workers live here?" Chumley asked conversationally as Kedd and Bureen steered them toward the largest office building, a completely white three-story structure with rectangular windows. Flagpoles had been erected out front, bearing violet banners emblazoned with white symbols.

"About two hundred eighty-eight," said Kedd. "Nearly two hundred eighty-eight more are stationed at smaller mines outside of this valley, and a crew of one hundred forty-four is clearing more land south of here."

"How lovely," Chumley said, absently rubbing his hands together. Dalton noticed his pocket still bulging with that mysterious squarish shape. Their captors must not have deemed it a threat, or they would have removed it from his person.

They entered the building. It smelled sterile, like new buildings do. A white-haired Haa'la woman with purple eyes and a narrow face regarded them blandly from behind a reception desk. Kedd conversed with her in their own language before switching back to English for Dalton and Chumley's benefit.

"We have taken other prisoners these past few weeks," Kedd said to them. "We've employed some of them in our gold and diamond mines, but you two might do just as well here. How do you feel about cooking or cleaning?"

Dalton, who felt much more coherent now that the last of the tranquilizer had worn off, let out a snort. "You're the jailers. Shouldn't you be the ones to decide that?"

"Like I said, we're businesspeople. You happened to be encroaching upon a listening post, so we had to get you out of the way in order to maintain our secrecy. Besides, our support staff here at headquarters got a trifle decimated when the natives attacked."

Dalton looked him up and down, taking in Kedd's solid white ensemble. "Your people have been in Richport. Why?"

"I'd rather talk about it in my office. Come this way, please."

Dalton and Chumley exchanged a glance before following Kedd down a bone-white corridor. Bureen stayed in the lobby to converse with the receptionist, probably making snide remarks about humans.

Kedd's office lay on the second floor, overlooking the polluted stream. Kedd motioned for them to sit in a pair of gray chairs.

"Would you like any refreshments?" Kedd asked, moving toward a waist-high cabinet. "I have grapefruit."

Something about the word "grapefruit" made the skin

tingle on the back of Dalton's neck, but he couldn't remember why.

"I'll have water," Dalton said. "Your kind does drink that, right?"

"Yes." Kedd regarded him with some annoyance, which made Dalton feel marginally better about himself.

"I'll take some too," Chumley said, raising a hand. Dalton noticed for the first time that a pair of binoculars hung around Chumley's neck. Where on Molorthia Six had he found binoculars?

Kedd handed them each a room-temperature bottle of water from the cabinet, then withdrew a grapefruit for himself and sliced it open with a small knife.

"As I was saying," Kedd went on, "would you prefer cooking or cleaning? We already have enough people in the mines and won't need more until the next mine is ready to open."

Dalton leaned forward. "How about you tell us why you've been sneaking around in Richport? I saw some of you lot, but nobody else could."

Kedd popped a slice of grapefruit into his mouth, chewed it, and swallowed it wearing a look of ecstasy. "Our cloaking devices scramble some of the signals going to your visual cortexes. It's not perfect tech, so sometimes people catch glimpses of us anyway."

"Why were you in town?"

"We were seeing if anything could be of use to us."

"You're talking about plundering. Theft."

Kedd's platinum blond eyebrows rose. "Am I?"

"That's what humans call taking things that don't belong to them."

"Which is ever so ironic."

Dalton had no response. Chumley twisted his hands together in his lap while making discreet glances around the room.

After a spell of silence during which Kedd consumed more of his grapefruit, Dalton said, "What about the forests down south? Are you burning them, too?"

"That will be our Phase Two project," Kedd said. "This year our efforts will focus on the northern hemisphere, and once we start turning a profit, we'll fly south and begin our work there."

"Burning all the forests, you mean," Dalton said. "To clear out the Greens."

"That would be the idea, yes."

"Will the forests be replanted once you're done here?" Chumley asked.

Kedd cocked his head to one side. "What do you mean?"

"Once you've concluded your business on Molorthia Six, will you be replanting the forests?"

A chuckle escaped their captor's lips. "Our scanners indicate that Molorthia Six has extra concentrations of gold, diamonds, petroleum, and a hundred other resources that make our other project planets look utterly worthless. Our work here will last many lifetimes—we're just getting started."

"What if my people worked with you?" Dalton asked.

Kedd gave his head a slow shake. "We prefer our own kind. We've only taken you into custody so you don't go sounding the alarm—for some reason, the Feds don't like us." Kedd smiled, showing his delicate yet sharp teeth again.

It made Dalton think of one of those spooky, deep-sea Earth fish with the dangly lights. "Now I'm going to give you two options: you can stay here and put yourselves to work, or you can try to walk back to your little city and tell your little friends about us and what we're doing. I'd like to see you survive the desert heat and any rogue Greens we might have missed."

Dalton knew he needed to formulate a plan, but he was too exhausted to think of one. "I can cook," he said, "but I've never done alien food."

"I'm sure you'll do your best," said Kedd. "And what about you?"

"I'll clean," said Chumley. "Now where will we be staying while we're here?"

"Why in the bloody hell did you split us up?" Dalton grumbled after Kedd left him and Chumley in a small "flat" of their own, which consisted of a bedroom-slash-sitting area and a bathroom with a shower. Clean, white uniforms were folded and stacked on the room's only dresser, waiting to be worn.

Chumley crossed his arms. "We can each gather intel this way—you from the kitchens, me from the cleaning staff."

"He already told us their plans! And if you haven't noticed, *neither of us speaks their language.*"

"It's still a good idea," Chumley went on, undeterred. "There could be plenty more he wasn't telling us. He's probably not even the boss of this place, because whoever's really in charge wouldn't have been hanging out in a secret listening post in the middle of the desert. Kedd is just trying to cover his arse by getting us out of the way."

Dalton nodded and sat on a cot that squeaked beneath his full weight. "Why did you tell him we were on a romantic getaway?"

Chumley's expression grew coy. "I had the feeling you were about to tell him exactly what we were doing."

"Had the feeling?"

Chumley sank onto the room's other cot, sniffed one armpit, and winced. "Look, Sheriff—Dalton—you've been kind to me—"

"*Kind?*"

"—and I don't want you to take this the wrong way, but you're a bit naïve."

Dalton clenched his fists. "Now just a minute!"

Chumley held up a placating hand. "You've led an innocent life, marrying your wife and raising your children, and when that all ended, you became sheriff because you couldn't help your family."

"So what?"

"What I'm saying is, you haven't lived a deceptive lifestyle one single day in your life. You *are* deceiving yourself, telling yourself you're the big, bad policeman, but inside you're just a dad."

"What are you talking about?" Dalton felt very cold, then remembered that was probably because they weren't in the desert anymore.

"You rescued me! You gave me food and a place to stay. I couldn't figure it out at first, but now I know you missed taking care of people you cared about. But I digress—I didn't think our captors should know we're police."

"Why does it matter if they do or not?"

"Because we don't know where they draw the line on violence."

Dalton could find no holes in that argument. "That's . . . actually kind of smart."

"I know." Chumley's eyes twinkled. "That's why I did it."

CHAPTER 14

The long, hot shower Dalton took prior to checking in with Kedd at his office did not improve his mood, nor did it improve when he crossed the ashy courtyard toward the office building.

He couldn't see why these people wouldn't just let them go, when Dalton was clearly on their side. Let every Green on Molorthia Six burn to a crisp! The whole world would be safe, if a little airless.

His heart skipped a beat as he rapped on Kedd's door.

Airless?

Would Molorthia Six really be airless, with all the trees and Greens gone?

Kedd's office door swung open, and the alien ushered him inside. Dalton nervously adjusted the starchy, all-white outfit he'd been given to wear.

"Where's your partner?" Kedd asked.

Dalton coughed. "He was still washing up when I left."

"Good—the two of you smelled terrible. Now come this way."

Dalton tried hard not to protest as he followed the Haa'la man out of the office, down a corridor and a flight of stairs, and into a stainless-steel, industrial-sized kitchen, where four other Haa'la people dressed entirely in white were laying out ingredients on a long countertop.

"Your supervisor is Maasha," said Kedd, nodding toward a tall figure Dalton guessed to be a woman. Maasha's platinum blonde hair peeked out from beneath a hairnet. "She studied English her first year at University, so I trust you'll handle things just fine here."

Then Kedd was gone, retreating the way he'd come. Dalton stared after him, wishing Kedd would smile and say, "Just kidding! Now let me take you home," but of course this was reality, where good things only happened to people who didn't deserve it.

Dalton turned to Maasha and stared up at her. She eyed him with a measure of disdain. She pulled a hairnet out of a box and handed it to Dalton, who grudgingly stuck it on his head.

"Pip-pip! You pots stir," she said gruffly, pointing to a row of cauldrons sitting on burners not yet lit. "No make meal to bottom pots stick."

Dalton remembered his Hindi and Spanish classes from a million years ago and felt his brain cells crying. "No pots stick," he said. "Got it."

Another worker dumped an assortment of ingredients into each of the cauldrons and lit the burners, and Dalton dutifully stirred each one as they boiled, not having the faintest idea as to how he could gather intel while supervising several hundred gallons of fetid alien stew. Various green and brown things that were neither peas nor beef floated in it like dead fish in a lake.

"Have you worked here long?" he asked after a time, knowing it was a stupid question since the mining base couldn't have been there more than a few months.

"Pip-pip! Work here from beginning," Maasha said without looking at him. She was busy chopping up something that looked like shallots and smelled like wet dog. "Feed family on Leeprau."

Dalton couldn't stop thinking about Molorthia Six running out of oxygen, and imagined children dropping dead in the street all blue in the face.

"Why get involved with the planet-killers?" he asked. "Aren't other jobs less . . . destructive?"

Maasha paused to process this, then said, "Pip-pip! My home is Leeprau, Land of Golden Suns. What happens to Molorthia Six, the Haa'la do not care."

Dalton went down the line again, stirring each cauldron in turn and hoping they'd have something more suitable for his own palate when it came time to eat.

"What if it happened to you?" he asked.

Maasha's thin brows knit together. One of the other cooks came over and consulted with her on another recipe brewing on the other side of the kitchen, and after they had gone away, Maasha said, "Pip-pip! Understanding, am not."

"Suppose," Dalton said slowly, "humans came to Leeprau and burned your forests and mined your minerals. What would you do?"

Maasha's expression grew most solemn as she did her best to decipher his words. Dalton knew that feeling well enough. Finally, she said, "Pip-pip! We would fight."

Chumley wondered what his grandmother would think if

she could see him now, rolling a cleaning cart down a hallway in an evil alien mining base, dressed in an all-white outfit designed by a race that had never developed the imagination to utilize any other color.

A housekeeper? she might have teased him. *Chumley, you could barely keep your room clean when you were a boy.*

He kept his room clean now, though, and had tucked it, snug within its portable universe, into the pocket of his borrowed work uniform for safekeeping.

The Haa'la woman in charge of maintenance had *pip-pipped* orders at Chumley for a few minutes in Haa'anu, and Chumley had just smiled and nodded and then headed to the first office along that hallway to begin cleaning it, even though the woman could have been telling him to strip and do the Chicken Dance, for all he knew.

He rapped on the plain, white office door, heard no reply, and shoved it open, rolling the cart inside. The office contained one desk and a few shelves, and Chumley wet a rag with a bit of cleaner and wiped all hard surfaces down so they gleamed, dust-free.

Then he plucked the tiny vacuum cleaner off the bottom of the cart, plugged it in, and ran it over the plain, white carpet.

It took him all of four minutes.

Chumley repeated the process in the next room, starting to feel a trifle bored.

He repeated the process in the third room, wondering how he could gather intel when he worked alone.

When Chumley rolled the cleaning cart back out into the hallway again, he came face to face with a dark brown-skinned man rolling an identical cart toward him.

"Oh, thank God," said the man, relief washing over his face. "Another human!"

Chumley glanced behind him to make sure they were alone, then lowered his voice. "Just what I was thinking. Do you have a moment?"

"Sure. It looks like you've already cleaned my block of offices."

"I might have misinterpreted my supervisor. All that pipping is making me a bit mad. What is it, anyway?"

The man cracked a lopsided grin. "Best I can tell, it means something like, 'May I have your attention please?' It's considered impolite to not use it. I've started hearing it in my sleep."

"I see." Chumley scratched his head, then pointed to the room from which he'd just emerged. "How about we talk in here?"

"Works for me," the man said with a shrug.

Inside the room, with the door closed, Chumley held out a hand and said, "Chumley Fanshaw. And you?"

"Keith Okpebholo," said his new comrade, pumping his arm up and down. Keith had closely-cropped black hair and looked nearly forty. "I've been here a week. Annaliese Jamison sent out ten of us to see why everything was on fire, and the next thing we knew, we'd been captured."

"I don't know Annaliese," Chumley said. "I'm new here."

"Oh, she's the sheriff in Paris. These creeps took our comm units, so we couldn't even report what had happened."

"I see they didn't kill you for being with the police."

"No, but they split us all up and sent everyone to different sites. I don't think they wanted us to stick together and plot anything."

"Have you learned anything important since you've been here?"

Keith snorted. "The Haa'la don't take us very seriously. I tried to tell them Annaliese would send an army after us, and they just laughed."

"Will she?"

The man shook his head, sadly. "You really must be new here if you don't know the answer to that."

"I see."

Keith rubbed the back of his hand across his forehead. "I've thought about escaping during the night."

"You could commandeer a vehicle."

"I don't know how to drive their stuff. I snooped around in one of their garages the other night, and I couldn't even figure out how to start an engine."

The sound of approaching footsteps out in the hallway made both their heads turn. Chumley held his breath, waiting for an angry Haa'la to burst in and berate them for fraternizing when work needed to be done, but the footsteps continued past their door and dwindled into silence.

"I'd better get back to work," Keith said after a moment of hesitation.

"Let me know if you hear anything important that might help us get out of here," Chumley said.

Keith just shook his head as he rolled his cart toward the door. "Sure thing. Just don't hold your breath waiting. Pip-pip."

"Did you learn anything?" Chumley asked, rolling onto his side on his cot to regard Dalton, who was doing his very best not to be ill from the headache raging behind his eyes.

"Yeah," Dalton said. "I've eaten better dog food than what I helped cook today."

"Dinner *was* a little strange," Chumley admitted. Dalton had spotted him at the far end of the communal cafeteria during dinner, but had been too busy following Maasha's orders to go over and compare notes.

"Don't ask me what was in that stew," Dalton said. "I'm just the bloke who had to *me pots stir.*"

"Sorry?"

"Never mind." He winced as another jolt of pain shot up through his neck and temple. "Gods, my head."

"I've got medicine, if you'd like some," Chumley said, then clapped a hand over his mouth in inexplicable wide-eyed horror.

Dalton sat up, the room swaying around him. "Where?"

"It was a slip of the tongue. Don't listen to me."

"Is that what you've got in that little box?"

Chumley's hand went to his pocket, where the little box in question stuck out like a squarish growth. "How bad is your headache?" he asked.

"I've had more pleasant concussions."

"Do you think you'll survive if you *don't* have any medicine?"

"What the hell kind of question is that? Do you have medicine, or not?"

"I do," Chumley said, glancing away from him. "And yes, it's in this box, but not in the way you're thinking."

Amazingly, this conversation was making Dalton's head hurt even worse. "Well, why don't you open it up and give me some before my brain explodes into bits?"

"Fine, fine. I just know I'm going to regret this." Chumley dug into his pocket and set a metal cube on his palm.

"You can't tell anyone about this," Chumley went on. "They were going to go on the market, but the manufacturer's funding fell through before they could make too many of them. I was lucky to get one of the early ones in return for a favor."

"What sort of favor?"

"I rescued the manufacturer's cat from a tree."

"You're pulling my leg."

"It was a very tall tree."

"Right," Dalton said at length. "So, what is it?"

"This," Chumley said, pushing a button on the side of the cube and setting the object on the floor, "is my portable universe."

A holographic doorway appeared midair. Dalton tried not to look overly impressed. Any child's toy could generate a floating lightshow, but he had the feeling this was something a bit more than a simple plaything.

Chumley rose from his cot, said, "Follow me," and walked through the holographic doorway, disappearing from sight.

Dalton blinked but remained motionless.

Chumley's head materialized through the hologram a moment later. "It's not hard," he said. "Just walk through it like you would any other doorway."

His head disappeared.

Dalton gingerly rose, his headache reaching critical levels.

He stared at the doorway a moment longer, shrugged, and walked through it.

He found himself in a cozy bedroom. A workstation occupied one wall, as did a bar, and a few windows looked out onto a well-maintained garden painted in the colors of twilight. A rodent cage, complete with shredded bedding, a water bottle, and an exercise wheel, sat on a table in the corner.

"Your pet's missing," Dalton said, as if that were the most unusual thing here.

Chumley emerged from a bathroom holding a pill bottle. "These are left over from my appendectomy last year," he said. "If they don't knock out your headache, nothing will."

"Did we just walk through a wormhole?" Dalton asked as Chumley placed the pill bottle into his hand.

"Sort of. I keep all my things in here. I thought I'd lost it in the fire, but then I found it in a pile of rubble before we left town."

Dalton squinted at his deputy, who'd shoved his hands into his pockets and was looking slightly sheepish. "Including your money?"

"All safe and accounted for."

"Then why didn't you book a flight off this stinking rock and go back to wherever you came from?"

"It wasn't in my best interests."

"Meaning?"

"Meaning you wouldn't have the best painkiller in the universe if I'd left. Just take one pill, though, because it's awfully potent, and I wouldn't want you to, well, you know. Die, or something."

Dalton let his gaze linger on Chumley's face before he unscrewed the cap on the pill bottle and swallowed one of them dry.

He handed the bottle back to him. Chumley dipped his head, went back into the bathroom, and returned with his hands in his pockets again.

As if by magic, the edge was already disappearing from Dalton's pain. He said, "You've had this cube thing since before we left town."

"Well, I didn't conjure it out of thin air."

Dalton glanced to the shimmering place where they'd entered the room. "Can anything from outside blow into here?"

"It depends. I can seal it off completely so nobody walks along and sees a holographic entrance floating midair." Chumley walked toward the wall and slapped a panel, and the shimmering vanished, leaving a plain expanse of blue paint.

Dalton regarded it with a frown. "We could have waited out the sandstorm in here."

"Yes. Technically."

"Technically?"

"I didn't want you to know about the Cube. You might have tried to steal it."

"I'm the bloody sheriff!"

"Which does not preclude one from committing theft." Chumley wagged a finger at him.

"I'm not going to steal your portable universe."

"To be technical, you'd be stealing the doorway, not the universe itself."

"What?"

"This is a different universe from the one out there." Chumley gestured vaguely at the place where the doorway had been. "That means it doesn't exist anywhere in our universe, and therefore can't be stolen. The Cube generates a doorway allowing us to enter the portable universe. Without the Cube, we have no way of getting inside."

"Can the Cube move?"

"Only if someone physically moves it."

"Ah." Dalton felt his briefly-acquired hope dwindling. "Then it can't help us escape."

"It could if we had someone smuggle the Cube onto a vehicle. I met a human named Keith earlier. He's a prisoner here, too."

Dalton licked his lips in thought, wishing he had a new toothpick to chew on. "We need to get a message to Carolyn. Do you have a comm unit in here?"

Mild amusement entered Chumley's eyes. "You do realize that those of us from civilized worlds don't use comm units, right?"

"Then how in the bloody hell do you communicate with people?"

"I had a sat-phone, but I didn't pay my bill so they canceled my service. Does Carolyn have an electronic address?"

"Probably, but I don't know what it is. Can you contact the Feds through your computer? They can arrest all of these Haa'la folks before they turn the rest of the planet into an ashtray."

Chumley's eyes widened. "You actually care, then?"

"I've decided I like oxygen."

"Well, let me see what I can do." Chumley planted himself in his swivel chair and woke the screen, then leaned forward and frowned. "That's odd."

"What?"

Chumley clicked at a few icons. "There's no net signal. Usually I can get *something*, even if it's weak."

"The Haa'la must not want humans sending messages right under their noses."

"I was hoping they wouldn't be that smart."

Dalton started pacing back and forth, racking his brain for ideas. "Kedd worked at a listening post south of here. Maybe we can have this Keith smuggle the Cube with us inside it onto Kedd's airship before he goes back. When Kedd falls asleep, we get out of the Cube and walk the rest of the way back to the motorhome, dig the spare comm units out of the sand, and call Carolyn. She notifies the Feds, the Feds arrest the Haa'la, and everyone lives happily ever after."

A grin spread across Chumley's face. "Do we know if Kedd is still here?"

"No idea."

"All right." Chumley rubbed his hands together. "How about we sleep on it? In the morning I can find out more, and see if Keith would be willing to help us."

"I like it," Dalton said.

It was as good a plan as any.

Chumley kept his eyes peeled for any signs of Keith as he rolled the cleaning cart through the workers' dormitories the next morning. He nodded politely at any Haa'la he passed, most of whom turned their noses up at him before continuing about their business.

Close to lunchtime, Chumley spotted Keith striding across the desolate courtyard between the dormitories and the office building, carrying a package of paper towels under each arm.

"Oi!" Chumley hissed, causing the other man to look his way.

Keith stopped in his tracks, looking furtive as a pair of tall, veiled Haa'la passed them, heading toward the large hangar just south of the compound. "Yes?" he asked.

"If you're looking for a good time, meet me and my friend in our bedroom during our two o'clock break," Chumley said, making an exaggerated wink.

Keith took one step backward. "Excuse me?"

"I'm sure it'll be worth your while," Chumley went on. "In fact, I'd dare to call it a *Great Escape*."

Keith's eyebrows shot upward. "Oh yeah?"

"Now you get it? Two o'clock, my bedroom. It's the third one from the end on the east side of the hallway. Has a squiggle on the door that looks like a crab."

"Duly noted. I guess I'll see you then."

They parted ways, and Chumley grinned to himself. That part had been easy enough.

He craned his neck toward the hangar, looking for Kedd's airship. He couldn't see it, but that might have meant someone had pulled it inside.

It didn't necessarily mean Kedd had already gone back to his listening post, did it?

Because otherwise their escape plan would be an incredibly short one.

Dalton didn't see Kedd as he crossed the open space between the dormitories and the offices.

He didn't see Kedd in the lobby or in the hallways.

He definitely didn't see Kedd in the kitchen, where he wouldn't have been anyway.

"Pip-pip! Morning that is good," Maasha said to him when he reported for duty. She wore a fresh apron and a new hairnet and leaned over a recipe book open to a page showing a picture of something green, gloopy, and possibly still alive.

"Uh ... good morning," Dalton said after a moment of delayed translation. "How are you?"

Her pale lips formed a frown, more confused than disapproving. "Pip-pip! What are you meaning?"

That gave Dalton a moment's pause. "It's just a friendly question. People ask how other people are as a polite greeting."

"Pip-pip! Why?"

"They just do. And—I'm sorry. I don't know what 'pip-pip' means, but you don't need to use it in English."

"Pip—my apologies. Always forgetting."

"Don't worry about it. What do the Haa'la say instead of 'how are you?'"

Maasha smiled, showing her many pointy teeth. "The Haa'la say, conquer world before set the suns? And we reply, always."

"Right," Dalton said, feeling slightly unsettled. "Now, what do you want me to do today?"

Maasha set him to work chopping tubers into cubes, and while he worked, he casually asked, "Have you seen Kedd? I wanted to ask him something."

"No Kedd today. Working, him."

Dalton's heart sank. "In the desert?"

"Yes."

"When will he be back?"

"It is unknown."

Don't panic, he thought. *There are other airships here, surely. We can smuggle ourselves out of here on a different one.*

"Do you know Kedd well?" he said a few minutes later, his hands already tiring from the repeated chopping motions.

"We are . . ." Maasha paused. "Cousins."

"Do you have a lot of family here on Molorthia Six?" Ordinarily he would have cursed himself for engaging in such mindless small talk, but he found he needed the company.

He imagined Darneisha watching him from somewhere, laughing.

"Kedd only," Maasha said. "Other family stay on Leeprau. Kedd ask, do I want job? Family are poor, I send money to them."

"Kedd hired you?"

"No, no. Nydo Base Corporation in charge. Ashi'ii is boss here, you see her in corridors?"

"I have no idea." Dalton made note of the name, not entirely sure how it could help him but knowing it wouldn't hurt. Who knew what information might give them an advantage here? The more they had, the greater their chances of escape.

The secret meeting they'd planned began four minutes late that afternoon because Maasha wouldn't let Dalton leave the kitchens until after he'd sterilized every surface following the noonday meal, which had smelled like a combination of cat litter and yeast.

The man Dalton supposed must be Keith sat on Dalton's cot with his arms folded across his broad chest while Chumley animatedly told him some rowdy tale about fleeing the police wearing nothing.

"How did you get away from them?" Keith asked, trying not to smile.

"I ran into an alleyway where someone had hung out their laundry to dry and stole clothes off of it. The police didn't recognize me dressed, so I was safe."

"And is that a true story, or are you just trying to impress our guest here?" Dalton asked, locking the door to their room.

Chumley placed a hand over his heart. "Sheriff, you insult me!" He looked back to Keith. "To make this short, Dalton and I need to get back to Richport so we can get word out to the Galactic Feds about the Haa'la here. We want you to help us."

"I already said I don't know how to drive their vehicles," said Keith. "Believe me, I tried."

"You won't have to drive anything," said Dalton.

"I'm not walking across that desert."

"You won't have to do that either." Chumley smiled. "You'll need to stay behind."

Any hope that had been on Keith's face vanished beneath a scowl. "No offense, but I'm liking this Great Escape plan less and less."

"Just hear us out," said Dalton. "I'm Dalton Kane, by the way," he added, remembering belatedly to introduce himself. "I'm the sheriff in Richport."

"Keith Okpebholo." Keith held out a hand, and Dalton shook it. "I've heard Annaliese mention you a few times. She sent me and some others out here to see what was up with the fires, and you can guess the rest."

"They didn't hurt you?"

"No; just put us to work. The people with me got sent to different sites."

"Anyway," Chumley went on after clearing his throat, "our plan is to have you smuggle us onboard Kedd's airship."

"He's gone," said Dalton, shaking his head. "Maasha in the kitchen said Kedd went back to his little listening post."

Chumley's face paled. "Then we'll have to find another airship."

"Hold on, I'm not following." Keith looked from Chumley to Dalton. "How am I supposed to smuggle two grown men onto an airship without getting caught? Stick you in a giant carrier bag and pretend you're mail?"

"Sort of, ish." Chumley pulled his portable universe out of his pocket and activated the doorway, then set the Cube onto the floor. "You two, follow me."

He strode through the doorway, vanishing in that uncanny way. Keith let out an impressed whistle. "Now that's some fancy tech."

When all three of them had gathered inside the portable

universe, Keith glanced around and nodded appreciatively. "Better not let the Haa'la know about this thing. They'd steal it and sell it to the highest bidder."

Chumley threw Dalton a look that said *I told you so.*

Dalton rolled his eyes.

"So, you two are going to hide in this . . . thing," Keith said. "Which I'm assuming is inside the metal cube? Did we shrink?"

"We're the same size as before," Chumley said. "Yes, Dalton and I will hide in here. You will smuggle the Cube onto whichever airship is leaving here next. When we decide it's safe, we exit the Cube."

"What if the airship just goes to another desert listening post? I don't think these people are bold enough to land a ship in one of our cities."

"We were counting on being left in the desert," said Chumley. "Once we know it's safe to get out, only one of us will sneak out of the ship. Say I leave Dalton inside the portable universe in my pocket and walk as far as I can across the desert. Once I start to wear out, I go inside the portable universe to rest while Dalton carries me in his pocket."

Keith scratched his forehead. "Don't you think there could be an easier way of getting out of here?"

Chumley gave Dalton an uneasy glance. "We haven't been able to think of one. We had hoped to board Kedd's ship because his listening post was near our wrecked transport, which contains our spare comm units. They confiscated the ones we had on us."

"Makes sense to me."

"But we can't do that, since Kedd is no longer here."

They sat in a contemplative silence for a short time. Somewhere outside, a motor burst into life and dwindled into the distance—probably someone heading off to the mines.

"When do we want to do this thing?" Keith finally asked.

"As soon as possible," said Dalton. "We'll find out which is the next airship scheduled to leave this base, and we smuggle ourselves onboard before they leave."

"Sounds like a piece of cake," Keith said, but by his tone, Dalton knew he didn't believe it.

PART 2

CHAPTER 15

arolyn Kaur sat behind her desk, kneading her forehead and trying to remember if she'd taken her blood pressure medication.

If she had, it wasn't working.

Errin poked their head through the office doorway. "Carolyn?"

Carolyn sighed. "What is it?"

Her assistant stepped fully into view, holding a datapad. "FCU are about to leave Richport. I thought you should know."

"Let them go. I've kissed their asses enough already."

"But surely as a sign of—"

"I don't care anymore. You may see them off, if you wish. You can tell them I'm in a meeting."

Errin opened their mouth as if about to object, but then simply said, "Of course. They know how busy you've been."

Errin disappeared, and Carolyn took the moment to bang her forehead on the top of her desk.

Nothing was going well at all.

For obvious reasons, FCU's departure of Richport had been delayed. Half the city still didn't have power after the storm. Half the roads were still clogged with sand and other debris swept there from who knew where. Four people were still missing, including Dalton Kane and Chumley Fanshaw.

Last night, after the most urgent matters had been attended to, Cadu Mão de Ferro led a small team out into the desert to retrieve the stranded sheriff and his deputy, only to find the wreckage of their borrowed motorhome with no people inside it. Cadu reported that they searched the desert within a five-kilometer radius of the wreck, finding no sign of the two men.

It was like someone had swooped down from the sky and swept them away, like so much dust. Had they tried to journey to the nearest settlement on foot and succumbed to the desert heat? Surely neither of them would be so stupid, but desperation could inspire even the sanest of people into madness.

Carolyn stood. She would take a page from Dalton's own book and take a brooding walk, to hell with whatever lies Errin had made up for Naomi Schwartzman.

She grabbed her canvas hat down from its hook, slipped on a pair of sunglasses, and left the office.

"Nice work, everyone," she said when she arrived outside and saw a small work crew dumping buckets of sand swept from the sidewalk into the bed of a waiting dump truck. "Richport is starting to look like a city again."

"Any word from the sheriff?" asked a young woman Carolyn recognized as Cadu's daughter, whose name she could never remember. Her clothes and cheeks were coated with grime from her work.

"No." Carolyn felt her expression darken. "But I'm sure he's fine wherever he is."

Perhaps speaking those words into being would make them true.

She turned down another street, making her way toward her cousin Slim's coffee shop. When she pushed through the doorway into the darkened interior, she spotted Gwendolyn Goldfarb sitting in a booth seat three meters away from her.

Honestly, the woman ought to have been institutionalized after she'd returned from the desert raving mad. She'd been disturbing the peace almost as badly as a salesperson, and it was only getting worse. Gwendolyn needed a safe place to stay where she couldn't harm herself or anyone else when she got into one of her fits.

"Good morning, Mayor," Gwendolyn said, a mug of brew cooling in front of her.

Carolyn drew up short, feeling a few shreds of guilt for her most recent thoughts. "Good morning, Gwendolyn. How are you?"

"I don't know." Gwendolyn's brows knit together, and the wisps of steam rising from her mug made Carolyn think the woman was some mystic about to impart tales of the future.

Stop that, she ordered herself. That had been Dalton's bullshit, not hers.

"Oh?" Out of kindness, Carolyn slid onto the seat across the table from her. She could order her own coffee later.

Gwendolyn's eyes grew glassy. "It's so confusing. Sometimes I can think and see so clearly, and other times, it's like a fog comes down and blocks everything from sight. My mind is full of walls."

"Like you're boxed in?"

"No, no." Gwendolyn shook her head. "These walls are placed at random and don't connect to each other. I can't see them until I run into them. It's so hard to think sometimes. In my mind I'm walking and walking, and *bam!* I run into a wall, and I try to find my way around it, and when I do I walk and walk some more until I run into another wall I can't see."

"What happens specifically when you run into one of these mental walls?"

"I'm not sure. I . . ." Gwendolyn looked down at her mug, then back up at Carolyn. "There's danger."

Carolyn's skin grew clammy. "Danger, where?"

"Everywhere."

"If this is some kind of prank, I find it in poor taste."

"They come from the sky," Gwendolyn said, her voice growing hushed. "They have your men and don't care that the world will burn."

Carolyn stood, placing both of her hands on the table. "How could you know anything about my men? Who has them?"

"Those who came from the sky. Those who burn the world. The People know. They saw, and they suffer."

"What people? Who came from the sky?" Carolyn was aware her voice was rising, and that a few of the other patrons were craning their necks to see her way, but she didn't care.

Gwendolyn coughed. ". . . can never remember once I'm past the wall."

It took several moments for Carolyn to understand that Gwendolyn was finishing the sentence she had so recently broken off from. Gwendolyn had hit one of these mental blocks while they were speaking, and some other part of her mind had briefly taken over for her.

"Gwendolyn," she said gently, "can you tell me more about the people who burn the world?"

"Good heavens, what are you talking about?" Gwendolyn chuckled and sipped at her coffee. "Who's burning the world?"

Wouldn't Carolyn like to know.

After Carolyn had finished her coffee—a double espresso topped with whipped cream—she marched down the street to her other cousin Monica Kaur's medical practice.

Sally, the receptionist, was sorting through patient files when Carolyn barged in. "Is Monica busy?" Carolyn asked, noting an empty waiting room.

"She's on her lunch break," Sally said, tossing her box braids over one shoulder. "Want me to let her know you're here?"

"Please do."

Sally disappeared down a hallway, and Carolyn could hear faint murmuring. When Sally reappeared moments later, she said, "Come on back!"

Like Carolyn's own office, Dr. Monica Kaur's practice was one of the few air-conditioned buildings in Richport, designed for patient comfort. Carolyn basked in the cool air as she made her way down the hallway toward the comfortably-furnished break room, where Monica, five years her senior, sat eating a bowl of masala channa, the smell of which made Carolyn's mouth water.

"What's troubling you today, cousin?" Monica asked with a faint smile when Carolyn rapped on the doorframe.

"Who says anything is troubling me?" Carolyn stepped into the room and sat in an unoccupied armchair.

"You only come here when you want advice."

That was true enough. "I'm worried about Gwendolyn Goldfarb."

"You know I can't discuss my patients, Carolyn."

"Who else is going to look out for her? I don't think she's got any family left."

"She was an Agarwal before she was married, and her mother was a Khoury. You'll find both families alive and well over in Fred."

"They must not be very good families, then, since they have nothing to do with her. Please, it would just be between the two of us."

"It isn't proper."

"It's my duty as mayor to take an interest in the wellbeing of my people."

Monica regarded Carolyn with narrowed eyes, then sighed. "Fine. I haven't seen her in here for six months. What's she done now?"

"I was talking to her this morning in the coffee shop. She has these blanking-out moments and starts prophesying, or something."

"Prophesying?" Monica laughed. "Didn't Sheriff Kane think she was predicting the future? I heard something about that from Sally. It sounds like *he* was having some kind of mental breakdown, not Gwendolyn."

"I thought so too." Carolyn glanced down at her hands, which she'd clenched into fists resting on the arms of the chair.

"Did they find the sheriff yet?" Monica forked more of her lunch into her mouth, and Carolyn wished she'd had a bite to eat before coming here.

"No." Since Carolyn hadn't come to discuss what might have happened to Dalton, she deftly steered the conversation back on course. "I want to know exactly what happened to Gwendolyn. It'll be our secret."

Monica shrugged. "You know the gist of it. She wanted to drive to Mount Olympus all by herself to visit old friends and got all turned around out in the desert. She was lost out there for something like two weeks before she somehow found her way back here on foot. Nobody ever found her transport. She probably drove it into a sand dune."

"Did she have any injuries?"

"A few bruises, but nothing major. She kept asking me if I would give her the brandy I had in my office cabinet."

"Did you have brandy in your cabinet?"

"I did." Monica's expression grew troubled. "I chalked it up to a coincidence, and I certainly didn't give her any. She was dehydrated, and I put her on an intravenous drip to help her recover."

"Did she say what had happened to her? Anything specific?"

"She said the People had found her and helped nurse her back to health. Those would have been hallucinations, of course. Nobody lives in the area where Gwendolyn was lost."

"How do you know?"

Monica tilted her head to one side. "What's this about, really?"

"I'm not sure. Gwendolyn seems to know things she

shouldn't. Dalton told me she was shouting about a fire in the sky not long before the hotel burned down."

"Another coincidence. They happen all the time, like how I dreamed that Slim and Jo were expecting the week before they announced they were having twins."

"Gwendolyn told me that people who came from the sky are burning the world and have my men."

"You mean Sheriff Kane and the new deputy?"

"She didn't specify, but who else? Monica, I need to know if it's in any way possible for Gwendolyn to have developed—oh, you're going to make fun of me for this one—"

"Psychic powers?" Monica asked dryly.

"I don't know how else to explain it! Lord, and I thought Dalton was mad for thinking that. But the way Gwendolyn was acting at the coffee shop . . . you should have seen her. It was spooky."

"I didn't know that word was in your vocabulary."

Carolyn shivered. "Have there been any documented cases of people with true psychic abilities?" She cringed inwardly even as she spoke the words; glad that only Monica could hear her.

"That's a very good question." Monica leaned back in her chair and folded her arms. "I read about a case on Pelstring Four where a boy of five or six cried out in his sleep that 'Mommy should watch out for the train.' It spooked his mother so badly that the next day she was extra-cautious when approaching a railroad crossing and nearly got plowed over because the approaching train indicator had quit working and didn't lower the gates."

"Who's to say that wasn't a coincidence?" Carolyn asked.

"Nobody's saying it was, or it wasn't. The fact is, the boy said it, and the next day it came true. The boy's parents had him tested, and those examinations revealed nothing out of the ordinary. Some researchers wonder if the intense connection between the boy and his mother allowed him to tap into some higher cognitive ability so he could save her life."

"Sounds a bit hocus-pocus."

"Yes, although it could have scientific grounds. Just because something doesn't make sense right now doesn't mean it won't in the future."

"So, Gwendolyn could have developed psychic powers, is what you're saying."

"Perhaps."

"Do you believe it, though?"

Monica stared down at what remained of her lunch and said, "I would need to run some tests on her. Even then, there's no way to prove that her 'powers' are nothing more than a string of coincidences."

"How many coincidences can you have before you can't consider them coincidences anymore?" Carolyn asked.

"That," Monica said, "remains the ultimate question."

Dalton reported back for kitchen duty that afternoon and got to work chopping more alien vegetables into cubes. Two of the other regular cooks were conversing in Haa'anu on the other side of the kitchen. Dalton wished he had a decent knack for languages—while he was starting to memorize some of their most common syllables, he had no idea what they meant.

"Pip-pip! Busy you?"

Dalton jumped. He hadn't heard Maasha's approach, and now she towered over him, making him feel like a small boy in trouble.

"What does it look like?" He gestured at the violet cubes that had once comprised something that looked like a giant zucchini, with some obvious key differences.

"Stop now." Maasha paused, thoughtful, then said, "You need get new delivery from ship in hangar. More food for all."

A spark of hope flared inside him, though he was careful not to show it. "A ship? From where?"

"From Leeprau. Go now, and bring them here."

Dalton wiped his juicy hands on a rag and undid his apron, grateful to get away from the stainless-steel room and the cluster of cooks.

He stepped out into the afternoon sunlight and felt a chill, not from any apprehension, but from the falling temperatures. He realized with a jolt that it must be autumn—seasons weren't a thing you thought about too much when you lived in an industrial-sized oven year-round. If there had been any trees left standing near the compound, they would have been changing from green to gold, almost but not quite like the ones he remembered as a boy on Earth.

Quite a few Haa'la were gathered near the hangar, rolling crate-laden carts toward various forms of ground transport. Dalton straightened his shoulders and tried to look tall as he approached the group of bustling Haa'la, the shortest of which stood centimeters above him. "Excuse me," he said to one Haa'la who surprisingly wore clothing of a pale gray instead of white like everyone else. "I need to pick up the supplies for the kitchen?"

The Haa'la pipped something at him and pointed toward the hangar door, probably telling him to go inside and talk to someone who could actually understand him. Dalton obliged, stepping through an immense bay door into a room housing four ships, one of which was in the midst of being unloaded. An even taller Haa'la stood at the base of a conveyor belt, scanning packages one by one as they rolled out of the ship before being loaded onto carts.

"Do you speak English?" he asked the Haa'la with the scanner.

The Haa'la spoke without looking up from his work. "Pip-pip! How can I help you?"

"I'm supposed to pick up supplies for the kitchen. Where—"

"Pip-pip! You will find four crates ready and waiting for you on the cart directly behind me, with more to come. My assistants will place your additional crates in the same place so you are able to find them on your next trip."

"Oh. Thank you." Dalton spied the cart and grabbed it, wheeling it toward the door.

He would have to find a clever way to ask about the other three ships in the hangar, namely who they belonged to, when they were leaving, and where they were going.

When he steered the empty cart back into the hangar ten minutes later, four more crates had appeared in the place he'd taken the first batch from. "Are there more after this?" Dalton asked, panting.

The Haa'la still didn't look up from his work, so efficient

was he at his job. "Pip—oh, right, I forget that isn't necessary. There are most certainly more after this. This is food for the entire compound."

"Were those ships full of supplies, too?" Dalton asked, nodding toward the others.

"No."

"Then what are they doing here?"

"They are parked. Good day, sir."

Dalton had never been too skilled at subtlety. Trying not to let his scowl show, he brought the second load of crates back to the kitchen for Maasha and her crew to sort out, and when he brought the empty cart back for the second time, he asked the now-annoyed Haa'la, "Are those airships or spaceships? I've always been interested in alien craft and wondered how you can tell which is which."

"They are airships," said the Haa'la, again without looking at him. "If you must know, the airships tend to be smaller than spaceships, and don't have the shielding needed to protect the occupants from the perils of space."

"Where do people go in the airships?"

That time, the Haa'la turned and regarded him with golden eyes ringed with a band of glowing amethyst. "Do you want to steal one and run back to your little human friends? You wouldn't survive long, anyway. Nydo Base Corporation operates on thirty-six worlds and has razed a dozen of them to the ground, and yours will be no different."

Dalton tried not to look cowed. "Couldn't fly one if I tried. And your people missed out on a big opportunity, burning all the forests around here. You could have sold them off as lumber instead."

"We burned the forests to burn the Greens as a safety measure. The minerals in your ground are more valuable than lumber, anyway. Why must you know about the ships?"

So much for a diversionary tactic. "I told you, they interest me. Living on Molorthia Six, we don't get many alien visitors. Your ships are much more interesting than ours."

"Anything about the Haa'la is more interesting than humanity," the Haa'la grunted, and refocused on his work.

He wondered if Chumley or Keith would have had an easier time extracting information from their captors, then did a double-take when he spotted a small shape darting around on the ground near the row of parked ships.

He squinted hard.

The small shape looked remarkably like a hamster, and it moved from one ship to the next as if giving them each a cursory inspection, which was not an action he would ordinarily associate with the typical rodent.

Dalton took a few steps closer to the hamster. The tiny creature turned its head toward him, let out a little *yip!* he wasn't even sure hamsters were supposed to make, and scurried off into a shadowy corner, where Dalton could no longer see it.

Shaking his head, Dalton grabbed the handles of his cart and steered it out of the building.

"What did you learn today?" Dalton asked.

"Hmm?" Chumley looked up from his wineglass, somewhat bleary-eyed. The two of them sat on the veranda inside

Chumley's portable universe, Dalton wishing the tranquil, digital garden before them was a real place he could go and relax in after a long day of chopping even more stinky vegetables.

"You were on cleaning duty again. Just wondered if you'd picked up on anything we could use."

Chumley's face had become lined with a nervous apprehension, and he took another sip of his wine. "I might have gotten some information from a Haa'la earlier."

"Might have?"

"I may have used some rusty flirting skills. I used to be very good at it, but they might suspect me, now."

"Do I want to know?"

"Probably not." Chumley dug in his pocket and withdrew a crinkled sheet of paper. "This is a list of the three airships parked in the hangar this very moment. Each one has a serial number stamped on the side. This one here—" he held up the paper and tapped the third item on his list, which looked like a string of indecipherable scribbles— "is headed to a listening post ten kilometers northwest of Paris tomorrow morning."

Dalton stood. "Then let's find Keith and have him smuggle us onboard."

"It isn't that simple." Chumley's eyes looked bloodshot. "I checked each airship for their serial numbers. They're all printed in Haa'anu, which makes them about as easy to read as cuneiform, and I realized my little Haa'la informant must have copied down the serial numbers wrong, because they didn't match what was on the paper."

"None of them did?"

Chumley shook his head. "So now I have to assume I'm going to be reported to whoever's in charge here, and I'll be punished accordingly for trying to catch a lift. It's only a matter of time before someone comes knocking at our door holding a set of handcuffs."

"Let me see that." Dalton took the paper from him and squinted in an attempt to decipher the alien text. "When were you able to sneak a look at the ships?"

"Oh, earlier." Chumley sounded oddly evasive. "I did it when everyone else was distracted."

"You mean when they were unloading the cargo?"

"That's right."

"I didn't see you."

"I'm very furtive."

"Come to think of it, the only thing I saw over there was a hamster. You ought to catch it and put it in your little cage."

Chumley's face seemed to darken a moment, but he made no comment.

"Anyway, what do you know about their language?" Dalton asked, returning his attention to the sheet of paper.

"Only what I heard about in school. I think instead of past and future tenses, they have tenses that describe what mood the speaker was in at the time, and whether or not they like the person they're talking to."

"That isn't very helpful."

"No."

"You've got a computer in there. Does it have translation software?"

Chumley's eyes lit up. "I think it does—and I shouldn't even need a net connection to use it!" He snatched up his wineglass and rushed back inside the bedroom-slash-office, and he was already firing up his computer when Dalton straggled in behind him on weary feet.

"Let me see, let me see . . ." Chumley muttered to himself, sitting in his swivel chair. Dalton drew up beside him, peering at the screen. "If I can scan this into the program, it might be able to decipher it."

"Need me to do anything?" Dalton asked.

"Just keep an eye on the security screen and make sure nobody's barged in and found the Cube."

Dalton looked to the screen displaying the interior of their dormitory. They did not appear to have company.

Chumley fed the paper through a scanning device, and a blown-up copy of the Haa'anu serial numbers appeared on the main screen. He clicked "Translate Now," then sat back to wait.

The computer hummed. Dalton found himself tapping his foot with impatience. He wanted *out* of here, dammit, and the sooner, the better.

Eventually, a soft ding issued from the computer's speakers, and a translated duplicate of the scanned paper appeared beside the scanned image itself. Dalton leaned forward to get a better look, and read, "The one you seek is in the middle. But beware, because transgressions are not taken lightly?"

Chumley put a hand to his forehead. "I'm an idiot."

"Looks like your informant didn't want you to lose your note and have someone figure out what was going on."

Chumley sighed. "So, it's the airship parked in between the other two. How simple."

"You don't think it could be a trap?"

Chumley chewed on his lip. "I don't know. But we have to risk it. Otherwise, your planet is toast."

"I don't see why you care. You could have run back home days ago."

A long sigh escaped Chumley's lips. "No, I couldn't have."

"Why not?"

"Because I can't." Chumley folded his arms and swiveled his chair around to face him. "I wasn't always a conman. My gran died after a long battle with chogavirus."

Dalton winced—chogavirus was rare, but ruthless once it started wreaking havoc on a patient's internal organs. "Sorry to hear that."

"The cost of her care and the cost of the funeral nearly bankrupted me. I was working fifty hours a week counting beans at my day job, and it still wasn't enough. I had to do something on the side to make up for it."

"You didn't have family who could help?"

Chumley shook his head. "Not on that side of the family. My parents fought a lot when I was a boy. One day it got out of hand and, well, I had to go live with Gran. She moved me to Pelstring Four so we could get fresh starts. She was my dad's mum, and he was her only child."

"That . . . must have been very hard for you."

"Yes. Well. That's life, isn't it? After I turned to some . . . new professions, law enforcement on Pelstring Four got on my tail, so I fled here, where I didn't think anyone would find me. I used a forged passport and paid cash to throw them off. If I go home, I go to prison."

"But you were still conning people even when you arrived here."

"I still have bills to pay off. I was hoping to wire in the payments through a dummy account so they couldn't trace where they'd come from."

"What were you planning on doing when the people here didn't get the tanning beds they'd paid for?"

"I'd have thought of something. I always do."

"Surely there was another way—"

"There wasn't."

"Why didn't you tell me this before?"

"Because it hurts." Chumley's shoulders drooped. "Gran raised me. She meant everything to me, taught me right from wrong, took me away from a family that did more harm than good. She'd hate what I became because of her illness. I hope she'd understand that I acted not out of greed, but out of desperation."

Ordinarily, Dalton would have said that surely there were plenty of other ways Chumley could have survived the financial aftermath of his grandmother's illness, and that Chumley just hadn't thought of them, but the expression of sorrow that had appeared on the man's face made Dalton keep his mouth shut. He understood pain, too, after all.

"So, the airship," Dalton said instead. "Shouldn't we go find Keith and have him stash us onboard?"

"Just what I was thinking." Chumley rose. "You wait here while I go find him."

Chumley stepped as lightly as a cat when he emerged from the Cube, feeling furtive even though the moment did not yet require it. The hour grew late, and the Haa'la who worked the day shift would be bedding down about now to dream sweet dreams of death and destruction.

He was primarily worried about the night shift people. There didn't seem to be as many of them, but it only took one to sound the alarm.

He opened the bedroom door and glanced left and right. The vacant corridor was lit with dim bulbs to mimic dusk while still giving off enough light to see by.

Remembering it was important to make it look as though he had business being where he was, Chumley straightened his shoulders and strode off to the right, toward the communal area in the center of the building where workers mingled between shifts.

As he'd expected, Keith sat in one of the white upholstered chairs, squinting at a magazine printed in Haa'anu. Keith glanced up when Chumley entered the room, then gestured with his eyes toward the room's other occupants, as if Chumley hadn't noticed them.

"Captivating read?" Chumley asked, taking the chair beside Keith's and slouching in it as if he planned on sitting there comfortably all night.

"I can't make any sense of it." Keith held up a page, which showed a photograph of a Haa'la couple holding hands while a wildfire raged behind them. "I think it might be like *Golfer's Digest*, only for people who demolish planets."

Three Haa'la stood near a snack machine, speaking in low tones but hardly giving Chumley or Keith the time of day. He couldn't tell if any of them were the one who'd given him information about the soon-to-be-departing airship.

Keith coughed lightly into his hand. "So, how are things?"

"They're absolutely spiffing." How much English did these particular Haa'la understand? "I do believe," Chumley went on, "that it might be in our best interests to use … colloquialisms of the highest caliber, in order that those who accompany us are less inclined to comprehend the intentions behind our speech."

Keith blinked at him. Then a conspiratorial glint appeared in his eyes, and he said, "Indeed? What news have ye of events yet to unfold?"

The Haa'la by the snack machine still hadn't looked their direction. "As I said, it is news most advantageous. Our … mode of conveyance has been identified. We need only our courier."

Keith set the magazine down on the small table beside him and rose. "Then a courier, you shall have."

They left the room together, and Chumley led Keith down the hallway toward the room where Dalton and the Cube awaited them. Once inside, Keith let out a long breath and said, "I haven't felt so nervous since I had to do improv in front of my whole drama class back at university."

"You're about to feel even more nervous." Chumley felt the increasing onslaught of his own apprehension. "You'll have to get us onboard the middle airship in the hangar without anyone seeing you. It's supposedly headed to a listening post close to Paris."

"That's perfect—I live there!"

"It's too risky to take you with us. We'd have to activate the doorway to let you inside after you place us on the ship, and the light might draw unwanted attention."

Keith's lip curled. "I understand, but it doesn't mean I have to be happy about it."

Chumley pushed the button to activate the holographic entrance to the Cube, then said, "As soon as this doorway vanishes, put the Cube in your pocket and make your way to the hangar. Like I said, it's the middle airship. Once we're securely onboard, get out of there as fast as you can and don't let anyone see you."

"Understood." Keith gave him a long look. "Best of luck to you both. Maybe I'll be the lucky one, getting to stay behind. You know, if things turn out wrong."

"I'm sure we'll be fine. And thank you." Chumley dipped his head and strode through the archway into his portable universe.

"Everything working as planned?" Dalton asked. He lounged on the swivel chair, picking his teeth with a toothpick Chumley had dug out of a cabinet for him.

"So far." Chumley prodded the panel on the wall to deactivate the entrance, and on the security screen, he watched Keith's hand loom large as he closed his fingers around the Cube. Then everything went dark, presumably because Keith had just put them into his pocket.

"And now we wait," said Chumley.

CHAPTER 16

Carolyn stood alone in her flat on the north side of the city, staring out at the star-speckled sky from her balcony window, grateful that work crews had gotten the rest of the city's power back on by sundown. A beeping truck with an attached sandplow rumbled by below her, clearing out the last of the mess. By fourteen o'clock midnight, Richport ought to be back to normal.

Well, almost normal. Her police force had yet to reappear.

Maybe she'd been too hard on Dalton. The man had been through an ungodly amount of stress, and the recent Green attacks had set it all off again like a big, nasty bomb.

She hoped she'd get the chance to apologize.

A soft rapping at her flat's door made her jump, and she sighed, wondering which fires she would have to put out this time.

She opened the door and blinked as she regarded Errin Inglewood, accompanied by none other than Gwendolyn Goldfarb, who was wearing one of her neon shawls again.

"What's going on?" Carolyn asked, her voice coming out colder than intended.

"I stayed late at the office, and Gwendolyn caught me right outside the door when I was leaving," Errin said, giving the old woman a sidelong glance. "She insisted she needed to see you."

"Well, come in, then." Dread bubbled inside of Carolyn as her visitors stepped past her and she closed the door. "Gwendolyn, what did you need to see me about?"

Gwendolyn's eyes were dilated far more than the lighting called for. "The ghosts are here again."

Her words added a chill to the room, which was admirable when one took the climate into account. "Errin?" Carolyn said quietly. "Could you please call Monica and have her come over as soon as she can?"

"Certainly." Errin stepped off to one side to make the call on their comm unit.

"Come sit with me," Carolyn said, leading Gwendolyn over to the couch. Once the elderly woman sat comfortably beside her, Carolyn said, "Tell me more about these ghosts."

"They come from the sky and burn the world." Gwendolyn looked toward the stucco ceiling as if expecting to see something there other than the textured paint.

"You mentioned something about that before. Are these ghosts alive or dead?"

"Alive," Gwendolyn said after a long pause. "But unseen."

"So, invisible people are coming from the sky and burning the world."

"Yes."

"And they've captured Dalton and Chumley?"

"Yes. Salt."

Carolyn felt taken aback by the hairpin turn in the conversation. "Salt?" she asked, making sure she'd heard correctly.

"Salt will win."

"What does that mean?"

"It will win!" Gwendolyn cried, and then her head slumped forward, her chin resting against her chest.

In a panic, Carolyn grabbed the woman's frail wrist and felt for a pulse, breathing a soft sigh of relief when she felt a reassuring *thud-thud-thud.*

"Monica is on her way," Errin said, pocketing their comm and looking grim. "Is there anything I should do while we wait?"

Carolyn gave Gwendolyn a long, hard look. "Maybe head down to Slim's and get more coffee. I have the feeling I'm going to need it."

Gwendolyn woke shortly after Monica Kaur's arrival with medical kit in tow.

"She seems fine," Monica said to Carolyn in the other room, where Gwendolyn couldn't hear them. "I can't do any deeper testing here, but everything so far indicates she's a perfectly healthy ninety-seven-year-old."

"Her mind's the problem, not her body."

"And she's sharp as a tack! You heard her ask how my cat Nibbles is doing. I'm sure I've only ever mentioned him to her once."

"Errin and I both witnessed her acting strangely. Maybe she should stay with you tonight, for observational purposes."

Monica put a hand on her chin. "We do have a spare room, and Gwendolyn shouldn't mind having the company."

"Good. Record everything she does and report all your findings back to me."

"But patient confidentiality . . ."

"She needs someone to care about her, Monica. That person can be me. Gwendolyn won't say no."

"Very well. But if she doesn't agree to sharing her medical information with you, you're out of luck."

Carolyn thought of the black smoke billowing on the horizon and wondered if they were out of luck already.

Stay calm, stay calm, Keith Okpebholo thought to himself as he moved from shadow to shadow outside the dormitories, slowly making his way toward the hangar with the magic cube in his pocket. His heart was practically in his throat, and he missed the long, boring years he'd spent in Paris, helping Annaliese keep the peace. He'd never had to do anything like this while working for Annaliese. This was like—like *espionage!*

Keith flattened himself against a dormant ground transport with giant wheels the moment he heard voices, and he held his breath as he waited for the Haa'la to pass.

He was almost there. He could *do* this.

When the voices receded, Keith darted out from his hiding place and paused behind another ground transport parked ten meters away, nearly dizzy with adrenaline. Ahead of him lay the hangar. The bay door nearest to him had been left open, and a dim light glowed inside.

He counted off ten beats and made one final mad dash to the side of the immense metal building. He poked his head around the edge of the bay door to make sure no guards had been posted, then tiptoed inside when he saw the coast was clear.

"Middle ship," he muttered. "Middle ship." That's what they'd said, right?

He peered up at the row of ships and frowned.

There were five various sorts of flying craft parked in a row—he remembered hearing the thrum of engines earlier, which must have been new arrivals to the base. Did Chumley and Dalton know about that? Probably.

Keith tugged the Cube out of his pocket and held it at eye level. "Good luck," he said, not sure if they could hear him.

Then he turned toward the middlest middle ship—one much larger than those on either side of it—and strode up the gangplank as if he had important business there.

Keith let out another impressed whistle when he stepped into a gleaming silver control room lined with glowing screens. Several swivel chairs looked cozy enough to sleep in. Fully aware he could be caught at any moment; he kept his gawping to a minimum and hurried down a corridor to find a decent spot to hide the Cube.

A vast storage room full of cargo toward the back of the craft looked just the place for it. Keith wedged the Cube between a crate and the back wall, then brushed his hands together, his work complete.

On his way down the gangplank, a tall Haa'la woman strode into the hangar, her face unveiled. Two others trailed behind her bearing holstered weapons.

"You! Human!" the woman bellowed. Her eyes were like licorice, her skin paler than marzipan.

"Me?" Keith asked, pointing stupidly at himself.

"What were you doing on my ship?"

Keith was fairly certain this was Ashi'ii, the Haa'la in charge of Nydo Base. He'd seen her stomping through the corridors a few different times while he cleaned them.

He swept into a bow. "Pip-pip! I was merely inspecting your vessel to ensure the safety of your passage."

"From whom did you receive those orders?"

Keith tried and failed to come up with a name.

Ashi'ii's guards stepped toward him.

Bugger, Keith thought.

"Did he put us in the right ship?" Dalton asked, squinting at the security screen and seeing only a solid wall in front of them.

"We can step out and take a look if you're feeling brave enough," Chumley said, lying back on his bed with his ankles crossed. "I, for one, don't want to risk being captured just yet."

"But if he got the wrong one—"

"Keith is an intelligent man. He works for your friend Annaliese, right?"

"Right . . ."

"And even if this isn't *the* ship we asked for, it's still *a* ship, and more likely than not, it will eventually do that thing which all ships do sooner or later."

"Sink?"

"Get us out of here."

Chumley's words held a certain amount of logic, and Dalton relaxed.

"And now we wait?" Dalton said.

"Not much else to do in the meantime, is there?"

They fell silent for a spell. Dalton felt suddenly uneasy.

"What?" Chumley asked, detecting his change in mood.

"If we'd been fast about it, we could have activated the doorway and let Keith in here without anyone seeing us."

"But the light—"

"Is probably less noticeable than a full-grown man sneaking around where he shouldn't be."

"Ah." Chumley paused. "Well, I'm sure he'll be all right."

"Right."

Dalton looked back to the security screen. Wherever Keith had stashed them was dark, and the Cube's external camera had painted the rather lacking view of the wall in the shades of night vision. "Wish he'd thought to leave us in a spot where we could see if we're on the move yet."

"Well, we can't get everything we want, can we?" Chumley looked at the time on the wall clock, which of course was far from correct.

"You know Molorthia Six has a twenty-eight-hour day," Dalton said.

"No wonder I feel like shit." Chumley regarded the clock again. "We'll wait thirty minutes before I go out and check on things."

"What if you're seen?"

"Then I get caught."

"What do I do, then?"

"You'll think of something. Why don't you try and get some sleep?"

Dalton ground his teeth together and then extracted

the last shards of toothpick from his mouth. "Don't see the point."

Stop being an arse, Darneisha's voice advised him from beyond the grave, not that she had a grave—none of them did. *Just lie down and shut your eyes before he chucks you out of an airlock.*

Dalton looked toward the veranda, where the digital garden rustled in a harmless, digital breeze. "I'll sleep out there," he said. "Let me know if anything happens."

Chumley watched the minutes tick by on the clock, then heaved himself off the bed and activated the archway. He took a deep breath and strode through, finding himself in a space so dimly-lit, he wouldn't have been able to see a Green standing two inches in front of him—the holographic light of the archway certainly didn't do much for illumination, which he supposed might be in his favor.

He held his breath, and he listened.

Chumley detected a hum so faint it lurked at the farthest edges of his hearing. The floor seemed to be vibrating, as well.

"Good," he muttered, and quickly retreated into the Cube.

CHAPTER 17

"S alt will win," Carolyn muttered as she lay wide awake in bed, unable to get comfortable. "Salt will *win?*"

She was, of course, fully aware that anyone who claimed to have portents of the future was full of shit. Soothsayers of old had either breathed in too many vapors, or they were pulling a fast one. Not that Gwendolyn was claiming anything—oddly enough, she seemed an innocent victim in the matter.

Carolyn had never been particularly religious. Sure, she made her way over to the gurdwara about once per month, but the fact that a Creator might be responsible for everything just seemed like too much mumbo-jumbo for her logic-hardened mind to take. Believing Gwendolyn might have developed psychic powers was its own sort of mumbo-jumbo, and it made Carolyn deeply uncomfortable to think it might be true.

What did she mean by salt?

She switched on her bedside lamp and sat up, then pulled open the drawer in her nightstand and removed from it a notepad and a pen.

Salt, she wrote at the top of the notepad, and underlined it twice.

Beneath it, she wrote, *What does salt do?*

-Adds flavor

-Melts snow

-Makes things float in oceans

-Kills slugs

She reread her short list. "Salt will win," she said again, and scratched at her temple. She was about to add *Preserves food* to her list when a shout rose from the still night air outside her flat.

"What now?" she hissed as she yanked her curtains aside and peered down at the street.

A man stood in the soft glow of one of the streetlights, pointing at a white-clad individual with one quaking finger. Pursing her lips, Carolyn jammed her feet into slippers and raced down the stairs, then burst outside to see what sort of incident needed defusing now.

The man was Louis Hopkirk, who lived in her building and often stayed up late blaring Kaktian opera music that made Carolyn want to jam icepicks into her eardrums. He gripped a paper bag in one hand, evidence of a late-night booze run. The person in white had disappeared, though Louis was still pointing as if they hadn't.

"Louis, what's going on?" Carolyn asked, skin prickling.

"That—that person just appeared out of thin air!" Louis's voice strained with disbelief. "I was about to get out my key, and ta-da!"

Carolyn squinted at the spot midair where the man pointed. It seemed perhaps a bit more shimmery than air was supposed to be.

"You see the person now?" Carolyn asked.

"You don't?"

"No." Carolyn paused as a knot of dread tightened in her abdomen. "Are they dressed in white?"

"Obviously! And they're holding a sack."

"I don't believe this." But she did, and hated herself for it.

Carolyn took one step closer to the shimmery place, and Louis gasped. "They just disappeared!"

The earsplitting wail of the sandstorm sirens cut through the air, and Carolyn whirled toward the west, where the police station lay, feeling shards of ice fill her veins.

"Louis, get inside *now*," she ordered, then broke into a run toward the station without waiting to see if he complied.

She knew it would be too much to hope that the blaring siren was experiencing a malfunction.

Several dozen citizens were already peering out their windows as Carolyn rounded a corner onto the street where the police station lay. She rushed up to the squat adobe building, where lights blazed behind the windows and the glass front door.

Cadu Mão de Ferro's bag-lined eyes met hers as she rushed into the building. He looked like someone who had missed a few weeks of sleep and then fallen off a cliff.

"What's happening?" Carolyn asked.

A croak came out when Cadu opened his mouth. He closed it, cleared his throat, then said, "I couldn't sleep, so I came in a few minutes ago to see if I could bore myself to death, and I thought I heard a noise like someone rummaging through cabinets. Don't know how anyone could have gotten in, though; the door was locked."

Her eyes narrowed. "So you were spooked, and set off the alarm?"

His face grew particularly grave. "I was more than spooked. When I switched the lights on . . . well, *you're* not going to believe it."

"Let me guess," she said evenly. "You saw a person dressed all in white, holding a sack while they looted the place, and then they disappeared."

Cadu's mouth fell open. "How did you know?"

"An identical person was just terrifying one of my neighbors."

Cadu ran his hands over his face. "That's at least two of them, then."

"Why did you turn on the siren?"

"To let people know there's a threat!" He blinked red, bleary eyes. "I wish Dalton were here."

"Dalton, who spends most of his shifts filling in crossword puzzles?"

"He'd know what to do. Or he'd at least pretend to. I just tell people how to stop themselves from bleeding to death while they wait for the medics to come rescue them. I don't know how to handle . . . this." He made a vague gesture in the direction of the door, and then his eyes widened. "Errin's here."

Before Carolyn could speak, Errin rushed into the station wearing a t-shirt and a baggy pair of shorts.

"How did you know what was happening?" Errin panted, looking from Carolyn to Cadu, their face ashen.

"What do you mean?" Carolyn and Cadu asked in unison.

"I was just about to call you! You know I live behind the hardware store? I woke up hearing a clatter, and I went over to make sure no one was breaking in. I peeked in one of the windows and saw tools lifting themselves off the shelves and vanishing." They let out a nervous little giggle. "I can't believe I just said that. Please don't fire me."

"Do you think the thieves are still there?" Carolyn asked.

Errin's sand-colored eyebrows shot upward. "You believe me?"

"Just answer the question."

"Well, I—I wouldn't know. The sirens started going off, so I came here to see why. I was hoping it wasn't another storm already."

"Cadu set off the sirens because he saw a thief vanish before his very eyes."

"A thief, in here?" Errin frowned, looking toward the row of open cupboards along the back wall of the main room, their shelves in disarray.

"I think they took some of the guns left over from Old Man Sondhi's day," Cadu said, rubbing at his eyes. "Joke's on them; we don't have any ammo."

"How is the siren going to help us stop a couple of thieves?"

"Cadu isn't thinking clearly," Carolyn said; then, turning to the emergency operator, asked, "When was the last time you got any sleep?"

"Before Dalton went missing. I think."

"All right." Carolyn put her hands on her hips. "Cadu, you stay here and do what you do. Errin, you and I are going to take a little look at the hardware store." She paused, thinking of Gwendolyn Goldfarb's mysterious words. "And bring some salt."

Every few minutes, Chumley risked exiting the Cube to see if the airship had landed. So far he'd entered the dark cargo hold three times, and each time, the faint hum of engines had indicated they were still in the air.

Shouldn't they have landed already?

The Haa'la had mentioned having listening posts out in the desert. They clearly possessed teleport technology, so they could have teleported out to their posts and saved themselves the time, but perhaps the airships themselves were the listening posts. They were probably scanning the airwaves for any mention of a Haa'la invasion, and at the first sign of trouble, they'd scamper off this rock and find some new planet to decimate.

On his fourth trip into the cargo hold, Chumley sensed that something had changed elsewhere in the ship. There remained the hum of the engine, but it sounded different somehow in a way that sent a chill straight into his heart.

A second fundamental change was equally alarming.

He hurried back inside the Cube and out onto the veranda, where Dalton was snoring softly.

"Dalton, wake up," he hissed.

Dalton grumbled something about salads.

"Dalton!"

"Huh?" The sheriff sat up and blinked as he gathered his bearings. "Have we landed?"

"I don't think so. Step outside so I can get a second opinion."

"On what?"

"Just come."

Dalton eyed him with some irritation and shook himself. "Fine. Next time you're asleep, I'll wake *you* up for no reason."

Outside the Cube, in the darkness of the cargo hold, Chumley flicked on the penlight he'd brought with him. The weak beam illuminated dozens of stacked crates labeled in Haa'anu script.

"What do you think is in these?" Dalton asked. "Supplies for the listening posts?"

"I'm not so sure." Chumley ran a hand through his hair. "I want you to jump up and down a few times and tell me what you think. But do it quietly, so nobody hears us."

Frowning, Dalton complied, and then a look of apprehension spread across his face. "I feel floaty," he said. "Like I've lost weight."

"That's what I was worried about."

"What does it mean?"

Chumley licked his lips. "You really don't want to hear this."

"I really do."

"Well, erm, Leeprau isn't a very big planet—I think it's about the size of Mars, or something."

"And?"

"The gravity is different."

Dalton's mouth fell open, releasing the toothpick shard he'd stashed there prior to their exit from the Cube. "We're on *Leeprau*?" he breathed.

"I don't think we are just yet. See, I've been on my fair

share of alien ships. They usually set their artificial gravity to match that of their homeworlds."

Chumley watched Dalton's face as this information sank in.

"Shit," Dalton said. Then, "*Shit.*"

"I'm sure it's not Keith's fault—"

"He's the one who put us on a bloody spaceship!"

"Shh! Dalton, you're going to—"

The door to the cargo hold whooshed open, blinding them with light from the hallway outside. A veiled Haa'la stood silhouetted in the opening, holding some sort of weapon that probably wasn't a water pistol.

Chumley shouted "Ha!" and tossed his penlight across the room, scooping up the Cube and stashing it into his pocket while the Haa'la was distracted.

The Haa'la looked back at him—at least Chumley thought they looked back at him; it was hard to tell through the veil. "*Pip-pip! Hee a'a'a mish aah!*" they shouted in their own language.

Both Chumley and Dalton lifted their hands to display their lack of weaponry. "We do not speak Haa'anu," Chumley said carefully. "Do you speak English?"

The Haa'la lifted their veil, revealing a stony, feminine face ringed in pastel hair. "I speak seven human tongues," she said, her tone lacking any sort of warmth. "Why are you on my ship?"

"We got lost." Chumley looked to Dalton, whose sun-browned face had become tinged with dread. "Could you show us the way out?"

The Haa'la grinned to reveal rows of pointy teeth. "We have an airlock. Would you like to leave by that route?"

"Erm, no. Where are we going?"

"Home." Two other Haa'la appeared in the doorway behind her as she said, "I am Ashi'ii. What I assume to be your accomplice was dealt with most harshly."

"What did you do with him?"

"Nothing that will cause him permanent damage," Ashi'ii went on smoothly. "It is bad business to destroy any member of the workforce."

Dalton's scowl deepened. "And what's all this in here? Stuff you mined out of our planet?"

"Of course. I'm overseeing its delivery to Leeprau."

"We can report you to the Feds."

Ashi'ii frowned at him. "How?"

Dalton glanced to Chumley and said, "We have our ways."

"Of course you do." Ashi'ii turned to her two comrades and exchanged a few words in Haa'anu, then stepped back as the others strode forward and seized both Chumley and Dalton as unceremoniously as if they were actual, literal criminals.

"Ow!" Chumley cried as the towering Haa'la dug their fingers into his arm and guided him toward the doorway. "Have a bit of mercy!"

"We are having a bit of mercy," Ashi'ii said as she watched them leave. "If we wanted you dead, we would have killed you already. Have a nice day."

"All right," Dalton said. "Now what?"

"I'm thinking." Chumley paced back and forth across the floor in one of the ship's cabins, where the two of them had been locked after their removal from the cargo hold.

"Well, think faster. I'm not spending the rest of my life trapped in some Haa'la prison." Dalton folded his arms across his chest and glared at the cabin's door, which looked solid enough to survive several nuclear blasts.

Chumley halted mid-pace. "Oh, biscuits."

"What?"

Chumley sank onto one of the narrow cots reserved for the ship's crew. "I can't go to prison, Dalton."

"Life of crime catching up to you, eh?"

Chumley's face grew long. "When I started doing ... things ... to pay for Gran's expenses, I knew the risks. Always thought I was too smart to get caught, always stayed one step ahead of the police, and now I'm right where I deserve to be. Might as well curl up and die." His shoulders slumped.

Dalton sat up straighter, alarmed at Chumley's change in demeanor. "Whoa now, let's not give up all hope just yet."

Chumley lifted his gaze to glower at him for a moment. "Remind me again, Dalton, where are we?"

"In a cabin on a spaceship. Maybe when we land, they'll just put us to work again." Dalton knew this was probably wishful thinking, and that life was easier when you expected the worst, but he didn't think he could stand sitting here listening to Chumley moping for very long.

"Ugh. I'm going inside my Cube. At least then I'll be locked up in comfort." Chumley pulled the device from his pocket, activated the doorway, and disappeared.

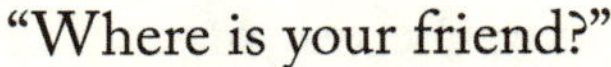

"Where is your friend?"

Dalton flailed awake. Ashi'ii stood over him wearing an expression of intense displeasure.

"I don't know," Dalton said.

"Is that so?" Ashi'ii planted her hands on her hips—an all-too-human gesture.

"He does that sometimes," Dalton added quickly. "Just up and disappears. He could be anywhere on this ship."

Ashi'ii showed her pointy teeth, then looked down at the empty cot across from Dalton, where the silver Cube gleamed in the glare of the overhead lighting. "What is that?"

Dalton ground his teeth together as Ashi'ii scooped the Cube up with her pale fingers.

"It's my good-luck charm," Dalton said. "I bring it wherever I go."

"It must not give you very good luck," Ashi'ii commented, turning the Cube over in her hands with interest. Dalton prayed she wouldn't activate the hidden button and push it.

He would have to distract her from examining it too closely. "I'm still alive, aren't I?" he said. "I've survived more than anyone else I know. Well, my sister-in-law did, too, but she didn't have her arm ripped off like I did."

Ashi'ii eyed him curiously. "You do not appear to have lost any appendages."

Dalton lifted his right arm and flexed his fingers. "I got a new one. We were attacked by the Greens. My entire family was killed, except my brother's wife. That was forty-six people dead. Even my wife and kids." A lump rose in Dalton's throat. He tried to force it back down, but it wouldn't move. "And . . . they ate my arm, right in front of me."

"My supreme condolences." Ashi'ii appeared contemplative. "And you credit your survival to this trinket?"

"It's just superstitious, I know," Dalton said, trying not to panic. "I was just lucky." If you could call it lucky.

"I will take this object with me," Ashi'ii said at length, pocketing the Cube. "We *will* find your friend—we're about to make planetfall, and once we've landed, every inch of this ship will be stripped and searched for him."

The Cube made her pocket bulge. Dalton's cantering pulse bordered on a gallop.

"Could I . . . could I watch out the window as we land?" he asked weakly. "I haven't landed on another planet since I was a boy."

"I suppose I see no harm in that. Come with me. If you attempt violence, you will be injured."

As Ashi'ii led him out of the room and down the corridor leading to the front of the ship, Dalton raced to think of ways he might reacquire the Cube from Ashi'ii's person and came up with nothing other than tackling her and wrangling it away from her—an act which would surely get him locked up again.

Three more Haa'la people sat or stood before viewing screens in the control room. One Haa'la operating a set of switches said something to their peers, and the blackness on all the viewing screens transformed into a star-studded field with an even brighter dot in the middle that was growing larger and starting to look an awful lot like a planet.

Dalton tensed, remembering how he'd watched Molorthia Six grow and swell on the viewing screen of the shuttle that had taken his family there so many years ago now. Molorthia Six was just a tad bit smaller than Earth and had one hemispheric ocean encompassing roughly 35% of the planet's surface area and another, smaller ocean close to its northern pole, which the young Dalton had thought resembled a watchful turquoise eye.

Leeprau stood out in stark contrast to his home. As details began to appear on the looming sphere, Dalton noted that Leeprau had more water than Molorthia Six, and a substantial amount of cities—a sliver of the planet Dalton had thought to be in the sunlight was actually billions of city lights glowing on the night side.

Dozens of space stations glimmered in their orbits about the planet. A few moons hung here and there, some of them also glowing with city lights. The right kind of person might have found the scene beautiful, but for some reason—probably the fact he and Chumley were not exactly here on holiday—it made him feel depressed and wish for his empty bed back home.

The ship shuddered as it angled toward the thin band of twilight dividing night from day. A Haa'la voice spoke through a speaker, and one of the crew replied into a microphone and shifted course a few degrees.

Dalton shoved his hands into the pockets of his trench coat, which he'd been able to launder in the Cube's bathroom prior to their escape. The space traffic controller said something else to the pilot, who shifted course yet again.

"What's going to happen to me when we land?" Dalton

asked, beads of sweat forming on his scalp. He wondered how Chumley was faring in Ashi'ii's pocket.

"You will be taken in for questioning. We have many interpreters at our headquarters in Vehenna. Someone there will speak your language, as I do."

"And after the questioning is over?"

"That depends on the results of the questioning."

He coughed lightly. "Who will be doing this questioning?"

"A Nydo Base representative who has more free time than I do."

Dalton's mind raced. If these Haa'la here were truly "businesspeople," as they claimed, that meant they were an independent enterprise, not sanctioned by any government. If he could get away from this lot and find the authorities . . . but could he pull it off?

He would see.

CHAPTER 18

Carolyn had woken Jill Benedict, the hardware store's proprietor, so she could unlock the door for them, and now she squinted in through the plate-glass windows before going inside. Shadows filled the store, not entirely dispelled by the single security light glowing behind the counter.

Jill stood aside in her dressing gown as Carolyn and Errin prepared to enter the shop. "I don't see anyone in there," Jill said doubtfully, her arms folded across her ample chest.

"Neither did I," said Errin. "But hammers don't just lift themselves off of hooks."

"Have a look, then." Lines appeared on Jill's face. "Should I stay here, or do you want me out of the way?"

"It might be safer for you if you went back to your house," Carolyn said. "We're not entirely sure what we're dealing with."

Jill gave a nod. "All right. Let me know if you learn anything."

"We will."

The proprietor vanished into the night, and Carolyn and Errin faced each other.

"Ready?" Errin asked.

Carolyn sighed. "I don't have another choice."

They stepped through the door, Carolyn straining her ears for the slightest sounds out of the ordinary. The intruder had probably gone away as soon as they heard the door unlock, but they might have left behind clues that might help determine their identity.

The floor creaked as they crossed the small, open space between the door and the ends of the aisles perpendicular to the front wall. A faint tinkle from elsewhere in the shop made Carolyn put her finger to her lips. Errin tensed beside her.

Very carefully, Carolyn removed a stun gun from her pocket. She'd borrowed it from the police station, hoping she wouldn't have to use it, but hoping had never really done her much good.

Errin withdrew their own borrowed weapon, and on an unspoken cue, the two of them stepped lightly through the hardware store past racks of shovels and sandblowers and spackling compound and whatnot, toward the place where the sound had come from.

Many shelves had already been emptied.

A light cough up ahead made Carolyn freeze for a moment. In the faint illumination from the security light, she watched as a box of nails rose from a display and disappeared, as if the air itself had swallowed it.

She set her jaw, aimed her stun gun, and fired a glowing burst of energy toward the vanished nails.

The air in front of them let out a startled yelp. There came a clatter, and a sprawling figure appeared on the floor next to a bulging sack of stolen wares.

The figure was dressed all in white. Carolyn did not feel surprised.

"Get the cuffs," she barked, striding forward with stun gun still in hand.

"Already have them. Here."

The figure moaned. Carolyn yanked the veil from over their face and regarded inhumanly-white skin. The being drew their lips back from razor-sharp teeth in a grimace but kept their eyes closed.

"What *is* that?" Errin whispered.

"I'm not sure, but I'd bet money they're not from around here. Help me sit them up."

Carolyn and Errin got on either side of the intruder and forced them into sitting position, then cuffed their wrists together behind their back before laying them back on their side.

"Look at this." Errin unclipped a white metallic object from the intruder's belt. "Do you think it's a comm unit?"

"Let me see that."

Carolyn took the object from Errin and found a button on the back. She pressed it—perhaps foolishly—and Errin let out a gasp.

Carolyn stood, alarmed. "What is it?"

"You've disappeared."

Carolyn looked down at herself. She didn't seem to have become invisible, but she would take Errin's word for it.

She hit the button on the object again. "What about now?"

"I can see you again. That's some interesting tech."

"The pulse from the gun must have switched it off the first time," Carolyn said, pocketing it. "Clever little intruder, hmm? Let's get them down to the station and wake them up."

In the long and dreary months following the annihilation of his family, Dalton had, under the urging of one of his old employees, sought counseling to help him work through this new and unpleasant life he found himself living.

His counselor had been a peppy young woman named Candace Murdock, who wore only pink and didn't believe in frowning.

One of the exercises she'd had him practice was "finding his happy place."

"Dalton," she would say in a voice typically reserved for puppies and small children, "you absolutely must find a place of calm inside of you. If you ever feel overwhelmed, you can go there to reset and recharge yourself."

Dalton had tried—he really did—but as the months passed, it became all too clear that finding his happy place was not meant to be.

Now, given that he was a prisoner on a Haa'la ship heading straight down to a Haa'la city where even more Haa'la might potentially torment him, finding his happy place might be ideal.

He thought of lying out on the veranda in the portable universe while digital plants glowed harmlessly just meters away from him, and imagined himself sipping at a glass of whiskey.

Angry shouting jarred him back to reality. Leeprau did not appear any closer on the viewing screen, and his alien captors in the control room were desperately flicking switches and stabbing buttons as if for dear life.

"What's going on?" Dalton asked Ashi'ii, who was bellowing orders at her subordinates.

She whipped her head toward him, eyes blazing. "Space Traffic Control shut down our trajectory. We're locked in place."

"They can do that?"

"We have to jettison in the life pods before the ship is terminated."

"*What?*"

"They. Are. Going. To. Blow. Up. This. Ship," Ashi'ii said, as if she were speaking to an incredibly stupid child.

"But why?"

"Never mind why!" She turned to her crew and barked more orders at them. They abandoned their controls and sprinted past Dalton down the corridor—this lot must not have been equipped with teleports.

"You're loading up in these life pods now?" Dalton asked, too stunned to comprehend the severity of the situation.

"Yes, but you are a stowaway. There is not enough room in them for you and your missing friend. It was nice knowing you, human, but you were foolish in getting onboard and will reap exactly what you deserve."

In a daze, Dalton watched as Ashi'ii strode down the corridor after her peers.

His vision narrowed to a point until she was all he could see.

She still had the Cube in her pocket, with Chumley more or less inside it.

Alarms started going off behind him in the control room.

It was now or never.

"Aaaargh!" he cried as he launched himself at her. She let out a yelp of surprise as he shoved her to the floor.

"Give me that Cube," he grunted as he fumbled for her pocket.

Since she was taller and more massive than he was, she got her bearings back easily enough and threw him off of her. "You're going to get me killed!"

"I just want the Cube!"

"I'm not going to—"

Outside in the blackness of space, two Haa'la sat in the cockpit of a passing space yacht on their way down to Okoka City, where they planned on spending the weekend sipping spiked yurba juice and eating injingji pie until they burst at the seams.

An unexpected orange glow blossomed through their forward viewport before dissipating into black.

Trinni, who was operating the controls, leaned forward and frowned. "Pip-pip. What do you think that was about?"

Her companion, Jonju, stood up and tilted his head to one side as he regarded a new patch of floating debris where moments earlier there had been a bulky cargo ship. Trinni had spotted it a short time before, angling through space a few hundred kushkims ahead of them.

Jonju said, "Pip-pip. Must be some unlucky bastard who crossed the wrong people."

"Pip-pip. Poor buggers."

"Pip-pip. Poor buggers indeed."

CHAPTER 19

Chumley had started to feel rather peculiar the moment he ensconced himself within his Cube to await his ultimate punishment, which was bound to be something equally humiliating and painful.

Stress, of course, was what made the room sway as if he were onboard a fishing boat on a storm-tossed sea, and as he sank onto his bed to steady himself, he thought of the dying Green he'd touched out in the desert before the storm hit, and how it had been so hurt and broken. Why hadn't he tried to help it? It hadn't meant anyone any harm; it had deserved so much better than what it got.

He slouched there for a time, pondering the poor creature and its fate, when without warning, the image of a fireball in space flashed through his mind's eye, and he sat up, heart racing. A fireball? In space? Had the Feds found Ashi'ii's ship and decided to blast it out of the sky?

He shook himself. What was he thinking? Like he would know if the Feds had found them, being trapped in here, a prisoner of his own making.

Still, the sense of alarm that had flooded him would not abate. He looked to his security screen and couldn't see a thing, meaning someone had stashed his Cube somewhere out of sight. Perhaps Dalton didn't want any Haa'la absconding with it.

In his mind, he saw himself activating the doorway, frantic as a madman.

He gritted his teeth.

What would make him frantic as a madman? An exploding ship?

Do it NOW.

Frantic as a madman, Chumley tore across the room and slapped the button to activate the doorway. He rushed out and saw that his Cube had been dropped on the floor in the ship's central corridor seconds earlier. Dalton and the Haa'la in charge were wrestling each other beside it.

"Get in!" he bellowed.

Both Dalton and Ashi'ii stopped, looked at him, and then over at the holographic archway flickering beside him. Dalton's eyes widened, and he threw himself into the safety of the Cube. Without missing a beat, Ashi'ii followed him inside.

Chumley paused, assessing his surroundings. No other Haa'la were in view.

The ship shuddered, accompanied by a loud rumble.

He swallowed and hurried back inside the Cube, deactivating the doorway.

On the security screen, fire erupted in a blinding burst, and when the smoke cleared, he could see the curving, cityscaped surface of a planet that could only be Leeprau floating before them like a great, bloated marble.

Slowly, he turned to Dalton and Ashi'ii, the latter of whom looked on the verge of erupting, herself.

"What . . . happened?" Chumley asked.

"That's what I'd like to know." Dalton glared at Ashi'ii, who glared right back at him. "Who blew up your ship?"

Chumley's skin crawled. He went to his minibar and poured himself a glass to help him not think.

Ashi'ii took her time in answering, as she was busy taking in the contents of the Cube and wrinkling her nose at most of it.

"Was it the Feds?" Dalton pressed.

Ashi'ii pursed her lily-white lips. "No."

"Then who?"

"Rivals." She sniffed. "Ones I'd hoped not to run into again. They must have operatives working for Space Traffic Control, and if they got a good look at our flight records, they'll know what planet we just left."

"How do you know it's them?"

"They announced themselves before they shot us down."

"Are they Haa'la?"

"Yes." Her scowl deepened. "They call themselves the Verdants. They've destroyed four of my cargo ships in the past five years, usually right after they've landed. Thank the gods they haven't found our main headquarters yet."

Dalton frowned. "What do they do that for?"

"They think Nydo Base Corporation and others like it are monsters. Actually, they think that way about any Haa'la who leaves Leeprau. They consider it an abomination for anyone to set foot on another world, like we're contaminating the universe."

"So, they're radicals."

"As radical as they come. And now they're going to destroy our base on Molorthia Six."

"But you just said they think it's an abomination to set foot on another planet."

"They're radicals. They haven't discovered logic yet." She shivered, then composed herself into a mask of calm. "It was smart thinking, stowing us in your vessel. Can you steer us down to the surface? The outside is small enough that Space Traffic Control won't see us on their scanners."

Chumley was already in the middle of pouring his second glass when Ashi'ii said this, and he looked up at her wearing a pained smile. "About that."

"Yes?"

"This isn't a vessel." He poured back a shot that burned its way down his throat like a falling meteor.

Ashi'ii's expression grew stony. "Then what is it?"

Chumley coughed, lightly. "It's a storage unit—where I keep my things. If it were a vessel, we wouldn't have stowed away on yours, now, would we?"

He hadn't thought a Haa'la's face would be capable of changing color, but Ashi'ii's deepened to a violet blue, which was probably the color of their blood. "So, what is the next step?"

"We stay in here until we suffocate from lack of oxygen."

A slow metamorphosis passed over the Haa'la's face. At first she appeared confused, then mirthful.

"You think we'll suffocate, do you?" she asked, her expression now wry.

"Well, yes. The Cube is floating out in space. If I open the doorway to ventilate it, all of our air will get sucked out."

Ashi'ii actually chuckled. "It's typical of humanity."

"What is?" Dalton snapped. He'd been brooding in the

corner, staring at his boots as if they would give him some answers.

"Your profound lack of knowledge about your stellar neighbors. Humans and Haa'la might look similar superficially, but we have vastly different physiologies."

"What, you don't need to breathe?" Dalton asked. "Doesn't help us any; *we'll* still suffocate."

"Of course we breathe! My species needs carbon dioxide to live, and our bodies convert it into oxygen when we exhale. Based on what I learned in university, your species is the exact opposite. This physiological balancing act will give us time to solve our dilemma."

"If you hadn't invaded Molorthia Six, we wouldn't *be* in this dilemma," Dalton reminded her.

She threw him a disgusted glance. "I'll hear no moralizing from the people who've conquered a hundred forty-four worlds and then some. Molorthia Six was never really yours. You just went there and made it yours—and now, it's mine."

"We could reach some sort of deal," Dalton said.

"Of course. Give me the money I would have earned from the sale of your planet's minerals, and I'll pack up my bags and call it a day."

Dalton bristled at the Haa'la's airy tone, and before this could devolve into even more of a mess than it already was, Chumley said, "How about you both have a good, stiff drink? We might be trapped in here for a while, and fighting won't help us keep our heads. Do the Haa'la drink alcohol?"

Ashi'ii let out a sigh. "What do you have?"

Chumley eyed the contents of his minibar. "Bourbon,

whiskey, some red wine, and champagne. Oh, and tequila, but I'm not sure if I have any salt to go with it."

Ashi'ii took a sudden, recoiling step backward. "You drink *salt*?"

Perplexed, Chumley said, "It goes on the rim of the glass; adds a little flavor. I'm guessing it's not quite your taste?"

"My *taste*?" Ashi'ii looked appalled. "It's barbaric!"

"How so?"

Genuine fear glinted in her eyes, and she took another step in reverse. "Salt in its pure form is deadly. If it gets on my skin, or if I consume it, I'll dissolve." She swallowed. "Please do not use that information against me. I mean you no harm." As if to prove it, she knelt on the floor and bowed her head.

Chumley looked over at Dalton, whose mouth hung open in astonishment. "*That's* why the food at the base tasted so bad."

"I'll be damned," Cadu breathed.

Carolyn and Errin had fashioned a rudimentary stretcher out of supplies from the hardware store and carried the inert intruder down to the police station. The being lay out on the long table in the meeting room now, uncuffed, and Carolyn's cousin Monica had arrived a short while ago, bleary-eyed and blinking, to examine them.

"It's true," Monica said. "This is a Haa'la, most likely male. He'll probably wake up within the hour."

"The Haa'la," Carolyn said, uncertainly. "Aren't they the ones the Feds have been investigating?"

"For raiding alien worlds and stripping them bare, yes," Monica went on, shining a penlight into the Haa'la's amber-yellow eye. The pupil contracted, but the alien didn't stir. "I saw a special about it when I was off visiting Punam for a few weeks."

"They're the ones causing the fires, then."

"I'd bet money on it. The Haa'la specialize in mining and drilling and probably needed to clear some land up that way."

"They've been looting, too." Carolyn nodded at the alien. "This one was stealing from the hardware store."

"Not just this one," Cadu said. "One was in here, too. And there was the one you saw outside your flat."

"What can we do about this threat?" Carolyn asked.

"You're the boss," said Cadu. "You tell us."

"I know almost nothing about these people." Then, remembering what she'd asked Errin to retrieve earlier, she said, "Errin, do you still have that salt?"

"Oh! Yes." Errin dug in the pocket of their pajama bottoms and withdrew a salt shaker. "But I still don't understand what we need it for."

Fully aware of how un-Carolyn-like this would sound, Carolyn said, "Something happened to Gwendolyn Goldfarb that's caused her to know things she has no way of knowing. She knew the hotel would burn down, for one. And she told me that 'salt will win.' Now either she and I have both gone bonkers, or there's something to it."

Monica's eyebrows rose. "You really don't know much about the Haa'la, do you?"

"I already said I don't. Why?"

"Salt is deadly to them. They don't even swim in their

own oceans, because even though the salt is dissolved, it can make them extremely sick."

Carolyn returned her attention to the Haa'la. Monica had lifted his veil from his head and pulled off his shirt to get clearer readings from his heart. (Monica had reported that his pulse remained steady at forty beats per minute). His skin was ivory, like a bowlful of heavy cream, and long, recently-healed scars stretched across his abdomen, as if made by sharp talons.

"What do you think cut him up?" Carolyn asked.

Monica frowned at the old wound. "Based on the spacing between the cuts? I hate to say it, but our boy here might have survived a Green attack not that long ago. I saw some of the remains from Piney Gulch."

A subdued silence fell over the room. Fully aware of the increasingly late hour, Carolyn said, "Can we give him a shot of something and wake him up?"

"I'd rather let him wake on his own; I don't want to accidentally kill him with human drugs. We'd better get him strapped down, though."

Before Carolyn could reply, the Haa'la drew in a gasp and sat up, wide-eyed at first, but then his expression morphed into a sneer. "*Pip-pip! Go a'a shim himms.*"

"Catch any of that?" Cadu muttered, drawing his stun gun.

"He probably just told us to go to hell," Errin commented, taking half a step backward. They were still holding the salt shaker, and when the Haa'la's gaze went to it, he let out a shrill cry and tried to scramble off the table, not realizing his ankles had been bound together.

Cadu squeezed the Haa'la's shoulder with his free hand and shouted, "Cuffs!"

Errin snatched the metal cuffs off the table and slapped one side around the Haa'la's left wrist, then yanked his other arm around and secured the other one. "I said we shouldn't have taken these off in the first place."

"It would have made it too difficult to examine him with them on," Monica said. She'd backed closer to the wall, her stethoscope hanging askew around her neck.

Errin picked up the salt again. Their Haa'la prisoner regarded it as if it were a cobra that could strike at any moment.

"Do you speak English?" Cadu asked the prisoner.

The Haa'la's jaw clenched, and he muttered something in his own language.

Cadu tried again: "Você fala português?"

The Haa'la made no response.

"Let me try," said Monica. She looked to their prisoner and said, "Tuannu punjabi aundi hai?"

This didn't work, either.

"Well," Cadu said. "Does anyone else have any ideas on how we can talk to this guy?"

Carolyn knew rudimentary Punjabi as well, which wasn't going to help. She looked to Errin and said, "Have you got anything?"

Errin bit their lip, concentrated a moment, and said, "Xereis na milas ellinika?"

The Haa'la's eyes lit up, and he replied, "Naí."

Cadu looked equally stunned and impressed. "What the hell was that?"

Errin folded their arms, a trifle smugly. "Greek."

"You're not Greek!"

Monica said, "The alien speaks Greek?"

"Hush, all of you." Errin refocused their attention on the Haa'la and said something else in words nobody else in the room could understand. The Haa'la said something in reply, and the two of them carried on in that same manner for several minutes.

Finally, Errin cleared their throat and said, "His name is Shoru. He would like it if we removed the salt from his sight."

"People in hell would like a drink," Carolyn spat. Fatigue was getting to her, and her head was pounding. "How do the two of you happen to know the same language?"

Errin said something else to Shoru. Then, "I had Greek roommates at university. Shoru learned it at his old university, where students could study alien languages as electives."

"All right," Carolyn said. "Ask him what he's doing in my city."

"And ask him how many more Haa'la are lurking around here," Cadu added. "That might be kind of important."

"Of course." Errin started to interrogate the alien further, when suddenly three white-veiled figures materialized just inside the meeting room door, pointing weapons at them.

"Pip-pip! Release your prisoner," one of them said, taking one menacing step forward.

"Or what?" Carolyn asked.

"Or we will rain combustible acid down on your city, just as we did to the forests."

Carolyn raised her eyebrows. "You'd burn your comrade along with the rest of us?"

The English-speaking Haa'la fell silent, but only briefly. "We will do whatever must be done to ensure the success of Nydo Base Corporation."

"And what does Nydo Base Corporation do here?"

"We operate mines and drills. It is a profitable endeavor, but your people may be too stupid to know that."

Errin, meanwhile, was making discreet movements at the far edges of Carolyn's peripheral vision. Carolyn realized what they were doing and thought, *I ought to give them a raise.*

"You should leave us," Errin said, their tone uncharacteristically dark.

"Or what?" the Haa'la asked.

"Or you'll pay the consequences."

Errin had been carefully unscrewing the top from the salt shaker behind their back. They flung it forward now, scattering granules over the three newcomers, who were all completely veiled and gloved, which probably saved their lives.

The three of them screamed and dropped their weapons as they clawed at themselves, clearly expecting imminent demise even though the salt couldn't get through their clothing. While thus distracted, Cadu slid in and gathered their weapons into his arms, then turned the guns onto them.

"Pip-pip! Why have you done this to us?" the lead Haa'la wailed, sinking to their knees. "If we remove our clothing, the salt will burn our bodies beyond recognition!"

"Maybe you should have thought about that before you threatened my people," Carolyn said.

"You have effectively declared war on the Haa'la race! We will bring our acid and burn you to the ground!" With a trembling hand, the Haa'la reached for an alien-looking comm unit clipped to their belt, pressed a button on it, and shouted out incomprehensible words that probably meant nothing good.

Carolyn sighed inwardly as she braced herself for whatever came next.

Maybe she should have stayed in bed.

Dalton huddled in Chumley's swivel chair, wondering how long it would be before the three of them would have to resort to cannibalism for survival. Not that all three of them would be resorting to cannibalism—the strongest of the bunch would undoubtedly become the diner; and the weakest, the entrée. He'd already checked the cabinets and small refrigerator, finding little more than a box of whole-grain cereal, a stale loaf of bread, jelly, a packet of cheese, and some yogurt.

If they stretched it thin, it might last them a week.

They'd been in here over an hour already. Ashi'ii had gone out to the veranda to be alone, and Chumley had helped himself to so much of his minibar already that he lay on his bed, making incoherent noises and throwing yearning glances at the empty hamster cage.

Dalton had limited himself to one shot of whiskey, which he'd slowly been nursing while he awaited their doom.

I could be home right now working on a crossword puzzle, he thought. Truthfully, he wasn't sure what he might be doing otherwise, since he'd lost all sense of time since boarding Ashi'ii's vessel. It had been night, then. Perhaps dawn was breaking over Richport now, or perhaps the sun was setting. He imagined Carolyn standing in her office shouting orders at underlings, envisioned Cadu drumming his fingers on his desk while he waited for emergency calls, and thought of Errin patiently maintaining peace and order as crises tried to erupt around them.

He envied them all.

Dalton, you're moping again, Darneisha's voice said in his mind.

I don't care, he thought back at her. *You'd be moping, too, if you were trapped in another universe with a limited menu.*

He pictured her standing over him with folded arms. *You'll stay trapped there if you don't use your brain and think.*

I've BEEN thinking, he thought. *If I activate the doorway, all our air will get sucked out into space, killing us instantly. I . . . don't want to die.*

That's a first for you, isn't it?

Dalton didn't know what to say about that. He took a microscopic sip of whiskey and licked his lips. *How can we get out of this Cube?*

By opening the door, of course.

That isn't an option.

Then you'll have to be patient and wait until an option presents itself. You're the bloody sheriff of Richport. You've fought hardships and won. You can win this, too, if you believe you can. Do something.

Darneisha's voice fell silent. Of course it wasn't actually Darneisha, but her memories living inside of him and twisting his own conscience into shapes he didn't want to see.

You're the bloody sheriff. Do something.

Could he do something about this situation? He didn't feel that smart or clever. He'd just always done what needed doing, and managed to survive because of it.

What could he do, stuck inside a Cube?

He swiveled the chair around to face the security screen sitting on Chumley's desk and gazed longingly at the planet that lay so far out of reach below them. He wasn't sure if Leeprau was truly bigger on the screen than the last time he'd looked, or if it was just wishful thinking.

He scratched at his nose, which still hadn't fully healed from his sunburn, and he thought about how Chumley had popped out of his Cube, urging him and Ashi'ii to hop in. How had Chumley known they were in any danger? There was no way to hear what went on outside the Cube when you were shut inside it, unless Chumley had some other trick up his sleeve he hadn't mentioned yet.

And Dalton had only clumsily tugged the Cube out of Ashi'ii's pocket about two seconds before Chumley appeared, so he couldn't have seen anything, either.

Dalton cleared his throat. "Chumley?"

Chumley lifted his head a few centimeters off his pillow. "Hmm?"

"I have some questions."

"Urgh."

Dalton opened his mouth, paused, then said, "Do you even know where you are right now?"

"I'm in my *kyooooob*." Chumley giggled, then groaned. "I told you I got it as a reward for saving someone's cat, didn't I?"

"I think so."

"Well, actually . . ."

"Look, I don't care where you really got it from. I just need you to focus."

"I didn't *steal* it." Chumley rolled his eyes. "See, there was this man, Bryan, who worked on the prototype. Met him in a pub, and he'd drank so much, he told me all about it. I thought if I could get my hands on it, I could sell it and use the money on Gran's expenses. But he didn't have it with him. I had to . . . I had to make him want to give it to me. And he did, eventually, as a gift. Took months, and then I left him because the Cube was the only thing I'd ever been after."

"You didn't sell it, though."

"I couldn't—too much guilt. I thought about finding Bryan and giving it back to him because I felt so ashamed about what I'd done, but I found out he'd been killed in an explosion at the plant not long after I last saw him. So I kept it." Chumley winced and put a hand to his forehead. "Oh, biscuits."

He hobbled up from his bed, rushed into the bathroom, and began retching into the toilet. Ashi'ii poked her head in through the other doorway and said, "What's going on in here?"

"A little bit of regret, I think," Dalton said, wishing he had a sufficient way of tuning out the noises from the bathroom.

"Disgusting." She disappeared again, the woes of humanity evidently beneath her.

There came a flush, and Chumley emerged from the bathroom, wiping his mouth with the back of his hand. "Somebody shoot me."

"How did you know to come out of the Cube and save us?"

Chumley shivered and sat back down on his bed. "It was in my head. Like when I touched that Green? I saw things when I touched it, and I saw things now. Then, I mean. I think I'm gonna be ill again."

He darted back into the bathroom, if swaying uneasily could be called darting, and Dalton jammed his fingers into his ears.

When Chumley returned this time, he flopped onto his side on the bed and curled into fetal position. "I saw the ship exploding in my head. I don't know how I saw it. I don't know if I *want* to know how I saw it."

Dalton's skin prickled. "You're talking about precognition."

"Doesn't make any sense. There's no such thing."

"Gwendolyn Goldfarb?" Dalton reminded him.

"I thought she was a loony."

"I don't think so. She knew too much."

"So you're saying . . ." Chumley's forehead wrinkled. "You're saying Gwendolyn and I have the same magic power."

Dalton's pulse raced the more he thought about it. "It makes sense, right? Only Gwendolyn's mind isn't what it used to be, so she doesn't *know* she knows the future. She just spouts off the things she sees as she sees them."

"But how did *I* get this power? I don't want it!"

"A good thing you have it, though. This is the first time it happened to you?"

"Right."

"Gwendolyn was more or less normal before she got lost in the desert."

"Getting lost in the desert causes magical powers?"

"Think about it. What did you do out in the desert that you'd never done before? That hardly anyone has ever done, and lived to tell about it."

Chumley blinked.

"It has leaves," Dalton pressed.

"You don't ... really?" Chumley frowned. "Could Gwendolyn have touched a Green, too?"

"Maybe."

"But she's not dead."

"You're not dead, either."

"Hmm." It was almost painful, watching Chumley's inebriated brain struggling to formulate coherent thought. "Didn't you say a Green ate your arm?"

Dalton's shoulder made an involuntary twitch. "Yes."

"Then why didn't you gain superpowers?"

"I have the feeling it wasn't trying to communicate with me."

"So you're saying ... a Green tried to communicate with me using its mind-powers, and I developed mind-powers because of it?"

"I can't think of any other reason. Same thing must have happened to Gwendolyn."

Chumley put a hand over his eyes. "Somebody wake me up."

"You're awake already." Dalton flicked his gaze over to the veranda door. "So, could you maybe try to foresee how we get out of this?"

"Gravity." Chumley rolled over onto his side, facing the wall.

"Is that precognition?"

A soft snore issued from the ex-conman.

With an aggravated huff, Dalton turned back to the screen. Before, he'd seen a sliver of black space past the curving disk of Leeprau, but now the planet's surface filled the entire screen.

"Gravity," Dalton said. "Makes sense."

CHAPTER 20

While the Haa'la were preoccupied with avoiding Imminent Death by Salt, Carolyn, Monica, Cadu, and Errin rushed past them and slammed the meeting room door shut, wedging a chair under the knob for good measure.

"That won't hold them," Errin said matter-of-factly. "Teleportation, remember?"

Carolyn cursed. "It spares me from looking at them."

"Unless they teleport into here."

"We should sound the alarm again," Cadu said, worry etched in deep lines on his face. "You know they've just called for reinforcements."

"And they said they'll rain acid on top of us," Errin said.

"They can have their damned prisoner!" Carolyn cried. "I just want to be left in peace!"

Monica, who'd remained silent until now, appeared ashen. "I should go home and check on Gwendolyn. She was asleep when I left, and I don't like leaving her alone."

Carolyn nodded. "Go, then. And be careful."

"I'll let you know when I make it back," Monica said. "So you know I'm safe."

Monica turned on her heel and left the police station.

Cadu cleared his throat after a minute of silence broken only by the wailing Haa'la in the meeting room. "Um, Carolyn?"

"What?"

"I'm at a loss here."

"You?" She wanted to laugh, but didn't. "You're one of the most cool-headed people I know. It's why you have this job. Someone can lop their hand off, and you talk them through it like you're sharing a recipe."

"But this is different!" Cadu blurted. "These people are going to destroy our city! With *acid!*"

"It will take time for them to get here." Carolyn's mind raced with ideas. "We can go door to door and evacuate everyone."

"But Carolyn, they can *teleport.*"

She put a hand to her throbbing forehead. "Individually, they can teleport. Maybe their ships can't."

"We can't make that assumption! We don't know anything about their tech—for all we know, they've already got a ship hovering over us ready to dump its load!"

Carolyn had nothing to say. In her silence, she could still hear the Haa'la in the meeting room moaning in agony— perhaps they wouldn't teleport with salt on their clothes, not wanting to contaminate their brethren.

She could also hear something swishing.

"What's that?" She looked from Cadu to Errin, who appeared equally baffled.

The swishing grew louder. It sounded like a thousand people wearing windbreaker pants jogging in unison, and then it stopped.

Carolyn's comm unit exploded into life. "Carolyn? It's Monica. I'm home, but Gwendolyn's gone. Do you want me to see if she's gone home?"

"Stay where you are," Carolyn ordered, momentarily forgetting that Monica was a relative and not an underling. Her feet drew her toward the front of the police station, and when she stepped into the lobby, she could see out through the long, glass door.

She didn't remember dropping the comm unit to the floor, but that's where Monica's voice came from when she said, "What was that noise?"

"Carolyn, what's the matter?" Cadu asked, coming up beside her.

Carolyn couldn't speak. Outside the police station door, filling the entire street for as far as she could see, were Greens, arranged in rows like an army.

Gwendolyn Goldfarb stood in front of them facing the police station, wearing a bright orange shawl and a wide-brimmed hat to match it, even though the sun wouldn't be up for hours.

Gwendolyn turned to the crowd of Greens, said something to them that Carolyn couldn't make out, and then turned back to the door and knocked on it. "Can you let me in?" she shouted. "My mind is clear for the moment, but I don't know how long it will last. I have something important to talk about."

Carolyn looked at the Greens and thought, *You don't say*.

The surface of Leeprau was definitely closer now. Dalton studied a denser clump of civilization in the center of the screen while Ashi'ii leaned over his shoulder to get a better look.

"Do you recognize that place?" Dalton asked her.

"No."

"It's your planet."

"Do you know every square *kushkim* of yours?"

"I was just hoping that . . ."

He trailed off as Chumley waddled over to join them. "Wass goin' on?"

"Oh, you're alive," Dalton commented, refocusing on the screen. "Ashi'ii and I were trying to determine where we'll hit once we make landfall." A new thought struck him; one he didn't quite like. "Will we survive entering the atmosphere?"

Chumley rubbed at his mouth. "Don't know. The Cube survived the hotel fire. I guess it was designed to be heat-resistant."

"What's our plan once we hit the ground?" Dalton asked.

Ashi'ii straightened. "We will find passage back to Molorthia Six so I can help my people fight."

"Why not just evacuate?"

Ashi'ii gave him a withering look. "The Verdants have a head start and will likely be there soon, assuming they were able to hack into my ship's flight log. If we evacuate, we will simply be followed, and the Verdants will kill us elsewhere instead."

"So, it's easier if you stay and fight."

"That's right."

Dalton thought long and hard; a task which had never come easy for him. "We could negotiate some kind of deal."

"You have the authority to do this?"

"No, but I know the people who do. They might help

protect you from the Verdants if you promise to stop burning all the vegetation."

"Protect us, how?"

"We have flamethrowers and boomstones."

Her head tilted to one side. "Boomstones?"

"Maybe you haven't found them yet—there might not be any in the forests."

"What are they?"

"Exploding rocks; sort of a bronze color. You throw them, they explode on impact. We have a few warehouses full of them."

Ashi'ii contemplated this, then nodded. "You want us to stop burning the vegetation, though."

"We'll run out of air eventually. Come to think of it, you will too."

She gave him a look, and he remembered that the Haa'la did not breathe oxygen. So much for solidarity. "We can discuss this more once we've arrived on Molorthia Six and I've had the chance to speak to Nydo Base. Can we at least agree on that?"

She held out a hand. Dalton grudgingly shook it. "It's a deal."

Carolyn opened the police station door, and Gwendolyn strode inside, her cheeks flushed with exhilaration.

The Greens stayed put but gently swayed in place like a forest on a calm, summer night.

"What . . . ?" Carolyn struggled for words. "Is this?"

Gwendolyn's eyes gleamed. "I must speak quickly," she said. "Before the walls return. When I was lost, some of the People found me on their way across the desert to a place of worship. A few of them wanted to kill me, but the rest were curious and didn't think I posed a threat. I suppose even a plant can tell when something is dying."

Carolyn glanced at the Greens again and fought to keep her pulse at a steady pace. "They were going to a place of *worship?*"

"They're a deeply spiritual people, Carolyn. They still remember when we first came here—they thought demons had fallen from the sky to destroy them."

"They must live a long time."

"The ones who found me nursed me back to health as best as they could and let me go. Maybe they wanted to study me to know their enemy better."

"You're making them sound intelligent!"

"They assured me their tribe would not harm me or any other human again as long as we kept our peace. Other tribes are not as understanding as they are."

"And that—" Carolyn nodded at the gathered masses— "is the tribe you met?"

Gwendolyn bowed her head. "They sensed things were going badly here the day before the hotel burned to the ground and started heading this way. They had to veer off course to get around the sandstorm, but here they are, ready to help."

Carolyn had to be dreaming. Reality couldn't have been half as baffling. "How are they going to help?"

"They say there will be a battle here, and soon. They will fight on our side because we share a common interest."

Errin stepped forward then, their expression grave. "Gwendolyn, how do you communicate with them? They don't speak."

"Touch them, and you'll feel their minds. I don't think . . ." The old woman's voice trailed off, and her gaze went to the ground. "So many walls."

Carolyn cursed. "I think we've just lost her again. Errin, go bring her a chair."

Cadu gave a light cough while Errin complied. "Um. People are going to start noticing all the Greens out in the street."

"Yes."

"If Gwendolyn is right and this bunch here aren't going to hurt us, shouldn't we tell people to leave them alone?"

"Good idea." Carolyn could practically feel her mind buzzing. In ordinary circumstances, she would have dismissed Gwendolyn's claims about the Greens as mere fantasy, but the gathered tribe waiting patiently as if for orders lent some credit to those claims.

Touch them, and you'll feel their minds, Gwendolyn said.

"Cadu," she said evenly, "I'm going to attempt communication with these creatures. Do not harm them, no matter what you see."

"But Carolyn—"

"That's an order."

She drew in a deep breath and stepped outside.

Leaves rustled in the light, nighttime breeze. The nearest Greens to her were at least two and a half meters tall, and they'd trained their eyestalks on her.

"Hello?" she said, suppressing a shiver. "Which one of

you is in charge here?" She looked up at the tallest of the Greens in the front row. It had four arms and blue-green leaves that appeared faintly iridescent in the light of the streetlamps.

A shorter Green stepped out of the line and reached out one of its lower arms, as if in greeting. Carolyn ground her teeth together to stop them from chattering as she held out her own arm in turn.

The Green curled its fingers—were they even called fingers?—around her wrist, and it was as if someone switched on a movie screen inside her mind.

She no longer stood in the center of Richport. Instead, she was whisked into a forest teeming with alien life—winged insects the size of pillowcases fluttered past her head, and eerie cries filled the air as some unseen predator found its prey.

Four Greens knelt beside a stream, filling jars with water. A peculiar sound came from above, like the hum of engines, which made the Greens look up at the sky and drop their jars in terror.

The Greens ran deeper into the wood, and the image faded out into another, where two Greens huddled together as still as they could while two human women in old-fashioned military garb marched through the forest holding what looked like machine guns. Carolyn was nearly overwhelmed by the sheer, visceral terror that the Greens felt at seeing these aliens intrude upon their home as if they owned it.

Something scurried through the underbrush, and one of the women opened fire while the other laughed, and the image shifted again so Carolyn saw a human man swinging an axe at a motionless Green, which let out a bloodcurdling scream as its left leg was severed.

We must kill the demons that fell from the sky, Carolyn thought. She caught glimpses of ichor and blood, and understood.

She opened her eyes, and the Green let go of her wrist and stepped back into line with its kin. "Why do you want to help us after our ancestors were so cruel to your people?" she asked, and even though she no longer touched the creature, she had the sudden mental impression that these Greens were here to help because it was the right thing to do.

She went on: "You don't know the Greens who attacked our city the other day, do you? They killed several of our people."

A few of the Greens turned and looked at each other, somewhat cluelessly. Carolyn got the distinct impression that nobody from their tribe had harmed any human since they had studied the Gwendolyn. "The" Gwendolyn? Dear Lord, she was starting to think like they did.

"And what about Piney Gulch?" she asked. "Your people slaughtered many of my people. They weren't even hurting anyone." She pictured the gorge as best she could in case that might help.

Another impression intruded upon her thoughts, clear enough this time to form words: *the place which you imagine is holy ground to one of the northern tribes. We know of no massacre, but we would guess that tribe did not want intruders in their place of worship.*

Carolyn started to feel a trifle dizzy.

We will help you now because there is a grave threat to this planet. New demons will fall from the sky, and we will do our best to help you defeat them.

"Others of your kind killed my people. How can we trust that you'll leave my people in peace while we fight the intruders together?"

The tribes that harmed you were not part of our number. They may have panicked when their homes burned. Those who panic do not think with clarity.

A cry rose from down the street. "Greens!"

Carolyn tore her attention away from the tribe and broke into a run toward the voice. "Do not harm these people!" she shouted. "They're here to help us!"

Of course, the Greens could have been lying, but she couldn't see what they might gain by doing so. If they wanted to burn Richport to the ground, they would have started already.

Carolyn caught up to the human figure, panting. It was Jae Liu, who worked as a receptionist at the salon where Carolyn got her hair done. Jae wore a terrycloth dressing gown and an expression of abject terror.

"Jae," Carolyn said calmly, grabbing their arm, "if you shout again, I'm going to lock you in the nearest prison cell and throw the key into a sand dune."

The young androgyne tugged out of Carolyn's grip. "But they're *Greens!* I couldn't sleep after the siren went off, so I decided to go for a walk, and nearly walked into them!"

"They're not typical Greens, Jae. These Greens are going to help us fight the Haa'la."

"The what?" Jae blinked, and Carolyn cursed herself

for forgetting that the presence of the Haa'la was not yet common knowledge.

"Alien invaders. That's why Cadu sounded the sirens earlier tonight. More Haa'la may be coming soon, and these Greens will help us fight them off. If you don't want to fight with us, you should go home and bar the doors."

Jae let out a whimper, then turned tail and fled.

"Holy shit, look at *that!*"

Carolyn turned to see yet another citizen standing in the street, this one holding a flamethrower. "Remain calm!" she ordered. "Do not fire on these Greens!"

She wished Dalton were here. With the way her luck was bound to go, her own people were going to wipe out their allies before the battle even began.

CHAPTER 21

Dalton remembered a time long ago when he and his family—that was to say, his parents and his brother and himself—had gone to an amusement park.

TerrorWorld had held many wonders for the seven-year-old Dalton, including costumed characters who roamed the park and jumped out at you when you least expected it. There had been a funhouse maze done up in disorienting neon colors that glowed under blacklights, a haunted lake ride where zombies rose out of the water and lunged at your boat, and restaurants serving such delicacies as Shepherd's Die and Beans on Ghost.

Most terrifying of all, however, had been the Terror Drop.

Dalton had been tall enough to ride the coaster, but only by millimeters. The Terror Drop was the park's crowning achievement: it had, at one time, been the tallest roller coaster on Earth, and the first drop was steep to the point of being vertical.

There had been no question that he and Rob would sit in the very front car. He remembered the ominous *clack-clack-clack* as the train climbed to the top of the first drop, and that final, yawning moment before the ride released them and let gravity do the rest.

His young stomach turned inside out when the car plummeted straight downward into a hellscape complete with bursts of flame, mechanical demons, and lots of red smoke that stung his eyes.

Dalton felt much that way now, as the great, bloated sphere of Leeprau grew even closer on the screen. Chumley and Ashi'ii had gathered on either side of him to watch what would become either their demise or their victory.

This drop, unlike the roller coaster, was thousands upon thousands of kilometers in height. They were either going to make it, or they weren't.

Dalton swallowed, remembering that as soon as he'd gotten off the roller coaster, he'd ambled to the nearest dustbin and vomited. Funny, the things you remembered at times like these.

A burst of flame flared across the screen, and Dalton sat up straighter. "What was that?"

"We've entered the atmosphere," Ashi'ii said dryly. "If we were actually *inside* the Cube, we would be feeling extreme turbulence."

The image on the screen shook. Dalton wondered if anyone on Leeprau was looking up at the sky right then, commenting on the pretty meteor.

They were above the night side of the planet now, and Dalton's stomach clenched as he watched billions of lights below them spinning like flecks in an out-of-control kaleidoscope.

"Do you think we'll make a crater when we hit?" Chumley asked.

"Depends on where we hit," Dalton grunted, not wanting to let his companions know the extent of his fear. "If we land in an ocean, we'll make ripples."

Chumley's face grew long. "If we land in an ocean, we'll drown trying to get out."

"Better hit land, then. Wouldn't want the fish to eat us."

"Our fish do tend to be quite large," Ashi'ii said.

The image on the screen spun even faster.

"Or we could land in a volcano," Dalton said.

"I don't know if we have any active volcanoes on Leeprau at the moment," Ashi'ii said. "We'd be more likely to land in a factory smokestack. We could fall straight down into a furnace."

Chumley put his hands over his ears. "Stop, it, both of you!"

They looked at him. Dread glistened in his eyes.

"Are your magical powers telling you what's going to happen next?" Dalton asked.

Chumley's jaw clenched. "No."

"Then shut up."

His deputy's lower lip quivered, and he turned and went out onto the veranda, closing the door behind him.

Ashi'ii said, "We're almost there."

The spinning lights of the cities below them looked awfully large now. Not that the cities themselves were spinning; the Cube's wild trajectory just made it look that way.

Dalton gripped the edge of the desk with both hands. Ashi'ii gripped his shoulder.

They held their respective breaths.

The cityscape grew closer, closer, and . . .

The screen went black.

Some of the tension went out of Ashi'ii, and she released Dalton's shoulder. "I believe we have landed."

Dalton nodded and swallowed, grateful they hadn't felt the impact, which surely would have killed them. "We're on the ground!" he called to Chumley, who failed to reply.

Waiting around in here all day didn't seem an effective course of action, so Dalton rose, squared his shoulders, and slapped the button to activate the doorway. As soon as the holographic exit appeared, smoke wafted in and itched his eyes, just like the special effects from that damned roller coaster.

"Ready?" he asked Ashi'ii. Chumley still hadn't appeared, and the door to the veranda remained closed.

"Just go," she said, irritated. "If he wants to mope in there, let him."

Dalton shrugged and strode out of the Cube.

He brought a hand up to cover his mouth when he entered an acrid cloud that the Cube had stirred upon impact. Ashi'ii appeared behind him, then bent and picked up the Cube. "Take a look at that," she said, holding it out for Dalton to take.

Dalton goggled at the device. Its surface was as shiny and silvery as ever, giving no evidence it had just fallen from space as a fiery streak.

He hit the button on it to deactivate the doorway and stuffed it inside his pocket.

"Right," Dalton said. "Where are we?" He blinked to see through the smoke and spied several Haa'la onlookers cowering together in a small cluster. Various midsize buildings rose in the distance, and lights mounted on poles illuminated rows of parked vehicles.

"We are in a parking lot," Ashi'ii said, dusting herself

off. "And that is a supermarket." She pointed at the nearest building. The sign on the front had red, glowing letters that Dalton couldn't read.

Ashi'ii cursed.

"What?" Dalton asked.

"We've landed in Hedjka."

"What's that?"

"A country on the other side of the world from mine. I can barely string two sentences together in their language. I need to find a translator who can help me book passage back to Molorthia Six."

She strode toward the gathered Haa'la and said something to them in Haa'anu. They gave her blank stares, so she kept on going toward the nearest street.

Dalton started after her, feeling almost floaty in the lower gravity, then looked back at the massive dent the small Cube had put in the parking lot. "Sorry about the crater," he said to the Haa'la who were still watching him. "We didn't know where we'd land."

"Tik-tik! No worries, friend," one of them said. "Nobody was harmed."

"Well, that's good. Nice day." He took two more steps after Ashi'ii and halted as something vital clicked in his increasingly-weary brain. "Wait—Ashi'ii! Get back here!"

Two hours later, Dalton and Ashi'ii sat side by side in the cramped cabin of a ship they'd chartered at the nearest spaceport.

"It's a good thing you have money," Dalton commented as he snacked on the unsalted nuts that had been provided for them. "I never could have paid my way off your planet."

"I should be the one thanking you for having that Cube. You know," she went on, "I've never actually spoken with someone from one of our project worlds before."

"No?"

"Not even once." Her gaze went to the porthole beside her head. It provided a view of unbroken blackness. "I never planned on getting into this business. It was a family thing. Lots of us from Leeprau are part of family businesses. We go out into the galaxy, we mine worlds until they're spent, we profit. I've got operations running on three dozen backwater worlds. Nydo Base Corporation is the third most profitable of our type on Leeprau."

"Does it ever get boring?" Dalton asked.

"Oh, there's never a dull moment when money's coming in." Ashi'ii paused, reflectively. "Do you think he's ever coming out of there?"

"Pardon?" Dalton asked, thrown by the change in subject.

"Your friend hasn't come out of the Cube."

"Right. I'll check on him."

They were the only two passengers on the flight, so Dalton had no shame in setting the Cube on the floor beside their seats and activating the doorway. He went inside, noting that the door to the veranda was still closed and the drapes were still drawn over its windows.

He rapped on the door.

Chumley didn't open it.

With a sigh, Dalton swung the door open and stepped

"outside" to see Chumley sitting there with his elbows propped on his knees, staring morosely at the digital garden before him.

"We're on a ship headed back to Molorthia Six," Dalton said. "Care to join us?"

"I figured you were dead," Chumley said, his voice hollow.

"We had to charter a flight. It was cheaper with only two passengers."

Chumley's shoulders shook. "I thought it must have been so bad outside that I'd die if I went out there, too, so I stayed here so I could suffocate in peace."

Dalton scratched his head, uneasily. "Ah. How about you come out into the ship with us?" It was then that Dalton spotted wood shavings clinging to Chumley's sleeve. "What's that?"

Chumley looked where Dalton indicated, flushed, and swiped the shavings to the floor. "Nothing."

"Was that from your pet cage?"

"I suppose it must have been." Chumley peered back out at the digital garden, not meeting Dalton's gaze. "Maybe someday I'll tell you about the hamster."

After a short, awkward silence, Dalton said, "What do you think about the Haa'la fighting these Verdants?"

Chumley flicked at another wood shaving clinging to his sleeve. "I say let them duke it out, and we can go home and call it a day."

"Can't object to that." Dalton felt a sudden stir of unease. Humans were as alien to Molorthia Six as the Haa'la. If the Verdants didn't like the Haa'la doing business there, what did they think about the humans?

"What's that look for?" Chumley asked.

"I need to ask Ashi'ii something. Come outside with me."

They emerged into the Haa'la ship. Ashi'ii was tapping furiously at a datapad she'd purchased immediately before they'd chartered their flight, since her old one had exploded into smithereens along with the cargo ship.

"What are the Verdants going to do to us?" Dalton asked her.

She lifted her head. "What do you mean?"

"I know what they're going to do to you, but what will they do to my people?"

Her lips formed a thin smile. "Were you hoping they would leave you alone? They hate colonialism, and I know they'd even try to bomb all the humans off of Pelstring Four if they thought they could get by with it."

Horror wrote itself over Chumley's face. "Have they attacked humans before?"

"Not yet, but I know that if they had their way, they'd kill every human on every world but Earth, melt the cities into slag, and return the planet to its natural state. Even if my company had never landed on your planet, it would have only been a matter of time before they came for you."

"But you don't know that," Chumley said.

"I've heard the rumors circulating. Don't count on them being merciful to you."

"Do you know when we're due to land?" Dalton asked, his stomach aching with apprehension.

"To use your terms, it should be about two hours." She made a face. "The Verdants have such a head start, it might not even make a difference at this point." She stabbed a finger at the datapad screen and cursed in Haa'anu. "I'm trying to put a warning through to our main camp, but the data connection in here is too spotty."

"What can we do about all of this?" Chumley asked, shoving aside a few crates and sitting on the floor.

"We can allocate tasks so we know what we're doing once we've landed," Dalton said. He took his seat next to Ashi'ii and thought, hard. "We need to arm everyone in all our cities. When we land in Richport, I'll put a call through to all the other mayors and sheriffs. Just about everyone has a cache of boomstones and flamethrowers."

"Likewise, I will contact my company," Ashi'ii said. "We don't know where the Verdants plan to strike first, so we'll have to plan for every contingency."

"Wouldn't it be safer for your people to evacuate?" Chumley asked.

Ashi'ii gave him a look.

"And what am I supposed to do when we land?" Chumley went on. "I'm not even a proper deputy."

"I'm sure Carolyn will put you to work." Dalton looked to the black porthole again, wondering what the mayor's reaction to this mess would be.

I should have taken up accounting like Mother always wanted me to, Carolyn thought as she guarded the rear line of Greens massed in the street. More citizens had emerged from their homes holding weapons, and the rest peered out into the early morning darkness from behind the relative safety of their windows.

The sun would be up soon. She could already see the sky lightening in the east.

"Remain calm!" she shouted for the thousandth time. "Do not harm these Greens! They've come to help us fight more invaders who are on their way!"

It did seem somewhat surprising that the rest of the Haa'la hadn't arrived yet. Cadu had run out to her half an hour ago to report that the Haa'la they'd shut inside the meeting room finally teleported away. Perhaps they were gathering to discuss tactics before wiping Richport off the face of the planet.

Errin appeared from the direction of the police station. "We've just heard from the spaceport," they said. "Four ships just entered the Molorthia System. The ID codes are the wrong types for human ships."

Carolyn swore. She'd thought the Haa'la would send ships from their mining base to obliterate Richport, but no, they'd had to go and call for backup from offworld! "I want to see this for myself."

"What happens when they land here?" Errin asked.

"Our new allies will help us fight them." She wondered briefly if the Greens might be wrong in their prediction. It wasn't in her nature to trust man-eating plants.

"I'll stay here, if you want to go talk to the people at the spaceport," Errin said. "I won't let anyone hurt these Greens."

Carolyn dipped her head. "Very well." She turned from her aide and shivered as she started past the ranks of Greens, who were either awaiting a signal telling them what to do next, or they'd decided to plant themselves in the street.

She borrowed one of the quads from the police station and rode out to the tiny spaceport, three kilometers southeast of town. The sun peeked above the horizon as she passed through the perimeter gate, and she skidded to a stop outside the small terminal, where two citizens dozed on benches out front beside their suitcases, waiting for their flight.

Carolyn strode to the Employees Only entrance and let herself inside.

She rapped on the door to the Space Traffic Control room. "It's Mayor Kaur," she said.

"Come in," called a voice, so Carolyn let herself into the smallish room cramped with screens, a holographic model of the Molorthia System, and other equipment she couldn't identify.

A man and a woman sat in swivel chairs. Nametags identified them as Dev and Nydia. "I've been told you've picked up some anomalies," Carolyn said, nodding at the three-dimensional planets hovering in the center of the room.

"Yes." The middle-aged woman cleared her throat and sat up straighter. "These four objects—" She stuck her hand into the middle of the Molorthia System, where blinking blips stood out like misplaced stars— "appeared a short time ago, and they're headed straight for us. They've just passed the orbit of Molorthia Eight and should be here in about thirty minutes, if they maintain their course."

"Errin Inglewood told me you believe the ships are alien."

The man named Dev cleared his throat. "All ships registered on human worlds begin with the same three digits—it's what designates them as human, and another three digits after those indicate their planet of origin. The registration codes on all of these are completely different."

"We ran them through our database to get a better idea of who's on their way here," Nydia said, her expression grim. "They're from Leeprau. That's the home of—"

"The Haa'la." Carolyn swallowed, uncomfortable. "They're the ones who looted businesses overnight. Maybe you didn't hear about it."

Dev swiveled his chair back toward her. "That's what that was about?"

"We heard the sirens," Nydia yawned. "We figured it would be safer if we stayed here. We don't change shifts for another three hours."

Carolyn watched the blinking dots. "Is there a way to get a message through to them?"

"Yes, but they haven't been answering."

"We think it might be a language barrier," Dev added.

"Give me the comm," Carolyn said. "I'll talk to them."

It may not have been the right protocol, but she was tired, dammit, and she'd be damned if she'd let any alien invaders ruin the rest of her day.

Dev passed her a large comm unit with far more buttons than her own. "It's set on a broad frequency. If there's a ship anywhere in this system, they're going to hear you."

"Good." Carolyn cleared her throat and pressed the Speak button. "May I have your attention please? This is Mayor Carolyn Kaur, of Richport on Molorthia Six. I have received intel that you, the Haa'la, will be landing on my planet with bloodshed in mind, but be warned—we will not hesitate to fight. We have powerful allies. You will regret landing here."

She paused, waiting for a reply.

None came.

The four blips blinked ever closer to Molorthia Six, and as Carolyn watched, a fifth blip appeared at the edge of the system from the same direction.

CHAPTER 22

A voice crackled out of a speaker near Dalton's head, making him jump.

"What did they say?" he asked, looking to Ashi'ii, who appeared to be struggling to understand their captain.

"Her accent is very thick, but I think she said we've entered the Molorthia System. Chumley, you'd better get inside the Cube before I get charged for an extra passenger."

Chumley dipped his head and vanished through the holographic archway, which in turn vanished behind him.

Dalton tossed his snack wrapper into the provided waste can and buckled his seatbelt, wishing he'd gotten some sleep.

The descent to Molorthia Six was uneventful. The ship shook as it entered the atmosphere, and Dalton felt surprisingly homesick as the green and brown landscape grew larger and vaster below them.

Dawn broke over Richport when they touched down at the spaceport. Dalton stumbled out into the daylight, feeling clumsy in the stronger gravity of his homeworld, and when he looked out at the tarmac, Carolyn of all people stood there waiting for him, dressed in her pajamas.

Carolyn blinked.

Dalton blinked.

"What the hell?" Carolyn asked, taking a step closer to him. Belatedly, Dalton realized she was holding a stun gun.

"It's a long story," Dalton said as Ashi'ii stepped out beside him. The door to their chartered ship whooshed shut, and the silvery transport trundled around to the back of the terminal to refuel before its trip home.

Carolyn continued to goggle at him and Ashi'ii. "Where's Mr. Fanshaw?"

Dalton tugged the Cube out of his pocket. "He's in here."

Carolyn pursed her lips and looked to Ashi'ii once more. "Who are you?"

"My name is Ashi'ii Nydo." The Haa'la bowed her head. "I would like to speak to your leader so we can gain a mutual understanding."

"I'm Mayor Carolyn Kaur. You can speak to me."

"Oh, good. I was hoping that—"

"First things first. Four alien ships entered this system ahead of you and are currently in low orbit. Know anything about that?"

Dalton's gaze shot to the sky, but of course he couldn't see anything. "They haven't landed?" he asked, heart thudding in dread.

"Not yet." Carolyn raised her eyebrows. "I'm assuming they're scoping out the best places to dump their combustible acid."

Ashi'ii's expression grew stony, even for a Haa'la. "We need to find a place to sit down and talk."

"About that." Carolyn appeared suddenly uncomfortable. "Dalton, some things have happened since you went missing."

He narrowed his eyes. "Like what?"

"Let me see if the spaceport will lend us an empty room."

"Why can't we just go to your office?"

"It's not a good idea right now."

Dalton turned to Ashi'ii, shrugged, and followed Carolyn into the building.

"Now what the *hell* happened to you?" Carolyn asked after they'd shut themselves inside the tiny breakroom reserved for spaceport employees. A minifridge hummed in the corner, reminding Dalton he was due for a hearty breakfast.

"Just one minute." Dalton eyed a legal pad and a pen, scrawled *You can come out now* onto it, and held it in front of the Cube, which he'd gently set on the breakroom table as soon as they'd gotten there.

"I really don't understand how—"

The holographic archway glimmered into life, and Chumley stepped into the room, smelling freshly-showered. "Did anyone miss me?" he asked, taking an empty seat and stuffing the Cube away out of sight.

Carolyn's mouth hung open. Slowly, she closed it and cleared her throat. "You have less than sixty seconds to explain what happened to you."

Dalton glanced to Ashi'ii, who nodded. "The sandstorm destroyed our transport," he said. "We were stranded. The Haa'la found us and took us prisoner. They've been mining up in the forests and burning off the vegetation to drive out the Greens. We tried to escape, things went wrong, and now the Verdants are here to destroy anyone who isn't native to Molorthia Six."

"Who are the Verdants?"

"They're Haa'la, like me," Ashi'ii said, looking resigned. "They consider themselves 'eco warriors' and try to undermine what my company and others like mine do."

"Meaning what?" Carolyn asked. If her eyes narrowed any further, they'd be shut.

"Say a company like mine comes to a planet and mines out most of the minerals. It's simply unavoidable that the environment is going to be damaged in the process."

"It would be avoidable if you didn't go there in the first place," Chumley sniffed.

"Nydo Base Corporation does not go public with the locations of its project planets," Ashi'ii said, ignoring him. "Mostly it's to avoid competitors moving in and fighting over resources. We typically select backwater planets where no one will bother us, but it's hard to completely avoid detection in a galaxy as populated as this one. The Feds learned what my competitors and I have been doing and declared us among the galaxy's Most Wanted for 'crimes against nature.' As if others haven't done worse."

Carolyn frowned. "And these Verdants were sent by the Feds?"

"Oh, no. They're a separate entity. The Feds would only like to see us imprisoned, whereas the Verdants . . ." Ashi'ii shivered. "When the Verdants locate a project planet, they destroy the mines, execute the workers, and clean up any damage that might have been done."

"And they want to do that here?"

"I'm sure of it. And if four ships are in orbit already, it

means they're scanning for strategic sites to attack—and they'll destroy your people, too, along with mine."

"But we haven't done anything!" Carolyn blurted, face red.

"You live here. That's crime enough for them."

Carolyn muttered a few four-letter words.

Dalton made an effort to keep his expression neutral.

Ashi'ii rose, her face grim. "I need to contact my people." She patted her pocket, withdrew a communication device, and began speaking in Haa'anu.

With Ashi'ii thus engaged, Carolyn turned back to Dalton and said, "There are Greens in town."

Her words hit him like a punch to the gut. "What?"

"I'm just warning you. They aren't hurting anyone. In fact, Gwendolyn Goldfarb vouches for them."

Dalton wondered if his brain had suddenly lost the capacity to translate human speech into meaning. "What?" he said again as a high-pitched tone began ringing in his ears.

"It seems Gwendolyn communed with a tribe of Greens when she was lost in the desert. She developed the ability to speak with them. They warn us of a battle and came to help."

"Greens are helping . . . us?" Dalton gripped the edge of the table to stop the room from swaying, but the next thing he knew, he was on the floor again, and Chumley was proffering him a bottle of water.

"Took a bit of a spill there," Chumley said, helping him sit up.

Heat blossomed over Dalton's cheeks. He yanked the bottle out of Chumley's hand and chugged it down in one gulp, then shakily returned to his seat.

Ashi'ii was still speaking on her device, and now Carolyn was doing the same with her comm unit. Seeing that Dalton had regained his senses, she ended her call and said, "Are you well enough to work, Sheriff?"

He shook himself. "You put me on indefinite leave."

"And I just so happen to need you. That was Errin. I forgot to tell you, the Haa'la from Nydo Base have declared war on Richport. Their first ship has been sighted coming over the horizon."

"I'm trying to tell them to stop!" Ashi'ii howled in frustration. "We have to fight the Verdants, not each other!"

"*Trying* to tell them?" Carolyn asked.

"They're taking matters into their own hands after these ... these human *scum* threw salt on some of my employees!"

Carolyn did an admirable job of keeping her composure. "Did you tell them the Verdants are here?"

"Yes! They said they will deal with them after they've dealt with the humans."

"Are they really going to dump combustible acid on Richport?"

"There's only a little bit left—it's on backorder and we're waiting on a new shipment to come in from Leeprau. By the sound of it, their fight is going to be more up close and personal."

Dalton got to his feet. "I've got to arm the citizens. Chumley, come with me."

He strode out the door, if trembling in his boots with every footfall could be called striding. Events blurred, and the next thing he knew, he and Chumley were riding a spaceport rental quad toward town, the wind riffling his hair.

He wondered where he'd left his hat this time.

Once they'd crossed into Richport proper from the open desert, Dalton could see that things were amiss. Hundreds of citizens clogged the streets, some of them making attempts to flee in vehicles that couldn't move due to the others blocking their way. Dalton and Chumley had to abandon the quad outside a candy shop on Cactus Street and run to the police station on foot.

As they neared the station, Dalton drew up short.

An uncountable number of Greens stood in the street. Cadu, Errin, and a few others stood at the perimeter of the gathered mass, trying to keep a bloodthirsty crowd back. Had these Greens actually come to help, or was it a trick?

Would this soon become a four-way battle—human versus Green versus Haa'la versus Verdant?

Spots flashed in his vision. He shook his head and tried to breathe, then continued forward.

Somehow he made it inside the station, and Cadu was suddenly standing with him and Chumley, panting. "Dalton? How did you get back here?"

"We need to arm everyone," Dalton croaked. He didn't feel fully connected to himself, like his eyes were ten million miles away watching the proceedings on a screen. "Errin says a Haa'la ship is almost here?"

"We're assuming that's what it is. It came from the north."

"More will be coming."

"What?"

Dalton hurriedly explained the situation with the

Verdants, and when he'd finished, Cadu said some words Dalton didn't think he'd ever heard the man say before.

"Dalton, we need to hurry," Chumley said, peering out one of the windows into the street.

Dalton closed his eyes, counted off ten seconds, and opened them. "We have to get to the weapons cache and arm everyone capable of fighting."

Cadu nodded, his lips drawn tight. "I'll do that. You can let the people know what's going on, since you seem to know a lot more than I do."

Shouts outside drew Dalton's attention to the glass door. A few of the people lingering at the edge of the gathered Greens were pointing at the sky.

Cadu hurried out the door without another word. Maxine of the City Watch peeled herself from the throng and followed him.

Chumley took one step closer to Dalton. "What are we going to do?"

"I was never supposed to be the sheriff," he said, more to himself than to anyone else. "I was a florist. People were happy with flowers. Flowers never hurt anybody."

"We've got to *do* something . . ."

In his mind, Dalton saw himself inside his old greenhouse, cutting the tulips and carnations he'd planted and arranging them just so in decorative ceramic vases that Darneisha made in her kiln and then painted. Imani and Kendra would play on the floor, picking up any petals that had dropped and sticking them into each other's hair.

"I was never supposed to do this," he said again. "I just needed a job. Sheriff seemed easy. Nothing ever happens in

Richport. It's the most boring place in the whole fecking universe."

Now Chumley was standing in front of him with his hands on his hips. "I was never supposed to be the deputy, either, but here I am."

"And here you are," Dalton said. "Just as useless as me."

"I don't know that I'm useless," Chumley said. "You know how I've survived this long?"

"By being a liar?"

"By being *adaptable*."

"All right," Dalton said. "How are you going to be adaptable right here, right now?"

Chumley put a finger on his chin. "When the ships land, I can disable their engines."

"And how, pray tell, will you do that?"

"There are things I haven't told you."

"Let me guess. You got paid to undergo scientific experimentation to help pay for your Gran's expenses, and now you can turn invisible."

"Not invisible, no."

Dalton folded his arms. "I don't have time for this. I need to go out there and start a fecking *war*, and your cryptic bullshit isn't going to help me or anyone else one fecking bit."

Chumley frowned at him. "My cryptic bullshit might be important. I want you to watch something. But back here, where no one can see."

Dalton supposed he should humor his deputy, because it kept him from going back outside.

"We'll go in my office," he said. "This way."

Once inside the office, Chumley closed the door and said, "I don't want you to harm me."

Dalton tensed. "Why would I do that?"

"Because I'm going to do something you won't expect."

"I might just harm you if you don't hurry up and tell me what's going on."

Chumley smiled, but only briefly. "Very well." He scrunched his eyes shut, and there came a sudden twisting of his features that made Dalton's head spin.

The next thing Dalton knew, a pile of men's clothing lay on the floor, with no Chumley inside them. He leaned forward, too stunned to comprehend the implications of this, when a hamster of all things wriggled out of the fabric and sat back on its tiny haunches to peer up at him. It had a white body and a light brown head, with one light brown patch near its rump.

"You have got to be fecking kidding me," Dalton said.

The hamster's pink nose twitched. Dalton squatted down and held his hand beside the rodent, and it stepped into his palm. The creature felt warm and soft, and Dalton resisted the urge to stroke it.

He held it at eye level. "Is that really you in there?"

The hamster nodded.

"I've heard about shifters," Dalton said. "Rich folks pay for the ability on the black market. It's illegal on just about every settled world."

The hamster let out a short squeak.

"But you didn't pay for it."

The hamster's head shook.

"They paid you?"

It nodded.

"Because you needed to help your Gran."

Another nod.

Dalton felt a grin stretching across his face. "Turn yourself back into you so we can discuss our next steps. I won't watch."

He set the hamster on the floor and turned the other way. He heard a squelching noise like something stretching, and Chumley said, "Not just yet, let me get my trousers on . . . you can look now."

Dalton turned back to him. Chumley remained barechested and held his shirt draped over one arm.

"Shifting has been around for decades," Dalton said. "Read about it when I was a boy and dreamed of turning myself into a bird to get away from my brother when he annoyed me too much." He paused. "Why would they have needed to experiment on you when the tech exists already?"

"They were working on transformations into smaller animals. Always before it had to be something roughly human-sized—something to do with mass redistribution. They gave me the experimental gene therapy, and about five thousand pounds less than they'd promised me."

"I saw a hamster in the hangar at the mining base."

Chumley raised his hand. "Hello."

"But . . . you have a cage and a wheel and everything. That's for you?"

"Whenever I'm stressed I, well, I go in there and run. It's very relaxing."

Dalton rubbed at his eyelids. "So, you're going to hamster

your way into the Haa'la ships and what, chew the wiring to bits so they can't leave?"

Chumley shrugged. "It might work."

"What benefit does that give us?"

"It gives us the chance to keep them prisoner here."

"I'd rather scare them away and have them never come back."

A wrinkle appeared in Chumley's brow. "Can an army of Greens and a few thousand inexperienced humans do that?"

"I don't know."

"Say we run them all off. What's to stop them from coming back with reinforcements?"

The sound of a door banging open spared Dalton from answering. To his utmost horror, Summer Kane of all people appeared in his office doorway, her eyes gleaming with murder.

"Someone in the street told me you came back," she croaked. Her strawberry blonde hair looked wild, like she hadn't brushed it in days.

"It's nice to see you, too," Dalton said.

His former sister-in-law stepped nearer to him, a blue gem twinkling from its chain around her neck. "I knew you weren't dead when they said you were missing. I knew it in here." She thumped her chest with one fist. "You're the last one. I would *feel* it if you died."

"I'm glad you believed in me. Now if you'll just—"

"But you know what I didn't know would happen?" She stepped even closer, forcing Dalton to scoot back against the wall while Chumley watched in grim amusement.

"What?" Dalton asked, because he honestly had no clue.

Summer dug into the pocket of her long skirt and withdrew a crinkled paper, which she smoothed out and held in front of Dalton's face.

It was an invoice.

Dalton read the line items and the prices, and winced.

"You had the motorhome towed back here to be fixed," he said, hardly believing she'd gone to the trouble.

"Are you going to help me pay for this?"

"Summer, I really don't have the time right now. You may have noticed the plant army?"

A commotion outside made both their heads turn. The door to the police station swung open, and someone shouted, "Sheriff, get out here!"

"Just a minute!" He focused his attention back on Summer. "We can talk about the bloody motorhome if we survive this."

Her face paled. "We've got to survive this. We have to, me and you, because that's what we do."

Dalton felt his jaw stiffen. "You're right. So go home and stay there. You live far enough outside of town that you might be safe. Where's your quad?"

"In the public lot. I drove into town early to pick up a few groceries and saw the Greens." Her eyes watered. "I don't know if I can get back there in time now."

"Then take one of the quads out back. We usually keep the keys in the ignition. And hurry!"

She stepped away from him and gave him a lingering look containing more emotions than Dalton could interpret.

"Sheriff, *please* get out here!" the voice cried again from the lobby.

"Go," Dalton said to Summer. "Take the quad, and don't look back."

Summer drew in a deep breath, nodded, and hurried out the back door.

Then Dalton turned and strode toward the front entrance.

Going outside was the last thing in the world Dalton wanted to do.

He did it anyway.

He was the sheriff, after all.

"What's happening now?" Dalton asked no one in particular.

"The ship just landed on the west end of town," said a young man with a mohawk, who held both a donut and a cup of orange juice, as if the coming spectacle was just some light morning entertainment and not potentially the end of all human life on Molorthia Six. "And those just showed up."

The young man pointed with the hand holding the donut, but he didn't need to. There was no overlooking the four gleaming ships that hovered a kilometer above the ground northeast of town. They were all round, like giant saucers.

If the Verdants were going to dump combustible acid on them like the Haa'la mining company had originally planned, then there was no point in fighting. The good citizens of Richport and their apparent leafy allies might as well curl up on the spot and wait for the fire to consume them.

But combustible acid might damage the environment, a little voice muttered somewhere in Dalton's exhausted mind.

So do bombs, Dalton thought back at it.

He wished he could send a message to the Verdants so he could beg for everyone's lives.

He wished he had an air conditioner in his house, too, but wishing wouldn't get him one.

Movement near his feet made him look to the ground. A hamster hunched there, peering up at him.

Dalton cleared his throat and said, "Where on the west side of town did the ship land?"

"Looked like near the quad dealership," said the young man with the orange juice and donut. "Or thereabouts."

"Thank you," Dalton said, and scooped the hamster into his pocket before it could make a run for it.

He hurried inside the station and out the back door, where one remaining quad sat alone. Hoping the battery had finally been charged, he hopped on the closest quad and gunned it down the back street that thankfully wasn't clogged like the one out front.

Dalton made two jarring turns and screeched to a stop when he spotted a silvery Haa'la ship sitting atop its landing gear beside the dealership, where dozens of new and used quads sat in dusty rows waiting to meet their buyers. He dug in his pocket until he felt something squirming, and withdrew the transformed Chumley, who chittered at him.

"Sorry," Dalton said. "I didn't want you to get trampled trying to run here on your own. Now see that ship?" He pointed. "Go do your worst to it—and try not to get hurt."

The hamster cocked its head.

"I don't want to have to find a new deputy already, that's why." He set Chumley on the ground. "Now, go! I don't care that these are Ashi'ii's people. They're Haa'la, and we can't trust them."

The hamster gave him a long look before turning tail

and scurrying off in the direction of the Haa'la ship. The gangplank had already been lowered, and at least two dozen veiled Haa'la stood outside, holding guns that looked a bit more menacing than the one they'd tranquilized him with out in the desert.

He wondered if Kedd or Maasha were among them. It was hard to tell with everyone dressed the same.

We would fight, Maasha had said when Dalton asked her what she would do if someone came to her planet and set it aflame. If she could admit that, would she understand that the humans of Molorthia Six were simply doing what they had to in order protect their own? Could she or any of the other Haa'la find enough empathy within themselves to call off the battle and leave?

He doubted it. Good fortune did not happen to Dalton Kane.

I've got to do something, Dalton thought when Chumley had vanished into the distance. Well, he could help Cadu and Maxine pass out weapons. That was something, right?

He took the quad to the warehouse where the city stored all the boomstones that the wind unearthed in the open desert. Cadu had slid up the giant bay door and was carefully lifting boxes off of shelves and passing them to Maxine, who in turn passed them to another volunteer who handed them out to a motley assemblage of citizens who had lined up outside.

"What are you doing here?" Cadu asked, hefting yet another box of explosive rocks off a shelf. "I thought you were organizing things at the station."

"I'm here to help you arm the people. The ship from

the mining base landed by the quad dealership, and they're already disembarking. Chumley is going to sneak inside and disable the ship so they can't leave."

"So we'll be stuck with them. Great. Here, you can bring down more boxes. Carefully, though, we don't want you to lose a limb." Cadu winced. "I mean, sorry."

"Don't worry about it." Dalton kept his expression neutral as he went to the nearest metal shelf and grabbed a sturdy wooden box off of it. Dozens of misshapen bronze stones nested inside, looking far too innocuous to be weaponry.

More citizens were lining up in front of the warehouse— someone in town must have been sending them their way. "Here," Dalton grunted, bypassing Maxine and the other volunteer and approaching the next person in line. "Take as many as will fit into your pockets. Just don't blow yourself up. That's right . . . there. Next!"

It was tedious work. He retrieved four more crates over the next ten minutes, his dread steadily building and making him wonder when he would pop.

After his most recent crate had been emptied, Dalton looked up at where the four Verdant ships had been, only to realize they must have landed.

He grabbed another crate of boomstones.

Carolyn fled the spaceport with Ashi'ii, who held on for dear life as Carolyn gunned the quad as fast as it would go.

"I'm so sorry," Ashi'ii kept saying. "Nothing like this has ever happened on one of my project worlds before."

"I'm assuming that's because you were too busy killing the locals to have anyone bother killing you," Carolyn said.

"We never killed the locals! Put them to work, yes, but never killed!"

"So the Greens just died all by themselves?"

"They're plants!"

Carolyn had to park the quad four blocks away from the army of Greens because the streets were so clogged, she couldn't get through. "Now go find your company and tell them not to be fools about this. We will *help* them if they agree to help us fight these Verdant people."

"I understand." Ashi'ii climbed off the quad and growled orders into her comm unit, ignoring the stares she'd begun receiving as soon as they came into view.

Carolyn wished she could stay with the alien to make sure she didn't attempt any treachery, but she needed to meet up with Dalton and discuss tactics. She almost laughed. Like she knew anything about tactics. The most tactical things she'd had to endure as mayor were budget meetings.

"Excuse me," she said, nudging her way through a throng of gawkers armed with flamethrowers. "Pardon me." She relaxed on her nudging a bit when she noticed several people holding boomstones. They'd already started unloading the weapons cache? Good.

She finally made it to the waiting army of Greens. Clearing her throat, she approached the one that had communed with her earlier and said, "May I speak with you again?"

The plant stepped forward. *Things have changed.*

"What?"

Our presence here has changed things.

"Is that good or bad?"

If we had not come, you would already be ablaze.

Carolyn thought of something as speckles of sweat condensed on her brow. "If your people have this kind of precognition, how is it the Haa'la—the new invaders—were able to hurt your kind? Shouldn't you have known about it ahead of time and escaped?"

Many did escape. Some remained in denial and refused to leave until it was too late. This too happened when your own people first landed among us.

Ah, Carolyn thought. *Typical.*

"So, what do we do now? How do we get the miners and the Verdants to leave us alone?"

You will fight them. We will help.

"But how? What should our strategy be?"

We will fight together.

Carolyn had the sudden desire to run her fist through something solid. She needed so badly to talk to Dalton. He was probably over at the boomstone warehouse, distributing the tiny bombs that were their only shot at survival.

She called him on her comm. "Dalton? We need to talk ASAP."

She got no response. It occurred to her that he might have lost his own comm when he was kidnapped by the Haa'la miners.

Errin stood nearby, remaining alert as they kept an eye on the humans armed with flamethrowers. "Dalton went to see where the Haa'la landed," they said to Carolyn without taking their gaze from the armed citizens who probably wanted to torch the Greens.

"And where is that?"

"West of town. Near the quad dealer, someone said."

"I thought he was going to help arm everyone!"

"Maybe he went there next."

Carolyn had already started dialing in Cadu's number before Errin finished their sentence. "Cadu! Is Dalton with you?"

"Yes ma'am," Cadu said.

"I need to speak with him."

"Just a sec—here."

"What?" Dalton growled. "I'm busy."

"We need to discuss how we're going to conduct this battle."

"I thought I was supposed to distribute weapons."

Carolyn breathed in deeply. "Yes, but I need your help."

There came a long pause. "And you're asking me."

"I don't know what to do, Dalton."

"That makes two of us."

"Well, maybe if you and I meet and put our heads together, we'll think of something."

Dalton's laugh sounded hollow. "Right. Where should we meet?"

CHAPTER 23

A subtle shift seemed to be occurring among the gathered citizens, Dalton noted as he steered the quad back to the street behind the police station. Those already armed were arranging themselves into ranks without anyone telling them to, and they had a tense, expectant air that made him worry they'd start lobbing their boomstones at the slightest provocation.

Carolyn waited for him in the main office area, sitting at Cadu's desk and tapping one foot nervously on the floor.

She was still in her pajamas.

"Where's Chumley?" she asked.

"Disabling a Haa'la ship." His gaze went to Cadu's desk, on which the emergency operator had posed action figures from one of his several dozen favorite films. "Maybe you should have asked Cadu to come back here instead of me. He might have picked up something useful in a movie."

"You'll excuse me if I don't think that movie battles and actual battles might have anything in common," Carolyn said. "For one, people in movie battles tend not to die for real. How are we going to organize them?" She jerked her head in the direction of the main entrance to the station.

Dalton sank onto an empty chair and put his head in his hands. "We can split them into groups."

"Okay. Then what?"

"There can be a distraction. Make the Haa'la think all the humans and Greens are in one place, while we send smaller groups around the back to catch them by surprise."

Carolyn perked up. "That's actually a good idea."

"It is?"

"Hell if I know. I'm running on no sleep." She looked down at herself and seemed just now to realize she was wearing a paper-thin top and flannel pajama shorts that barely reached a quarter of the way down to her knees. "Oh, dear God."

"If it makes you feel any better," Dalton said, "half the folks outside are still in their pajamas, too."

"Just what we need." Carolyn rubbed her eyes. "A sleep-deprived army. Do you still have any of that garbage coffee around here?"

Dalton pointed at the door to the meeting room. "Help yourself."

"Gladly." She rose and disappeared through the meeting room doorway.

Dalton felt briefly lost, then said, "I'm, er, going to go out and talk to the people." He thought about the best way to go about doing that, then remembered how Old Man Sondhi, the previous sheriff, would go to the roof anytime he needed to make important announcements, which usually involved letting the citizens know about the upcoming town potluck.

He dug an ancient bullhorn out of a closet in the back hallway, ascended the dusty stairwell to the roof, and strode across it until he stood above the street where the Greens and humans had gathered.

He cleared his throat and held the bullhorn in front of his face. "Ahem. Excuse me. This is Sheriff Dalton Kane speaking."

They know who you are, you dolt, he thought. *Just get on with it.*

"We, um, want to take the Haa'la by surprise. So we need to split everyone into groups. If your last name begins with A through M, stay here, in front of the station. If your last name begins with N through S, meet in the street behind the station. If your last name begins with T through Z, meet in the town square."

Several hundred citizens and plants stared up at him. Then the humans got moving, like a tide separating from itself.

The Greens remained in place, the gazes from their eyestalks locked onto him. He tried not to feel dizzy; these Greens hadn't killed anyone yet. Did they know the difference between a human and a Haa'la? It might be hard to tell, for a plant.

Once his citizens had gone to their respective meeting places, Dalton strode toward the back of the station and eyed the two hundred or so people comprising the N through S group. About half of them were armed already, either with flamethrowers or boomstones.

He spoke into the bullhorn again. "Those of you without weapons, go to the weapons cache, arm yourselves, and come straight back here to await your orders."

He went to the front of the building and repeated that command to the larger group gathered there. Then he hurried back down the stairs and out to the street, ignoring the walking plants as best as he could, and made it to the town square.

Pleased to see that nobody had yet taken down the stage they'd assembled for Frontier Care United, he hopped up onto it and repeated his command yet again to the T through Z group.

Back at the station again, Dalton found two comm units and put them into his pockets. Carolyn sipped at a mug of steaming coffee and grimaced.

"I've divided everyone into three groups," he said to her.

"I know," she said. "I have ears."

"You should take charge of one of the smaller groups. We can be in contact with each other at all times."

"There's something you're forgetting." Carolyn chugged the rest of her coffee in one gulp and shivered. "You didn't tell the Greens what to do."

"I can't exactly divvy them up by last name now, can I?"

"No, but you can let me talk to them before I take charge of a group. Do you have any spare flamethrowers around here?"

"Hall closet," Dalton said.

"Good." Carolyn disappeared a moment and came back with a weapon nearly as long as she was tall. "I'll take charge of T through Z and see if Errin won't take N through S."

She strode out the door without another word. Dalton hurried back up to the roof. From his position above the town, he could catch the slightest glimpse of the Haa'la miners' ship out by the quad dealership.

He couldn't see the Verdant ships. Too many buildings stood in the way.

Directly below him, Carolyn was having a one-sided conversation with the Greens. Then, as if it had been choreographed beforehand, the plants broke into three separate groups, the two smaller ones migrating toward their human counterparts.

Dalton had to close his eyes to spare himself the sight, but all he could see behind his lids were a picnic shelter and playground area splattered with blood and dismembered limbs, so he opened them again and stared up at the sky.

His comm crackled, making him jump. He could see Carolyn down below, looking up at him. "Dalton, Ashi'ii just contacted me. *Do not* send anyone to attack the Haa'la miners. I repeat, *do not*."

He breathed out the tiniest sigh of relief. "They're going to cooperate with us, then?"

"That's what she says."

Dalton paused. "I don't believe it."

"On second thought," Carolyn said, "I'll take my group around behind the miners and keep an eye on them. Just in case."

"Pip-pip! You had no right to ally yourself with the humans! Do you have any idea what these people *did*?" Kedd screamed.

Ashi'ii stood with folded arms before more than a dozen dozen of the most able-bodied employees from Nydo Base. They'd gathered in a dusty street not far from where they'd parked their ship and had armed themselves with the weaponry they'd originally used to keep the Greens at bay before realizing the Greens were immune to the blasts.

She'd been told that the remaining forty-eight dozen members of her workforce had taken cover, hoping that the Verdants' scanners wouldn't find them.

"Pip-pip! The humans outnumber us," Ashi'ii said. "We need to band together to stop the Verdants from killing everyone on this planet."

"Pip-pip! Humans threw salt on Jakaaki, Mishnam, and Florvis. And you want them to live?"

Ashi'ii felt a stab of hatred toward the humans, having to remind herself that Dalton and Chumley had been with her and weren't responsible for such an infraction.

"Pip-pip! I've been listening to their comm calls out in the desert day after day," Kedd went on. "They are the most boring, vapid, and insipid beings I've ever had dealings with. They speak of nothing useful, but if left to rally together, they will murder us all with salt."

Ashi'ii turned back toward the town. She couldn't see any humans from her current position. She couldn't see where the Verdants had landed, either, which made her more nervous by far. How many Verdants were there? Could her miners overpower them?

"Pip-pip! We absolutely must work with the humans," Ashi'ii said.

"Pip-pip! Never! We attack the Verdants first, and then the humans. This is not negotiable."

"Pip-pip! Don't forget who is in charge here."

Kedd moved his veil aside and glared at her. "Pip-pip!

You are in charge at the base. Here, I can do what I please. I advise you not to get in my way."

Dalton called Errin's comm. "Errin, take your group out and around town and try to sneak up on the Verdants from behind."

"I don't know how much sneaking we'll be able to do, when half of us are plants."

He closed his eyes and counted to five. "Sometimes I think you have too much common sense for your own good."

"Just trying to keep everyone alive." They lowered their voice. "And just so you know, this isn't easy for me, either. My sister is still in the hospital after the attack at the hotel."

"Sorry to hear that."

"If we can keep the Verdants' attention fixed on the town, they may not notice my group coming up behind them."

"How do we do that?"

"We'll have to consider the resources we have available."

"We don't have any resources!"

"We have to come up with something. A lot of lives depend on it."

There was no arguing about that. Dalton looked back down at the A through M group below him and spotted Lennox McTavish and Gurmeet Singh standing among them, huddling close to each other and looking as if they'd rather be a few kiloparsecs away by now.

Dalton held the bullhorn in front of him. "Mr. Singh. Why didn't you join the N through S group?"

Gurmeet jumped and peered up at him. "Because if I'm going to die today, it will be with Lennox." He grabbed Lennox's hand as if to prove it.

An absurd idea was beginning to take shape in Dalton's mind. "Do you still have your musical instruments?"

Gurmeet's face screwed up in confusion. "You mean my sarangi, and his bagpipes?"

"That would be them."

"What do they have to do with anything?"

"Go get them. We need to distract the enemy, and I can't think of a better way to do it."

Below him, the two musicians looked at each other, nodded, and darted off. Dalton knew it wouldn't take long for them to collect their instruments; Gurmeet only lived one street over and Dalton was pretty sure Lennox had moved in with him not that long ago.

He contacted Errin again. "I've got a distraction in progress. I'll let you know when to start circling around."

"What's the distraction?"

"A concert."

"A . . . concert, sir?"

"It's going to be very loud."

"And you think this will work?"

"No idea. But the Verdants won't be expecting it."

Dalton made his way down the stairwell into the station and stepped out the front door into the street. Gurmeet and Lennox soon came into view with their respective instruments. "We haven't really perfected anything yet," Gurmeet said.

"Doesn't matter. I want you to be as loud and obnoxious as possible."

Lennox's cheeks flushed pink. "Obnoxious, sir?"

"Just get in here."

Dalton ushered them inside the station and over to the wall-mounted manual control panel for the siren system.

The sirens switched on naturally when high winds activated the sensors outside of town. They could also be switched on manually from inside the station. There was some way to switch all the sirens over to loudspeakers, a trick that Old Man Sondhi had accidentally discovered during his tenure as sheriff and that Dalton only knew about because he'd been walking out of the bank one day and heard the man's voice say, "—this switch do—Oh, shit!" broadcast out of the pole-mounted siren speakers at several hundred decibels.

He squinted at the control panel. Some of the switches were so worn, he could barely read their labels.

A dusty grille in the center of the switches was likely the microphone. A switch to the right of it read "MA UAL SI EN."

Having nothing to lose at this point, Dalton flipped the leftmost switch and flicked the microphone grille with his middle finger.

A deafening THUD echoed through the town, causing several dozen citizens to scream.

Dalton cleared his throat. "Sorry to disturb you," he said, glancing at Gurmeet and Lennox, both of whom gave him wary looks. "This is your sheriff speaking again. I'd like to introduce you to two fine musicians." He turned from the microphone and whispered, "What do you call yourselves?"

"Sikh Highlander." Lennox's cheeks turned pink. "We've been trying to come up with something better."

"Sikh Highlander!" Dalton said into the microphone, then stepped away from it. "Keep playing until I tell you to stop."

The men gingerly stepped up to the microphone and moved their instruments into position.

"Which one should we do first?" Lennox whispered.

"What about 'My Old Molorthia Home'?"

"I can never get the ending right."

"Maybe 'O Danny Boy'?"

"But we only just started that one!"

Dalton was aware that their whispers were being magnified and blasted over the town.

He pinched the bridge of his nose.

"I know!" Gurmeet said, forgetting to whisper. "We can do 'Just Dance'!"

"Oh, *gods* no," Dalton said as Gurmeet strummed the opening notes of the ancient song.

Some of the people out in the street peered in through the glass door wearing concerned expressions.

Dalton's comm crackled. "Dalton, what in God's name are you doing?" Carolyn asked.

"Distracting our enemies. Now try to get a visual on the Nydo Base folk."

He keyed in Errin's number before Carolyn could object. "You'd better get your group moving."

"I'm on it."

Dalton resisted the urge to tap his foot in time with the beat of the music. Despite their claim that they weren't very good, he thought Sikh Highlander might have a bright future in entertainment ahead of them, assuming they didn't end up being massacred today.

He gave them the thumbs-up and returned to the roof. The music blared from the siren speakers so loudly, he had to scream into his bullhorn before anyone so much as noticed him.

"All of you need to stand by!" he shouted at the A through M group. "Errin and Carolyn are taking their groups around to—" A particularly loud succession of notes drowned out his words, even with the bullhorn amplifying them. "Oh, hell. Stay put and pay attention. If the Verdants come into view, don't attack until I say so."

Ashi'ii and Kedd went ahead of the rest of their group to scout out the precise location of the Verdants. The bastards had killed too many of her people already, and destroyed months' worth of income during their other attacks over the years. She'd been lucky so far, she supposed, that they'd only ever managed to destroy her cargo ships.

Other companies had not been so fortunate. Oreega Incorporated, for example, had lost half its employees when the Verdants wiped out their silver mines on Gaspind Lora, and the entirety of Interspace Materials had been decimated when the Verdants found their bases on Korsha Two, Hulitzporgia, and Tomm.

Kedd flickered into view ahead of her, his veil fluttering in the wind.

"Pip-pip! Your shield is down," Ashi'ii said.

Kedd clawed at the invisibility shield clipped to his waist. "Pip-pip! I thought I charged it this morning. Damned tech."

"Pip-pip! At least you have one." Since Ashi'ii's job was largely administrative, she had never bothered to issue herself a shield, because the chances of her needing to hide herself from humans all the way up at the base were next to zero. Kedd and his ilk, who spent their days monitoring human communications channels and looting anything they thought they could sell, were another story.

Kedd clicked the button on the device a few times. "Pip-pip! Do you see me?"

"Pip-pip! Yes, and I'm sorry, but we need to keep moving."

Her colleague cursed, and the two of them proceeded to dart from building to building with weapons drawn, peering around corners and spotting a few humans peeking out from behind their curtains. They were the least of her worries. They would burn along with everyone else.

Ashi'ii poked her head around the corner of another building and nearly dropped her weapon. She was far more suited to a desk than to this, and her nerves showed it.

"Pip-pip! What is it?" Kedd hissed.

"Pip-pip! The enemy, of course!"

"Pip-pip! Which one?"

"Which one do you think?"

Kedd gaped at her, and she realized she'd forgotten to *pip-pip*. Hanging out with humans overnight had evidently rubbed off on her.

"Pip-pip! You should apologize for that," Kedd growled.

"I don't have time for this. *We* don't have time for this! Just *look*."

Kedd glared at her but acquiesced.

They stared around the corner together, carefully.

They'd reached the northern edge of town. All four Verdant ships were in view, and about twenty-five dozen of their "eco-warriors" mingled outside, wearing armor instead of veils and toting guns big enough to kill a pod of whalebeasts.

"Pip-pip! This is not their ordinary method," Kedd said, ducking back out of sight behind the adobe building. "What do you think they're doing?"

"The Greens are in town," Ashi'ii said, receiving another reproachful glare from her subordinate. "The Verdants won't burn the town if it kills the natives."

"That's absurd!" Kedd exclaimed, then clapped a hand over his mouth in horror.

Ashi'ii nearly levitated out of her shoes when Dalton's voice boomed out of a pole-mounted speaker across the street from them, announcing something about a Sick Highlander. She didn't know what a highlander was, or why Dalton would need to tell everyone they'd been taken ill, but her thoughts were interrupted by some cryptic, amplified whispering, which was then followed by a blast of what could only be music.

"Pip-pip! What is *that*?" Kedd breathed, staring up at the speaker.

Ashi'ii never had the chance to answer. There came a shout, and the sound of a blast, and the next thing she knew, Kedd lay at her feet, his veil blown off his face and blood seeping out of a wound on his chest.

Two Verdants strode toward her without fear.

She couldn't stay and help Kedd. If she did, she would

not survive. Maybe she wouldn't survive anyway, but she could try.

She fired off two shots of her own weapon and darted around a corner into an alleyway between two three-story flats. The music blasting out of the speakers made it impossible to think straight, and maybe that was the point.

Several doors lined the alleyway, and cans of waste sat beside them. Ashi'ii tried one of the doors at random, smiled a sort of malicious glee when it opened without resistance, and hurried inside what appeared to be the flat's laundry room, if she were to guess from the rows of low machinery and the smell of soap.

She turned the locking mechanism on the handle and shoved a cardboard box full of detergent over to block the door for good measure, then raced to think of her next steps.

The Verdants had seen her. She could ditch her clothing and pretend to be human by stealing some unattended garments, but the Verdants would want to kill the humans, too, so it would be pointless to change clothes.

She wedged herself into a corner and sent a call through to Melyip, who managed the copper mine thirty *kushkims* from Nydo Base. "Pip-pip! Kedd is down. The Verdants got him."

"Pip-pip! That is unfortunate to hear. What is our next step?"

"Pip-pip! Send half our people around behind the Verdant ships. You'll find them on the northern edge of town in close formation. The noise all the humans are making should distract them from noticing us if we are careful."

"Pip-pip! Acknowledged. Sending backup your way right now."

Chumley did not enjoy being a hamster, per se. The minute size of his animal form made him prone to many accidents, such as being stepped on by humans and being eaten for dinner by cats. He could shift back into human form at a moment's notice in order to save his life, but that would only result in indecency and awkward explanations.

Being tiny did have its advantages. Nobody would be expecting a rodent to sneak onboard a ship.

After Dalton left him by the quad dealership, Chumley made a beeline for the ship from Nydo Base, without making it look like a beeline. A rodent with a purpose could not be trusted.

He skirted a few of the quads and had to hide in the shade of a potted palm tree for at least half an hour to avoid the scrutiny of the gathered Haa'la, who appeared to be discussing tactics in their own language. Every time he prepared to rush toward the metal ramp leading into the open hatch, one or two of the Haa'la would either step in front of it or turn his direction as they scanned what was visible of Richport from their location.

If he'd been human, Chumley would have been sweating bullets. This was taking too long! He didn't know what this lot was waiting for. Most of the Haa'la had gone off on some errand, so maybe the ones left here were simply guarding their ship?

Dalton's voice boomed over the town, loud and clear. Chumley huddled closer to the pot as he tried to make sense of the sheriff's words. A concert? Why in the world was he announcing a concert?

A cacophony of sound followed some deafening whispering, and when Chumley realized it was music, he noticed the Haa'la guarding the ship had stepped away from it and were staring perplexedly at a pole-mounted speaker a block away from them.

Not daring to miss his chance, Chumley hurried up the metal ramp and into the cool interior of the ship.

His hamster nose twitched. He hated when it did that. While the genetic splicing that had given him this ability had been altered enough to let him keep his mind and his eyesight while in animal form, it did not eliminate animal instincts. In this form, he constantly had to resist sudden urges to gnaw on wood and stuff his cheeks full of seeds.

Faint voices carried toward him from deeper in the ship. Chumley raised himself on his hind legs and sniffed the air. Three Haa'la were still onboard—he could detect their unique alien scent.

Please don't notice me, he thought as he scurried close to the nearest wall and kept his rodent eyes peeled for any instrument panels he might prise open.

The sound of heavy footsteps thudded through the floor beneath him, and he instinctively wedged himself as deeply into the corner where the wall met the floor as he could. Three sets of thick, white boots the size of houses strode past him without stopping.

Thanks, he thought weakly before moving onward. Dalton had no doubt caused the distraction for a reason.

He scurried here and there, stopping every few seconds to sniff the air again. He could smell where the Haa'la had been, but nothing indicated to him which way the engines might be. His diminutive height made it impossible to navigate, because he was too damned short to see where he should be going.

Taking an immense gamble, he shifted back into human form, to hell with indecency.

Now at his normal height again, Chumley turned in a full circle to evaluate his surroundings. A thick, metal door stood ajar ahead of him. Something hummed inside, so he hurried through the doorway and closed the door behind him.

Machinery towered over him—the ceiling in here was double the height of the one out in the corridor. Lights blinked and screens showed dots and lines that didn't mean a whole lot to Chumley but probably meant something vital to the functioning of the ship.

He rubbed his hands together and stepped forward.

The most important part of destroying machinery was to do it in a way that would not result in one's immediate incineration. Chumley felt a burst of adrenaline as he flipped open an instrument panel and stared at a tangle of orange and violet wires.

A noble person intent on defeating the enemy would gladly sacrifice their own life for the cause. Aside from the fact that disabling this ship would make hardly a dent in the present crisis, Chumley wasn't all that noble. He'd swindled people out of their money, for goodness sake! What kind of hero did that make him? Maybe sacrificing himself would be better in the end, because he wouldn't have to keep living with the guilt.

Maybe he could blow up the ship. He wondered if dying hurt. He wondered if there was even anything afterward—probably a lake of hellfire for him, which would be just his sort of luck.

Still, he had to do something. Destroying this ship might cause only a ripple, but ripples could become tidal waves. Or so he'd read somewhere.

He had to hurry, though. He'd been inside the ship too long already.

He drew in a deep breath, closed his eyes, and reached for a wire to yank out of the wall.

As his fingers closed around it, he thought of Dalton, and paused.

Dalton may have been all gruff on the outside, but he'd saved Chumley's life the day the mob attacked him. Not many people had saved Chumley's life before other than his gran, who'd whisked him away from England, never to return, the week after Chumley's father had had enough of Chumley's mother and stabbed her six times in the chest with a kitchen knife.

Dalton had offered Chumley a new start, just like Gran. It would be nice to get to know Dalton a little better and pay him back for his kindness.

Chumley eyed an orange wire, gripped it in one hand, closed his eyes again, and gave it a tremendous tug.

The wire snapped easier than he'd expected, and he

landed hard on his bare arse. Blinking tears out of his eyes, he looked up at the panel and smiled at the sparks spitting from it. He may have only disabled the bathroom exhaust fan for all he knew, but it was a start.

He went from panel to panel, yanking out two wires here, three wires there, and wincing as some of the sparks stung his fingers. Then he noticed a cabinet in one corner and flung it open, rejoicing when he realized it was a storage place for tools, including a giant spanner the length of his arm.

He picked up the spanner and tested its weight in its hands. Could probably do a bloody lot of damage if he used it wrong. He held it like a bat and was about to swing it into one of the screens showing the flashing lights when a white-gloved hand grabbed him by the arm and spun him around.

The veiled Haa'la stood a foot taller than him. He didn't think it was Ashi'ii, so he clubbed the alien in the head and watched, transfixed, as they released his other arm and slumped to the floor.

Wasting no time, he bashed the screen in.

The lights flickered, and an alarm began to whoop somewhere deeper in the ship.

He knew that sound. A system had gone critical, which was good because that's what Chumley had come here to do, but it was also bad, because Chumley was still inside the ship.

He broke into a run, still gripping the spanner. A second Haa'la stepped into his path, and he swung the spanner at them but missed as the alien dodged out of the way. The Haa'la lifted up some kind of blaster weapon—

—and Chumley was speeding along the floor in hamster form with no memory of having shifted.

Shots rang around him. The lights went out, but he could see the glow of daylight through the open hatch. He put on an even greater burst of speed—

And the world exploded into flame.

CHAPTER 24

Carolyn and her group had been edging around the western side of town, crawling on their stomachs in the dry bed of the Rosa River so nobody would see them. Dalton's insane concert had entered its third song, and maybe it was working because so far, the Verdants hadn't shown up to annihilate them.

When she judged that they had reached the approximate vicinity of the quad dealership, Carolyn poked her head up to get a visual, flamethrower still strapped to her back.

The dealership and the Nydo Base ship parked there lay roughly half a kilometer in front of them. Only a handful of Haa'la lingered in front of it, the rest hopefully having gone off to face the Verdants under Ashi'ii's guidance.

She wondered if communicating with the Greens would give her precognition like it had given Gwendolyn. Precognition would greatly help in these circumstances, but right now the only thing she perceived from the Greens in her group was that they thought this furtiveness was pointless.

We don't want to kill these Haa'la, she thought back at them. *They might be on our side.*

"What's our next move?" asked a man who'd been tagging along at Carolyn's elbow for the past ten minutes. He squatted on his haunches beside her, covered in dust.

"We keep an eye on this lot." She nodded at the Haa'la. "We don't make any moves until they do. Understood?"

"I say we rush them and blow them all to kingdom come."

"They're supposed to be cooperating with us. Remember?"

"A bloody alien is a bloody alien. We blow them up, half our problem's solved."

"Do you have any military experience?" she asked him.

"No. And neither do you, Mayor."

She clenched her jaw. "We will attack only if they begin attacking our other citizens. That's a final order."

There came some more muttering among other members of their group. The Greens among them sat on the ground like a bunch of giant, misplaced houseplants.

Two of them had put hands to the sides of their heads, as if covering their ears.

"What—" she started to say, when a rumbling sound issued from the Haa'la ship and smoke and fire billowed from its open hatch in an acrid cloud. Several of the Haa'la who remained there dropped to the ground while the rest lifted their blasters at full attention.

"I think their engines just went critical," said the man beside her, a boomstone clenched in his grimy fist.

"Yes," said Carolyn.

"Gives us one less thing to worry about."

She smiled grimly, but then frowned. Ashi'ii would not be happy about this, and angry people tended to act, well, angrily.

She wondered where their supposed ally was right now, and how much longer that supposed alliance would last.

Ashi'ii had not been brought up to be a warrior, and like most non-warriors in the middle of a combat zone, she opted to hide.

Luckily for her, a laundry room had plenty of crannies in which she could squirrel herself away. She counted off two rows of six washing machines, and squeezed herself into the second one from the end. The lid just barely closed over her bulk.

She waited for the Verdants to break in and find her.

Her comm spat out a hiss of static. "Pip-pip! The Verdants are in sight." It was Melyip, sounding exhilarated.

"Pip-pip! Now wipe them off the face of this planet," she whispered. "I don't care how you do it. I just want them dead."

"Pip-pip! Yes, ma'am."

A low, muffled *whumpf* shook the washing machine, as if something deep within the bowels of Molorthia Six had come awake. An explosion?

"Pip-pip! Bad news, ma'am." This time, it was Ondrow, who had been left behind to guard their ship. "It appears our ship's cooling system overheated. Um . . . it blew up, ma'am. And we believe that Jumaah and Klikket were still inside."

Ashi'ii felt dazed. Klikket was her cousin, and one of her closest confidantes. Steeling her emotions, she cleared her throat and said, "I thought you all were instructed to guard the ship."

There came a long pause. "Pip-pip! We are guarding

it, ma'am. Or were. There's no more ship to guard. I mean, there's pieces of it left . . ."

"You must not have been guarding it very well, then!"

"Pip-pip! We saw no intruders. Jumaah and Klikket thought they heard something and went back inside to investigate, but they must have heard the system about to blow. It might just be an unfortunate accident, ma'am. It's been a long time since we had the ship in for servicing."

But Ashi'ii knew it was no accident. In the darkness of the washing machine, she saw red. She would mourn for her fallen people later, Kedd included, but for now, she would have to fight. "Pip. *Pip*," she spat. "This is *war*."

A door burst open, probably body-slammed from outside. Ashi'ii held her breath as heavy footsteps crossed the floor. She thumbed the power button on her comm so Ondrow wouldn't unintentionally give away her position.

Low voices spoke not in Haa'anu, but Hindi—another human language with which she had extensive knowledge due to its prevalence. She strained to hear them through the metal washing machine lid.

"We should leave that one and get back to the others."

"I thought we were instructed to eliminate everyone except for the natives."

"We're wasting time if we're going to hunt them down one by one. I see none of the native life forms in this sector, so we can ignite the whole block."

"But what if the fire spreads and harms the natives?"

There came a spell of silence during which Ashi'ii contemplated the fact that these Verdants were speaking a human tongue. Haa'la did not converse with each other in human tongues, which meant that these two were not Haa'la at all.

"This entire settlement will have to be razed to the ground sooner or later," the first human said. "And when this one is gone, we move on to the other settlements and deal with them."

"Even if natives die in the process? This isn't what I signed up for."

"You're going to learn that sometimes there are casualties no matter how careful we are. Don't get me wrong, I'd have been happier if we were allowed to bomb the mines right off the bat, but the boss says there's a high concentration of miners here in this town, so this is what we have to do. Let's rejoin the others and see what they want us to do next."

More footsteps and the creak of a door indicated the pair's departure.

Ashi'ii's pulse thudded. It was bad enough having Haa'la kill Haa'la, but having *humans* kill Haa'la was an abomination she wasn't willing to accept. The damned Verdants must have done some recruiting on Earth since her last run-in with them.

She let out a breath and climbed out of the washing machine, switching her comm back on as soon as she was upright. "Pip-pip! There should be no further delay. Attack the Verdants as soon as you're ready."

Dalton began to fidget once Carolyn and Errin's groups departed. He'd played a few battle video games as a child, but the key difference between a game and reality was that the game gave you multiple lives. Blow yourself up, you get a fresh start a few seconds later, nothing to see here.

The street below teemed with anxious people who seemed more terrified at the so-called "friendly" Greens that had come to help them than the prospect of being butchered by Haa'la. Dalton paced the roof of the station as Sikh Highlander continued their music recital, wishing he had something inspiring to say to the crowd, many of whom may be dead by sunset.

He just wasn't an inspiring person. He'd never had much to say, even back in those days when he grew flowers in a greenhouse. You didn't have to say anything to flowers. You watered them, made sure they got enough sunlight, and clipped them when the time was right. Darneisha dealt with the customers far more than he ever did. She'd always seemed to have the right words to say, like a font of wisdom and politeness that never ran dry.

A long-forgotten memory dredged itself up suddenly in his mind, and it took him far away from the plains of battle, back into the happy past.

Kendra and Imani had sat on the floor playing with painted building blocks one evening while he and Darneisha relaxed on the sofa with the news screen on. A reporter had been giving grim updates from a violent dispute over on Rama Seven, where three nations were beating themselves into a bloody pulp for reasons not apparent to any outsiders. Theories about the origin of the skirmish abounded, but the war had been going on for so long at that point that nobody could remember what started it. Now they just fought because they could.

"Why are people fighting?" Imani asked, tears in her eyes as the screen showed images of body bags lined up in rows.

"I don't know, honey," Darneisha had said, drawing her daughter close to her side and giving her a squeeze. "But the important thing to remember is that sometimes there are good people fighting back to make sure there's never any fighting again."

"Do the good people die, too?"

"Sometimes. It's sad, but they do it so someone else's life might be better."

It had been a lot for a six-year-old to take in. It was a lot for anyone to take in, really, especially when you were the one ordering the good people to fight back and die.

Dalton resisted the urge to lean over and vomit. Why couldn't life be like a video game?

A video game . . .

He remembered something.

He held the bullhorn in front of his face again, wishing for a moment that the music blaring over the town wasn't quite so loud. "You need to construct barricades!" he bellowed. "Block off streets to seal yourselves in!"

The building shook, ever so slightly. He peered off to the west and saw a rising cloud of smoke. Since it did not seem to be harming him at the moment, he chose to ignore it and refocused his attention on the citizens and plants gathered below.

"In fact," he went on, "we can build them in a way that funnels the Verdants in toward us. Then we can trap them inside and deal with them. I need people on roofs with boomstones!"

Feeling almost gleeful, he rushed back down the stairs and into the station. He tore a map of Richport off the wall and snatched up a magic marker on his way out the door.

Panting, he stopped outside the station and spread the map out on the ground. He knew these streets better than he knew the backs of his own hands, but he needed to show everyone else his plan.

He began marking barricades here and there, designed in such a way that would draw the Verdants in toward them, like herding field beasts into the slaughterhouse. Errin and their group would need to provide an impetus to get the Verdants moving, but Dalton didn't doubt that it could be done. This plan made *sense*.

"Errin!" he barked into his comm unit. "Are you there?"

"Affirmative! We're in sight of the Verdant ships. We can see a few dozen Haa'la from here, but I don't know how many are still inside."

"When I give the signal, take your group and charge them. Drive them toward Lily Street with everything you've got. We'll push from the other end and trap them in the middle, and our people on the roofs will take care of them."

"I didn't know we had people on the roofs."

"We will soon. Stand by."

He finished marking all the places where the barricades should go and then held up the map so the people nearest him could see it. "We need to install barricades in these precise locations! Use your automobiles, your kitchen tables, anything that will make it hard for anyone to get through—then report directly back to me once they're in place. And everyone whose last name starts with M needs to get up on the roofs here, here, and here." He paused to draw in a breath. "We're going to trap them and rain boomstones down onto them until they're dead. They'll never even realize what hit them."

CHAPTER 25

As the citizens of Richport scurried off to form barricades after examining Dalton's map, fewer and fewer humans remained in the street. The Greens that stayed behind towered over the scant humans who'd opted to linger with their giant flamethrowers, ready to incinerate the plants at the first wrong move.

Dalton didn't want to look at the Greens, nor could he take his eyes off them. It was no wonder the first settlers on Molorthia Six had mistaken them for great, bloody trees. The Greens here stood so still it was like their feet had grown roots, anchoring them into the street.

While he waited for the barricades to be moved into place, he checked in with Carolyn. "Any updates?" he asked.

"The ship we were monitoring exploded a few minutes ago," she said dryly. "You may have noticed?"

Dalton's heart stuttered. "Chumley was supposed to be disabling that ship, not blowing it sky-high."

"He may have set it to blow on a delay and got out before it ignited."

"May have?"

"I haven't seen him."

If Chumley had still been in rodent form, Carolyn may not have spotted him at all from her vantage point, and Dalton fervently hoped that was the case.

He decided to change the subject. "What are you doing now?"

"I've split my group in half. Some of them are still in the riverbed, and the rest of us are moving in closer to town to get a fix on the Haa'la again."

"Let's focus on the Verdants," said Dalton. "They're the ones planning on murdering everyone."

"Have you alerted the other cities?"

At first, Dalton couldn't think of what she was talking about. Other cities . . . ? Oh. Other cities. *Right*. "I'm on it," he said, and hurriedly dialed Annaliese up in Paris.

"Annaliese?" A static hiss was just barely audible beneath the sound of Gurmeet and Lennox's music. "Do you copy?"

"Dalton! Last I heard, you'd disappeared!"

"No time to explain. Richport is under attack."

"Oh my God! Is it the Greens?"

Dalton scratched an ear. "Um, no. The Greens are actually helping us."

"Is that music?"

"Ignore it. Some of your missing people are up in a Haa'la mining base."

"I'm having a hard time following this."

Dalton didn't think he'd really have the time to explain every last detail to every other sheriff on the planet, but he had to remind himself that nobody else knew what was going on here. "Aliens called Haa'la built an illegal mining base up in the forests. They've been burning the forests to drive out the Greens. A bunch of eco-warriors called the Verdants have just landed to kill all the other Haa'la and the humans as well. They're here in Richport, and if we can't stop them, they'll destroy every settlement on the planet."

Her tone turned sour. "Why the hell would they do that?"

"It doesn't matter why! Just get your people mobilized, and maybe send someone to go rescue your people from the base, if the Verdants haven't destroyed it yet."

Annaliese said some choice words. "Thanks for letting me know," she said, and the call ended.

Dalton had just dialed up Janelle in Cloud City when several of the inert Greens loitering in the street straightened and fanned out as if creating a line of defense. He couldn't suppress a shudder as he watched them move—it reminded him too much of that day in Piney Gulch. He ought to give himself an award for not blacking out again already.

Why would Greens want to help humans? Shouldn't they be on the side of the Verdants?

Were these Greens *being nice*?

The earsplitting music fell silent.

Amplified whispering issued from every siren speaker.

"That's all the songs I know."

"We started on 'God Save the Queen' a few weeks ago."

"But we never finished it!"

"We could start over from the beginning?"

"But my hands are tired! Oh gosh, do you think everyone can hear us?"

Dalton forced himself to breathe. In the distance, he could hear the sound of blaster fire.

Shapes and colors spun behind Chumley's eyelids. He forced them open and winced—it felt like weights had been tacked to them.

Smoke wafted through the air above him. He coughed and rolled over onto his side. He lay on a patch of rocky sand that felt about as comfortable as you'd expect. Shouts and heavy bootsteps drew his attention, and he watched dazedly as a gaggle of veiled figures marched past him with blasters raised.

They gave him no notice.

He sat up and looked down at himself. He wasn't wearing any clothes.

Why wasn't he wearing any clothes?

He strained to replay the most recent events. He'd been in his flat looking for suitable worlds on which he could hide from the police, and then . . .

Oh.

Right.

He shifted back into hamster form as another group of Haa'la rushed past, armed to the teeth with blasters.

I blew up their ship. He giggled, or he would have if he hadn't been a hamster. *I blew up their ship!*

He still had four other ships to take care of, though. It would take him too long to run there like this, and running there in the nude would draw unwanted attention, so he would have to find some clothing.

His nose quivered. If he could find some laundry hanging out to dry somewhere . . .

The sound of many blasters firing in quick succession made him twitch, and yet another batch of Haa'la came through, yelling what was probably profanities. They didn't appear to be organized, like a true army would be. This was what happened when you handed weapons to a bunch of angry miners: mayhem.

Honestly, Chumley couldn't see how anything good would come of this day. There was no military on Molorthia Six; it had never needed one. Colony worlds usually didn't until they got invaded for the first time. Then it was all, *Hey, we should organize a formal government so we can organize a formal military*, and within a few generations the former colony would just be a regular world that more pissed-off people split off from to go settle their own uninhabited planets. It was like the circle of life, or something.

Chumley's tiny, furry body backed up against the side of a block of flats as a troop of what could only be the Verdants came into view. They wore armor and carried guns that meant business, and they shot down three of the Haa'la without batting their eyes. Not that Chumley could see their eyes; they were wearing helmets. They also looked about the height of skyscrapers, but that was to be expected since Chumley was currently small enough to fit inside a teacup.

One of the surviving Haa'la squeezed off a shot that hit one of the Verdants in the helmet, which sparked and crackled as if it had been electrified. Another Verdant cut down the remaining Haa'la as the one with the damaged helmet tore it off their head and threw it to the ground in disgust. Long, black hair spilled over armored shoulders, and Chumley blinked his hamster eyes in astonishment.

He had seen this woman before. And he was fairly sure her name was Naomi Schwartzman.

She stared down at the fallen Haa'la, her face as stern as Chumley had seen it on the day she gave her little speech in the town square. "That's five of them down, at least," she said, sounding almost bored. "Pity we can't get this done any easier."

Chumley hardly heard as one of her companions replied to her. If this was Naomi Schwartzman, then the Verdants might be on the humans' side after all! The Verdants must have picked her up from whatever city she was supposedly inspecting at the moment. Would they have had the time to do that, though? Of course they had; Naomi was here.

He couldn't disable the Verdant ships if they were actually here to help the humans. Since it was now pointless to remain in hamster form, he shifted back into himself and held up his hands in a sign of peace.

"Oi!" he shouted. "Ms. Schwartzman!"

She and the other Verdants turned and stared at him, probably wondering why he wasn't wearing anything.

"Who the hell are you?" she asked, coolly.

"It's … I'm Chumley Fanshaw. The deputy here. Remember? You gave a speech in front of the whole town just the other day."

She gave him a blank stare, and then smiled.

Chumley tried not to notice that her companions had their weapons trained on him.

"You think I'm my sister," she said.

Chumley felt his heart hammering faster and faster. "You're not Naomi?"

"Naomi is four years younger than I am. My name is Magdalene."

"I don't understand."

"Don't you?" Her eyes sparkled like black diamonds. "We suspected that Nydo Base Corporation was running operations somewhere in this sector. Naomi knows what I do and dragged Frontier Care United out this way to spy on things while the Verdants were otherwise engaged."

Chumley tensed. "What do you mean by that?"

"She means we were busy bombing Horgon Base on Mendiron Two," growled a helmeted man beside Magdalene.

"Does that mean . . ." Chumley gulped. "That Frontier Care United is a sham?"

"Oh, it's a real charity." Magdalene shrugged. "Naomi and I have always been close. She tells me her secrets, I tell her mine. The day after she landed here, she sent me a message describing the wildfires, but it wasn't confirmation enough that Nydo Base Corporation was responsible. But when a Nydo cargo ship reentered the Leeprau System about thirteen hours ago with Molorthia Six registered as its planet of origin, well . . ." Her lips twisted into a dark smirk. "Luckily we'd just arrived back from Mendiron Two. We restocked our supplies and headed straight here."

"You've come here to save us, then. From the wildfires, and the attacking Greens, and the Haa'la miners?"

Neither Magdalene nor her comrades replied. Her expression didn't even change, so Chumley tried a different approach. "It would help us all to know that you're on our side. We can even leave the fighting to you since we're not experienced."

"You really are a sad little person," Magdalene said, looking him up and down in disgust. "I contacted Naomi when we arrived, and she'll be requesting emergency evacuation for her team if she hasn't already. Now we have a job to finish."

Chumley was on the ground running away in hamster form half a second before blaster shots rang out again.

Indignation burned within him as he rushed around a corner and tucked himself beneath a vehicle parked outside a two-story adobe building. So, two sisters, each fighting for the frontier in their own way: Naomi, who supposedly wanted to better human colony worlds, and Magdalene, who wanted to purge those worlds of foreign inhabitants.

The Schwartzmans must have had very strange family reunions.

He remained under the vehicle a few minutes longer. Nobody found him, and he began to feel lonely as more blaster shots and cries of agony filled the air.

I'm scared, Gran, he thought. *I've made a mistake in coming to this planet, haven't I? I thought I might evade the authorities here, and now I'm going to die in a great, bloody battle. No one will ever know what happened to me, or even remember me.*

A body thudded to the ground next to the vehicle. It was a human being, wearing sand-colored clothing that smoldered from the shot that had brought them down. He could see no other details, but he knew without a doubt that this was a citizen of Richport whose only mistake had been in defending their home.

The shots moved off toward the distance. Chumley crept out of his hiding place, scanned the street, and shifted back into his normal shape when he saw the coast was clear for the moment.

He knelt beside the body. They appeared androgynous, with closely-cropped hair and eyes glazed over in death. Blood seeped from the front of their shirt and stained the street.

They weren't even holding a weapon. The only thing clenched in their hand was a key. Chumley pried it from their grip and examined the keychain, noting it had the number "2C" stamped on it.

He stared at the building beside him. It could have been a block of flats, certainly. Perhaps this person had lived there. Perhaps they had loved ones waiting for them anxiously inside.

What should I do, Gran? he thought.

He imagined her saying, *You should do what is right.*

Chumley gritted his teeth, checked his surroundings, and hurried up the stairwell leading straight off the street.

It took no time at all to find 2C; there must have only been six or eight flats in the whole building. He rapped on the door, and when nobody came, he used the key and let himself inside.

It felt cool inside the flat, by Molorthia Six standards. "Hello?" he called to the living area, where a small table and reclining chair sat in front of a screen. There wasn't much in the way of clutter, and not too many places where scared people might hide, so he strode into the small bedroom and tore through the dresser in search of something that might fit him.

So sorry about this, he thought at the poor soul lying in the street below. *I don't think you'll be needing these anymore.* He tugged on trousers that were an inch too short in the leg, shoved his feet into shoes that made his toes feel like sardines, and pulled a shirt over his head that was tight enough to show his abs through them.

He looked at himself in the full-length mirror on the back of the bedroom door and tried not to laugh. This was neither the place nor the time for laughter, but it escaped his lips anyway, and the sound of it chilled him.

He sobered up quickly and searched for supplies. A comm unit lay on the table. Pocketing it, he moved into the kitchen and stared at the array of items that may or may not benefit him in his present situation.

In his mind, he saw himself donning a metal colander on his head and strapping it in place under his chin using a curtain cord, then rushing out into the street brandishing a kitchen knife at the Verdants, but if that was his Green-related precognition kicking back in, he was going to ignore it. A person could do only so many ridiculous things and live.

Chumley rushed back into the bedroom and eyed a computer terminal sitting on a desk in the corner. Its screen was alight, and he hunched over and typed "how to contact the feds" into the search bar.

It took him to an important-looking page written in serious-looking font. Several options were listed, including Galaxy's Most Wanted. He clicked on it and scrolled through an impressive list of criminals-at-large until he spotted "Ashi'ii Nydo, Nydo Base Corporation."

He clicked Ashi'ii's name and skimmed over her list of crimes. He would rather report the Verdants, but he felt time running short, so he clicked the option for Report.

The face of an extremely-cross human woman appeared on the screen. "Greetings, good citizen," she said, as if reading from a script. "You have chosen to report on the activity of Ashi'ii Nydo of Leeprau. What is your name?"

Chumley wasn't about to provide his real name, since it was somewhere on a Wanted list as well, though for theft and fraud, not environmental devastation. "Dalton," he said quickly. "Dalton Kane."

He heard clacking as she typed the information into her computer.

"What is your report?"

"Ashi'ii is on Molorthia Six. Her company has been lighting wildfires and looting the cities here."

There came more clacking. She looked back at him and said, "How do you know?"

"Because I met her, and she introduced herself! Now her people and the Verdants are having it out in Richport, and lots of people are going to die if your lot don't come and help put an end to things!"

"Is there an electronic address we can use to reach out to you for more information?"

"You don't need more information! Just get your people out to Molorthia Six before anyone else dies!"

"It's our policy to record the electronic address of each person who reports information about wanted criminals. It's to weed out hoaxes."

"I don't have an electronic address right now!" he cried. At least, not one he was willing to give out. In hindsight, he probably shouldn't have impersonated Pelstring Four governor Elroy Ghosh and drained half his bank accounts, but it *had* paid off some of Gran's innumerable medical bills. It had been his last big crime before scampering off to Molorthia Six.

The woman on the screen squinted at him, and something in her expression suggested she didn't believe a word he'd said. "I—I hear gunfire!" Chumley spluttered. "I've got to go!"

Cursing himself, the Haa'la, the Verdants, the Feds, and life in general, he scrambled out of the bedroom, went back to the kitchen, put a metal colander on his head, strapped it into place with a curtain cord, and armed himself with a kitchen knife. As he closed his fingers around the black, polymer handle, he remembered skipping into the kitchen of his boyhood home to show his mother the neat stone he'd found out in the garden, only to find her sprawled on the tiles gasping for breath as the life poured out of the great, ragged wounds in her chest.

His father had stood over her clutching a knife not too different from the one Chumley held now.

Chumley tilted it in the light, watched the blade gleam, and swallowed a large knot in his throat.

He was not his father, but he would kill with a knife to defend the innocent.

When a vision told you something, you shouldn't ignore it.

Dalton was able to contact four other sheriffs before some of the people he sent off to set up barricades trickled back into view, covered in sweat and dust. "We blocked Apple Street with three buses," reported a tall woman in a maroon Desert Van Lines uniform and cap. "Half a dozen people stayed inside the buses with flamethrowers, for when the creeps come by."

That hadn't been part of the plan, but Dalton dipped his head in acknowledgment. "Well done."

A heavyset man jogged past the fanned-out Greens and halted beside Dalton with his hands on his knees. He wore a dingy, canvas backpack bulging with boomstones. "I parked. My truck. Across Juniper Alley."

"Good," Dalton said. "Good." He made checkmarks next to both Apple Street and Juniper Alley on his map. Only sixteen more streets to go before the funnel was properly in place.

Over the next ten minutes, he checked off the barricades for Wax Street, Rock Street, Molorthia Avenue, Fisher Lane, and Circle Court. Each second that passed as he awaited news for each barricade lasted roughly ten years.

Errin's voice startled him. "Any news yet?"

Dalton twitched and lifted his comm unit back to his mouth. "We're still waiting on eleven barricades."

As he said this, a teenage girl reached him, panting, and said, "We've blocked off Harrison Street."

"Ten barricades," Dalton said as he made the appropriate mark on his map. The girl had a bow and a quiver of archery arrows strapped to her back—probably the only thing she had on hand to defend herself with.

His heart ached. No child had any business being in a warzone—but he would not tell her to stand down.

"Half the Verdants have dispersed already," Errin said. "It's hard to see from where we are, but I think they're fighting the miners. What should we do?"

Dalton closed his eyes and visualized the barricades that had already been placed. It wasn't enough for his plan to work. "Give me five more minutes, and I'll get back with you."

Someone ran up to him and told him that six quads and eight tables had been dragged across Curry Street, with armed citizens crouching behind them like soldiers in a trench.

He marked another check on the map.

Another someone came to report that the barricade was in place along Turmeric Lane, and that they'd seen bodies on the ground in the distance.

He marked another check on the map.

Dalton watched with sadness as his people worked together. He recognized most of them, but their names had begun to elude him, as if his mind was protecting itself against the losses to come.

After five minutes had come and gone and more reports came in, there remained two unguarded streets: Pear and Willow. He had no way of knowing if the barricades were there and those reporting them had been delayed in getting back, or if something had happened to them before they had the chance to place the barricades, but he could feel his time drying up like a puddle after a rare desert rainstorm. "I need people blocking off Pear and Willow Streets *now!*" he shouted into his bullhorn. Into his comm unit, he said, "Errin, you have my permission to attack the Verdants."

"Acknowledged," they said, and the comm went quiet.

He wondered if he'd ever see Carolyn's aide alive again. Errin never thought of themself; only ever wanted what was best for the town and quietly did whatever was necessary to make sure Richport operated like a greased wheel.

And it wasn't just Errin in danger. *All* of these people were in danger. He thought of all the people he saw on a daily basis—the postal workers, the retail employees, the families going for walks in the evening when the sun wasn't so hot—and he imagined them lying broken in the sand, never to enjoy the tranquility of their little corner of the universe again.

Dalton wished he had some whiskey. Whiskey would make things better. It would make them seem better, at least.

The Greens who'd stayed with Dalton's group sprang into sudden motion and swished out of sight up the street. Citizens screamed, and a burst of flame gushed across the street as someone fired their flamethrower on pure instinct.

"You lot need to stay with us!" Dalton shouted at the plants' retreating backs. He felt both disappointed and relieved to see them go. "Oh, never mind, then." He strode down the street after them and looked up at the buildings on either side, saluting the citizens perched atop them with their boomstones.

He contacted Cadu on his comm unit. "Cadu? Where are you?"

"Someone said we're raining boomstones from the roofs, so I loaded up a cart with even more of them and started passing them up to people. Wait, I see you now."

Dalton caught sight of a hand waving from the other

side of the Curry Street barricade, and saw the top of Cadu's coily black hair.

"Good," said Dalton. "You can join them on the roofs when you're done, if you like."

"I just might do that."

"Good luck, Cadu." Dalton swallowed. "I just want to say . . . it's been good working with you."

"Was that a compliment? Should I be worried?"

Of course you should be bloody fecking worried, Dalton thought, but he said, "Stay safe," and turned back toward the police station to arm himself.

A water pistol full of weed killer would have no effect on their current attackers. Dalton passed Gurmeet and Lennox, who were bickering off in a corner away from the speaker, their instruments abandoned on Cadu's cluttered desk, and threw open the supply closet, which appeared much emptier than he remembered. He plucked an antique flamethrower off the bottom shelf, checked to make sure it had fuel, and slung it over his shoulder.

Gurmeet and Lennox fell silent and watched, solemnly, as Dalton went back outside.

A minute later they joined him, minus their instruments but with the boomstones they'd received earlier.

"We ran out of songs," Gurmeet said miserably.

"It's okay," Dalton said. "You did good."

"We did?"

"We're still alive, aren't we?"

The men thought about this. Lennox cleared his throat and said, "You called the other sheriffs?"

"Some of them." Dalton scanned the street, feeling proud

and sad that his people were armed and ready. "They can't send us any backup, though. They don't have a way to get here in time to make any difference. They're just going to arm themselves and be ready and waiting for in case we fail today."

"What's our objective, exactly?" Gurmeet asked. "Aside from winning, of course."

"We kill the Verdants before they kill us."

Dalton squared his shoulders, and Lennox squirmed. "I haven't killed anyone before."

"Well, you'll have to bloody start. It's either them or you." Dalton marched past him and nodded at the other armed citizens, who returned expressions of grimness that made a yawning pit form in his stomach. Blaster fire from more than a kilometer away made him wince, though he did his best not to show it. He'd panicked at the sight of a plastic bag not too many days before; he would have to prove he was a man worthy of his position.

He lifted up his bullhorn again. "When I give the signal," he said, feeling nauseated, "you all attack."

CHAPTER 26

Chumley darted from parked vehicle to parked vehicle in human form, keeping his newfound kitchen knife pointed in front of him. He'd found a stray metal dustbin lid to use as a shield and was trying his darnedest to make his way toward the Verdant ships to work his wonders on them as well. Crossing long distances was much faster when you were a human, but it also made you an easier target.

He crouched down low and waited while a clump of Haa'la miners strode past, one wearing a veil covered in scorch marks. Blaster bolts took the lead miner in the chest, and they crumpled to the dusty street while their comrades shot back.

The Haa'la passed. Chumley emerged from his hiding spot behind a parked van and stared at the dead miner. Their own blaster lay on the ground beside them, and Chumley took it and slung the strap over his shoulder, feeling quite heroic to be armed with not one, but two weapons.

He rushed across the now-vacant street, squeezed himself between two buildings, and then saw them.

The four Verdant vessels had parked in a sort of diamond shape. A group of humans and Greens, led by Errin Inglewood, pummeled dozens of Verdants with everything they had. Blood oozed down Errin's face, but Chumley wasn't sure if it belonged to them or someone else.

He watched as a Green lifted a Verdant off the ground and tore them into shreds.

Chumley bent over and vomited, which surprised him because he wasn't entirely sure how there could be anything in his stomach at this point. Between the heat and the gore, he was amazed he was even conscious.

A helmeted person in Verdant gear lifted a blaster and aimed it at Errin, who'd become momentarily distracted by the carnage. Without thinking, Chumley stepped out from the narrow alleyway and shot Errin's would-be killer in the back, dropping them to the ground.

Errin lifted their gaze and met Chumley's. They offered him a grim smile and dodged to the side when another Green lifted another Verdant off their feet.

Chumley didn't let his focus linger enough to see the rest.

He shot a bolt at another Verdant and missed, then took a shot right in the dustbin lid, which electrified and caused him to drop it with an "Ow!"

He managed to squeeze off two more shots. The blaster clicked empty—it had run out of charge—and Chumley waved the kitchen knife feebly, like a mouse brandishing a toothpick at a cat. Two Verdants actually cocked their heads at him in apparent curiosity before taking aim at him.

It was at times like this when Chumley wished he could turn himself into a sparrow and sail away out of sight. He had to settle for turning himself into a hamster, which he did again without blinking an eye.

He didn't know if anyone was chasing him. He resisted every rodent urge to scurry into a hole and stay there until the danger passed, and made straight for the open gangplank of the nearest ship.

He had work to do, and he'd do it if it was the last thing he did.

Hot blood ran down Errin's face. Their veins buzzed with adrenaline; their senses ran on pure instinct. They only had about half a dozen small boomstones in their pack, and it felt woefully inadequate. The Greens fighting with them were a force of nature all by themselves, and Errin wondered if it might be wiser to take a step back and let them do all the work.

So far, the Verdants hadn't really moved toward Dalton's barricade funnel, though quite a few of them were now dead and in pieces on the ground, which was just as good.

It was the "in pieces" part that made Errin's stomach churn. These Greens appeared no different from the ones that had attacked the hotel and very nearly killed their sister Jeanette just a few days ago. The plants had the potential to turn on them at any moment, in which case Errin would be ready and waiting with weaponry of their own.

The battle went by in a blur. At one point they spotted Chumley Fanshaw wearing a metal colander like a helmet. He shot one of the enemy in the back, and Errin acknowledged him with a smile.

They lost sight of him as the minutes passed. Errin tossed a boomstone at a clump of Verdants, and shut their eyes against the sudden concussion. The humans and Greens had managed to force this part of the Verdants about twenty meters closer to the barricade funnel. It wasn't a lot of progress, but Errin wasn't about to complain. They'd only lost about ten humans so far, and all of the Greens were still intact, save for some scorched leaves.

But where had Chumley gone? Surely he hadn't abandoned them after making an effort to help. He'd just saved Errin's life, after all.

Just when Errin was starting to think they might be able to drive this remnant of the Verdants right where they needed to go, more of the bastards appeared from around a corner.

"Get them all!" Errin screamed, voice raw. Maybe they'd been screaming this whole time and hadn't even realized it.

The Greens surged forward in front of the humans in one single mass, driving the Verdants back. The Verdants shot at the Greens, but it was like throwing sparks at a forest.

"Toward the funnel!" Errin cried at the Greens. "Send them toward the funnel!"

They couldn't even see any Verdants now through the line of advancing Greens.

A rumble behind them made them drop to the ground. A blast of heat and smoke wafted over the street, scorching the back of Errin's sweat- and blood-soaked clothing.

Then all grew still.

Errin rolled over and sat up. One of the Verdant ships was no longer a ship, exactly. It was more like twisted, metal components that used to be a ship.

"Did we do that?" asked a woman in Errin's group. The

tip of her ponytail was singed, and a hole smoldered in the brim of her straw hat.

"I don't know." Errin frowned, looking for any human movement around the remains of the ship, but saw nothing.

Dalton had walked far enough up the barricade funnel that he could see where his batch of Greens had gotten to. They waited about a third of the way down, poised and ready.

His hands shook at the sight of them. Hell, *all* of him shook.

And now he could hear part of the battle coming toward them from the northern end of the funnel.

He peered up at the roofs of the taller buildings around him. Citizens stood at the edges holding sacks of boom-stones: regular people turned into killers out of necessity.

The tips of flamethrowers poked from the open windows of a Desert Van Lines bus parked across a side street.

Again, in his mind, Dalton could see the broken bodies of his family lying at the bottom of Piney Gulch five years earlier. He'd seen a shoe with an ankle sticking out of it that he was fairly sure had belonged to his young cousin Gia. A tiny hand lay beside a tricycle next to the blood-soaked play-ground. A head . . . dear God, a *head* belonging to his brother Rob had lain beside some shrubs like a unique lawn orna-ment. Its expression had been one of permanent surprise.

Dalton's thoughts whirled faster and faster.

The Verdants were coming up the street, chased by Greens from the other end.

Greens, who had destroyed everything good in Dalton's world.

Greens, who could kill his people as easily as the Verdants.

As if on cue, the Greens on his end surged forward to help pin the Verdants in the middle.

Dalton imagined the dismembered limbs, the entrails, the grim silence of death where laughter had reigned mere moments before.

He remembered the bright blue eyeball peering at him from where it lay on the ground. He'd struggled to place the eye in a face he'd known, but his mind had shut down completely then. He'd crawled to the playground tunnel to die. The next thing he'd known, he was in a hospital, minus an arm.

How had he forgotten the eyeball until now?

The Greens . . . were going to kill . . . *everyone*.

Dalton held up his bullhorn. "Stop!" he cried. "Stop it, all of you! There will be no more fighting today!"

Someone tugged on his sleeve. He turned and realized that Lennox McTavish hovered at his elbow.

"What do you want?" Dalton growled.

"Erm, we're all going to die if we don't fight. You said."

"We'll have to find some other way then, won't we?" He lifted his bullhorn again. "You lot on the roofs, retreat!"

"Sir, you're not making any sense," Lennox went on, softly but urgently. "If we don't fight, we'll die anyway."

"Then we'll . . . surrender to the Verdants, or something. Work out a deal."

Something leafy reached down in front of Dalton and yanked the bullhorn out of his hands.

It was a Green, of course. It tossed the bullhorn onto the ground and stomped it flat.

Dalton stared up at it, fully expecting the plant to kill him. It held still for what felt like a long time, but was probably only a few seconds. All four of its eyes focused on him, and it seemed to be studying him just as much as he was studying it. He'd never truly contemplated just how alien the Greens looked . . . or how intelligent.

And he'd *killed* one the other day.

"I'm sorry," was all Dalton could manage to say.

The Green's gaze lingered a moment longer before it turned and rejoined its group.

Dalton stared helplessly after the plants. A faint murmur from the roofs made him jerk his head up. Half a dozen people frowned down at him as if unsure of his most recent order.

He cupped his hands around his mouth. "I said, no fighting! You hear? We can't be like them! We can't be murderers, too!"

He felt a tap on his shoulder. He whirled, half-expecting a stray Green to be sneaking up on him, but it was only Gurmeet, whose cheeks had flushed in something like rage.

Gurmeet's fist shot out and struck Dalton in the temple.

Dalton crumpled like a disintegrating house of cards. As stars danced in his eyes, he felt himself being pulled off the street.

A door opened, and he was dragged into dimness. The air smelled of garlic and tea leaves. Hands forced him into a chair, and a rope began winding its way around him from his chest down to his ankles. Where had they gotten a rope? Why were they doing this to him? It wasn't fair, it wasn't—

"Should we really have done that?" Lennox whispered, somewhere out of Dalton's line of sight.

"We have to defend ourselves," Gurmeet said matter-of-factly. "My grandfather did not come to this planet so his grandchildren could die like pigs."

A door clicked shut.

Dalton opened his mouth to call after the men, but the only thing that came out was a croak. Many things had happened to Dalton in his thirty-five years, but getting punched in the temple wasn't one of them, and he decided he didn't like it very much. Ice! He needed ice. And then he needed to get back out to the street and tell everyone to stand down.

He wiggled to try to get the rope off. He wiggled again, when nothing happened. He tried to stand up with the chair still attached to him but lost his balance and crashed to the floor on his side, feeling even more nerves explode with pain.

Dalton said a bad word.

And no one was around to hear him.

CHAPTER 27

Several things happened.

Carolyn, whose group had crept in to investigate the remains of the ship from Nydo Base, approached some of the white-clad miners and was about to wave them over to see if they needed any help when the lead miner lifted a blaster and began firing at the humans, as if Ashi'ii had never tried talking any sense into them. The shots hit two of her people, and the rest of her group charged the Haa'la, throwing boomstones at them without mercy.

Errin, whose shirt was now ripped in at least four places and whose hair was most certainly charred beyond immediate repair, let out a battle cry as they raced down the barricade funnel behind a line of Greens. Body parts wearing Verdant armor lay on the dusty street. This would haunt their nightmares for years to come—if there were years to come.

Ashi'ii fled the laundry room and found an abandoned blaster lying on the ground. Technically it wasn't *abandoned*, as its Haa'la owner lay next to it, but that was just semantics.

She rushed out toward the main bit of fighting. Her people pummeled the Verdants as hard as they could, but the Verdants kept on coming like a stubborn tide. But wait— what was that? *Greens?* They were going after the Verdants, scooping people off their feet and plucking their limbs from their bodies like petals from flowers. Her vision wavered and went black.

Gwendolyn Goldfarb sat at a table, her eyes round with awe. She wasn't sure whose table it was, or why she was there, but pictures danced in her head like ballerinas. Ballerinas tall like the trees, ballerinas dripping crimson rivers . . .

She stood, pushed her chair in, and strode out the door.

Dalton lay on Gurmeet's kitchen floor, hearing screams outside and cursing Sikh Highlander with every foul word he knew.

Small explosions made the room shake. He wished he could crawl inside Chumley's Cube and stay there, but it was back in his office at the police station, and the logistics of getting there while bound to a chair were a bit too compli-cated for his aching mind to work out.

The screaming seemed to go on for hours. Dalton wept

awhile, though he would never tell anyone this. Blaster shots went on for so long, he could scarcely remember what life had been like before their incessant reports filled his ears. Maybe this was the way life always had been, and he'd only dreamed of a time free from war.

Eventually, the sounds of the battle grew quieter and then stilled into silence. Dalton could hear his own heartbeat, and he held his breath as he waited.

More time passed. Dalton fell into a daze, both thirsty and hungry, and so exhausted he could hardly remember his own name. A door creaked, and a woman stood over him.

"Darneisha?" he whispered, for he could speak no louder. "Is that you?"

A hand more wrinkled than a raisin reached toward him and clasped the fingers of his right hand. "It's Gwendolyn, Sheriff."

"Gwendolyn?" He squinted up at her, and her ancient brown face wavered into focus. "What the hell are you doing here?"

"You're trapped. I came to help."

"But the battle . . . !"

"I believe," Gwendolyn said, "it is finished."

Gwendolyn was too frail to pull Dalton to his feet, so she found scissors in one of Gurmeet's drawers and cut him free of the chair.

"How did you know I was in here?" Dalton asked, rubbing his arms to try to get the circulation back into them.

Gwendolyn didn't answer. He supposed she didn't really need to. She went to the door and pulled it open, sending a blinding ray of midafternoon sunlight across the floor.

Gingerly, Dalton followed her out the door, dreading what he might see.

His breath caught in his throat once they emerged from Gurmeet's house. This was worse than Piney Gulch; this was *bigger*. All along this block lay bodies and parts of bodies. Two mangled Greens lay in the street, but the rest were humans and Haa'la. He recognized some of the humans, feeling too stunned to even remember their names.

Gwendolyn took Dalton's hand and led him past the worst of it, back toward the police station. Citizens stood at the edges of the streets, watching him with hollow eyes.

Dalton drew to a stop twenty meters from the police station door. He couldn't bring himself to go inside. "Gwendolyn, what do I do?" he asked, as if an ancient woman with a fractured mind was in the proper state to be dishing out advice.

"Two broken halves make a whole," she said, as if that meant everything.

He spread his arms wide. "This isn't two broken halves. This is thousands of broken people."

She dipped her gray head. "Do your duty." Then she turned and walked away from him.

He went inside the station. Debbie Harper, whom he'd fired, sat at her old desk, cleaning the blood off of Cadu Mão de Ferro's arm. Her mousy hair hung in a limp ponytail down her back.

"Hi, Debbie," Dalton said weakly.

She gave him a long look. "Hi, Sheriff."

"You know you don't work here anymore."

"I just came to help."

Dalton looked to Cadu. "What happened?"

Cadu winced. "I don't really know. It was all so fast, you know? One moment I'm tossing boomstones, the next I'm lying in a pool of my own blood. Maybe one of my stones bounced back at me."

"I'm . . . I'm glad you're okay."

"Me too. I'd been planning a GatorMan marathon for this evening, anyway. Can't miss that *ow that hurt*."

While Cadu continued to writhe under Debbie's ministrations, Dalton looked to Carolyn, who sat off to one side speaking into her comm unit and typing notes into a datapad. Instead of interrupting her, he looked to Errin Inglewood, who was haggard to the point of being unrecognizable.

"Are you all right?" Dalton asked them.

Errin sat in a swivel chair tapping their foot frantically against the floor, arms folded tightly over their chest. "I fought," they said. "I really did. And—I see now. Piney Gulch. I know what you saw. And . . . and . . ."

"It's okay," Dalton said, though it wasn't. "Have you seen Chumley?"

"Maybe two or three hours ago, over by the Verdant ships. He saved my life, I think. I was so distracted by everything, and he shot a Verdant who almost got me. A Verdant almost got me!" Their eyes were round and haunted. "Nobody ever cares about what I feel or think. They just expect me to do everything I'm supposed to, no questions asked. Good old reliable Errin, that's me. I bet they don't even know I have a life outside of kissing Carolyn's arse. But now I'm somebody important. Because I *fought*. And I *won!*"

They giggled, and the sound of it turned Dalton's blood into ice water.

"Errin," he said gravely, "I give you permission to take the next whole year off of work. To hell with what Carolyn thinks."

Carolyn was so busy with her conversation that she didn't even look their way.

"How do you get the pictures out of your head?" Errin asked.

You don't, Dalton almost said but, opting to be nice for once, he said, "I don't know. But when I find out, I'll let you know."

Errin nodded, and swallowed.

"You're sure you haven't seen Chumley recently?" Dalton said.

"I'm positive. We saw each other by the Verdant ships not long before one of them blew."

Dalton's heart stuttered. "Did any of the others explode?"

"I'm not sure. Our Greens chased the Verdants into the funnel, and we went in after them. Then once the fighting stopped, I came straight here."

"You could have gone home."

"I live alone, Dalton." A hint of tears appeared in the corners of Errin's gray-blue eyes. "And being alone is the last thing I want right now."

"Have you talked to your sister?"

"Not yet."

So you might not even know if she's alive, Dalton thought.

"Listen, Errin . . ." Dalton swallowed. "If you ever want to sit and talk about this, let me know, okay?"

They nodded. "Okay."

"Well, take care," he said, feeling hollow. "I need to see about a few things."

He strode into his office and took off his grime-covered trench coat. He held his arms out in front of him and glanced from his hands down to his scuffed boots to make sure all of him was present and accounted for, then went to the cabinet in the corner and helped himself to a bottle of Kentucky bourbon he'd been saving for a special occasion. It felt like divine fire trickling down his parched throat.

Once he felt sufficiently numbed, he plucked the Cube off his desk and activated the doorway the way he'd seen Chumley do, yet when he stepped inside, the portable universe was unoccupied.

"Chumley?" he asked the empty room, then stepped back out into his office.

He shut the Cube inside his desk drawer for safekeeping.

For a moment he felt the world wobble, as if he'd just stepped off that Terror Drop ride. What was he supposed to do now? His deputy may or may not be missing, quite a lot of people were dead, and all he felt like doing was going home and sleeping for the next five or six years.

Well, for one, he could go try and *find* his deputy. Chumley might be out there helping the injured. He might not necessarily be . . . indisposed.

It took every ounce of fortitude in Dalton's body to slip his coat back on, don a spare Stetson from the hall closet, and step back out into the aftermath. Everywhere he looked, he could see people standing around bloody and bewildered as if waiting for someone to tell them what to do next.

"If you're hurt, go to the hospital," he said as he passed a woman with a charred shirt. Then, to a man kneeling beside a fallen comrade, Dalton said, "I'm sorry for your loss."

He spotted Maxine of the city watch standing guard over three Haa'la miners she'd roped together with a clothesline. Their veils had all been removed and tossed aside, and their eyes blazed with fury.

Dalton nodded at her. "Nicely done."

"We'll need to put a call in to the Feds," Maxine said matter-of-factly. "I've heard these people have been causing some problems other places, too."

"Find someone to help you take them to the brig," Dalton said, referring to the little-used Richport jail that hadn't held a prisoner in more than two months. "And make sure they don't have their teleports on them. Have you seen Chumley?"

Maxine's head shook. "I'm afraid not."

Dalton let out a curse. "If you see him, tell him to go straight to the station."

"Will do." She paused. "The Greens are all mingling in the town square. You might want to see what they want."

Panic rooted him into place. "You want *me* to talk to them?"

She cocked an eyebrow at him. "You led a band of them just a short while ago, didn't you?"

While Dalton wouldn't have exactly called what he'd done "leading," he understood her point. "I'll call Carolyn," he said. "See if she won't come with me."

By some miracle he caught Carolyn on her comm, and he invited her to join him in the town square. On his way there, he spotted Dr. Monica Kaur squatting beside a fallen citizen with her medical kit open beside her. She gave him a grim nod, which Dalton returned in kind.

He rounded a corner into the town square and shuddered at the sight of the Greens, who'd banded back together and stood in neat rows facing him, as if he'd been expected. A dozen or so Richport citizens stood at their perimeter holding flamethrowers, presumably in case of sudden moves.

He coughed and cleared his throat. "Hello there," he said. "Erm, thank you for helping us."

The Greens remained unmoving. It was like trying to strike up a conversation with a garden.

The buzz of an approaching quad made his head turn, and he caught sight of Carolyn, still in her pajamas, weaving her way through the battle's aftermath. She parked beside Dalton and dismounted with a grunt. "I've requested medical assistance from Paris," she said.

"Good."

"They're sending over ten doctors and five nurses, plus a bus full of supplies. They said they'll be here by sundown. Now what can I do for all of you?" She looked up at the Greens, hands on her hips, and one stepped forward with two arms extended—one for her, and one for Dalton.

Dalton remembered hands like those wrenching his old right arm from his body.

"It wants to communicate with you, Dalton," Carolyn said. "It knows you hold some level of authority here."

"And how does it know that?"

"Because it can see inside my head. Just touch it, Dalton. They're not going to hurt you."

"But my family . . ."

"These Greens have never even been to Piney Gulch. Now *please*. Can we just get this over with?"

He hated her in that moment, but he knew she was right. He reached out his hand. The Green's twiggy fingers curled around it—

—and his mind opened as if a lid had been pried off of it. He saw lush forests where Greens danced until his thoughts snapped back to the moment at hand.

"Thank you for helping us," Carolyn said to the Green who had greeted them. "Your people fought bravely today."

We lost fourteen of the People, said a voice inside Dalton's head that made him recoil, though it was less of a voice and more of a succession of ideas that approximated a voice. *We will mourn them.*

"I'm very sorry," Carolyn said. "Will you be going home now, or did it burn?"

Our home is in the southern forests, which the demons have not yet touched. Our brethren from the north have been joining us.

"I don't understand why you helped us," Dalton said, sounding a bit sourer than he probably should have. "The Verdants wanted to kill all of us. Shouldn't you have wanted that?"

Your kind does not harm us in the desert. The foolish People who invaded your city should not have done so.

"That doesn't explain why you helped us."

The new demons would have defiled our sacred lands with . . .

Dalton couldn't detect the word, but he had the sudden mental image of barns and tilled fields sprouting vegetables.

"You didn't want the Verdants to establish farms?" he said.

None who are not the People may set foot in our forests or plains. Our lands are sacred. The desert is damnation. We do not care if your People live in the desert, for it is a hell we enter only when necessary.

"But, farms." This still did not fully compute in Dalton's mind. "The Verdants wipe out colonies and plant *farms?*"

It is an abomination.

"All right, all right. So the Verdants are hypocrites. *You* could have attacked the Verdants *after* they wiped all the humans off the planet. Then you wouldn't have had to worry about any of us bloody humans again."

We are being kind.

"What?" He spat the word as if it had a bitter taste.

We could have done as you just said. But we are being kind.

"Wait just a minute," Carolyn said. "After all of this, you still don't want us to go to the forests?"

There came a long pause. *That was never part of our agreement.*

"But I thought as a show of solidarity between us, we might be able to visit each other. You send ambassadors here, we send ambassadors there. Establish trade, or something."

We do not need you. It is only because of our kindness that you live.

Dalton opened his mouth to speak, but every Green turned by some unspoken signal and shuffled one by one out of the town square. The citizens holding flamethrowers kept them at the ready but did not fire.

"I'll be damned," Carolyn said.

"That makes two of us."

"I really thought this tribe might be able to work with us indefinitely."

"If I don't see another one of them again, I'll be a happy person."

"But Dalton, they *helped* us."

"Yeah. One bloody tribe out of how many? And look at all of this!" He pointed at a row of sheet-draped bodies that a handful of citizens were stacking onto a flatbed lorry. "Is this what we want for our town?"

"We would all be dead otherwise," Carolyn said coldly. "And you know it. We fought, we had help, and we won. Don't you get it? *We won.*"

It felt like a hollow victory.

"Have you seen Chumley yet?" he asked, to change the subject.

"No." Carolyn blew a strand of hair out of her mouth, then put a hand on her stomach. "God, I'm hungry. Do you want anything?"

Dalton's appetite had fled with the Greens. "I've got things to do."

He turned away from her and chose a random direction to set off in, his thoughts in a muddled daze. He passed a bloodied group of Verdant prisoners, saw a young girl passing out food and bottled water to people on the streets, and froze when he saw a South Asian man talking animatedly to a reporter for Richport's measly news outlet.

He took five steps closer to the man, and his heart sank when he realized it was not Chumley Fanshaw, but Dhruv

Das, who worked at the law firm that had handled the estates of many of those lost at Piney Gulch—Chumley and Dhruv had similar builds.

Dalton's fists clenched, and he stomped past them, continuing on his way.

Dalton eventually found his way back to his home, which had been completely untouched by the battle, as it lay at the far end of town. He let himself inside, hung up his coat and hat, and rolled up his gray shirtsleeves, then stared at the empty room.

After Piney Gulch, when Dalton lay in the infirmary having his arm regrown in a tank, he thought he'd finally learned the meaning of loneliness. There was no Darneisha at his side to give him moral support, there was no Kendra or Imani to giggle and fidget in the hospital room while they waited for their daddy to get better.

He couldn't call his brother Rob to tell him how bloody miserable he felt. He couldn't brood to his parents that his world had ended, and he couldn't ask his cousins to smuggle spirits into the hospital for him.

Cadu, who had been a couple years ahead of him in school and remained a friendly acquaintance more than an actual friend, surprised him by coming to see him in the infirmary, bringing in a portable screen and forcing Dalton to watch something called *Star Wars*, which was performed in such an archaic version of English that they had to use the subtitles to understand it. Luke, the main character, lost his aunt and uncle and barely batted an eye. Dalton decided immediately that Luke was not to be trusted. When normal people lost loved ones, they did not go off on epic space quests, except perhaps for revenge.

When the ancient film concluded, they'd chatted for a while, and Cadu casually mentioned that Sheriff Sondhi would be retiring soon, and Cadu dreaded to see what kind of pompous young sheriff would replace him. Dalton had had no reply and drifted off to sleep.

No, the true meaning of loneliness was when you were discharged from the infirmary with a new arm and a clean bill of health, and you got to go home.

What was home, when the people who belonged there were gone?

Dalton peeled off his boots and his clothes and went into the shower to get the grime off of him, not completely sure why he felt so broken now. Maybe it was because Chumley had given him some measure of companionship these last few days. Chumley hadn't known him before Piney Gulch, so there was no unspoken expectation that Dalton should just get over what had happened and be a normal person.

He stepped onto the bathmat and toweled off, then grimaced at the man in the mirror. He ran a hand over the stubble on his chin and said to hell with it.

He climbed into bed and stared at the ceiling until he fell asleep.

CHAPTER 28

The next day passed, but if asked to recall the tiny details, Dalton couldn't have said much about them. He chatted with Carolyn—Errin had been conspicuously absent—and patrolled the streets to see if he could be useful. Every citizen but him seemed to have something important to do. People cleared away rubble, patched up damaged buildings, and solemnly gathered the dead.

The brig held forty-one prisoners. Seventeen were Haa'la miners, including Ashi'ii (or so he'd been told), and the remaining twenty-four were what was left of the Verdants.

Interestingly, six of the Verdant prisoners were human. Cadu had performed a cursory census on the lot when they'd all been brought in, but Dalton didn't have the energy or willpower to look at any of them. It was their fault there'd been a bloody battle. Putting Dalton in the same room as all of them would not end well.

Dalton did do something later that day that surprised even him.

He sat in his office and called Summer on his comm.

"Hi," he said, his stomach tight.

"Dalton?" Summer sounded startled. "I didn't think you'd call."

"Just wanted to see how you were doing. I assume you made it home before the fighting started?"

"I did." She paused for a long time. "I thought about turning back and helping . . . but I just couldn't do it."

"I hear you."

"You do?"

"Yeah." Dalton let out a breath and imagined both Darneisha and his brother Rob standing in the corner with folded arms, intimidating him into doing the right thing. "Listen, I was thinking, maybe we could get together sometime. Talk about old times."

"Really?" Summer laughed.

"How does next Saturday sound? You can stop on by my place for dinner."

"I'd be glad to."

"It's not a date," Dalton added.

"Oh, *gosh*, no! You and I, together? That would be like an antimatter explosion."

At least there were no misunderstandings there. "I'll see you on Saturday," he said, and ended the call.

On the morning of the second day, Dalton felt marginally more like his miserable bastard self and made of pot of his terrible coffee in his office. He glowered at the filing cabinet in the corner, willing all of his problems away, when there came a soft rap at the door.

"Come in," he barked, straightening his shoulders.

The door opened. It was Errin, holding a datapad and looking freshly-showered. Their sandy hair had been cut shorter to get the burns out and glistened as if they'd just styled it with mousse.

"Good morning," Errin said.

"Good morning." Dalton squinted at them. "How are you holding up?"

"I didn't think it was your custom to ask about other people's wellbeing."

"Consider me soft at heart. Don't tell anyone."

Errin's lips formed a wry smirk. "I'm coping. But I came in to give you some reports Carolyn wanted to share with you. She's still been trying to contact the Feds. Apparently most of their operators are busy."

"What are the reports? And sit down, you don't need to keep standing there like a member of the waitstaff."

Errin blushed and pulled out a chair. Once settled, they said, "As far as we can tell, the death toll of our citizens currently stands at one hundred and ninety-seven. I can read you a list of names."

Dalton felt sick. "That isn't necessary. But . . ." He dreaded to ask it, but he had to. "Chumley. Has anyone . . . found him?"

Errin scrolled through the list on the datapad screen and shook their head. "Three of the bodies haven't been identified, but they don't match his description."

Dalton bit his lower lip in sheer frustration. "Have there been any reports of a hamster running around anywhere?"

A crease formed between Errin's eyebrows. "A hamster?"

"Little furry thing, runs around on a wheel."

"There have been no reports about hamsters." Errin frowned. "Are you all right?"

Dalton could feel an invisible hand squeezing his heart. No, he wasn't all right. Chumley was dead—he just knew it. He must have died in hamster form during the battle. They would probably never even find his body.

Instead of answering, he said, "What are the other reports?"

"FCU contacted Carolyn's office this morning. They'll be making their way back here sometime today."

Dalton had already forgotten about bloody FCU. "I suppose they'll be telling us what wonderful sorts of gifts they'll be bestowing us with."

"I suppose so." Errin's gaze went out of focus, appearing reflective. "What would you want them to give us? I mean, really. I don't mean air conditioners."

Dalton put a hand on his chin. "What I'd like," he said at length, "is to have some way to protect us all against bastard alien scum. For all we know, Nydo Base is still up and running. One of Ashi'ii's people can call in reinforcements from Leeprau, and they'll just start looting and setting fires again."

"Not if Carolyn gets through to the Feds in time."

"Let's hope she does, then. I can't handle this kind of thing again."

"You did well, though. Organizing us like you did."

"I spent half the bloody battle tied up in Gurmeet Singh's kitchen. How is he, by the way?"

Errin scrolled through the datapad. "His name isn't on a list of the dead."

"What about Lennox McTavish?"

"He's not on it, either."

"Good," Dalton said. Then, "Are you busy right now?"

Errin glanced up in surprise. "Not particularly. Why?"

"How about you come and help me find a hamster?"

"I wish you'd tell me why we're doing this," Errin said as they and Dalton picked through the rubble of the Verdant ship that had gone kablooey. "It makes you seem unstable, no offense."

"It's not my place to tell you."

"So you're keeping a hamster's secrets."

"That's right."

Errin kicked over a warped chunk of metal. "Are you sure you don't need a medical evaluation?"

"I'm fine." Dalton lifted up a tangle of singed wires and tossed it aside. They'd been digging through the mess for half an hour now, and hadn't found so much as a rodent hair.

Maybe there was no point in keeping Chumley's secret. If Chumley was dead, then it didn't matter that he'd had an illegal procedure performed on him.

If Chumley was dead . . .

Dalton sat back on his heels, hot tears burning the corners of his eyes. "Chumley can turn himself into a fecking hamster," he said.

Errin straightened, mouth open. "He what?"

"You heard me. He wouldn't want me telling anyone, but . . . " Dalton's gaze traveled across the rubble and the ravaged street beyond it. "It doesn't matter now."

"I'm very sorry," Errin said softly.

"I hardly even knew him!" Dalton stood again and kicked a hunk of ship that made his foot sting through his boot. "But he didn't deserve to die like this."

"No," Errin said. "He didn't."

Their comm crackled. "Errin? Have you talked to Dalton yet?" It was Carolyn.

"I have." Errin gave him a sidelong glance. "Right now I'm . . . helping him clear some debris. Did you need me for anything?"

"Just tell him FCU is due back here in an hour and a half—they just updated me. I'd like him to be there. And I *finally* got through to the Feds. Would you believe they told me someone turned in a tip about Nydo Base *two days ago* while the battle was going on?"

"And they didn't do anything about it?" Dalton snapped.

"They said the person wouldn't provide an electronic address, so they thought it was a hoax."

Dalton couldn't believe it, but then again, he could. He was about to muster up some sort of snide reply when he caught sight of a family of three disembarking from a nearby flat—mother, father, and little girl, who gripped a cage against her chest.

Without thinking, Dalton broke into a run toward them. The family halted, giving him wary looks.

"Good morning, Sheriff," said the man, who had a butterfly closure sealing part of his forehead shut. "Can we help you?"

Dalton looked down at the cage. A hamster nestled inside it. The creature was mostly white, with brown markings.

"Where are you taking that?" he asked, his heart thumping in disbelief.

"To the vet," said the little girl. "We found him outside our door when the fighting stopped, but he looks sad and won't eat."

"The vet says they're open," said the mother. "We checked."

Dalton stared at the hamster. The hamster stared up at him, its beady eyes gleaming.

"I'll take it from you," Dalton said. "Give you the day off so you can relax. You live here?" He nodded at the building behind them.

"That's right," said the father. "But you don't have to do that; we're fully capable of—"

"Sheriff's orders. I'll get this little fellow taken care of and have him back to you by the end of the day. I'll even pay for his, erm, treatment."

The little girl looked up at her parents, who nodded. She passed the cage to Dalton and stepped back. "I named him Mister Skweeks," she said.

"I'll make sure the vet takes good care of Mister Skweeks," Dalton said solemnly. "Now you folks try to go and enjoy yourselves, if you can."

He strode away from them, and Errin fell into step beside him. Once the two of them had rounded a corner onto another street, Errin said, "Is that him?"

The hamster was now frantically biting one of the metal bars as if to gnaw it in half. "It's him," Dalton said.

"Then how are you going to explain to a child that her new pet isn't coming back?"

"There's a pet store next to my bank. I used to take my girls in there to look at the animals." Dalton held the cage up at eye level. "All right, Mister Skweeks. You're coming with me."

Chumley emerged from his Cube looking rather cross. "I wish you hadn't told them about me," he said, throwing a look at Errin, who occupied Dalton's extra office chair and wore a look of mild amusement.

"I thought you were dead," Dalton said. It hurt him to say it. "And I have questions."

Chumley leaned against the filing cabinet with a huff. He wore a lilac button-down shirt and khaki slacks that bore not even a wrinkle. "If you must know," he said, "the explosion knocked me unconscious. The next thing I knew, I was in a cage in a child's bedroom. You do realize I can't shift back into myself if I'm in a cage; I'd get crushed to death."

Dalton suppressed a smile. "So. Mister Skweeks."

Chumley's cheeks flushed. "Shut up."

"You've got to admit, it's cute," Errin commented.

"We'll have to come up with a plausible story for your disappearance," Dalton said before Chumley could let out a retort. "Any ideas?"

Chumley scratched at an ear. "You could say I was knocked senseless during the battle, and a kind family who chooses to remain anonymous took care of me."

Dalton thought it over and then nodded. "That works. We'd better get to the pet store before FCU gets here."

"FCU is coming back?" Chumley gaped at him.

"Yes, why?"

"She told me they'd evacuate!"

"Who's she?"

"Magdalene Schwartzman. This is crazy."

"Who's Magdalene?" Errin asked, sitting up straighter.

"Long story—I ran into some Verdant people during the battle. One got shot in the helmet so she ripped it off, and I thought for certain it was Naomi Schwartzman, but she said no, her name is Magdalene and that Naomi is her sister. She said the two of them trade information back and forth and that the only reason FCU came here in the first place was so Naomi could gather information about Nydo Base and pass it on to the Verdants, since the Verdants were busy killing someone else at the time."

Dalton blinked. "Repeat that, please?"

Chumley did, slower this time, and Dalton felt his fists clench as his deputy's words sank in.

"So FCU doesn't give one flying feck about us."

"I don't know. The others might not know about Naomi's connection to the Verdants."

A thought entered Dalton's head then, and he stood. "We have Verdant prisoners in the brig."

He strode out of the room, hearing Chumley and Errin's footsteps following him. Cadu sat at his desk, and his eyes widened at the sight of Chumley.

"Where did *you* come from?" he asked in disbelief.

"He snuck in the back," Dalton said before Chumley could speak. "He's gathered some intel I need to follow up on in the brig."

Judging from Cadu's expression, he didn't believe a word

Dalton had just told him, but thankfully he did not press the issue.

The brig lay in a separate building beside the station and contained four wide cells with iron bars. Dalton pushed through a connecting doorway and nodded at Debbie, who apparently had been chosen for guard duty, as she sat in a folding chair just inside the door looking bored beyond all reason.

It served her right for the salad.

The cells were so full, it was almost inhumane. Someone had been smart and grouped the Nydo Base miners and the Verdants in separate sections across from each other. They hurled insults in Haa'anu, which would have amused Dalton if these people hadn't been responsible for his people's deaths.

Dalton strode up to a cell containing a smattering of humans. "Do any of you speak English?" he barked.

"I do," said a tall woman who unfolded herself from the hard bench on which she'd been sitting. She strutted up to the bars and looked him up and down as if he were a worm. "Colonizer," she spat.

The woman looked remarkably like Naomi.

"Magdalene, I presume?" Dalton said. Chumley and Errin drew up beside him, the latter with their datapad out, ready to take notes.

Magdalene's lip curled, but she made no comment.

"It's funny, you calling me a colonizer," Dalton went on. "Since your lot came here to colonize it in your own way."

Her expression turned neutral. "What do you mean?"

"Your lot may pretend to hate the fact that life spread to the stars, but the Greens showed me what would've happened if you'd had your way on this planet. Is it typical for the Verdants to start farming on the worlds they target?"

"No." Magdalene's mouth twitched. "But Molorthia Six abounds in resources; we did some research on the way here and decided that the plains beyond the forests are some of the most fertile in the galaxy. We were going to build farms and feed the poor."

"Yeah, well, the Greens didn't want you to do that, did they? So they ripped your lot to shreds. You may have noticed." For perhaps the first time in his life, he felt grateful toward the beings that had brought his own world to an end, which conjured such dissonance inside of him that for a moment he thought he might be ill. Recovering as quickly as he could, he said, "The Feds know you're here. I don't know when they're coming, but you'll be answering to them. See— you might think you're noble, going along and smiting this lot—" He jerked his head toward the miners in the two cells on the other side of the room— "but it turns out that most people aren't very happy with you."

"Humans and Haa'la never should have left their own planets," Magdalene growled. "We try to make good of the disasters they wrought."

"How honorable of you," Dalton said. Then, "Magdalene, you're coming with me." He fished a pair of cuffs out of the depths of his trench coat. "There's someone I'd like for you to see."

Dalton sent money and the cage with Errin so they could

pick up a new hamster for the little girl ("I don't care if it doesn't look exactly like Chumley; you can tell her it looks different because it isn't sick anymore!"), and then he and Chumley herded a restrained Magdalene out of the police station and down the street to Carolyn's office.

"What's the meaning of this?" Carolyn asked when they made it inside. "Naomi?"

"Not Naomi," Dalton said, feeling smug for knowing something Carolyn didn't. "But we're going to wait here for Naomi."

"You can't keep me bound like this," Magdalene sneered as Dalton forced her to sit in one of Carolyn's chairs. "I have rights!"

"Not on this planet, you don't."

"You've really brought it upon yourself," Chumley added. "Don't blame us."

Carolyn's mouth opened and closed a few times. Then she cleared her throat and said, "FCU should be here in a few minutes."

In fact, they arrived five minutes later in a Desert Van Lines bus that belched Naomi and her crew out into the dusty street. Dalton greeted them at the curb, wearing a manic smile that scared even himself.

"Good day to you all," he said, sounding falsely gracious. "Have you had a safe journey?"

"It went as well as can be expected," Naomi said in her clipped, professional tones. "We were sorry to hear of the battle that took place here." There was a hint of unease in her expression that Dalton probably would have missed if he didn't know the truth.

"We can discuss it inside," Dalton said.

A sardonic spring appeared in his step as he led FCU into Carolyn's building and down the short hallway to the meeting room where city council gathered twice a month. Carolyn waited alone at the head of the table; her face schooled into an even expression that did a remarkable job of masking the rage Dalton knew was broiling within her.

"Please sit, all of you," Carolyn said. "I'm glad to see you've all made it back safely."

"It's good to see you remain in good health, as well," Naomi said as she and her cohort occupied the mauve cushioned chairs arranged around the rectangular table. All of them still wore their black business suits, and Dalton hid a smirk at the fact that the paler-complected members of her party were suffering from colossal sunburns.

"Yes," said Carolyn. "We seem to have just survived the worst battle this planet has ever seen. Unfortunately, a couple hundred people from our community did not."

"A fact I am terribly sorry to hear." Naomi pulled a datapad out of a black messenger bag, laid it on the table in front of her, and activated its screen. "It is not customary for us to enter war zones."

"Ah, but how could any of us have known it would become a war zone?" Carolyn mused. "On the day of your arrival, we'd only suffered minor attacks from the Greens. And I don't use the term 'minor' lightly, as people were killed then, too."

Naomi nodded in commiseration. "It is most lamentable."

Dalton, who had opted to remain standing near the door for reasons of practicality, couldn't wait to wipe the cool indifference off of Naomi's face.

"So." Carolyn folded her hands together, her eyes gleaming. "I trust your visits to our sister cities went well?"

"They went as smoothly as could be hoped." Two of her cronies made silent nods, as if for emphasis. "It's truly impressive how your people have been able to eke out an existence in such a hostile zone. Mayor Zhao in Cloud City said this region only receives rain three times per year."

"We take our water very seriously," Carolyn said. "I trust you've already discussed your plans with my counterparts, then?"

"Not as such." Naomi exchanged a glance with the woman next to her, who of course didn't utter a word. These people were nothing more than drones. Dalton wondered what would happen if you lit a fire under their chairs.

Carolyn's eyes narrowed a fraction. "What do you mean?"

"You were our first point of contact, and you're mayor of the largest city on the planet, so we will give our information to you, and only you. You may pass the information on to the other cities as you see fit."

"I see." Carolyn paused. "So, what's the verdict?"

Naomi lifted the datapad a few centimeters closer to her face. "We have reached a unanimous decision that—"

A cry echoed down the corridor and in through the meeting room's open doorway.

Naomi stiffened. "What was that?"

Dalton coughed and peeled himself from the wall. "That would be our prisoner."

"You have a prisoner in the mayor's office?"

"It's not typical," Dalton admitted, "but we wanted to

bring her over here to commemorate this special occasion. Oh, Chumley!"

He heard a thud, followed by a curse. Dalton stomped from the meeting room and threw open Carolyn's office door. Magdalene was on her feet with her hands cuffed behind her back, kicking at Chumley's shins as hard as she could and mostly missing since Chumley kept dodging out of the way as he tried to regain control over her.

"A little help, here!" Chumley exclaimed.

Dalton strode forward, ignored the glob of saliva that Magdalene spat into his face, and seized her by the left arm.

"Grab her other arm," Dalton said. "We're taking her in."

Chumley complied, and they forced Magdalene out of the room and down the hallway. It was like trying to steer an angry bronco that had developed the ability to swear.

Together, Dalton and Chumley shoved her through the doorway into the meeting room, and hurriedly closed the door behind them.

Magdalene had frozen. In fact, everyone in the room had frozen. Dalton wished he could take a picture and frame it.

"What are you doing here?" Naomi hissed, the color draining from her face.

"What do you think I'm doing here?" Magdalene's eyes blazed.

"Magdalene here has an interesting story to tell," said Dalton. "Chumley?"

Chumley cleared his throat and stepped forward. "During the battle in which the Verdants so rudely attacked us, I ran into Magdalene. She works for the Verdants. She told me that she asked Naomi to scout out our planet to see if Nydo

Base had set up operations here. You can admit that FCU was never going to do anything to help. You were just acting as spies." He glanced over at Dalton as if for approval, and Dalton nodded.

The woman next to Naomi looked stunned—the first expression Dalton had ever seen on her face. "Is this true?"

Naomi's lips quivered. She looked cornered, and Dalton suspected she would try and finagle her way out of this situation using corporate doublespeak. "In a way," she said.

"In *what* way?"

"Magdalene did ask if I'd come investigate this planet. They'd had their suspicions that Nydo Base was operating out of the Molorthia System, and Molorthia Six made the most sense out of all of them. We knew there would be a lot of ground to cover, but we agreed that if Nydo Base was here, there would be some disruptions indicating their presence."

Disruptions, Dalton thought. *Ha.*

"So you came to snoop on our planet, using FCU as a cover," said Carolyn. "Which seems like such a waste of time since you knew the Verdants would wipe our cities off the map once they had confirmation of Nydo Base's location."

"I didn't know they were going to attack the human settlements!" Naomi cried. "I thought they would only target the mines!"

"Are you really that naïve?" Magdalene laughed, an ugly sound. "I thought you knew what we did to planets like this one."

"But not to humans! It's never been to humans!"

"*These* humans subjugated a vulnerable species. They deserved to die just as much as the Haa'la."

"*They* subjugated *us*," Dalton said, but he didn't think anyone heard him. Naomi let out a snarl and launched herself over the top of the table toward her sister, as if they were no longer women in their forties, but rival children battling over toys.

Two of the FCU grabbed Naomi before she could reach her sister. The Schwartzmans swore at each other, calling each other things that would have made a nun blush, and Dalton opted to defuse the situation by guiding a flailing Magdalene out of the room and stuffing her back inside Carolyn's office with a rueful-looking Chumley.

When Dalton returned to the meeting, a new argument was underway.

"How dare you insinuate that I was in league with my sister!" Naomi cried at Carolyn, her face awash with an angry flush.

"You already admitted you were scouting out our planet for her."

"I didn't know she would try to kill you! You know what?" Naomi paused to glance from Carolyn to Dalton. "I don't have to put up with any of you. We're going to the spaceport, and we're going back to Earth." She crammed her datapad into her messenger bag with a particular viciousness and strode toward the door, making a gesture for her people to follow her.

"But what about the donation?" Dalton asked, heart hammering in sudden alarm.

"You're not getting one."

Dalton stood and watched helplessly as FCU exited the room.

"Well," Carolyn said, brushing her hands together. "That's that."

"But . . . but the air conditioners . . ."

"We don't even know if that's what they were going to give us. And if you want air conditioning that badly, you can stay here in the municipal building, or order one yourself."

The Feds arrived later that day, piloting a bulky prison ship that would have more than enough room for those shut inside the brig. As the prisoners were led single-file out the door of the police station toward the waiting transport, Dalton stopped Ashi'ii and said, "I suppose I have to thank you."

She scrunched her pale face at him. "Why?"

"You told me about the Verdants. It was useful information."

"I did what I could to help. My people wouldn't listen."

"That's people for you. I hope you have fun in prison."

She scowled at him. "Don't think I'll be there long."

"You're in cuffs."

"I'm Ashi'ii Nydo. I have a business to run. This won't stop me."

The Fed agent guiding her rolled his eyes and said, "Come on, we haven't got all day." He led the Haa'la into the transport, out of sight.

Dalton didn't see how Ashi'ii could start up her operations here again that easily. He'd been told that the Feds had landed in the forests and raided Nydo Base prior to their landing in Richport. As far as anyone could tell, all the

Haa'la had been captured, and the few humans the Haa'la had put to work had been rescued and dropped back off in Paris, including a rather cross Keith Okpebholo.

Dalton and Chumley rode out to the spaceport as the sun hovered lower on the western horizon, and they watched together silently as the prisoners were guided from the transport to the great, hulking Fed ship, and stayed to see it rise into the air and grow into a smaller speck that vanished in the twilight haze.

"Well," Chumley said. "That was interesting."

"It was."

"Do you think Ashi'ii will really find her way back here?"

"I sure as hell hope not. We've got enough things of our own to worry about."

"What are we going to do now?"

"We're going to go home and sleep, and in the morning we'll go to work and carry on like always. We've got to work on your target shooting some more. Seems like we got sidetracked from doing that." Dalton gave him a sidelong glance. The wind gusted stronger, and a damp scent hung in the air indicating a rare, incoming rainstorm. "Unless you don't plan on staying."

"Oh, I'll stay." Chumley ran a hand over his inky black hair. "I'm not sure why, but this place is starting to grow on me."

"That's Molorthia Six for you," Dalton said. "It's the most miserable damn armpit in the universe, but we call it home. Speaking of which, what do you want for dinner?"

Fat droplets of water were already spattering the ground when they made it back to the adobe house on the far eastern edge of town. Dalton took the easy route with dinner and heated a frozen pizza, and he and Chumley dined out on the back patio beneath the canvas awning, not caring they were getting soaked with every gust of wind.

Dalton imagined that the rain had been sent to wash away the blood of battle; the planet cleansing itself.

They ate in silence, listening to the raindrops fall like tapping fingers, and when they'd finished and pushed their plates back and the deluge fell in greater earnest, Chumley said, "I've been wondering something."

"What?"

"The Haa'la at Nydo Base had posts in the desert so they could listen to humans. I thought they were listening for any signs that the humans had discovered them so they could evacuate if necessary—but they didn't evacuate when Ashi'ii told them the Verdants were coming. It just doesn't make sense to me."

Dalton had been wondering the same thing. "Could be the Haa'la were going to attack us the moment they heard a transmission mentioning we'd found them. Not evacuate."

"Then why didn't they just attack the humans as soon as they landed in the first place? It seems like it would have been easier for them in the long run."

Dalton thought about it some more. "Could be they were being kind."

"Kind?"

"Weirder things have happened, trust me on that." He thought of the Greens in Richport—not the ones that had killed at the hotel but the ones who had fought the Verdants and won. He said, "We could go back inside, if you want."

"I think I'd like to stay out here a bit," Chumley said, dabbing at his mouth with a soggy napkin. "It's not supposed to rain often. I need to absorb as much of it as I can and save it for a sunny day."

Dalton let out a chuckle, then frowned at himself. "The Rosa River is going to be full for a while," he commented as water ran down his scalp and into his eyes. "We could go swimming one of these days."

"I like swimming," Chumley said, a boyish twinkle appearing in his brown eyes. "I've thought about installing a pool in my Cube but haven't gotten around to it. I'd have to get rid of the veranda."

"And we could go for night hikes," Dalton went on. "I always liked doing those. It's been a while, though. Probably five or six years."

"I don't think I've ever been on a night hike."

"They're better than day hikes when you live in a desert. You get to see more wildlife, too, like the great desert stinkworm—don't think I've ever mentioned those to you. Ugly little buggers." The rain thickened suddenly, as if God himself had switched on the universe's largest faucet. "We'd better get inside before we drown ourselves."

Chumley nodded. They gathered up the empty plates and the pizza pan and dragged themselves, dripping, inside. Then Dalton stood at the back door watching the rain sluice downward, thinking about all the lives that had been lost, and reminding himself of all the lives that had been saved.

The constant pall of grief that had lain over him for the

past five years hadn't gone away, but it felt lighter somehow, as if someone had lifted up a corner of it and let a little light in underneath, which of course was a silly thing to visualize in the middle of a monsoon.

It was nice being not as sad about things, though. He could go through life feeling not as sad about things. And while he didn't think himself a happy man by any means, that small distinction made all the difference in the world.

I know my family will never come back, Dalton thought at the sky. *But maybe having a friend is the next best thing.*

He shook himself and turned from the pane. "Chumley, go grab a couple glasses. What was it you were saying about Kaktian rum?"

EPILOGUE

Pelstring Four was said to be the gem of the Milky Way Galaxy, not that there was a whole lot to compare it to, given that humanity had yet to travel more than a hundred and fifty light years away from Earth in any direction.

Most planets that had been discovered and then explored were either airless worlds boasting more rocks than life forms or overgrown gas giants that didn't have ground to stand on. Others were already occupied.

Pelstring Four was different. It had a twenty-four-hour day, just like Earth. It had one sun and one moon, just like Earth. It had a 407-day year and four distinguishable seasons in its northern and southern hemispheres, none of which ever got too hot or too cold.

Thirty million humans made Pelstring Four their home, and the population was growing at a steady one percent increase each year. All seemed to be going well.

Seemed being the operative word.

The view out the penthouse window on the top floor of the Shikhar Building in Nuevo Pradesh City showed lush gardens in full bloom for the season, but Governor Elroy Ghosh was too agitated to enjoy it.

He stood at the window, gripping a bottle of mineral water in one trembling hand, having just downed his afternoon dose of Nerzopan. The pills just took the edge off his anxiety. He couldn't go full mellow today because he had several important meetings lined up for the next four hours, and it was never a good idea to be too agreeable when you walked into one.

A soft rapping on his door made him drop his bottled water, which glugged into the carpet. Swearing, Elroy snatched it up and said, "Come in!"

Jyoti Benoit, his assistant, stepped into his office, her hair tied back into a severe bun. She held a large manila envelope in front of her. "I've received a message for you, sir."

"A message?" Elroy made an effort to keep his hands still. Rumors of his affliction had been circulating among his staff, and he did his best to quell them.

She held the envelope out for him to take. The flap was open—he could tell it had been sealed at one point.

Elroy's eyebrows rose as he took it from her. "You've read it?"

"I have." Her mouth twitched. "It's your own policy, remember? We have to check for threats before passing any physical correspondence on to you."

Elroy could hear his own heartbeat banging out a staccato tempo as he slid a white sheet of A4 paper out of the envelope.

Four words were printed on it: *He's on Molorthia Six.*

It had been initialed at the bottom with the letter B.

He read the message twice more, then looked up at Jyoti. "Do you understand what this means?"

"I assume you're looking for someone, and that whoever you hired to track them down has found them. Would you like another nerve pill? Your hands are shaking like crazy."

"I don't take nerve pills," Elroy said through clenched teeth. He turned away from her toward the window and felt his mouth broaden into a grin.

He's on Molorthia Six.

Elroy slid his sat-phone out of his pocket.

Chumley Fanshaw was going to regret the day he was born.

TO BE CONTINUED . . .

ABOUT THE AUTHOR

J. S. BAILEY enjoys writing speculative tales that keep readers on the edges of their seats. She has published eight novels and twenty-two short stories, with more on the way. Bailey is fond of long walks in the woods, British television, and lots of burritos. She lives in Cincinnati, Ohio with her husband and cats. She has never met a man-eating plant, and plans to keep it that way.

Follow J. S. Bailey on social media at:

> facebook.com/jsbaileywrites
> instagram.com/jsbailey_author
> twitter.com/jsbailey_author
> mewe.com/p/jsbailey1
> goodreads.com/jsbailey

www.ingramcontent.com/pod-product-compliance
Lightning Source LLC
Chambersburg PA
CBHW050851210726
48290CB00004B/1173